Dedication: To my Phoobs, for loving me through all of my highs and lows.

Also, to anyone who's ever felt like you aren't enough. You. Fucking. Are.

sweet little
NOTHING

LK FARLOW

THERE ISN'T a single cell of my body that doesn't ache.

It's the kind of hurt that pierces your skin and sinks into your veins, your bones, your fucking soul. It's the kind of pain that eats away at you like poison, consuming all of the good within you until all that's left is a shell.

I stumble, tripping over my own feet as I cross my bedroom. "So fucking stupid," I mutter, righting myself. I flip on the light as I enter the bathroom, recoiling at the bright light. Win in my eyesight.

I guess seventy-six days of crying will do that, huh?

My fingers tangle in my limp, dirty hair, and I wince as I tug on the knots, my past and my present colliding in my mind, morphing into a single mangled nightmare.

"As long as you love someone, this is okay," my stepbrother once said to me, his soft tone a stark difference to his cruel words. I wanted to tell him I didn't love him. I wanted to yell and shout and scream for help, but my fear of him far outweighed my self-preservation. The last time I called for help, he brutally ended me; when my mother asked what happened, I told her I tripped and hit the dresser.

She believed him, too—didn't even ask me.

My heart beats raggedly, like someone ripped the already damaged organ from my chest, shredded what was left of it, stomped on the pieces, and then hastily shoved the tattered remains back beneath my ribs.

"You like that puppy my daddy brought you?" Rob asks, and I nod. "Then you better do what I say or he might just disappear."

"Stop, stop, stop!" I plea, the words a garbled cry to the universe. I want it all to go away, for the memories of then and the horrors of now to all stop. But I learned long ago there's no one out there listening. Not to the likes of me, anyway. My own mother didn't even hear my cries as I begged and pleaded for her to take my side.

"Not enough." I pivot in a wide circle, clipping my hip on the vanity. "Never enough. Stupid!"

Tears cloud my vision as I struggle to breathe. I want... *I need* the pain to stop. For my past to stop haunting me. For the taunts and leers to go away.

I'm a top spinning out of control, desperate for someone —*anyone*—to save me from the path my own self-loathing is shoving me down. If I'd have been stronger—smarter—none of this would've happened to me.

I thought a fresh start would be the cure, but like a dark cloud, my secrets and scars followed me. And now, this place, what should have been a safe haven, is as tainted as the home I fled.

All because of Sterling Abbot—Rob's best friend. With a torch in one hand and a pitchfork in the other, Sterling's on a mission to make me pay for my alleged transgressions against my stepbrother.

"You thought you'd get off scot-free? That you'd run away and hide your sins? Not on my watch. You ruined him,

his entire life, and now I'm going to ruin you. I'm going to dismantle everything you've ever loved. I'm going to dissect you, take you apart, and scatter the pieces. You think you regret spreading your legs for him? You're going to regret spreading those lies even more. Take a seat, Emmalyn. Class is about to start."

My breaths heave in and out of my lungs as a humorless laugh slips past my trembling lips. God knows, there's not a single person on this planet who cares enough to try and pull me from the murky depths of my misery. *If anything, they'd press their boots to the back of my head and hold me under.*

My hands shake as I press down on the lid, pushing to the right.

"Dammit," I cry as the orange bottle slips, and my blessed relief falls to the floor. The tablets scatter and roll around my feet as I fall to my knees in a desperate attempt to gather them.

With one hand clutching pills, I grip the edge of the vanity and pull myself back to standing with the other. The reflection staring back at me is the face of a stranger. She looks like me, but different, too. The face in the mirror is how I feel inside—worthless... empty... hollow.

Already gone.

I watch as she raises her hand and jams the pills into her mouth. The plasticky outer-coating quickly gives way to a bitter taste. Her face puckers, and so does mine.

She is me, but she's more than me. She's all of my hurt and bitterness and suffering personified. She's the part of me that's broken beyond repair—used up and dirty, unwanted and unloved. She's the voice urging me to end it all. I've fought her for so long, but now... my fight is gone.

With a flick of my wrist, water pours from the faucet. I

lean down and suck the liquid into my mouth, my throat working overtime as I swallow it all down.

With the bottle empty, I collapse back down to the floor, the water still running.

I sit slumped against the tub for God knows how long, waiting—praying—for death. For relief. Time has no meaning here.

A fine sheen of sweat covers me as my vision blurs. My head feels heavy, and my stomach churns as unwanted visions plague me behind my heavy, drooping lids.

"If you loved me you, wouldn't do this," I sob as Rob smiles cruelly down at me.

His lips curl into an ugly sneer. "If you really loved me, you'd give freely. Then I wouldn't have to take."

But I don't... I don't love him.

And because of him, no one will ever love me. Not that it matters. Nothing matters. Nothing about me matters to anyone. I'm a waste of space, wasting away.

I try to laugh at my own morbidity, but no sound comes out. My body sways and I slump sideways, banging my head on the side of the tub.

I struggle against his hold, but it's no use. "Love is kind," I whisper brokenly. "And you're a monster; you're incapable of love."

His gaze darkens as his hand around my throat tightens, crushing my windpipe. "And you're a little bitch. Always walking around here, teasing me." Rob skims his index finger over the apple of my cheek and I flinch. "You're pure, but don't worry, Em. I'm going to dirty you up real good."

The phone rings again... or maybe it's my ears.

Who would even call me? Not even Stella, my one and only friend on campus, would care now—Sterling made sure of that.

My heart thunders in my chest.

Someone knocks on the front door.

He's never taken things this far before. "Rob, please. Please don't." *Tears stain my cheeks as my pleas for him to stop pour out of me.*

I vomit into my lap as the sound of my name reverberates through the house. *No, that's not right. There's no one— I'm hearing things.*

Even though my eyes are closed, I'm weeping. Sobbing for my stolen innocence.

"You're mine, Em." He fists my hair with the hand that isn't wrapped around my throat. "Mine."

A sob breaks free as he destroys my virtue with just one thrust. Countless tears paint my cheeks as I force my mind to drift away to somewhere better... somewhere safe.

"Emmalyn!" someone—*no one*—yells as tremors overtake my body.

Only one person calls me that, but he wants me gone, too. I wonder if he'll smile when he hears the news? It might be the first time I make someone happy.

Someone bangs on the door. "Emmalyn!" His voice sounds crazed, worried even. *I must be dreaming, because Sterling Abbot doesn't give a shit about me.*

The door splinters open, and everything goes dark.

"HOW ARE YOU HOLDING UP, MAN?" I ask, drumming my fingers on the mahogany bar top. It's inlaid with satinwood and has the kind of patina where you can't tell if the wood is centuries old or newly made to look it.

My lifelong best friend peers at me over the rim of his crystal glass, a storm brewing in his dark gaze. "Fucking peachy."

"Self-pity doesn't suit you." I'm a shit for being so blunt, but everyone at Club Roble babies him. They all treat him like he's as fragile as a Fabergé egg—priceless and delicate—when really, he's nothing more than an entitled, overprivileged, and undersupervised son of a bitch.

Beau, in that moto jacket, has been my best friend for as long as I can remember.

He seems unfazed by the truth in my words. "Little bitch is trying to ruin me," he growls. "How do you think I'm doing?"

I spin on my stool to face him fully. "What are you going to do?"

"Simple." His lips curl up in a devious smile, and he

tosses back the remaining whiskey in his glass. "I'm going to ruin her right back."

"Isn't Em—*she* leaving for college?" I almost slip up and say her name. I guess I do coddle him a little, but this is out of self-preservation, because Rob goes apeshit at the mere mention of her name.

"Actually" —he pins me with a cold stare— "I need your help."

"How can I help?" I regret asking no sooner than the words pass my lips. The calculating gleam in his eye all but promises I'm not going to like what he says next.

"Dad says she's going to Central Valley."

An uneasy feeling settles in my gut. Is it merely a coincidence for her to end up at the same school I'm doing my apprenticeship at?

It doesn't feel like one.

No, it feels like a carefully planned step in Rob's revenge plot.

This is his battle to wage, but something tells me I'm about to be drafted as an unwilling soldier.

Helping a friend wronged is one thing, being nothing more than a means to an end is quite another.

"What's with the look?" my best friend asks, his voice infused with steel. His temper is hair-trigger, and I know from experience that I do not want to be in the line of fire when it goes off.

"Nothing, man. There's no look."

"You think it's okay for that little bitch to get off scot-free after what she did to me?" His chest heaves as he struggles not to go full-on Hulk. "You think it's no big deal she told everyone with a set of fucking ears that I raped her?" His volume increases with each unfounded accusation. He lunges at me from his stool, and I've had enough. "Maybe you fucking think—"

"What I think"—I bite out the words, fisting his shirt with both hands while holding him at arm's length—"is you need to fucking chill. I've got your back, Rob. Always. I just need to make sure it's in a way that doesn't compromise my future."

Rob slumps back down into his seat and hangs his head. "She compromised mine," he mumbles under his breath.

It's on the tip of my tongue to tell him that being told you have to wait for the media shitstorm to blow over before being promoted isn't quite the same as losing your job. But I digress.

"She'll get hers," I say, trying to reassure him.

He swings his gaze back up to mine, his face a blank mask, void of any and all emotion. "Even if it fucking kills me."

His vow sends an arctic chill down my spine. I try to shake it off as Rob being Rob. As long as I've known him, he's been a surly fucker with an attitude problem unlike any other.

Unfortunately, the older we get, the worse he gets. And at some point, I fear he'll cross the line he's been toeing and dive head-first into the darkness.

In the blink of an eye, he's settled and calm, with his cool mask in place. "Will you make it to Levi's party tonight?"

I bring my glass to my lips, sipping at my drink to buy myself some time. The way Rob can seamlessly move between personas is... unnerving, to say the least. "Unfortunately, no. I need to get on the road before the sun rises if I want to make good time."

Rob cocks his head to the side, studying me, looking for

the lie. Luckily, my words are as true as they are not, which is probably my saving grace.

"Right. It's a long drive."

Exhaling out a relieved breath, I nod. "Got a lot to do before the academic year starts."

"I'm counting on you," Rob growls, his dead eyes hard on mine. "Don't fuck this up."

"I've got your back, man."

Again, Rob appraises me for a long moment before finally nodding.

"A FRESH START."

I mumble the words under my breath for what has to be the billionth time as I drive up the narrow, winding road that leads to the secluded Central Valley campus.

I've said and thought those three stupid words so many times over the past nine months, I almost believe they're true.

God, I hope they're true.

My breath catches as the campus comes fully into view. The pictures in the welcome packet definitely sold this place short.

Nestled into the side of the mountain, the campus is spread out in a lush valley, perfectly hidden away behind a thick forest.

Honestly, it's charming, which only fuels my hope of this place being my fresh start.

The grounds are overflowing with students and their families, laughter ringing through the air as old friends reunite after a long summer.

If I had to sum up the Central Valley campus in one

word, it would be *happy*. This place radiates happy and maybe... just maybe... all of this bustling life and laughter is a good omen of what's to come.

I guide my Honda—while a nice ride to the average person, it may as well be a jalopy compared to most of the cars in this lot—into a free spot and kill the engine.

All around me are students decked out in the latest name-brand fashions. They look golden and shiny and untouched by the darker side of life. But I know, probably better than most, not to judge a book by its cover.

I manage to suppress my doubt before stepping out of the car, nearly hitting a passerby with my door. "Sorry—"

"Oh my God! Fucking watch it, you broke bitch!" the gorgeous blonde screeches as she shoves past me, effectively knocking me back into the driver's seat.

"Sorry," I whisper in her wake, willing myself not to cry. This is my fresh start, and I refuse to let one mean girl ruin it.

After a deep breath, I lock my fragile emotions back into their little heart-shaped box and exit the car. As I lean back into the car to grab my messenger bag, a creeping sensation washes over me, simultaneously prickling my skin and causing sweat to bead on my hairline.

Someone's watching me.

"Just breathe," I mutter to myself, securing the strap of my bag over my shoulder.

Inhaling deeply, I hold my breath for two counts before exhaling. I repeat this measure twice before ducking back out of my car and peeking around.

There are people everywhere, but none of them are paying any special attention to me.

I am no one here, and *I know no one here*, and this is still my fresh start.

I quickly smooth down the soft jersey fabric of my favorite sweatshirt—a second-hand thing I scored from the local thrift store back home—and grab my duffel bag from the trunk. Aside from a silken stuffed rabbit given to me by my paternal grandmother at birth, my pillow, and a winter coat, all of my belongings are on my person.

Eighteen years on this planet, and all of my worldly possessions fit into two bags and a pillowcase. It's kind of sad, really.

I keep my gaze on the ground in front of me as I make the trek across the parking lot to my dorm building.

While mommy dearest hasn't ever done much for me over the course of my life, she managed to score me one half of a two-person suite—rare for a freshman, or so I'm told.

As thankful as I am for the privacy it will afford me, it in no way makes up for the fact that she all but pawned me, and my wellbeing, for a cushy lifestyle.

The dorm building looks more like a mountain lodge from the outside, with its stone and wood exterior, steeply pitched roof, and massive windows. Here's to hoping the inside is as nice.

Plastered across the front, right over the grand entryway, is a banner that reads *Welcome Wildcats!* Beneath the banner, there's a desk, and behind the desk, there's a pretty redheaded girl, with a bored look on her face.

"Hey, I'm, uh, checking in."

She perks up at the sound of my voice, her previously thinned lips are now upturned in a beaming smile. "Of course. Name and ID?"

I fish my driver's license from my wallet and pass it to her.

"Emmalyn. That's a pretty name."

"Just Emmy."

"All right, Emmy. I'm Abigail, a senior, and one of the RAs of this dorm. Not yours, though. I'm on the second floor, and you're on the third with Melanie."

"It's nice to meet you." My voice shakes, and I ball my hands into fists, digging my nails into the flesh of my palms.

She smiles a genuine smile, most likely chalking my behavior up to nerves. "Here are the keys to your room and mailbox. As I mentioned, you're on the third floor, suite three-hundred three. You'll take a right out of the elevator, second door." Abigail passes me a set of keys along with a folder. "There's a map in there, along with an itinerary of Welcome Week events."

"Thanks," I whisper, hating how meek I sound.

While I was never the life of the party, I used to at least be able to carry a basic conversation without sounding like a frightened child.

"It's what I'm here for." She tilts her head to the side, studying me. "Do you have your student ID card yet?"

"No."

"You're gonna want to get that ASAP. You can get it over at the tech center—it's on the map. Your ID card is basically your life. It will get you in and out of this building, along with many others. I would highly suggest getting it today. You'll have to be buzzed in without it, okay?"

I nod. "Yeah, yes. I'll go right now. Thanks."

I start to turn away, but Abigail calls after me. "Don't you wanna put your stuff up first?"

My cheeks heat. "Oh, yeah. Sure."

Her lips tip up in a grin. "C'mon, I'll let you in."

Falling in line behind her, I wait patiently as she swipes her badge in front of the sensor. The light flashes green, and Abigail pushes the door open before stepping to the side and allowing me to enter.

"Elevator is on the left, stairs are to the back right. Mel will be around, and I'm sure she will come by and introduce herself."

"Thanks," I say again, undoubtedly sounding like a parrot.

"No problem, Emmy. Welcome to the Wildcat fam!"

As I enter the building, I almost wish I could bottle her pep and use it to help get me through the dark days. Sure, they're fewer than there were, but memories of what happened still loom over me like my own personal dark cloud.

Today, though, the sun is peeking through those clouds, and I plan on taking full advantage of the sunlight. So to speak.

The inside of the dorm building is every bit as luxurious in the lobby as the outside suggests. From the slate flooring and comfy couches in the lounge area, to the exposed wooden beams overhead, this place looks more like a coveted vacation spot than a college dorm.

I follow Abigail's directions to the elevator, though I could have found it regardless; it is a straight shot down the wide hallway.

Worry over meeting my roommate sets in as the car climbs to the third floor. What if she's like the girls back home?

Mean, petty, and black-hearted.

Even worse... what if she's nice? What if she sees through my mask, straight down to my broken core? What if she pulls at the thread holding all of my secrets inside me? What if she wants to try to fix me up, like I'm some old dilapidated house?

My soul is far too tarnished for a little TLC to make it shine.

It's black. Rotten, through no fault of my own. Not because I'm bad, but because of bad done to me. The kind of bad that leaves a mark so dark, sometimes I wonder if I don't wear it like a beacon.

The elevator dings and then the doors part, chasing away the rumble of thunder in my mind.

Anticipation thrums heavy in my chest as I approach my suite door. My heart feels as if it might actually beat clear out of my chest as I slide my key into the lock.

I inhale deeply and hold my breath as I swing the heavy, wooden door open.

Except, when I step inside, I'm alone. I'm only half relieved; if I'm being honest, I would have preferred to get the meet-and-greet out of the way.

The main living space is cozy in a generic sort of way, with a deep navy couch and a low-sitting coffee table. There's a modest-sized flat screen television mounted on the wall over a console table. And in the kitchen, there's even a small eat-in table with two chairs.

Undoubtedly, my mother would turn up her nose at these accommodations, but me? I'd take them a million times over the shiny mansion she calls home. That place is nothing more than a polished facade hiding poisonous lies and treacherous memories.

I check out the bathroom before peeking my head into the bedroom on the left. Judging by the fluffy purple duvet covering the bed, pictures on the walls, and string lights going from one side to the other, this room is claimed. Unfortunately, nothing about the room gives me any hints about its occupant.

Please God, let her be a nice, normal girl.

Unlike my suitemate's room, which is full of life and

somehow already looks lived in, mine is bare bones. A complete blank canvas... a fresh start.

I place both of my bags at the foot of the bed and then fish my phone from my back pocket. I unlock the screen with my thumb and pull up my text messages. Only, I don't have anyone to text. There's no one waiting to hear from me. I doubt mommy dearest even cares if I made it here okay.

Lord knows, she didn't bother to even check on me once over the past two days I spent driving here from Texas.

Sighing, I lock the screen and repocket the device.

For a moment, I sit here in total silence, letting the calm of the room wash over me. I'm sure it makes me foolish to put so much hope in this place being the turning point for me, but it's like the old saying goes, *if not now, when?*

If things don't get better—if *I* don't get better—I'm not sure what I'll do. I'm hoping, since I've already experienced rock bottom, that up is my only option.

Then again, I know better than most just how unfair life can be. Sometimes, it seems like the universe actually takes joy in kicking people while they're down.

I know it did for me.

The sound of the door unlatching snaps me out of my pity party. Instantly, I'm on high alert, my breaths sawing in and out of my lungs and my heart ricocheting around in my chest like a wayward bullet.

Please be nice. Please be nice. Please, please, please.

"You must be Emmalyn."

I force my eyes open and look toward the voice. My suitemate is striking, with long sandy hair, pale blue eyes, and bronzed skin.

"Um, Em-Emmy is fine."

"Nice to meet you, Emmy." Her eyes crinkle as she smiles. "I'm Stella."

"It's nice to meet you, too," I croak, feeling more self-conscious than ever. You only get one chance to make a good first impression and knowing my luck, this girl is going to think I'm a capital 'L' loser.

She studies me for a moment, squinting as she takes the time to really look at me.

My closet back home is filled with designer labels, but I didn't bring any of it when I left. These days, my clothes are more for comfort than style. And while we're not dressed dissimilarly, I still feel out of place under her scrutinizing gaze.

Finally, she nods. "Sweet." She eyes the two bags on the floor. "Do you need help bringing the rest of your stuff up?"

I swallow roughly. "Um, no. I... this is pretty much it."

Silence descends with me sitting awkwardly on the bed while she stands in the doorway. Oddly enough, it's a comfortable silence—the kind you'd expect to exist between lifelong friends, not virtual strangers.

"Well, what are you doing then?" she asks, intentionally not commenting on my lack of worldly possessions.

"The tech center. I need to, uh, go there and get my student ID card."

Her glossy peach lips tip up. "Perfect. Me, too. Let's go!" Before I can refuse, Stella crosses the small space, wraps her fingers around my wrist, and hauls me up from the bed. "C'mon, we can grab a bite to eat after."

After spending so much time ostracized and the butt of everyone's jokes, having someone actually want to spend time with me feels foreign. However, I'm so tired of being alone, and if Stella wants to be friendly toward me, I'm certainly not going to stop her.

Here's to hoping it doesn't blow up in my face.

I manage to grab my messenger bag from the floor as Stella drags me out of my room. "So, where are you from?" she asks.

"Texas."

Stella lets out a low whistle as we step into the hallway. "Long way from home. Won't you miss your family?"

It's on the tip of my tongue to say no, but such an honest reply will only invite questions I have no intention, much less desire, to answer. "I'll manage," I say instead.

"You're stronger than me. I've lived here in Central Valley for my entire life. My parents literally live like five minutes away."

"Then why are you living on campus?" I ask before I can think better of it. *Great. Now she probably thinks I'm rude.*

Instead of snapping at me, she laughs and shrugs before punching the button to summon the elevator. "Wanted the full college experience. These are supposed to be the best years of our lives, right?"

"That's what they say." I step into the elevator behind her, wishing like hell I wasn't so rusty in social situations.

Stella grins and hits the button for the ground floor. "I think I'm gonna like you, roomie. I really do."

Much to my surprise, I find myself grinning right back at her. With Stella at my side, maybe Central Valley really will be my fresh start after all.

"OH MY GOD," Stella cackles. "At least you're smiling in your picture. I look like I'm constipated!"

She waves her freshly printed badge in my face to prove her point.

I try to hold in my laughter, but it is a fruitless pursuit. "You really do."

"Shut up." She elbows me as we meander down the sidewalk. "—"

"Say cheese." ...er s... ...ing with cheese."

It takes a second for my words to click, but as they do, Stella dissolves into laughing. "Oh my God!" she wheezes.

"A—" I say ..., awkwardly patting her back.

She swings up, dodging my hand from her. "I am amazed. I actually now know you have a sense of humor beneath that doom and gloom."

"Whatever," I mumble under my breath.

"Hey," Stella's laughter dies off. "I meant no offense. It's normal to be a little *in your feels* girl. You just moved like five states away to attend college. You're allowed to be sad and shit. I'd probably cry forever if I moved away from my family."

"Nah, you'd be fine."

"What makes you say that?" Stella asks, stopping in the middle of the sidewalk.

Despite the burning in my cheeks, I shrug. "I don't know. You just seem... strong."

"I'm glad you think so. Some days, I think—" She shakes her head, clearing away the clouds that were creeping into her pretty blue eyes. "Never mind. You wanna go to Target and get pretzels and Icees?"

Stella's transparent in her deflection, but I'd be the pot calling the kettle black if I were to say anything, so instead, I resume walking and say, "Most definitely."

"Do you drive?" she asks before slapping her palm to her forehead. "Blonde moment! It's not like you teleported from Texas."

"We all have them," I assure her, twisting a lock of my dark brown hair that's escaped my braid around my fingers. "Even those of us on the dark side."

"You're cool driving us, though?"

"Yup. I'm in the lot in front of the dorm."

Like an unwanted companion, anxiety churns in my gut as we near the parking lot. Stella seems cool, but what if she's the kind of girl who will think less of me because my car is out of date?

No, Emmy, stop it. Don't self-sabotage out of fear. You're better than that and Stella doesn't deserve to be the victim of said fear.

"This is me." I stop at the trunk and dig my keys from my bag.

"Nice ride," she says, skimming her hand appreciatively over the body.

If she were anyone else, I'd assume she was being disingenuous, but Stella's face is completely open and honest. She truly believes my little old Honda is nice.

"Thanks. Bought her myself," I say as I duck into the driver's seat.

"Does she have a name?" Stella asks once she's buckled.

"No..." I hedge.

The bubbly blonde to my right gasps. "What? You *have* to name your car. Everyone knows that, Em."

My heart slams against my chest in tandem with my foot slamming against the brake pedal. Stella braces herself on the dash as the momentum of my sudden stop sends her forward.

"What? What is it?" she asks, her voice trembling slightly.

Embarrassment renders me mute.

"Emmy, are you okay? You're totally freaking me out."

My breath stalls in my chest and my hands sweat against the leather of the steering wheel. I pinch my eyes closed and try to regulate my breathing.

Sensing something is deeply wrong, Stella softens her voice when she speaks again. "Hey, it's okay. Deep breaths, right?" She says each word slowly, with a deliberateness that tells me this isn't her first rodeo with panic attacks.

"Everything is okay. You're okay."

I nod as I exhale.

"Do you think you can pull the car to the side of the road?"

I nod again before peeling my lids open and guiding my car to the shoulder. Thankfully there are no other vehicles in sight.

"What happened just now?"

So much for her thinking I'm normal. Now she knows I'm a freak.

"You don't have to tell me, but I'm a great listener."

"It..." I swallow hard. "It was the name. I, um—"

"Say no more." Stella waves a hand in the air. "I'll never use it again. Promise."

Relief washes over me instantaneously. "Thank you."

"We all have our shit, girl. No worries. Now, if you're good to drive, I need some cinnamon-sugar goodness, stat."

"Yeah, I am. Just tell me where to go."

"Didn't you luck out?" she asks as I pull back onto the road. "A bomb-ass roomie and your own personal very local tour guide."

"OH. MY. GOD." Stella pops the last of her pretzel into her mouth. "I swear, they put crack in the cinnamon. There's no other explanation."

"That good, huh?" I ask as I toss my trash.

"Girl. You'll have to try one next time. You'll never get that salty garbage again."

"I happen to like my salty garbage, thank you very much."

"Yeah, yeah. Well, we all have our flaws."

I can't help but laugh at her antics. Stella is a breath of fresh air and exactly what my life has been missing for the last nine months. Hell, probably longer, seeing as all of the people I thought were my friends were the first to turn on me when shit hit the fan.

"You mind if I grab a few things?" I ask.

"Girl, first thing you need to know about me? I will never say no to a Target run. This is my literal happy place."

I grin. My former friends wouldn't be caught dead shopping at Target. Yep, Stella is everything I've been missing and more.

We each grab a shopping cart and, through some unspoken agreement, head toward the home section of the store.

"What all do you need?" I ask as we peruse the aisles.

"Need?" Stella spins in a wide circle before turning down the next aisle. "I don't know, but Target will tell me. Trust the bullseye."

I roll my lips inward to keep from laughing. "If you say so."

"I know so! It's like, science, or something."

"Or something," I snort, tossing a basic white duvet insert into my cart.

"Trust the process, Emmy. Trust the process."

"You're crazy." A giggle punctuates my words.

"The best people are."

For the next half hour, we continue up and down the aisles, stopping when something catches our attention, until our carts are full.

Stella's is a mishmash of things, while mine is loaded down with essentials, since I came to Georgia with nothing more than a single bag of clothing, my phone, and beloved laptop.

Oh, and Oreos—but those are essential for me.

"Are you going to any of the Welcome Week events?" Stella asks as we load our bags into the trunk.

"I don't know." I shrug. "I read online you should, but..."

"But nothing! Personally, I plan on hitting up the ice cream social tonight."

"I do like ice cream."

"Perfect. We'll go together."

And just like that, I have plans with a friend on my first night at college.

SOMETHING PULLS ME FROM A DEEP, dreamless sleep. My eyes pop open and I bolt upright in my bed, desperately searching the small room for what pulled me from my slumber.

Goose bumps cover my skin, sweat beads my brow, and my heart is thundering in my chest. My body is on high alert; I just don't know why.

I clutch my fisted hand to my chest and will myself to calm down. In, out. Deep breaths.

When that doesn't help, I count back from one hundred.

By the time I've gotten to single digits, my breathing has returned to normal, and I'm able to take stock of the situation.

The realization of what has me so out of sorts hits me like a punch to the gut.

I slept.

No tossing, no turning. No nightmares. No waking up crying with the sheet twisted to my chest.

How sad is it that sleeping through the night is such a foreign concept to my brain and my body that I still woke up terrified?

Baby steps, I suppose.

Rolling to my side, I grab my phone and check the time. It's five past eight, which is easily the latest I've slept in years. I listen for sounds of life from Stella, but the suite is quiet. She must still be sleeping.

I fling off the covers and swing my feet over the edge of the bed. First things first: a steaming hot shower.

Some people say their best ideas happen in the shower, but for me, my mind goes totally blank the second I pull the curtain closed. It's like the water washes my worries right down the drain.

If only they'd stay gone.

Once I'm squeaky clean, I towel off and dress in a pair of cut-off shorts and another thrift store sweatshirt; this one is tie-dye and reads *Poor Little Rich Girl* in swooping cursive. I love it mostly because my mom loathed it.

I braid my damp hair and slather my face with moisturizer before brushing my teeth and calling it good. It's easy to be low maintenance when you have no one to impress.

By the time I pad back into the kitchen, Stella is awake and pouring herself a cup of coffee. "Want some?" she asks through a yawn.

"Always."

She passes me a mug, which I graciously accept. Stella stares wide-eyed as I sip down the piping beverage.

"What?" I ask.

"You just drink it... black?"

"Oh, um, yeah," I say, looking down into my mug. Mom always said cream and sugar make for thick thighs, so I learned to like it without. "Force of habit, I guess?"

Stella pulls a face as she moves to the fridge and loads her mug with some kind of flavored creamer. She takes a sip and sighs. "Ah, sugary goodness."

We drink our beverages in silence for a minute, before Stella randomly bursts out laughing.

"What?" I ask, because seriously... who just cracks up out of nowhere?

"I was just thinking. I'm blonde and like lighter coffee. You're brunette and like dark coffee." She shrugs and takes another sip. "I don't know, it just made me laugh."

"You're ridiculous," I tell her. "And I love it."

"Duh. I'm lovable AF." She finishes her mug and refills it. "What are your plans today?"

"I need to get my books, but that's pretty much it."

"Oh my God! That reminds me—we haven't compared schedules or anything! What are your classes? Do you know your major?"

"Psych major," I say, ducking my head, before rattling off my class schedule.

"Oh, we have history together!" Stella remarks, rinsing her mug and then the carafe. "I'm an education major. Every woman in my family since basically the dawn of time has been a teacher."

"That's really cool." I mean it, too, seeing as the only degree my mother ever earned was her *Mrs.*

Stella nods. "Most people think I want to teach because it is expected of me, but I truly have a heart for it. The thought that I could impact a child's life... to help them on their path... I don't know, it makes me happy."

"I think that's amazing."

"Thanks! So, do you know what you want to do with your degree?"

Right as I go to reply, there's a knock on our suite door.

Stella checks the peephole on the door before unlocking it and swinging it open. "Hey, Melanie," she says in greeting, waving the lanky brunette into our space.

"Good morning, ladies," she chirps, stepping into the room with a folder clasped under one arm.

"Hey," I murmur, glancing down toward the floor.

"We didn't get to meet yesterday," Melanie says, stepping closer to me. "I'm the RA for your floor. I stopped by yesterday, but y'all were out."

"Sorry." I wipe my hands across the front of my shorts. "I'm Emmy, it's nice to meet you."

"Nice to meet you, too." Melanie smiles, seemingly unbothered by my sudden bout of nerves. "This is for you," she says, holding the folder she brought with her out toward me. "It's a little welcome pack from me to you. You'll find the dorm rules, along with some useful info."

"Oh, thanks." I clutch the folder to my chest.

"For sure. Are y'all settling in all right? Getting along okay?"

I step back and let Stella take point. "We are. Emmy and I are a match made in roomie heaven."

Melanie beams. "Glad to hear it. If you ladies need anything, my number is on the last page in your welcome packet."

"Perfect. Thanks so much." Stella walks her back to the door.

Our RA offers us one last smile before stepping back into the hallway.

"She seems nice," I murmur, hating myself a little for shutting down in her presence.

Stella nods before smoothly changing the subject. "Let me get dressed and we can head to the bookstore together."

I pop my now cold mug of coffee into the small

microwave and sip on it while Stella gets ready. Luckily, she's fairly low maintenance as well and doesn't keep me waiting long.

———

THE SUN IS high in the sky and shining brightly when we exit the dorm. It's unseasonably warm out, which is why the chill skittering over my skin has my back stiffening and the fine hairs on my body standing on end.

It's the same feeling as yesterday, as though someone is watching me. It's a fight not to frantically search for the prying eye that has my skin feeling like it's covered in ants, itching and crawling.

"Are you okay?" Stella asks, somehow tuned in to my discomfort.

As discreetly as possible, I survey our surroundings.

Once again, there isn't anything or anyone suspicious.

I shake off the feeling and force a grin. "Yup, just got a chill."

"Do we need to go back so you can change?" Stella nods down toward my shorts.

"No, I'm good," I assure her. After all, paranoia isn't something you'll find in the weather app on your phone.

She regards me, doubt darkening her pale eyes, before finally nodding. "Okay. Let's go."

We fall into step together, making our way across the campus to the student center, where the campus bookstore is housed.

It takes a few minutes for the feeling of being watched to fully dissipate; luckily, Stella is a talker, and her endless chatter quickly distracts me from my demons.

"Do you plan on going to any football games?" she asks

as we enter the student center.

"I don't know. It's never really been my thing before." The lie rolls off of my tongue so easily it should worry me. But that part of my life is in the past, locked away under lock and key.

Plus, it's really only a half-lie. I don't know football from any other sport, game-wise. I only ever cheered and shook my pom-poms on the sidelines. I was too busy nailing my stunts and routines to ever bother learning the actual game.

"Well, I plan on experiencing every college-y thing there is. So that means you're going to at least one game with me."

"Every college-y thing?" I raise a dubious brow.

"Yes. Every." Stella wags her brows and leans into me. "Including ditching my V-card."

My eyes widen at her candor, and she laughs.

"Don't look so scandalized, Emmy. It's the twenty-first century; women can talk about sex."

"No, right, of course, they can." I pinch my eyes closed and shake my head, dispelling the dark thoughts that try rolling in.

"Have you"—she leans in, so only I can hear her—"had sex?"

Dread drops into my gut like an anvil, the weight of it threatening to plummet me straight into the bowels of hell.

Misreading my misery for embarrassment, Stella nudges me with her elbow. "No worries, Emmy. Just because women *can* talk about sex, doesn't mean they *have* to." She laughs under her breath. "My mom would love you... she says modesty is a woman's best accessory."

I offer her a grateful smile at her easy reprieve as we step into the bookstore.

"Let's split up and grab our books and then afterward, maybe we can get some food?"

"Sounds good."

ANOTHER NIGHT of peaceful sleep down, and hopefully a lifetime more to go.

Seriously, a girl could get used to not waking up sobbing or screaming.

Stella has plans with her family today, which leaves me on my own. Apparently, they do a big family dinner after church.

Remembering the little campus cafe, I decide to throw on a slip dress, throw my hair up, and fur-lined Van mules. I brush my teeth, spray a little dry shampoo in my hair and call it good.

The air is slightly cooler in the city compared to yesterday, but I like the bite of it against my skin. It reminds me that I'm alive and well.

I take my time and wander as I walk, not really thinking about anything in particular. Which is why it comes as a total surprise when I slam right into a wall.

No. Not a wall, per se. Unless you count rock-hard muscles as a wall. It certainly feels like one.

"Oh, God. I'm so, so sorry." I take a step back, but

still have to crane my neck to look at the behemoth of a man I just plowed into. "Are you... okay?"

Mr. Muscles grins down at me. "Pretty sure I should be asking you that. You slammed into me pretty hard, sweets."

I can feel my cheeks heat to near nuclear levels. "I'm fine," I squeak.

"That you are. Got a name?"

My knees threaten to drop me on my ass, not out of attraction, but fear. All at once, it dawns on me how close this giant, strange man is. He could do anything to me, and I'd be helpless to defend myself. He's built like a brick shithouse, nearly three times my size.

"Um." My entire body shakes as I back away from him.

"Hey, whoa." He holds his hands up. "I'm not going to hurt you, sweets. You're safe."

I don't realize I'm crying until he reaches out and wipes away my tears.

Is it possible to die from humiliation? I scoff at myself. I know good and well it's not, because if it were, I'd have been six feet under long ago.

"S-s-sorry," I stammer out the single word, wishing like hell I could teleport myself back to the safety of my suite.

Mr. Muscles smiles down at me in a way that's far too soft for his size. "You're good, no apologies needed." He takes a small step back, his hands still held out in front of him. "Let's try again. I'm Gabe, and you are?"

"Emmy."

"It's nice to meet you, Emmy." He reaches out to shake my hand, but seems to think better of it and lets his arm drop before I can clasp his hand.

"It's, um, nice to meet you, too. And I'm... really sorry for running into you." I toe at the ground. "And I'm sorry for being such a mess, too."

"What did I say? No apologies needed." He winks. Any other guy, and I'd scoff, but somehow Gabe makes it work. "Am I allowed to ask where you're headed?"

I hesitate to answer him, a fact that doesn't escape him.

"Before you go thinking I'm a stalker, I'm only asking because I'm hungry and was hoping you'd do me the honor of joining me."

I gulp, torn on how to reply. On one hand, Gabe's intentions could be strictly platonic; on the other... well, I'm not even remotely prepared to consider the other. For a second it felt like he was flirting, but I'm so out of touch with anything resembling romance that I can't be sure.

"Listen," he says, leveling me with a look that's as warm as it is stern. "No offense, but you remind me a little of a lost puppy, and I've never been able to resist feeding a stray. So, brunch, on me. No strings, no funny business. Just a meal between potential friends."

I weigh his words, searching for the truth. When I don't see as much as a hint of deception in his crystalline green eyes, I find myself accepting his invitation.

"I was actually on my way to eat, so um, I guess we could do it together. Eat, I mean. We could eat together."

Gabe quirks a brow, like he's not quite sure what to do with me.

That makes two of us, Mr. Muscles.

"Where were you headed?"

"Holy Roasters."

He rumbles his approval. "After you."

I shoot him a weak smile and resume walking.

"You're a freshman, right?" Gabe asks.

"That obvious?"

He imitates a dog whimpering. "Little. Lost. Puppy."

Indignation burns in my chest. "I was doing just fine until we collided."

A deep, masculine chuckle is his only reply.

"What?"

"Sweets," he sighs. "You were walking with your eyes trained on the ground like it held all of the answers to the universe. I'd been standing still when you walked into me. You legit didn't notice me. I'm six-five and two-hundred-and-eighty pounds. I'm kind of hard to miss."

"So, maybe I was a little distracted?"

He reaches past me, holding the door to the cafe open for me. The smell of fresh coffee and cinnamon greet me, beckoning me inside.

"Or..." He lets the door close behind him. "Maybe you didn't want to draw attention by making eye contact with anyone."

Or maybe I felt like someone was watching me and the feeling made me want to crawl in a hole and never come out... potato, po-tah-to.

"Something like that," I murmur, scanning the menu.

Gabe hums thoughtfully, but the barista greets us before he can reply.

"Welcome to Holy Roasters, what can I get y'all today?"

The beast of a man behind me prompts me to order first. "Um, a coffee, black, and a cinnamon roll."

"And you?"

"Oh, we're separate," I mumble, but Gabe talks right over me. "I'll also take a coffee, black, but with room for cream. A green smoothie, a breakfast burrito, a banana, and a blueberry muffin."

My jaw practically unhinges at the amount of food he orders.

"Gotta keep my figure." He winks and pats his belly.

"That'll be twenty-two fifty."

"But, we're not—"

Gabe bustles me behind him and then passes the barista his card, paying for my order along with his, despite my protests.

"Y'all's coffees will be at the end of the bar, and we will bring the rest out when it is ready."

Smooth as butter, Gabe maneuvers me to where our steaming paper cups are waiting. Gabe adds a healthy dose of cream and sugar while I simply pop a lid onto mine and call it good.

"How about that table by the window?" he asks, not actually waiting for me to reply.

Our seats offer us an unfettered view of both the cafe and the campus. I ignore the bustle around me and focus on the students milling about on the other side of the glass. People watching has always been a hobby of mine; there's something about assigning stories and traits to strangers that thrills me.

Maybe it's because, for a short time, I can see everyone as good. Who knows?

"Zone out much?" Gabe asks, knocking his knee into mine.

"Just taking in the scenery."

An employee drops off my cinnamon roll, along with his mountain of food.

"Where are you from?" He takes a massive bite of his muffin, sending crumbs scattering across the table.

"Texas, you?"

"Alabama, but only just past the state line."

"What made you decide to come to Central Valley?" I ask, for lack of anything more interesting to offer. Plus, if I keep the focus on him, it won't be on me.

"Football."

"Oh, yeah? Is the program good?"

His cheeks spread into a shit-eating grin. "Nope."

As much as I hate to admit it, he's got me, hook, line, and sinker. "Explain."

"Dad wanted me to play ball. Mom wanted me to get a degree. This was a middle ground. It's Mom's alma mater, so Dad couldn't say no without making her feel bad. And, technically, I'm on the team. It's a win-win. You know, aside from the actual games. Those are definitely a loss."

"I guess you aren't trying to go pro?"

"Not even remotely. I'm working toward a communications degree."

"Oh, that's cool."

I'm so enthralled in our conversation, I don't even realize I haven't touched my own food, until Gabe asks if I plan on eating it.

I pinch off a bite and pop it into my mouth, my eyes falling shut as the flavors serenade my taste buds. Cinnamon, vanilla, and a hint of orange play a symphony in my mouth. "Oh my God." I lick some of the cream cheese icing from my thumb, moaning softly before going back for more.

"Sweets," Gabe groans.

I divert my attention from what I am now calling my crack roll to him. "Yeah?"

He shakes his head. "You really are clueless, aren't you?"

"Excuse me? Rude."

"You have to know you're a total babe, right?"

All I can do is stare at him in utter confusion.

Gabe sighs like he doesn't know what to do with me.

Well, back at ya, buddy, you're about as easy to understand as a Rubik's Cube.

"Emmy, I'm gonna level with you." He drags his eyes over me in a way that leaves me more baffled than breathless. "You're like, fuck-hot. Tall, toned, with curves in the right places. You've got a pretty face and pouty lips. Great hair. You're easily a ten."

My cheeks blister with what has to be third-degree burns as he basically takes stock of me like I'm a piece of cattle.

"Gabe, I—"

He waves away my protests and bulldozes on. "You're innocent and sweet and pretty much every college boy's wet dream."

I'm all but two seconds from bolting. This brunch is easily the weirdest I've ever experienced, and that's really saying something since I broke bread with Satan himself on a weekly basis, smiling like nothing was amiss.

"I think I should go," I whisper, pushing my chair back from the table.

"I'm not hitting on you, sweets. Chill."

"Um."

"Listen, you're cute. Hot, really. But I'm currently more into dicks than chicks."

His confession keeps me in my seat.

"I'm... so confused. Gabe, what is... what are you... just what?"

He sighs. "I guess I did get a little off-topic. My point was you need to be more aware. Of yourself, of your surroundings. You're a pretty girl, and you wear your innocence on your sleeve for all to see. There's plenty of people ready and willing to prey on that. That's all I was trying to say."

"No offense, but you went about it in a really weird way."

"Yeah." Gabe slouches down in his chair and scrubs his hands over his face. "Zach laughs all the time over the fact that I'm a communications major who majorly sucks at communicating."

I laugh at his admission. "Is Zach your…"

"Boyfriend? Yup. For over a year now."

"Do you like girls, too?" I ask, immediately wishing I could stuff the words back into my mouth.

His green eyes twinkle as he regards me.

"Why? You interested?"

I cough out an unintelligible reply.

"Kidding. But yes. I'm into the person, not what they're packing below the belt, you know?"

For the first time since I ran into him, Gabe looks self-conscious. "I think… that's perfect. Brave and perfect."

My behemoth of a friend grins. "I knew I was going to like you, sweets."

We chat for a few more minutes before tossing our trash and heading out. "Let's do this again soon, yeah?"

I nod. "Yes, for sure."

It's not until Gabe's out of sight that I realize we never exchanged numbers.

Oh, well. I suppose if our friendship is meant to be, it will find a way.

The weather is mild, and I decide to use the rest of my afternoon to explore the gorgeous, sprawling campus. If anything, maybe it will help orient me by the time classes start in a few days.

Twenty minutes into my exploration, I stumble upon a wooded walking trail. The temptation to venture down it is too great, and I find myself stepping off the sidewalk and onto the narrow, leafy path.

The sounds of the campus fade away as those of nature

wrap around me. Branches rustle as the wind whispers through them, carrying birdsong with it.

In the distance, I can see the peaks of the mountains rising up into the sky, cementing the fact that I'm no longer in flat-as-a-pancake Texas anymore.

Thank. God.

If I never step foot back into that godforsaken state, it will be too soon.

Don't get me wrong, I have nothing against the actual landmass. But every bad memory I have happened there, and I just... I can't handle the idea of returning. Escaping to eastern Georgia is my fresh start and I am going to make the most of it so I never have to return to the four walls that masquerade as a home.

Eventually, I reach the end of the walking path and have no choice but to head back. As I approach the mouth of the trail, the hustle and bustle of the campus comes crashing back into focus.

People are scattered about, but there's one in particular that has me frozen, as fear and confusion tear through me, rooting me in place.

I squint against the harsh light of the sun, hoping... praying... begging that my eyes are deceiving me.

I'm hallucinating; I have to be. Even if the erratic thumping of my heart says otherwise.

Because directly across the street, front and center, is the devil's right-hand man. His piercing gray eyes are locked on me, and his lip is curled in a snarl.

I want to run, or at the very least to look away, but my fight or flight instinct seems to be stalled, rendering me completely immobile.

I'm a sitting duck in the face of a wolf. A hungry wolf, with very sharp teeth, if the way he's glaring at me is any indication.

My vision tunnels as he steps off of the sidewalk, moving toward me with a single-minded focus.

Move, dammit! Run! I shout at myself, and yet, I may as well be a statue for how still I remain.

He grins as he nears. It's a feral sort of smile, one that promises pain, retribution, and punishment for my perceived crimes.

He's more than halfway to me when I finally unfreeze. I don't think twice, I just run, the sound of his cruel laughter chasing behind me.

I'VE SEEN Rosalyn a few times on campus now. She always looks so meek and mild and innocent.

She's convincing, too, with her eyes always on the ground and her soft, murmured words. Hell, I was almost ready to call the whole thing off, my friendship with Rob be dammed.

Until I remembered it was all a ruse, I know the kind of girl she really is.

Trouble.

[illegible]

And she had an obvious case of buyer's remorse.

I watched her for a few seconds when I saw her venturing out of her building along with an unreadable expression on her [illegible].

At first, it was hard to read, but I quickly saw it for what it truly [illegible].

The moment of unfettered guilt in her gaze when she saw me was all the confirmation I needed.

And when she [illegible] shake my head at her idiocy. Innocent people don't run. Why would they when they have nothing to hide?

If she thinks running away somehow absolves her of her sins...

She's wrong.

A pound of flesh is owed, and I am more than happy to collect on Rob's behalf. I'll make her suffer ten times over for what she did to him.

Emmalyn has no idea what's in store for her. She foolishly thought she could upend my best friend's life and then scurry away to Georgia, like a scared little mouse.

Too bad for her, Rob somehow managed to arrange for her to end up here.

With me. Her very own big, bad wolf.

She's backed into a corner now and doesn't even know it.

Game on, little mouse. Game on.

FOR THE SECOND day in a row, I bolt upright in bed, gasping for air while tears stain my cheeks.

"It's okay," I console myself. "You're okay. He's not here."

I repeat the words over and over, until the lingering wisps of my nightmare wither away and my heart rate returns to normal.

Logically, I know that Sterling Abbot isn't here, in Georgia. He's back in Texas with all the monsters, doing rich boy things like ruining the lives and crushing dreams.

After sprinting all the way back to my dorm, I scoured the school's website for any mention of him. Much to my relief, my search came up blank. There's no trace of a Sterling Abbot at Central Valley.

For a split second, it crosses my mind that he could be a student here, but I brush that notion aside. Surely a man like him would go to Ivy League and not a small-town private college.

Don't get me wrong. Central Valley is still the kind of school where money talks, especially *old* money. It has top-notch academics and produces graduates that go on to do great things. But in the circles my family runs in, prestige is power, and I'm not sure this charming little town offers enough of it.

It is, however, highly unfortunate that the devil's right hand has a doppelganger here, of all places.

Sterling was a fixture in my childhood home. He and Rob were practically bosom buddies—with their wet nurses, because God knows their mothers wouldn't risk sagging tits. The devilish duo grew up together and, truth be told, for a long time, I used to secretly pray Sterling would come over.

Because if he was there, then Rob was too preoccupied to mess with me.

Sterling sleeping over was typically the only reprieve I ever got from my stepbrother sneaking into my bedroom at night.

Not to mention, the many times he sought me out just to say hi or ask me about my day. In such a cold, frigid household steeped in hate, he was often times my only bright spot.

As silly as it sounds, I always fancied him a knight, sent to protect me. Now I know those were childish wishes, but at the time, the notion helped me get by.

Seeing him though—well, seeing his lookalike—sent me into a tailspin. Those darkly familiar and striking features of his stole away every bit of safety and security I've acquired since arriving here. Seeing him thrust me back into the hell I've spent the last nine months clawing my way out of.

Hopefully, if I'm lucky, I'll never see him again.

Except, when am I ever lucky?

A QUICK GLANCE at the clock tells me I still have a few hours before I need to be up. But the thought of what horrors might await me in my slumber has me swiping open the Kindle app on my phone.

There's nothing like a good book to steal you away from your troubles. Truly, without the escape reading provides, I may not have survived at all. When all of my friends and family turned on me, fictional characters wrapped me in their words and fit back together my mangled, barely beating heart.

Before I know it, I'm several chapters deep, and Stella is banging on my bedroom door, shouting for me to get up. "Girl! We're not going to have time to stop by Holy Roasters if you don't get it in gear. I need coffee, Emmy. Need. It."

I swipe out of the app and check the time. *Holy crap, it's after eight!*

"I'm coming!" I fly out of my bed and throw on my favorite high-waisted leggings, stuffing my feet into my Vans. I slip a cropped neon-pink hoodie over my bralette, toss my hair in a topknot and call it good.

"Are you ready?" Stella asks as I race past her on my way into the bathroom.

"Nearly!" I call back, shutting the door behind me.

I emerge five minutes later as put together as a girl can be in under ten minutes. "Ready," I murmur, grabbing my messenger bag from the couch on our way out of the door.

"Are you nervous?" she asks as we emerge from the building.

"Only a lot."

Her answering laugh causes me to grin.

The sun is shining. The sky is blue. I'm safe. And today is the first official day of my future. Come hell or high water, I'm determined to make the best of it.

Surprisingly, the line at Holy Roasters is relatively short; we're in and out in under five minutes, with our coveted caffeinated beverages in hand.

"Let's get lunch after?" I ask when it's time for us to go our separate ways.

"Duh." Stella rolls her eyes, as if it was a given. "Let's meet at the fountain in the quad?"

"Perfect."

She heads left down the sidewalk, while I enter the building to the right.

The hallway is packed with students and faculty alike, but I'm far too concerned with counting the room numbers to pay them any mind.

Ever since realizing Professor Ellison is both my Psych 101 prof *and* my academic advisor, I've been determined to make a good first impression. The man has serious clout in the world of academia. He's supposedly working on the second book of a three-book deal.

And while I hate the dog and pony show of the society I grew up in, I know having something as small as a recommendation letter from Professor Ellison could be potentially game-changing for my academic future.

After passing it twice, I finally find the number I'm looking for. First day jitters hit me full force as I enter the classroom.

Psych 101 is the first step to securing my future as a victim advocate, and I'm willing to do anything, to face anything, to make this dream a reality. Even if that means stepping out of my comfort zone—i.e., sitting in a room full of strangers.

The inside of the classroom is nothing special; it's your basic setup, with rows of desks on either side of a central walkway. At the front of the room, there's a podium, as well as a projector screen.

Behind said podium is Professor Ellison himself. He's thoroughly engrossed in something on his laptop screen, not paying any attention to the students entering the room.

Many of the seats are already filled, but I manage to claim a desk near the center of the room. Close enough to the front to have a good view, and far enough from the back to show I'm no slacker.

At nine on the dot, Professor Ellison strolls over to the door and closes it before returning to the podium. He stares out, his gaze moving over the room like a cool breeze.

He clears his throat and introduces himself. "Welcome to Psych 101. I'm Professor Ellison." His voice is the kind that commands attention. He nods to a guy in the front row. "You there, pass these out."

The kid scrambles out of his seat and grabs the stack of papers, handing one to each student before hurriedly returning to his desk.

"Before you is your class syllabus. It covers everything you need to know for this class. Please take a moment to read over it. If you have any questions or concerns, please first ask my TA. If he is unable to assist, you may then email me with an appointment request to discuss it."

The room falls silent as we all scan over the pages. Only, I never make it past the third section, a name from my nightmares is typed neatly in bold letters that practically jump off of the page.

Teaching Assistant/Coordinator: Sterling Abbot.

I scrub at my eyes with the heels of my hands before blinking and reading the page again. Surely my eyes are playing tricks on me. They *have* to be. Because, if they're not, that means my past—the one I'm so desperately trying to escape—is catching up with me before I've even had a chance to truly be free.

But when I look down at the page again, his name is still there, mocking me cruelly.

My palms sweat as I clutch the sides of my desktop, debating whether or not I should flee. My breaths come in short pants while my heart hammers in my chest like someone stabbed me with a syringe of adrenaline.

I can feel moisture gathering in the corners of my eyes; I'm about to break down crying in the middle of my first college class.

Central Valley was supposed to be my fresh start, but it's becoming clear this is nothing more than a long-distance prison—that the freedom was just a carrot to lure me into a trap.

On autopilot, I begin shoving things back into my bag. I can't… the thought of facing him is pure agony. Maybe I can get transferred to another class?

I sling the strap of the bag around my shoulder and shoot out of my desk, ready to make my escape. I barely make it to the end of the aisle before the door swings open and Sterling waltzes in.

He's even more imposing up close, with his sharp jaw and hawk-like gray eyes. He's tall and brooding, and utterly lethal.

The sight of him, up close and personal, has me swaying on my feet. My skin somehow is pebbled with gooseflesh and sweaty at the same time.

Instinctively, I avert my eyes from his, hoping I'll be able to slip past him without any resistance.

I should have known better.

"Emmalyn Grace Price." His voice is low, a taunt meant

only for me. The sound of it sends shards of ice through me, freezing me from the inside out. "Going somewhere?"

"Um… I, um," is all I manage to stammer out.

He grins, but it isn't a kind gesture. In fact, it lacks any warmth whatsoever. It's cold, detached, and brutal. He steps closer and leans down into my space. "You thought you'd get off scot-free? That you'd run away and hide your sins?"

I shake my head back and forth, adamantly wanting to refute him, but I can't seem to find the words.

"Not on my watch. You ruined him, his entire life, and now…I'm going to ruin you. I'm going to dismantle everything you've ever loved. I'm going to dissect you, take you apart, and scatter the pieces."

He keeps his voice low, and his face soft. I want so badly to push past him, to run out of the door and never look back. A fact he uses to his advantage. To anyone else, it probably looks like he's consoling me, the young nervous freshman.

"You think you regret spreading your legs for him? You're going to regret spreading those lies even more. Now, take a seat, Emmalyn. Class is starting."

I gulp, unable to move, to speak, to breathe. It feels like my entire world is collapsing, like the walls of this classroom are closing in on me, like they're going to bury me alive.

Sterling's eyes light with something akin to mirth as he regards me, watching the panic, fear, and pain play out across my face like a movie.

"Scurry back to your desk, little mouse." He takes a threatening step closer to me and, like the coward I am, I whirl around and race back to my seat, hating myself for allowing him to have any kind of power over me.

I bury my face in my hands, knowing I just made a fool

of myself, not only to him, but to the entire class, and even worse—in front of my academic advisor.

"Ah, Mr. Abbot," the professor chortles, as if he found our interaction amusing somehow. "How nice of you to join us."

"Good to see you, Professor Ellison." I swear to God, his wicked gray gaze lands on me as he says, "I'm *thrilled* to be here."

Sterling crosses the room to stand with the professor. "This is Sterling Abbot, my TA for this class. He will handle the day-to-day basics, and should be your point person for most things."

You can do this, Emmy. Get through the next hour and then you can figure things out.

"Mr. Abbot, if you will." Professor Ellison gestures to the podium, stepping out from behind to make room for Sterling.

"To get things started, we're going to do an activity called *Stand Up*."

My heart is pounding so hard that my pulse thunders in my ears, effectively blotting out his voice. Which is a blessing and a curse.

A blessing, because the sound of his deep, gravelly voice both terrifies and enthralls me.

A curse, because I have no clue what's happening at the moment, other than students seem to be standing at random.

I will myself to calm down. *Professor Ellison is here, he won't allow anything to happen. Breathe.*

The panic rushing my system begins to wane.

That is until the professor up and leaves the room.

Without him here, what will Sterling do? At this point,

I can only hope he has enough professionalism to spare me his wrath while inside the classroom.

Waves of tittering laughter raise up around me, yanking me from my internal worry.

"Miss Price," Sterling bites out.

My eyes fly up to his. Judging from the pinched look on his face, this is not the first time he's called my name. Which means they're all laughing at me.

"Y-yes?"

"Is there a reason you're not participating?"

I stare at him, doe-eyed.

"Have your legs suddenly quit working? Or perhaps you think you're too good to participate?"

"Um." I try to swallow, but my mouth feels like it's full of cotton balls. "If you could just... um... remind me what we're doing. Please?" My voice wobbles, right along with my pride. Less than ten minutes in his presence and I'm wilting like a daisy beneath the sweltering sun.

Sterling rolls his eyes, looking as pleased as he is perturbed.

"Since you haven't been paying attention, I'm calling out descriptors. You're to stand if they pertain to you. Surely you aren't so dull that none apply?"

My cheeks burn as his words hit their mark. "Right. I'm sor—"

Sterling cuts me off. "Let's try this again, this time with Princess Price participating."

Anger wells inside of me so fiercely, it nearly blots out the embarrassment.

"Now that I have *everyone's* attention, let's try this again. But first, please apologize to your classmates for wasting their time, Miss Price."

"What?" I sputter. He can't be serious.

"You heard me." He raps his knuckles against the podium. "Please don't make me repeat myself."

Bile rushes up my esophagus, but I force it down. "Fine. I'm sorry for wasting y'all's time. It was rude, and I will do my best to ensure it doesn't happen again."

"Satisfactory," he murmurs, his soft voice in direct contrast with his hard eyes. "Please stand if any of the following words have any at point applied to you. Once the next is listed, take a seat if it does not also apply."

Sterling draws out the anticipation, dragging his gaze around the room, before honing in on me. "Stand up if you are a liar."

A few uneasy titters go up.

"Come on, everyone lies," he goads, his focus still locked on to me.

I quickly glance around the room; my classmates look as uncomfortable as I feel.

Eventually, a guy toward the back of the room stands. Then a girl to the right of me, followed by several more students.

Maybe he's not out to get me. Maybe he's just a hardass in the classroom.

On trembling legs, I join the group standing.

Sterling smirks.

"Stand up if you've ever had regrets."

I remain standing, because who hasn't had regrets?

"Stand up if you're selfish."

I go to sit down, because selfish is definitely not a word I would use to describe myself.

Sterling's not having it though. "Remain standing, Miss Price."

"Why?" I whisper, feeling defeated but unwilling to admit it.

Ignoring my question, Sterling addresses the class. "I do not tolerate lies. Of any kind. Not to me, and not to yourself. Keep that in mind before returning to this class on Thursday. Show up ready to be real, or don't show up at all. Class dismissed."

In a flurry of motion, we all begin packing away our belongings. Luckily, most of my stuff is already in my bag from my failed escape attempt at the start of class.

I'm nearly to the door when Sterling calls after me. "Miss Price, a word?"

I gulp but turn and head toward him, determined not to show any more weakness to the likes of him. "Yes?"

"I know what you did," he says for my ears only, "and I intend to make you pay."

A million replies race through my brain, yet my mouth won't form around a single word. Instead, I glare while willing myself not to cry.

"That's right. I know. Now, run along, and if you're a good girl, maybe I'll play nice."

Still, I can't seem to bring myself to speak. And even if I could, I'm not sure I'd trust myself not to make a fool of myself. So, I do the only thing I can. I turn around and bolt.

CHAPTER 8

EMMY

I READ over her rapid-fire texts and slink down deeper into my despair. Because in addition to being a spineless coward, I'm also the worst friend who bailed on my lunch plans with Stella. Instead hiding out in the relative safety of our suite.

The smart thing would be to feel safe anywhere, knowing he's here, and in order to set up Bruno's vendetta as his own.

Guilt over ghosting my best friend weighs on me as I text her back.

ME
Sorry. I'm not feeling well.

Not a total lie.

STELLA

Want some soup?

ME
Sure, thanks.

I don't want soup. I don't want anything, other than to wake up and find this whole day is nothing more than a nightmare.

Only, I know this is real. Of course it is. Why would anything ever go my way? Honestly, you'd think the universe would give me a break after everything, but no. Here it is, knocking me down yet again.

I'm still wallowing when Stella enters our suite. "Emmy?" she calls, her voice soft.

"You can come in," I call back, unwilling to leave the cocoon I've created beneath my covers.

She steps into my bedroom, thankfully with no soup container in sight. "You look rough, babe."

I give her a wry laugh. "Thanks."

"Just calling it like I see it." Stella shrugs unapologetically before plopping down beside me on my bed. "What's going on?"

"I'm—"

"Don't you dare say sick." She shakes her head, her blonde locks whipping around her face. "I may not know you all that well *yet,* but I do know a lie when I hear it. You're not sick. You're just not. So, what gives?"

How much do I tell her? Will she think differently of me? Will she think I'm a liar? A slut?

A million different outcomes race through my mind as Stella stares expectantly, waiting for my reply.

"It's just. Um. Some bad things happened back home and coming here was supposed to be my fresh start." I sniffle as the tears I've been holding back all day finally break free. "But someone from home is here and I... I can't."

My sniffles give way to chest-heaving sobs.

"Hey, it's okay." Stella reaches out as if to hug me, but drops her arms at the last minute, taking my hand in hers instead. "You're okay."

"I'm not. I'm not, I'm not." I draw my knees to my chest, and repeat those same three words over and over, my head shaking side-to-side.

"Emmy, stop it!" Stella shouts. The unexpected sharpness of her tone instantly pauses my breakdown. "There, that's better. Now, listen. Everyone has a past. Everyone has demons. Everyone, babe. Even the freaking pope. But that doesn't mean you let them rule you."

"How?" I whisper, my voice hoarse from crying.

"By dealing with it. Head on."

"What do you mean?"

"Who is this person? Can you avoid him?"

I shake my head. "He's my TA."

Stella cringes. "Ooh. Can you talk to the professor? Change classes?"

"The thought of changing crossed my mind. Do you think I could?" A small seed of hope blooms in my chest.

"Log in and check. You should be able to request it through your portal."

I'm still not ready to leave the comfy warmth of my bed.

Luckily, Stella understands my puppy eyes and grabs my laptop for me.

"Thanks," I murmur, as I pull up my web browser and log in. Except, every time I try and submit a request to change the class, an error message pops up. "Ugh!"

"What's wrong?" Stella asks, leaning into my space to look at my screen. "Oh. That blows."

"What do I do?" My earlier panic threatens an unwanted encore.

"Try your advisor?"

"That's a good idea."

I exit out of the portal and open my student email.

Professor Ellison,

I am emailing to request a meeting with you about my class schedule. I tried adjusting it via the portal, but keep running into an error message.

Thank you in advance,
Emmy Pierce

"There," I say, feeling moderately better. "Now all we have to do is wait for him to reply."

"And pray like hell he accommodates your request," my roomie unhelpfully adds.

"That, too." As I move to close my laptop, a whoosh sounds, alerting me to a new email. "He replied!"

"That was fast! What's it say?"

"That he can see me tomorrow at noon!"

"You know what that means?"

"What?"

"No more panic until you know for sure there's something to panic over. Okay?"

Slowly, I nod. "Yeah. Okay."

Stella grins. "Good. Oh, and it also means you owe me a meal. I tried getting soup, but it looked inedible."

I can't help but laugh. "What sounds good?"

Her eyes flare wide. "Babe. I skipped lunch for you. I'd eat just about anything."

"So, we should go back for the soup?"

"Okay, anything except that."

"Let's order a pizza?" I suggest.

"Only if we follow it up with ice cream and a chick flick."

"Can do."

The rest of the night is spent stuffing our faces and watching *Sierra Burgess Is a Loser*. It's easily the best night I've had in a while.

But then sleep comes, and my past sinks its claws into me during my REM cycle.

"Stupid little bitch." My former best friend Nichole glares at me with nothing but hatred in her cool blue eyes. "You'll get what's coming to you."

While her cruel, venomous words sting, they're nothing compared to the betrayal I felt when she took Rob's side. The way she dropped me like I was nothing to her, after sixteen years of friendship... that almost hurt more than my own mother turning her back on me.

Laughter and jeers follow me down the hall, each one more cutting than the last.

"Ugh, watch out. Wouldn't want to catch an STD." Stacie, the cheer squad's newly minted captain, takes an exaggerated step away from the center of the hallway.

Her boyfriend wraps a protective arm around her and glares at me, as if I can somehow taint his precious little girlfriend by proximity alone.

His best friend, however, has no qualms about getting

close to me. "Hey, baby." The meathead jock steps into my path, crowding me. "Twenty bucks and I'll let you suck my dick."

"She's not worth it," Aaron, my first love and the boy I thought I'd marry, scoffs. "Pussy's like parking in a two-car garage. Shit was so loose, I felt like I was fucking a cup of water."

Tears burn my eyes, and shame paints my cheeks. It doesn't matter that we never even made it past second base. I'm now the school slut, and it's everyone's word against mine.

Unwilling to let them see my pain, I shoulder past them and walk away with my head held high. As soon as I turn the corner, I let the mask drop, breaking into a dead sprint toward the bathroom. Once I'm safely inside, I break, letting my tears fall as my heart breaks all over again.

***

THE NEXT MORNING dawns overcast and misty—perfectly somber to match my mood.

I wake up early enough to wash and dry my hair. I want to make a good impression on Professor Ellison, which I guess is kind of stupid after trying to flee his class yesterday. He probably thinks I'm some immature brat here on Daddy's dime.

Still, I take the time to dress nicely, throwing on a simple cotton dress that straddles the line between professional and relaxed.

I make it through two hours of class—one of history and one of science.

Thankfully, they're both easy days. We go over the

syllabus in both classes, do a few ice breakers, and in science, we also tour the department.

I send up a small prayer of thanks, because God knows my mind is preoccupied.

All I can think of is meeting with Professor Ellison. If he's not able to help me, I truly don't know what I'll do.

I'd like to say I'm strong enough to withstand whatever Sterling may have up his sleeve, but the truth is, I'm really just... not.

I only have minutes to make it to Professor Ellison's office after my science class ends. My power walk turns to a full-on sprint when I realize I'm cutting it close, and I manage to make it to his office at twelve on the dot.

A shiver works its way through me as I knock. Shuffling sounds from behind the door, and then it swings open, revealing the last person I wanted or expected to see.

He regards me disinterestedly before his lip curls into a sneer. "Are you coming in or not? My time is valuable, Miss Price."

"Um." I dart my eyes around the room, looking for Professor Ellison. Surely he's around here somewhere. Why would he set up a meeting and not show?

"Um," he mocks in a high pitched tone. "Drop the act. Either come in or leave."

"I... I'm supposed to have a meeting with Professor Ellison."

"Which he so kindly left in my capable hands."

I gulp. I'm pretty sure the only things his hands are capable of right now is strangling me.

"Stop wasting my time." Sterling's voice is a low growl that sends flutters of fear through my belly.

"Are you going to let me in?" I ask, sounding one-hundred percent braver than I feel.

Smirking, he steps back a fraction of an inch. If I want into that office, I'm going to have to press myself through the microscopic opening between him and the door.

Our chests brush as I cross the threshold. The hint of contact between us sends shivers down my spine.

Aware of his effect on me, Sterling laughs as he pulls the door closed behind us.

"To what do I owe the *dis*pleasure of this visit, Miss Price?"

He remains standing, and so do I. He's already taller than me, I'm not about to give him an ounce of additional power over me.

"I think you know." My voice is flimsy, even to my own ears, but I pretend not to notice.

He nods thoughtfully. "I'm sure I do, but I think I want to hear you say it."

Squaring my shoulders, I force my gaze up to his. "I would like to be transferred into a different section."

Sterling rubs his chin with his thumb and forefinger. "That's too bad."

"Why?" I ask, even though the sinking feeling in my gut says I already know.

He's not going to make this easy for me. It wouldn't surprise me for him to outright refuse me, if only out of spite.

"All of the other classes are full."

"All of them?" I ask in disbelief.

A dark grin tugs at the corners of his mouth. "Every. Single. One."

"Then I'll drop the class!" I shout, my voice far too loud for the small space.

He advances toward me, boxing me back until he has

me caged against the wall. My chest expands and contracts rapidly. His uninvited nearness makes my pulse go haywire.

"Sure." He leans his right forearm against the wall, dipping his face toward mine, so we're eye to eye. "You could, but I wouldn't advise it."

"Why not?" I whisper.

Sterling brings his left hand up and trails his knuckles over my cheek.

Suddenly, I'm thankful the wall is at my back to support me, because his touch—as unwanted as it is—has my entire body off-kilter. Whether it's the juxtaposition of the threat in his words and the softness of his touch, or simply fear, I'm not sure. Either way, I hate that a man as rotten as him can make me feel anything at all.

"You're a psych major, right?" He pauses and I nod. "Then you need this class."

"I can take it next semester."

"No, I don't think you can."

"Why?" I want to stomp my feet at the injustice of this whole situation.

I'm the one who was wronged, in the most atrocious of ways, and yet I'm also the one being punished.

"Because, little mouse, if you drop this class, you'll derail your entire college career."

"That's not... that's not true."

"Isn't it?"

I know there's a shred of truth to his words. I guess what it really comes down to is how much I'm willing to endure to make my dreams a reality. Yesterday, I was willing to do anything to cement my future.

Plus, what's the worst Sterling Abbot can truly do to me?

I CAN SEE the implication of my words as they hit. She knows I'm right, she knows if she drops this class, she won't be able to take at least one of the classes she wants next semester.

However, I need to make sure she stays.

Emmy falling into my lap like this is too good of an opportunity to pass up, and I'm damn sure willing to play dirty if it ensures she gets what's coming to her.

"Well..."

"I... something to me," I cut her off, my words intentionally...

"V..."

"You're showing too much, in that little dress."

...den...my... ...tion. "What? It's... it's just a dress..."

"She..." I reach down and finger the material of the hemline, my knuckle ... the soft, smooth skin of her thigh. "This is barely ... public."

Wetness gathers on her ... her lashes, but she doesn't speak. In fact, she doesn't even move. She's as still as a statue.

"I'd hate for it to get back to the dean that you came to your professor's office and propositioned him." I click my tongue and slowly shake my head back and forth. "I imagine having such a blight on your record would be troublesome. Especially given your past."

"You're a monster." Her voice breaks and the brimming tears spill over.

I step away from her, a smug look on my face. "You know what they say... takes one to know one."

Her entire body is practically vibrating in anger. I fucking love it.

"You wouldn't!"

"Wouldn't I?"

"It's... you'd be lying!"

"That's your area of expertise, is it not?" A sharp bark of laughter punctuates my words. "Poor little Princess Price. So eager to ruin the lives of others but whimpers and whines when she's paid back in kind."

"You don't know what you're talking about," she whispers vehemently.

She's good. Convincing. But I know better. She's a foolish girl prone to poor choices. A selfish girl. A liar. And it ends here. I won't let her ruin someone else's life. No, I'll ruin hers instead.

"I know exactly what I'm talking about."

She tries to shove past me, but I'm not quite ready to let her go.

"Not so fast."

Emmy tries again to push past me, and now I'm pissed.

"I said *not so fast*." I grab her wrists and mercilessly shove them into the wall over her head. She struggles against my hold, but her fight only excites me. I squeeze her delicate wrists even tighter as I press against her with my hips.

She stills instantly at our intimate position. But sex is not what I'm here for, even if the thought of fucking her until she's sobbing my name is tempting enough to have me rocking a semi.

"What?" she hisses the word, anger and frustration and fear, all dripping from the single syllable.

"You will stay in this class. You will take whatever I dish out. And you'll do it with a goddamn smile."

"Why are you doing this?"

She sounds so small, so broken. *All the easier to break her more.* "You know why, and I won't hesitate to rain down hell on you if you don't play my game, Emmalyn. You deserve all of this and more."

Resigned, she shakes her head. "Am I free to go?"

I release her wrists and step away. "As free as a bird with clipped wings."

She doesn't waste a second and flees toward the door. I expect her to haul ass out of here without sparing me a second glance, but instead, she surprises me and pauses. "You're wrong. I know you don't believe me, but you are. You're so very wrong."

And with those parting words, she slips out of the door, leaving me to wonder when she became such a skilled liar.

I RUN out of the office like the hounds of hell are nipping at my heels, because they are.

I run like my life depends on it.

Despite my entire body shaking like a leaf, I run all the way back to my dorm building, not caring even an iota about the shouting and glaring students I leave in my wake.

My entire world is imploding, collapsing in on me, and I have no clue how to stop it.

"Damn it, open!" I swipe my badge in front of the sensor for the third time. Finally, it flashes green, and I dash through the door, bypassing the elevator for the stairs.

The thought of only waiting a second for the car to come would be enough to push me over the edge into full-blown hysteria.

I'm breathless and covered in a fine sheen of sweat by the time I burst out of the stairwell.

My hands shake as I attempt to slide my key into the lock.

The sound of the elevator doors parting, followed by footsteps, sends a fresh bolt of terror zipping through me.

At this point, I may as well be trying to thread a needle rather than insert a key into a lock.

The footsteps grow closer, sending my entire being, mind and body into overdrive.

"Just do it, damnit!" I mutter, finally shoving the key into the hole.

I disengage the lock and throw the door open right as someone calls my name. "Emmy!" The voice is familiar, but I'm taking no chances.

Without responding, I race into my suite and slam the door behind me, promptly locking it again.

"It's okay. You're safe." I press my back against the door and slide to the floor, pulling my knees to my chest. "Just breathe."

Overhead, the doorknob rattles, and I scramble up from the floor and into my room, slamming and locking that door as well. I dive beneath my covers, burying myself in them.

If the monster can't see me, it can't get me.

"Emmy!" A sharp knock on my bedroom door follows. "Emmy, you're freaking me the hell out. Open the door."

"It's only Stella," I whisper to myself. But still, I don't move. I *can't* move. My body is locked in place, my muscles seemingly paralyzed with fear.

"Please open the door. I need to know that you're safe."

I will myself to move. To speak. To do something to let my friend know I'm okay.

"I'll get Melanie if I have to." Her words are thick with worry—worry for me.

I can't even begin to recall the last time someone worried over me.

It's that worry that has my muscles unclenching enough to haul myself from the bed.

The second I unlock the door, Stella pushes through it,

her eyes wide and her lips trembling. "Are you okay? Talk to me, Emmy. I'm begging you."

"I'm..." I manage to croak, then the tears start anew.

"Babe, you're seriously freaking me out. Do you... is there anyone I can call?" She slides her phone from her back pocket. "Your mom?"

"No!" I shout, knocking the slim device from her hand.

She stares at me in shock. "Okay. That's fine. On one condition."

"Anything." My voice is desperate... pleading. "Anything!"

"You gotta talk to me."

I shake my head back and forth, nerves outweighing logic. But Stella cuts her eyes at me in a way that has me changing my tune.

"Okay," I whisper. "But... you can't... you have to promise not to judge me. Do you promise?"

Stella tucks a strand of honey-colored hair behind her ear. "Yeah, I promise."

"Can I change first?" I glance down at my outfit, and the ghost of Sterling's citrusy male scent burns my nostrils. "And maybe shower, too?"

"Yup. I'll be here when you finish."

I nod my thanks and then grab a fresh pair of leggings and my coziest sweatshirt before darting to the bathroom.

I'm half tempted to throw out the clothes I'm wearing, but ultimately decide washing them will be sufficient. The thought of giving him more than I already have pains me. He doesn't deserve any part of me—not my tears, not my worry, and definitely not my time.

With the water scalding hot, I step beneath the spray and scrub away the remnants of his touch until my skin is pink and raw.

I towel off, throw on my clothes, and twine my damp hair into a braid. I don't feel better, per se, but I feel clean, and that's something.

When I step back out in the living area, the scent of freshly brewed coffee greets me. "Thank you," I murmur, graciously accepting the mug Stella passes me.

The warmth of the beverage comforts me; if only it could also give me courage for the talk we're about to have.

"Let's sit," she says, nodding to the couch.

I sit pressed against the arm, my shoulders slightly hunched and my legs pulled up, with my coffee balanced between my knees and chest.

Stella offers me a throw blanket, but I decline, mostly because I don't want to move. She claims the spot beside me and smiles a soft, watery smile. "Talk to me."

"I don't know where to start," I admit, tears already pricking.

"I hear the beginning is a pretty good place."

"My dad died when I was eight. I don't even think grass had grown over his grave dirt when my mom remarried." My heart constricts painfully in my chest, aching for a man I hardly remember. "Robert, my stepdad, he was okay. Rich as the devil. He never really paid me much mind."

I shrug and then drain my mug, leaning forward to place it on the coffee table. "His son, Rob, on the other hand... he took notice of me, and not in a good way."

Memories better left dead and buried assault me, flashing through my mind like some D-List horror movie reel.

"How old are you anyway?" asks the little boy with an angry mouth from the top of the stairs. He stands up there like some kind of lonely king, lording over the manor.

"Almost nine," I tell him, glaring.

"So, eight then. A baby."

I stomp my foot on the cold marble floor. Mother told me he's a pre-teen, so we're almost-kinda-sorta the same age. "I'm not a baby!"

"Then prove it."

"How?" I ask, wanting more than ever for my new brother to like me.

I've always wanted a sibling, but Mom says you couldn't pay her to have another baby. So, if a stepbrother is all I get, I'll take it.

He starts down the hall. "Follow me," he says, looking at me over his shoulder, his eyes daring me.

I dart up the stairs after him, my Mary Janes tap-tap-tapping as I run. "Hey! Wait up!"

"I don't wait for babies."

Huffing, I push my little legs faster. "I'm not a baby!"

"Yeah, you said that." He slows his pace as we near a section of the house I've never explored. "Time to put your money where your mouth is."

"What's that mean?" I ask, trying to peer around him.

He smirks in that way boys do before they pull your pigtail. "It means you gotta show me you're brave. Because I don't hang out with losers."

"Well, I'm not a loser either!"

Rob turns his back to me and steps into a small alcove. I notice a door to the right; it's one of those tiny ones that even I have to duck down to walk through. His lips twist in a way that makes me question if I should trust him or not.

"Get in," he says, opening the door.

"In there?"

"Unless you're... scared." He spits the word like it's worse than cold broccoli dunked in puke.

And I am. Scared, that is.

The dark is where all of the big-bads hide, but I'd rather get grounded for a month than let him know I'm scared of the dark.

"Fine," I say, my voice shaking.

I step into the small, dark room. The air is hot and smells like my grandma's closet. I don't like it.

"There!" I shout triumphantly. "I did it!"

"Not so fast," he says when I try to step back into the alcove.

"What?"

"Just walking inside is lame. You gotta stay inside."

"For how long?" My neck itches at the thought of staying in here.

"Until I say so."

I try to swallow, but there's a lump in my throat. "Fine."

With a look that can only be described as evil, Rob swings the door shut.

I close my eyes and count to sixty, while Rob shuffles around outside of the door. "Okay! Let me out now."

A cold laugh sounds from the other side of the door. "No. I don't think I will."

"What?" Fear slithers down my spine.

"I said no. You'll stay here for as long as I want you to. Who knows... maybe I'll never let you out."

I push against the door, but it doesn't budge. He's blocked it somehow. "Rob! Let me out!"

He laughs but doesn't say anything.

"Rob! Please!" My voice breaks as I begin to cry. "Please let me out."

"Told you you were a big baby. And babies get punished."

"I'll scream," I threaten.

"Do it. No one will hear you."

Stella's eyes are damp as she asks, "Did he leave you?"

"Yeah." I tug my sleeves down to cover my palms, using the soft cotton to wipe my tears. "He did."

"How long?"

"Until the next morning."

"What?" Stella shouts, outraged.

"Yeah, and because I missed dinner—he told my mom that I refused to come downstairs, and she was too lazy to check on me—so she punished me by not letting me eat the next day."

"What in the hell is wrong with your family?"

A bitter laugh escapes me. "This was only the start."

Stella cringes. "I'm so scared that I already know where it ends."

I stare blankly ahead, not answering.

"Emmy, did he... did he *hurt* you?"

"Are you asking if he hit me?"

"And other... stuff..."

I give a sharp nod, and she bursts into tears, crying as though my hurts are her own.

"Oh, Emmy. I'm so sorry." She reaches out, as if to hug me, and while I'm not a huge fan of physical contact, I lean into her embrace and let her comfort me. "You don't have to tell me anything else, but I'm here if you ever want or need to talk. Or even just to cry. I'm here, and I'm not going anywhere."

"Thanks," I whisper, tasting the salt of my tears.

After several long minutes, she releases me. "I have to ask..."

"What?"

"Where does Sterling fit into all of this?"

"He's Rob's best friend."

"So, it's some bro-code thing? Because, babe, that's some bullshit."

"Yeah, it is." I nibble on my lower lip, debating whether or not I want to say more. "After Rob...after he...no one believed me. Everyone turned against me, even my own mother. Everyone back home says I ruined Rob's life. When in reality, he's the one who destroyed me, over and over."

Stella places her hands to my cheeks, holding my gaze on hers. "You. Are. Not. Broken. Do you hear me? You've survived unspeakable things. You're not broken, or damaged, or a victim. You're a freaking survivor, and some white-collar loyal lapdog isn't going to take away or degrade everything you've worked so hard to overcome!"

Her cheeks are rosy, and her chest is heaving by the time she finishes. Her words aren't empty; they're a vow, and the power behind them settles over my soul like a balm.

For the first time in a long time, I truly have someone in my corner... someone who gets me. And my God, it's good to be got.

I'VE BEEN COUNTING down the hours until today's class.

A twisted sense of pride at her easy defeat has me wanting to pound my chest.

I emerged from our first battle the victor, and while the taste was sweet, I want to win the war.

"Hey, Sterling," a blonde coed coos as she enters the classroom. I'm tucked back behind the podium, waiting to see if my little spitfire is going to show up today. I nod, both in greeting and in subtle dismissal—one blondie isn't picking.

"I was wondering, do you offer tutoring? I'd hate to fall behind."

"It's the second day of class," I deadpan, cocking my head at her. Studying her, she's a looker with perky tits, tan skin, hazel eyes, and curly blonde hair.

She's got mean girl written all over her, and as shitty as it is, I'm already weighing her usefulness. She twirls a strand of hair around her finger and bats her obviously fake lashes. "Of course. This class is so important." She licks her lips and drags her eyes over my body. "And I'm always down for a little extra credit."

It's on the tip of my tongue to tell her no, but alienating her certainly won't endear her to my cause. Instead, I lean in, just enough for her to think I'm interested. "I'll keep that in mind…" I trail off, waiting for her to offer her name.

"Summer," she says.

"Perfect, Summer. I look forward to calling on you in class."

She grins, like I've offered her a ride on my dick.

I turn back to the papers I have gathered on the podium, hungry anticipation for Emmalyn's arrival gnawing at me.

At the last minute, she strolls into the room with her head held high and a small smile on her face.

Well, that won't do.

Thanks to her late arrival, most of the seats are full. She heads toward an open seat in the center of the room. As she moves down the aisle, her bag knocks into Summer's desk, sending the cell phone perched on the edge crashing to the floor.

"Stupid bitch," Summer swears under her breath, loud enough for most of the room to hear.

I let it slide, though, because the shoe most assuredly fits.

"I'm so sorry!" Emmalyn's cheeks are as scarlet as the letter branded on her lying little soul as she scrambles to retrieve the phone.

"Get your hands off of my stuff!" Summer snatches the device back, glaring as though Emmalyn's touch alone has somehow tainted her phone.

Emmalyn's eyes take on a glassy sheen, but she continues to the open desk without replying.

"Now that everyone's here and the show's over"—I glare

at Emmalyn, and she slinks down in her seat—"let's get started. Today I'm assigning the first group project of the semester. You'll be grouped in pairs and are expected to work together, as a unit, to do the research and the writing. You will also be required to give a presentation."

Murmurs along with a few groans fill the room. I let them have their moment before continuing.

"For this project, *I* will be assigning groups." I begin rattling off names until there are only two left. Summer glares at me, while Emmalyn's are downcast in a sad sort of acceptance.

"Summer, you're with—"

She cuts me off before I can finish. "You can't be serious!"

I narrow my eyes. "Oh, but I am."

"Sterling," she whines.

"There will be no complaints over your pairing, nor will there be any changes. If you can't work together like mature adults, you'll take a zero." I drag my steely gaze from one side of the room to the other. "Which I wouldn't recommend, as this is worth a hefty percentage of your grade."

Another chorus of murmurs and groans ring out, but I pay them no mind. There's only one person's reaction that's of any interest to me, and much to my dismay, she's wearing an impenetrable mask of indifference.

"For your project, you'll be writing a research paper on social cognition." I go on to outline the finer points of the project before telling them to find their assigned partner. "I'll give you a few minutes to discuss the project with your partner, please be sure to exchange contact information."

The students scatter across the room in search of their partners, save for two. Summer sits with her plump lips curled into a vicious snarl, while Emmalyn looks more like a frightened field mouse.

The two glare at one another from their desks, both unwilling to make the first move.

I already know who's going to cave first though, and it's not going to be the snotty blonde.

As if on cue, Emmalyn slips from her seat and trudges over to Summer.

I hide my interest in the screen of my laptop, pretending to read while discreetly watching the two from the corner of my eye.

"Um, what days are you—"

"Okay, no. Stop."

"What?" Emmalyn's brow furrows.

Summer rolls her eyes. "I'm not free, any days, none at all, to work with you."

"But it's a group project. It requires both of us."

"Your point?"

"My point is you can't expect me to do it all."

I'm mildly shocked by Emmalyn's backbone. She's always been on the meek side, so seeing her stand up to Summer is... unexpected.

As is the reaction her fire—as small as the flame may be —is having on me.

I recline slightly against the back of the desk chair, no longer bothering to pretend I'm not watching them. They're both too engrossed in their showdown to notice.

"I can. And I do."

"That's not fair."

Summer shrugs, unaffected. "Life's not fair."

Emmalyn's cheeks redden as her anger grows.

I allow their standoff to continue for another minute

before dismissing the class and returning my attention back to my laptop, in earnest this time.

A shadow falls over my keyboard causing me to glance up.

"Yes?" I ask, affecting a bored tone.

"Can we talk, please?" Emmalyn rakes her teeth over her lower lip.

"What about?"

"My partner." She cringes, but presses on. "It's just, I don't think we can work together, and—"

"I'm going to go ahead and stop you there." I push my chair away from the small desk and stand. "There will always be people who are difficult to work with, Princess Price."

"I understand that, I do. It's just—"

"It's just that you're a spoiled brat. But guess what?" I lean down and in, nearly pressing my lips to her ear. "You're in the real world now." Unable to help myself, I skim my nose over the shell of her ear, and she shivers, a response I file away for later. "Better get used to it."

As if on autopilot, she nods as she backs away before turning and running for the door.

I follow her into the hallway, watching in satisfaction as she once again flees from me.

That is until she runs into a blond version of the Hulk.

"Sorry!" she cries, as the giant reaches out to steady her. "Oh, it's you."

"Long time no talk, huh, sweets?"

I can't see her entire face from where I'm standing, but I can see enough to know she's smiling warmly at him.

"I wasn't sure if I'd run into you again."

He reaches down and rubs the ends of her dark hair between two of his fingers. "I've been looking for you."

"Really? Well, you found me."

He lets her long locks drop and then reaches into his back pocket for his phone. "Let's exchange numbers, yeah?"

She rattles off her number, and I repeat it in my mind, committing the seven digits to memory.

"Perfect, I sent you a text so you'll have my number. Feel free to save me as Stud Muffin or something equally charming."

She laughs, and the sound of it grates against my every nerve.

I don't realize how much until my jaw aches from me clenching it.

Emmalyn Price is mine. Mine to punish and mine to play with.

"Or, I could save you as Gabe?" she says with a laugh, and when he does, too, red tinges my vision.

Somehow, my reaction to seeing her interact with him... it goes beyond Rob and his vendetta, and while I know it, I'm wholly unwilling to admit it.

Princess Price and her impending destruction is nothing more than a favor to a friend. I'm angry over her talking to him, because I don't want him to suffer the same fate as my best friend.

Once a liar, always a liar.

That's my story, and goddamn it, I'm sticking to it.

"SPOILSPORT," Gabe jests, grinning.

"That's me."

"Are you okay?"

It's on the tip of my tongue to nod my head yes, to lie and say everything's okay. But I don't. Because even in Gabe's comforting presence, my anger still boils and bubbles like a witch's cauldron.

"No." I admit my confusion and, though we're virtual strangers, he wraps his meaty arms around me and pulls me close.

"Let me take you to lunch."

"It's past lunchtime."

He refuses to do this with me. "Brunch then, Emmy."

I shake my head. I don't know why I'm being so difficult. Maybe because I don't want a pity meal.

"Brunch it is, then. Changed your mind. Now, let's go."

"Are you sure?"

"A hundred and—"

"What?"

He rolls his eyes. "I'm one-hundred-and-one percent sure I'd like you to join me for brunch."

"Smartass."

"Always." He smirks. "Let me text Zach really quick."

"I don't want to interrupt your plans."

Gabe heaves out a long-suffering sigh and wraps his arm around my shoulders, guiding me out of the building. I'm probably imagining it, but I swear I can feel the burn of someone's stare against my back as he leads me out into the sunshine. "You aren't interrupting. You were invited. Plus, we're just going to the dining hall."

"Thanks, Gabe."

He presses his palm to his cheek and flutters his long lashes. "I know, I know. I'm a great guy."

As we approach our destination, Gabe drops a bomb on me. "So, you gonna tell me what had you so upset?"

"Do I have to?" I ask, halfway hoping he'll let me off the hook and halfway hoping he'll press for more.

"Yes," is his single word reply.

I turn to look at him, surprised to find his lips pressed into a thin line and his face set in stone. "Um…"

He reaches around me and pushes open the door to the dining hall, letting me enter before him. "It's obvious to anyone with eyes that something upset you. Bottling things up is a shit way to dealing—trust me. Let it out. You'll feel better, and maybe… maybe I can help rid you of what ails you."

I snort out an unintentional laugh. "God, I wish."

"Uh huh, tell me more." Someone yells his name, and he reroutes us toward the sound of it. "Hold that thought, sweets."

He blazes a trail through the cavernous room, me hot on his heels. He stops in front of a table occupied by a handful of people, but he only has eyes for the tall, dark-skinned man seated at the center.

This must be Zach.

Even seated, his presence is commanding. He stands to greet us. "You must be the mysterious Emmy I've heard so much about."

He gives me a once-over, and I return the favor. Zach is made up of long lines and compact muscles, an obvious athlete. He's taller than I thought he'd be, but still shorter than Gabe; though I think everyone is shorter than the bear of a man to my left. His dark hair is woven into tight braids which are secured with an elastic at the base of his neck. With his wide smile and friendly eyes, I can instantly tell he's good people.

"That's me," I say, suddenly feeling shy. "It's um... it's nice to meet you."

"It's good to meet you, too. Now, let's eat. No offense."

"None taken."

"Workouts were brutal this morning," he says, rounding the table so we can walk together.

"Do you play football, too?"

"Yes," Zach says, but Gabe's voice spills over his.

"No."

They share a laugh, leaving me to stare between them in confusion.

Zach shrugs. "It's called football everywhere on earth except here."

"Be that as it may, in the great state of Georgia, it's..."

"Soccer," Zach mumbles begrudgingly.

"Oh!" Understanding dawns. "I get it!"

Zach gives me an amused look before herding us into line. The guys grab enough food to feed a family of four, while I settle on a kolache with a fruit cup.

We bypass the table Zach was at when we came in and cluster into a smaller, more intimate table instead. They both dig into their meals, while I pick at my fruit. I feel strangely comfortable with the two of them, but the events of class still weigh on my mind.

Gabe finishes his first sandwich before pinning me with a look. "About earlier?"

I sigh. "I was hoping you had forgotten."

Zach rolls his lips in to smother a laugh.

"Go ahead and say it, babe."

"An elephant never forgets."

Gabe gives an exaggerated, dry laugh. "Ha-ha. Never gets old."

"You love it."

"I love you; I *tolerate* your smartass mouth."

"Now I know you're lying. You *really love* my smartass mouth."

"Sure, when it's stuffed full of my dick."

"Too true," Zach muses.

I've never been around this kind of PDA. But if I'm being honest... I like it.

"Now hush," Gabe scolds. "Emmy here was about to tell me why she was upset when I ran into her earlier."

"I just..." I shake my head. "I don't know."

"Talk to me, sweets."

"The TA for my Psych 101 class hates me."

"I'm sure that's not true," Zach says.

"No. It is. We have... a history. He's best friends with my stepbrother, and yeah, he hates me, and is determined to make me miserable."

"Why does he hate you? You seem cool as hell to me."

I turn slightly toward Zach. "It's a long, messed-up story."

"CliffsNotes, sweets."

"Right." I swallow roughly. "Um. My stepbrother and I have a really bad relationship. Like, really bad. And some things happened and I spoke up, and no one believed me. Now he's determined to ruin my life and has apparently enlisted the help of a friend to do it."

"Some things?" Gabe asks, a blond brow arched.

I nod, unwilling to elaborate. But I think both of these men are smart enough to put two and two together.

"Why didn't anyone believe you?"

"Because he's a Pearson, and while that doesn't mean much here, it means a hell of a lot back where I'm from." I shrug. "He's basically Texas royalty, and it was my word against his."

"What about your parents? Didn't they—"

"Dad's dead and my mom chose her husband over me."

"Man, fuck them!" Zach declares. "We're your daddies now."

I don't mean to, but I can't help but laugh.

"Yeah, that sounded bad."

"So bad," Gabe agrees with his boyfriend. "But I dig it. Daddy Gabe. It's got a ring to it."

"Y'all are crazy."

"The best people are, sweets. The best people are."

WATCHING Emmalyn eat lunch with those two jocks has my heart racing and my blood pumping.

As irrational as it may be, I need to know who these two men are. I need to know who they are to her. How close they are to her.

I need to know it all.

I tell myself it's because I need to know my enemy and knowing the enemy she keeps is paramount to taking her down.

But what I tell myself while watching doesn't make it true. And if the way my gut twists in anger at the sight of her— head tipped back, laughing at something one of them said— is anything to go off of, I'm absolutely lying to myself.

Because if she truly was the victim, in what universe is it okay for her to do what she did and then go on living her best life like she's not a lying, backstabbing, disloyal bitch.

As much as I want Rob Bell to flog her, saying she destroyed his life, she originally did it for, after all, money talks. But my earlier thought from the glass lingers: what if she were to do the same to a guy who doesn't have pockets deeper than Mary Poppins' bag? What then?

It's not fair to let her potentially ruin someone's life.

I'm drawn from my enraged musings when the trio stand to throw their trash away. The blond giant takes hers from her and disposes of it with his own.

They stroll out of the dining hall, and I follow behind them at a safe distance, listening to as much of their conversation as possible.

Which, unfortunately, isn't much.

I'm half tempted to call my first foray into stalking a bust. That is until the trio stops in front of a dorm building. Specifically, Lookout Hall, which is a strictly female dorm. Which means, unless they're here to add another person to their merry band of assholes, Emmalyn lives here.

Holy shit. In one day, I've managed to acquire both her phone number and her dorm hall. This is one-hundred percent what winning feels like.

I linger as the three chat for another few minutes, then finally Emmalyn turns and retreats into the building. Unfortunately, they continue down the path in the opposite direction of where I'm waiting.

I don't let the strike-out bother me though; today's still a win.

I'm about to head back to the psych building when a familiar voice calls my name from somewhere behind me. I debate hauling ass, but she catches up before I can.

"Sterling Abbot! I thought that was you." She bats her lashes and wraps her arms around my middle, pressing her breasts against my chest in a bone-crushing hug.

"Melanie." I reluctantly return her embrace.

She's nice, but clingy. I took her out with me to a party once *as friends* as a favor, and she all but growled at any female who got within a five-foot radius. Clearly our friendship never progressed.

"What are you doing over here in my neck of the woods?"

"Just enjoying a little fresh air."

She laughs like I've just delivered a witty punchline.

"How've you been?" I ask when she doesn't speak.

"Really good. *So* good."

"Glad to hear that, Mel."

Her eyes sparkle at the abbreviated version of her name. "Is this your dorm?"

"Yep. I'm an RA, too." Her eyes widen, and she gently smacks a hand against my chest. "Oh my God! And you're a TA, from what I hear. How crazy is that?"

"So crazy," is my dry response.

Melanie beams up at me, not picking up on my tone in the least. She's an attractive woman, but the *marry-me-and-give-me-babies* streak runs a little too deep with her.

We both start to speak at the same time, and I quickly offer for her to go first.

"We should catch up some time," she murmurs, stepping closer.

Instantly, I regret not speaking first. Because now, instead of some generic parting words, I find myself reluctantly saying, "Sure, what did you have in mind?"

She nibbles her glossy lower lip. Instantly, I compare it to Emmalyn's much fuller ones, which only serves to piss me off. Hot or not, Emmalyn Price is a fucking she-devil. "Well, there's a party this weekend at the Delta Psi house."

The thought of partying with her again sends a shudder through me. Until she adds, "It's the first party of the year, and me and the other RAs are getting all of the girls to go."

"Girls as in the ones who live in your dorm building?" I ask, suddenly interested.

"Yeah, we like to think it's a good way to ease them into the college party atmosphere."

"Text me the details," I tell her, mentally reminding myself to unblock her number as soon as I walk away. "And I'll meet you there."

"It's a date." Melanie pops up onto her tiptoes and presses a kiss to my cheek.

She says something else, but I'm too busy plotting to pay her any more attention.

"DO WE HAVE TO GO?" I whine, tossing myself back onto my bed.

"Babe. It's our first real college weekend. It's a rite of passage. We *have* to." Sadie continues rifling through my closet. "Plus, Melina said she really wants us all in attendance."

"Ugh!" I drag my hands over my face. "Fine."

"Yay—and you have to wear this skirt with a top I have!" She tosses my favorite, most worn-in denim skirt my way. I've had that damn thing since I was fifteen. It's distressed and soft-as-hell now.

"What else?" I ask suspiciously.

"Just trust me?"

I can't help but laugh. "Solid maybe."

"Please?" She pleads with big puppy eyes.

"I'll try." I concede. "But no promises."

She smiles. "Good enough. Do you need to shower?"

"I'm good," I say. I already showered this morning. Plus, I can use the free time to do some research for my psych paper, since I'm doing the work of two people.

An hour later, Stella emerges from the bathroom looking like a Victoria's Secret model with her blonde hair styled in soft, beachy waves and her face made up in a way where it's hard to tell if she's wearing makeup or is simply blessed with perfect skin.

All I have to show for my sixty minutes is a sizable list of source documents to hunt down in the library and online.

"Do you want me to do your hair?" she asks, but I wave her off.

"Nah, I've got it. You finish getting ready."

I plug my flatiron in and begin the process of smoothing out my long, thick, nearly waist-length hair. Once it's silky-straight, I start on my makeup.

I waffle for a moment between subtle and bold. Old me would have gone bold, with dark eyes and bright lips. Current me prefers to blend in. But tonight, I think I'll marry the two sides of my soul and do a smoky eye with a nude lip.

It's a silly thing to read so far into, and yet somehow, it feels like one of many baby steps to reclaiming myself.

"Okay," Stella says, walking back into my room dressed and ready. If my top is anything like hers, it doesn't bode well for me. "Put this on."

She passes me a top; well, a scrap of cotton fabric masquerading as one, anyway.

I give her a dubious look, but she's not having it. "You promised you'd try."

She has me and she knows it. I grab the top from her and toss it onto my bed alongside the skirt. I hesitate for only a minute more before stripping down and pulling on the outfit of Stella's choosing.

The top almost fits like a sports bra, with the hemline

hugging the top of my rib cage. My skirt sits at my waist, leaving a strip of flesh on display.

"You look hot!" Stella exclaims.

"I feel naked. And it's cold outside."

"It's like fifty."

I give her a deliberately blank look. "Cold."

She huffs and grabs a flannel shirt from my closet. "Here, wear this, too."

"And boots?" I ask, sliding my arms into the sleeves of the oversized button-down.

"Fine."

Between my lace-up boots and the flannel, I feel a little more like myself. "What time are we heading over?"

Stella checks the time on her phone. "Now!"

We each grab our ID badges and step out into the hall. Melanie is already there, along with the other girls on our floor.

"Okay, ladies, a few guidelines before we head over. Your roommate is your buddy. Stick together at all times. I mean it. Gotta pee? Go together. Gotta puke? Go together. Found a hottie you want to hook up with? Well, maybe don't bring a friend, then, unless that's your thing."

She winks before continuing, completely clueless to her contradicting and dangerous advice. "I'm technically supposed to tell y'all not to drink, but I'm not an idiot. So, while I am heavily suggesting that you not, keep these tidbits in mind if you do. Do not accept a drink from a stranger. If possible, make your own. Do not be the drunkest person at the party. Do not fall asleep at the party. And most importantly, *beer before liquor, never been sicker*—that saying exists for a reason, ladies."

Melanie begins walking toward the elevator. "Oh, and, ladies, have fun!"

Most of the girls break into excited chatter, but I'm a big ball of nerves. I haven't been to a party since my junior year of high school. I went from being the life of the party to a social pariah almost overnight.

The thought of attending one now has me feeling a little queasy and a lot keyed up. My only saving grace is that aside from a handful of girls from the dorm, I won't know anyone. And more importantly, they won't know me.

There's a bite to the night air, but the walk to the Delta Psi house passes quickly—probably because we're all under-dressed for the weather.

The sound of thumping bass hits half a block before the frat house comes into sight. The music is cranked up so loud it nearly shakes the ground beneath our feet.

Anticipation rockets through me. *Just breathe, Emmy. You've got this.*

By the time the house comes into view, the sounds of laughter and yelling can be heard over the music, but just barely.

People spill out onto the lawn, some drunk, some dancing, all having a good time.

Stella nudges me with her elbow, and I look over to see her grinning like a fool. "This is my first party," she confesses. "I wasn't ever allowed to go to any in high school!"

She sounds downright giddy. Her enthusiasm is contagious, though, and before I know it, I find myself smiling back at her.

We're each given a red Solo cup at the door and instructed not to lose it. Inside, there are more people than I ever thought possible. It feels like the entire campus has to be in attendance.

"Drinks or dancing?" Stella asks, as eager as a puppy.

I don't drink. Ever. So, dancing is an easy answer.

She doesn't think twice about my preference and happily drags me out to the dance floor—a.k.a. a section of the living room where all of the furniture has been shoved against the walls.

The song changes to something fast with a heavy bassline. I feel self-conscious at first, only gently rocking my hips in time with the beat. But Stella dances like she's auditioning for a job at a strip club. She swings her hips and shakes her ass like her life depends on her getting the job.

Seemingly fed up with my mild moves, Stella wraps an arm around my waist and pulls my body in close to hers. She locks our hands together and twirls herself in a wide arc.

We're both laughing and grooving by the time the song ends.

"You've got moves," she accuses.

"I used to love to dance."

"What made you stop?"

"I love this song!" I cry, rolling my body to the beat, hoping it will distract her from questioning me further.

"Me, too!" She begins twerking, not caring for a single second that she's horrible at it.

As we spin and twirl, I envy Stella's free-spiritedness. I have no clue what trials she's faced in her life, and I'm certainly not so self-involved to think I'm the only person with an ugly past. But her ability to be so in the moment is one I envy. A lot.

"Oh my God!" Stella pants as yet another song comes to an end. "I need a drink!"

Miraculously, we both still have our cups clutched in our hands. I let her lead the way through the house and into the kitchen. While still crowded, there are considerably fewer people in here. We don't have to shout to be heard.

"What're you drinking?" she asks, her eyes flitting from the keg in the corner to the liquor bottles lined up on the island.

"Water."

"Water?" Stella's eyes practically bug out of her head.

"Yup. I don't drink."

She looks at me speculatively, and I'm sure at any moment she's going to ask the same question everyone asks... *'Ever?'*

Because the thought of someone not wanting to drink, even socially, is so foreign to them. But to my surprise, she simply nods and says, "Cool." She grabs my free hand, tugging me along behind her. "Let's ask the guy manning the keg where to find you some water."

"Hello, ladies. Two?"

"One," Stella says, batting her lashes, turning up her Georgia charm. "And my friend here would like water. Preferably in a sealed bottle."

He fills her cup and then directs us to check the sink. At first, I think he's being a smartass, but quickly realize the sink is being used as a cooler and is packed full of ice and bottled waters.

"You wanna check out the rest of the party while we hydrate?"

"Um." A soft laugh escapes me. "I'm the only one hydrating."

Stella rolls her eyes. "Same difference."

We take a lap around the house, exploring the different areas. For the most part, it really is like every college party I've seen in movies. There are drunk students engaging in all kinds of questionable activities everywhere I look. Two beer pong tables are set up on the back deck, and there's a fire burning in one of those fancy pits in the lawn beyond it. The basement is nothing more than a haze of pot smoke; the skunky smell makes me scrunch my nose. We don't venture upstairs, but judging from the PDA happening as couples venture up the grand staircase, I can easily assume the rooms up there are reserved for hookups.

By the time we make it back to the living room, Stella's cup is empty and she's ready to dance again, if the sway in her hips is anything to go by.

Me, though? I'm ready for my jammies, my bed, and a good book.

But I know Stella won't be ready to leave for at least a few more hours, and since she got stuck with me as her party buddy, the least I can do is stick around long enough for her to have a good time.

A guy approaches as she dips and sways. He wraps a beefy arm around her waist and pulls her body flush against his. She startles momentarily and then catches sight of the Greek god of a man behind her, welcoming him with a blinding smile.

"I'm going to be right over there!" I yell, gesturing vaguely to the other side of the room. "I won't leave. You don't either."

She nods as she grinds her ass into her dance partner's groin. Stella was adamant she wanted the full college experience, and she's well on her way to getting it.

I weave my way across the room, bobbing and dodging my way through the throng of revelers until I reach the expanse of wall I plan to occupy until it's time to go.

The spot offers me a clear view of the room. I pick out familiar faces here and there: girls from the dorm and people from my classes. No one I want to speak to, though, so I keep my place against the wall, watching and taking it all in.

"Waiting for your next victim?" a cool, dark voice asks from my left.

"What do you want?" I ask without turning around. His voice alone sends shivers down my spine. God only knows what seeing his smug smile and sharp jaw would do to me right now.

Stupidly, I let my guard down tonight. Every single fiber of my being is telling me to run, but I refuse—partly because the thought of making a scene in front of all of these people has my skin feeling tight and itchy, and also because I refuse to give him the satisfaction of seeing me run away... again.

Sterling leans in, his breath tickling my neck and his body warming mine. "I'm just saying. Dressed the way you are, you must be looking for a good time. And I can't help but wonder..." He trails off, skimming his nose down the column of my throat before scraping his teeth against the sensitive flesh where my neck and shoulder meet.

"Stop it!" I pray for my voice to come out firm and commanding, but seeing as God abandoned me long ago, I sound raw and needy. Which is a lie. I am a lot of things in regard to Sterling Abbot—angry, frustrated, hurt—but definitely *not* needy.

I try to shoulder-check him, but he bands an arm around my waist and pulls me in closer, bringing my back flush with his front. The feel of our bodies pressed together has my heart slamming against my ribs as arousal and disgust battle for dominance inside of me.

Judging from my roiling gut and damp panties, it's a tie.

"I don't really think you mean that, little mouse." He rubs small circles over my exposed midriff with his thumb, and I nearly sigh in pleasure. It's been so long since someone's touched me with a soft hand that I can almost convince myself he's someone else. Someone kind and caring. Someone who will value me and help me and most importantly of all, *believe me.*

But then he keeps talking and breaks the stupid spell. "I think you like having my attention. You probably like *any* guy's attention. Don't you?" He nudges his erection into my back, as if to prove his point.

Tears brim my lashes as I clench my thighs together. Here and now, I'm not sure which of us I hate more. Probably me, because what in God's name is wrong with me that I'm getting turned on by the touch of a bully?

Because that's what Sterling is, isn't he? A bully.

"Get away from me!" I growl, my voice stronger this time around.

But Sterling only chuckles.

"Why are you doing this?"

"You know why," he murmurs the words in my ear, dipping his index finger beneath the waistband of my skirt. "You deserve *every single thing* coming your way."

"What?" It's like I'm caught in some kind of limbo; I'm here physically, but my mind... it's in some kind of alternate universe. It's somewhere harsh words and soft touches belong together.

I'm so preoccupied trying to unravel the *what* of the night that I don't see it coming. I don't see *her* coming.

"Get away from my date, you slut!"

"What?" I ask again, still feeling untethered, like I'm floating through space, barely able to make out what's happening right in front of me.

The feel of ice-cold liquid dripping down my face yanks me back to reality.

I swipe a hand over my eyes, wiping away both the beer and my tears. "What? Why?" I swing my gaze back to Sterling, who's no longer touching me.

"Don't fucking look at him!"

"Melanie?" I ask, bewildered at my RA's behavior.

She scoffs. "I don't know how they did things at your high school, but it's shitty to make a move on someone else's date!"

"I didn't know. I swear!"

Sterling scoffs as he rounds me to stand beside Melanie. "I told her to stop. To leave me alone." He sounds so convincing that I almost believe him. "I told her to go away, but she wouldn't listen."

Melanie plasters herself to his side and glares at me.

"That's... no. That's not true!"

"Girls like you are the reason good men cheat and marriages end!"

Lamely, all I can think to say is, "Good men don't cheat."

Melanie presses her fingertips against my chest and shoves me back into the wall. "If I ever see you anywhere near him again, there will be hell to pay." She pushes me again and I whimper, which makes her grin. "Do you understand?"

"Yes," I whisper, desperately looking over her shoulder for Stella. But I don't see her anywhere.

"Good," Melanie spits the word at me before turning to Sterling. The sight of them together turns my stomach—and not with jealousy.

They're a perfect pair, seeing as they're both sociopaths. Who in the hell behaves this way?

Who lets their tormentor touch them the way you let

yours touch you? the small, ugly voice in my brain asks. *Not just one man, but two.*

Black spots obscure my vision and the floor shakes and rolls beneath my feet. *Just breathe,* I tell myself, but I can't seem to take in a breath.

My chest heaves as I gasp and sputter. I tug at the high neckline of my shirt, desperate for air. But it's no use. I stumble against the wall and collapse down onto the floor.

Someone in the distance calls my name, but I can't move. I can't breathe. I can't do anything other than lie here and beg the universe to help me. Because once again, I'm that eight-year-old girl in the closet, unable to help herself.

"Emmy!" Cool hands wrap around my shoulders, gently shaking me. "Oh my God! Emmy, are you okay?"

My head lolls to the side and I stare blankly, not really seeing.

"Did you take something? What's wrong? We need to get you out of here."

"Is your friend okay?" an unfamiliar masculine voice asks.

"I don't know!" She shakes me again. "Will you... will you keep an eye on her while I call someone?"

"Yeah."

The party continues around me, but I'm not here anymore. Not really. I'm back in space, only this time, instead of floating, I'm hurtling toward a black hole.

"Just hang tight, babe. Help's on the way."

THE SOUND of dull but furious voices rouses me from my stupor.

"The hell were you doing at a party anyway, Luna?"

Where am I? And who the hell is Luna?

"Why do you even care?" my roommate asks with more fire in her voice than I've ever heard. "You gonna tattle on me?"

"You're acting like a b—"

"What can I say? You bring out the worst in me."

A soft, a little laugh sounds, filling the space around us.

"N—are you going to help me get her inside or not?"

"As long as you keep up your end of the bargain, I'll help."

Samson. "You might not think much of me, Samson Carter, but I'm not a liar."

"You don't have the first clue of what I think of you."

Two loud slams finally unseal my eyelids, allowing me to take stock of my surroundings. We're at the dorm build-ing. *How the*

I don't get to finish the thought when a strange man flings open the back door and reaches for me. Panic swarms and I scream at the top of my lungs.

"Stop! Get away from me!" I kick and thrash, all coherent thought lost in my struggle to get away.

"Holy Shit, Luna! Get your damn friend before she kicks out my teeth!" the deep voice booms, making me shiver in fear.

"Emmy!" Stella's worried voice cuts through my terror. "Emmy, stop!"

"Stella?" Her name comes out scratchy and thin. "What... where?"

"Shh, we'll talk inside."

"Who?"

Thankfully, she understands what I'm asking, despite not being able to string more than two words together in a sentence.

"That's Samson. He's a... he's someone I know. He brought us home, and he's going to help get you inside, okay?"

My pulse hammers at the thought of some random guy touching me, but Stella's quick to soothe my distress.

"I've known him since I was in diapers. He won't hurt you. Okay?"

"Okay," I whisper, and she moves out of the doorway, making room for Samson to try again.

I whimper when his broad shoulders obscure my vision. He grits his teeth and asks, "You gonna try and kick me again?"

Just breathe. He's not going to hurt you. "No."

He leans into the car and helps me out and onto my feet. "I've got it," I say, even as my knees wobble beneath me. Gritting my teeth, I press my palm into the side of the car and focus on breathing and holding myself up.

"Are you good to head inside?" Stella asks.

"I, um. Yes, I think."

"I'll help you." Stella wraps an arm around my waist, and I wrap mine around her shoulders. Every step is grueling, not because I'm hurt but because I'm tired. Like down to my bones, through my marrow, to my soul tired.

We slowly make our way from the parking lot to the dorm building. At the door, Samson turns to us. "Gonna need your card, Luna."

"It's in my back pocket."

He balks, looking unsure.

"Oh my God!" Stella cries. "It's a freaking pocket. You might graze a little ass cheek. It won't kill you."

"It fuckin' might," he grumbles before sliding his hand into her pocket.

A wave of dizziness rushes me, and I sway in Stella's arms.

"Whoa! You okay?"

I nod. Or at least I think I nod. "Just need to... bed."

"Are you sure she isn't on something?"

"Positive," Stella growls, helping me over the threshold and into the lobby. "Now either call the elevator or go home. We don't need your negativity."

"No, just my ride." He's all attitude as he swaggers ahead of us toward the elevator. He curls his hand into a fist and pops the side of it against the *up* arrow.

Inside, he repeats the gesture, hitting the button for the third floor. The contents of my stomach rush up toward my throat as the cables begin pulling us higher. I gag a little as I slap my free hand over my mouth.

"Swear to God, if she pukes on me…"

"Stop being an asshole, Samson!" Stella scolds, already sounding like the teacher she's studying to become.

I force myself to swallow. "I'm fine."

In our suite, Stella helps me into my bed with a promise to check on me in five minutes. I wave her away, too exhausted to care about anything other than my head hitting the pillow.

Only, when I close my eyes, he's there, waiting and ready to torture me some more.

"You deserve every single thing coming your way," his voice taunts, wrapping around my body like a vise, squeezing and squeezing, tighter and tighter, until all of the air is expelled from my lungs.

I shoot upright, a scream lodged in my throat. "Why is this happening?" I wonder aloud. "What did I ever do to deserve this?"

Muffled voices filter into my room from the crack under the door. After a few minutes, I hear a door open and close, before the sound of the lock turning reaches me.

Followed by, "Emmy, can I come in?"

I groan out my permission for her to enter.

"Are you okay?" Stella asks, crossing the small space to my bed. She perches on the edge of it and reaches down, smoothing my sweaty hair away from my face.

"I-I don't know."

"What happened? You literally went from fine to on the floor in the span of a song."

"St-Sterling."

A fire lights in her blue eyes, making her look lethal. "What did he do? Do I need to kill him? Swear to God, I know how to get rid of a body, babe."

"Um…"

"Just say the word. No one will ever find his sorry, no-good, rotten ass."

"No," I barely manage to croak the word as I shake my head. "No."

"What did he do to you?"

I heave out a sad sigh. "Nothing more than I allowed."

The admission nearly breaks me. It's a reminder of how weak I am. How weak I've always been. I've been on this earth for eighteen years and spent a decade of them being abused at the hands of my stepbrother.

I quietly took his mistreatment, over and over, and the few times I tried to speak up, my pleas were cast aside as the whining of a bratty child.

I should have pushed harder. Tried harder.

But I didn't. I let him victimize me. Over and over and over again. When he finally took it too far and I went to the authorities, I was all but laughed right out of town.

What would a fine young man like him want with a child like you?

Nice girls don't tell lies. We thought you were a nice girl, Emmalyn. Don't you want to be nice?

He's got his whole life ahead of him, Emmalyn. Surely you don't want to leave a dark mark on his future.

And yet, no one cares about the one he left on me. On my heart… my soul.

"No! Nope." Stella sounds fierce, protective. "That doesn't fly with me. He *did* something to you and I want—no, I *need* to know."

"Just mind games."

Stella stands from the bed. "What drawer are your jammies in?"

"Second from the top."

She grabs a pair of flannel pants and a tank top and passes them both to me. "Get changed. I'll be right back."

I strip out of my wet party clothes but don't put on my pajamas. I need a shower.

"What are you doing? Are you okay?" Stella asks as I step out of my room in only my undergarments.

"Just need a shower."

"Okay. Can I... can I sit in the bathroom while you do it? To make sure you're okay?"

I nod, secretly grateful to not be alone.

We trek into the small bathroom, and I step into the tub and pull the curtain closed. I toss my wet bra and panties out and turn on the water, cranking the temperature to scalding.

Stella chatters aimlessly as I stand under the hot spray, letting it wash away the scent of cheap beer, wishing it could wash away the memory of his touch.

"Did he pour his drink on you?" Stella asks as I rinse the shampoo from my hair.

"No. Um. That would've been... Melanie."

"What?" my suitemate shrieks.

I'm nearly too tired to tell the whole sordid story, but I know Stella, and she won't let me sleep until she knows it all.

"I guess they were there together. And she thought I was flirting with him and got really, *really* mad. She said some not nice things to me and then tossed her beer in my face."

"And he let her believe that? That you were with him?"

I scoff out a laugh. "He encouraged the notion."

"That little dick weasel!"

Even though she can't see me, I shrug. "It is what it is."

"No, ma'am. It is not."

"Stella, I love that you want to help, but—"

"But nothing! Tonight, you sleep. And tomorrow?" She pauses for dramatic effect. "Tomorrow, we plot!"

STELLA DIDN'T LEAVE my side for the rest of the weekend. And I mean that literally. We spent Saturday, Sunday, and Monday—which was blessedly a holiday—cozied up in our dorm room watching chick flicks, eating takeout, and plotting my payback.

Ultimately, we both decided the best form of revenge against Ste... *nothing.* He's clearly after a reaction, and if I refuse to give him one, he can't win.

However, I also agreed I can't let him steamroll me either. I have to be fierce, which means taking no shit when it comes...

"I'm serious, Stella," I say as we walk through the quad, "if he's an asshole, just give him space. Don't let him know he's getting...

"...and you can tell me all about how you shut his ... down."

"And you can tell me all about Samson," I counter, already knowing it, because I asked about him at least twenty times over the last three days, but she shut me down each and every time.

"Toodles," she calls over her shoulder with a finger-wave before breaking into a run toward her building.

I roll my eyes at her antics, but press on toward my destination, albeit slowly. While I don't want to be late for Sterling's class, I definitely don't want to be early either. When it comes to his class, it's bare minimum and nothing more.

I make it to the classroom with two minutes to spare, marching right past Sterling's smug, stupid face, all the way to a desk in the very back of the room.

For the next one-hundred-and-twenty seconds, I sit on pins and needles, waiting for him to fling some low-handed, shitty remark my way. But he doesn't even look at me.

It's as if I'm not here. Invisible.

And how completely wrong is it—how completely damaged am I—that him ignoring me bothers me?

I don't want him to torment me, not at all. But after three days of prepping on how best to deal with him, I guess it's a little disappointing.

Or at least that's what I'm going with. Because while I *am* a little weak, I'm not a freaking doormat. At least, I don't want to be.

At exactly nine, Sterling closes the door. He dives straight into his lecture, still ignoring my presence completely. His eyes skip over me as he speaks and he never once calls on me when he asks questions.

Not that I'm volunteering, but still.

Instead, I busy myself furiously taking notes. Sterling Abbot might be a piece of shit, but he brings the topics we study to life. Once I get back to my dorm after lunch, I'll recopy and color-code them.

There's something about the repetition that really cements it all in my brain.

"Quiz time!" Sterling's voice booms through the room, causing shivers to dance across my skin. A few groans rise up, but he shakes his head and slaps his palms down onto the podium. "I don't want to hear it. You should have completed the required reading for it, so if you don't do well..." He allows his words to taper off and shrugs— "That's on you."

I grin to myself, confident I'll ace the quiz. I not only read the assigned material—*twice*—but I also read several related articles and studies just to make sure I had a good grasp on it.

On a scale of one-to-ten, right about now, my confidence is a twenty.

Except, when I look down at my quiz, none of the material on it was covered in the reading.

No, no, no.

I ball my hands into fists and scrub at my eyes, hoping like hell my mind is playing tricks on me. *It has to be.* There's no other option. Only, when I reread the page, none of the words have changed.

This can't be happening.

How is this happening?

After everything with Rob came to a head, I threw myself head-first into my studies. It's not like I had friends, much less a social life, so preparedness became my bestie.

I know I did the right reading. I know it.

My breathing accelerates as I rack my brain, trying to figure out how I messed this up.

I'm about to fail the first quiz of the semester and it's all my—*oh my God!*

My brain rockets back to the email I received last

week alerting me to an error in the syllabus. At the time, I didn't think anything of it. Mistakes happen all of the time.

But why wouldn't we have gotten an updated version of it in our class portal?

Why wasn't the update mentioned in class?

Understanding hits me with the force of an arrow plunging into a bullseye.

This wasn't a mistake at all. I didn't mess anything up. I was *sabotaged.*

Anger pulses within me, like the beat of an angry drum. My blood boils and my jaw clenches as I fight the urge to march down to Sterling's desk and let him have it. But master manipulator that he is, I know he'd only turn it around on me.

He wants me to make a scene. I'm sure of it. So sure, I'd bet every pretty penny of the inheritance my dad left me. He wants me to throw a fit, to beg and plead.

Well, I won't give him the satisfaction. I refuse.

Instead, I put my pen to the page, and answer the questions to the best of my ability.

I try not to let it get to me as one-by-one, my classmates hand in their papers and exit the classroom. Minutes trickle by until, eventually, only the two of us remain. The smug grin on his face as I stand from my desk and head his way is all the confirmation I need.

"Tell me," he says, kicked back in his chair, looking as regal as a king. *An evil king.*

"Tell you what?" It's a struggle to control my voice. I want to lash out at him, to scratch him with my claws and wound him with my sharp tongue.

"How do you think you did?"

"We both already know the answer to that, don't we?"

His grin widens, and it takes my all not to knock it from his face.

"You're a real piece of work," I seethe, wondering not for the first time how someone that attractive can be so awful. Shouldn't men like him have some kind of marker to denote the evil in their blood?

You know very well they don't, my inner voice cruelly reminds me.

He shrugs before adopting a careless pose. "I hear it takes one to know one."

"For a grad student, you sure sound like a schoolyard bully."

Sterling tips his head back and laughs. My eyes are drawn to his Adam's apple, seemingly transfixed by the way it bobs as the tenor of his voice winds itself around me like a toxic fog.

He has the kind of laugh you could live in, get lost in, if only he weren't so wicked.

"You think you're so clever, that you can hurt me. But you can't, Sterling. It's not possible." *To break me any further,* I add in my head.

"Guess I'll have to try harder."

"Your loyalty's misplaced," I mutter under my breath This man here before me, he's so different than the boy I used to know. He's sharper, more cunning, colder.

While he wasn't ever particularly sunny, he was still a bright spot for me, because his presence in our home always meant as a reprieve from Rob's torture.

"What was that?"

"One day…" I sigh and shake my head. "No, you know what? Forget it. I'm not wasting my breath trying to plead my case to you. You're nothing more than a lapdog. News-flash, your master is a sociopath."

I crumple my quiz and toss it down onto his desk before spinning on my heel and hoofing it toward the door. I'm over him, over his antics, and desperately in need of pizza.

Preferably multiple slices with extra cheese, black olives, and bell peppers. And a side of ranch.

He calls my name just as I reach the door. I slow my pace but keep moving. "Have a great lunch."

Somehow, his parting words sound more like a threat.

Freaking psycho.

"STUPID, ARROGANT, NO GOOD JACKASS," I swear under my breath as I stalk across the campus like a woman on a warpath.

I'm enraged, barely hanging on by a thread, and in serious need of carbs. *God help anyone who stands between me and my pizza.*

"I'll show him."

"Show who?" Stella asks, appearing at my side, seemingly out of thin air.

"Jesus Christ!" I whisper-shout. "Where did you come from?"

"Uh, I've been walking beside you for like two minutes."

"Really?"

"Yup," she says with a pop of the P. "I showed up right around *no good jackass.*"

"Huh." I must have been deep in my feels to not notice my best friend at my side. Which only serves as a reminder of my lacking self-awareness.

No wonder Sterling was so easily able to pull the wool

over my eyes; I may as well have my head in the damn clouds.

"I take it class was bad?"

I groan. "More than bad. It was awful."

Stella shoots me a sympathetic glance. "Let's get some food and you can tell me all about it."

"Please tell me you want pizza," I plead, fully prepared to stand in line alone if need be.

"Babe, I always want pizza."

"Good, because I need it. *Need. It.*"

"Then you shall have it." She links her arm with mine and steers us toward the entrance.

Inside, various tantalizing scents greet us, but I only have one thing on my mind.

Dough, sauce, cheese. Dough, sauce, stabbing Sterling in the face, cheese.

Okay, so more than one thing.

"So, you want to tell me what happened?" Stella asks softly, gauging my reaction.

"Well, I'm ninety-nine percent sure I just failed our first quiz." I grab two slices of my beloved pizza. "And I'm one-hundred percent certain he set me up to do it."

"Set you up how?"

"Remember last week when my syllabus changed?"

Realization dawns in her eyes. "That rat!"

"Yup. He's vile."

She nods. "All the pretty boys are."

"Pretty boys like Samson?" I ask, hoping today's the day she finally spills her guts. God knows I could use the distraction.

"Nice subject change, Emmy. Real subtle."

"Whatever." I roll my eyes as I swipe my card and key in my PIN.

An angry beep sounds, causing my cheeks to burn. "Oops. Must have hit a wrong number."

The guy behind the kiosk rolls his eyes as I re-enter my code, making sure to press the correct keys this time, but the results are the same.

"Are you sure you're entering it correctly?" he asks, sounding beyond bored.

"Positive." I glance back at the growing line behind me. "Could you... um... enter it manually?"

"Sure."

I pass him the card and he keys it in on his side. Whatever he sees on his side has his brow furrowing. "Your account is locked."

"Locked? What? Why?" Uneasiness snakes its way through me.

"I don't know. Just says it's locked by a faculty member."

"What?" I ask again, more in outrage than in search of an actual answer. Because there's only one person to blame for this, and he's already at the top of my shit list.

"You'll have to go over to student services to get it fixed," he says, right as Stella offers to cover my meal.

"That won't be necessary." My tone is low and lethal as I slam my tray down onto the counter. Turning, I stalk toward the exit, a righteous fire burning through me. If Sterling Abbot thinks he can break me so easily, he's got another thing coming, and I plan to hand-deliver it.

"Emmy, where—"

"Talk later!" I call over my shoulder without looking back. I'm a woman on a mission, and there's not a thing on this earth that's going to stop me from finding him and giving him a good, swift kick in the balls.

OFFICE HOURS ARE A FUCKING JOKE.

Every single meeting thus far has been silver-spooned brats either offering to suck my cock for a higher grade or a good word with Elijah for their referral letter.

Pathetic. The whole lot of them.

With only fifteen more minutes on the clock, I begin packing up. If someone happens to drop by, I'll wrangle up an acceptable excuse for my absence. Because I can't sit here another second without losing my mind.

I've been half-certain the little mouse to pay me a visit, but it seems she's even more cowardly than I first imagined. She can't even bring herself to confront me when I pretty much expected to intentionally setting her up to fail.

She's no more pathetic than the girls in here offering to fall to their knees. At least they're willing to chase after what they want so badly, she always just hides.

It's not like I really expected more, I'm not sure why I expected more from a woman of her caliber. Liars are inherently weak, and Priscilla Price all but built her throne on tall tales and falsehoods.

I check the time on my phone once more—ten minutes left. I cross the small office, raising my hand to flip off the lights and call it a day, when the door flies open with enough force that I have to jump back to keep from getting smacked in the face.

"What in the—"

"You have some nerve," Emmalyn fumes, as if summoned by thought alone.

Her eyes are molten and her cheeks tinged crimson as her unbridled rage fills the air around us, weighting it, making it hard to breathe.

I pull a carefully blank face, careful not to show her the physical effect she's having on me. I cock my head to the side and pout. "Aw. You mad?"

"Fucking furious." She shoves me back and enters the room fully, throwing the door shut behind her.

"Good," I growl, stepping into her space. I have no qualms about using my height to intimidate her. By hook or by crook, she will break.

As predicted, she retreats, but the solid wood of the door halts her progress, leaving her trapped. "I hope it burns through you like a wildfire and razes every bit of happiness you have left."

"Why are you like this?" Her plump lower lip wobbles, and some sick part of me delights in knowing she's trying not to cry.

I wonder which tastes better? The salt of her tears or the sweetness of her lips?

"Why are you a liar?" I counter with a mirthless laugh.

"I'm not." She shoves at my chest again, but I don't budge. Not even an inch. Instead, I box her in closer, holding her captive in a cage made of my flesh and bone.

"You are." I dip lower, bringing my gaze level with hers.

"You are, and you know it." This close, I can see the flecks of gold and honey that streak her irises. She's captivating, utterly stunning. Too bad she's also a duplicitous bitch.

Her breathing accelerates, though out of anger or my nearness, I can't say.

"I'm. Not. A. Liar." Her voice breaks on the end as a single tear falls, rolling down her cheek, over the corner of her mouth, and off her chin.

I unplant one hand from the wall behind her and drag my finger over the wet path before stroking my fingers over her silky dark hair.

Her breath shudders and my lips turn up in a devious grin. I affect her, just as she does me. I'm sure of it.

But there's only one way to know for sure.

I gather her long strands in my fist and tug sharply, jerking her nearer. A small gasp escapes her, yet she makes no move to push me away.

Interesting. So very interesting.

With her trembling lips only a hairsbreadth away from mine, she asks, "What... what are you doing?"

I give her hair a hard yank, leveraging her mouth to mine. "Anything I want, little mouse." I rasp the words against her pillowy lips, so soft and tempting, full and pink. They'd look phenomenal with my dick sliding in and out of them.

"Get away from me," she says, even as she clutches at the front of my shirt, pulling me closer.

Her pupils are blown wide with want, and I can practically feel her heart thundering in her chest.

"Now, you don't mean that." I wedge my right thigh between hers to drive home my point.

"Don't..." she protests weakly. Her fight is giving way to the white-hot need churning between us. I can tell she hates the way she reacts to me, but damn if this delicious development doesn't open a million new doors, each one a straight shot to her demise.

I grin darkly, already laying the groundwork as I claim her mouth in a kiss that's as hot as it is demanding. I expect her to at least keep up the ruse of fighting me, but instead, she opens greedily, sucking my tongue into her mouth like it's her favorite flavor of lollipop.

Emmalyn Price kisses the same way she lies, with a practiced ease that borders on familiarity.

We use our lips, teeth, and tongues as we funnel our mutual hatred for one another into this mind-fuck of a kiss, licking, sucking, and biting at each other until all that's left is a simmering desire threatening to boil over at any moment.

"Sterling," she whimpers, rocking against my solid thigh.

I nip at her lower lip, dragging my hands down her body to her ass.

Understanding my silent command, she wraps her long, toned legs around my waist.

I thrust into the hot space between her thighs. A deep groan rips from my chest, and then—

The sound of a door slamming down the hall has us breaking apart like two horny teens caught in the act.

Chests heaving, we regard one another. Lust and anger duel for dominance in Emmalyn's dark gaze, while I run the numbers on how to play this to my advantage.

Our chemistry is undeniable, and I'd be an idiot not to find a way to exploit this burning attraction we seem to share.

"What the..." Emmalyn whispers, seemingly caught somewhere between confusion and outrage as she tries to push away from me like she wasn't just rubbing herself all over my leg. "What just happened?"

Still processing this new turn of events, I don't answer her immediately.

"Sterling?"

My name's a question, one filled with equal parts loathing and longing.

"Shh." I press my index finger to her kiss-swollen lips. "Go back to your dorm, Emmalyn."

"But—"

I lean down and stamp her lips with one last chaste kiss before stepping away from her. "Go."

She stares at me for a moment, but doesn't make me tell her to go a third time.

I chuckle darkly as she squeaks out a barely audible reply before turning and bolting out the door.

THE SOUND of Sterling's laughter, dark and deadly, chases behind me as I shoot down the hall toward the exit.

Confusion slows me as my brain and body battle, the two no longer functioning as a cohesive unit.

While my brain screams for me to run far and fast, my body, the stupid traitorous wench, is trembling with need, hungry for his touch.

I'm half tempted to turn back and demand answers. But my pride and my legs pump me along faster, carrying me away from the confounding, swirling feelings he's stirring in me.

The air nearly blasts me as I barrel out of the building.

The campus is full of students, all laughing and smiling and living while just doing and existing. And even then, just being.

They have never tasted my distress. Because in that office, with Sterling's body pressed against mine... I felt normal.

How sick is that? Just how completely messed up am I?

Through my tears, I notice a little alcove to my left and

duck into it. I collapse onto the stone bench and draw my legs to my chest, wrapping my arms around them.

Tucked away and out of sight, I let myself break down and sob silently.

Over and over, I replay our kiss as I rub my index finger over my lips, recalling vividly the way Sterling's lips felt against mine, the way he tasted.

It's been nearly a year since my stepbrother stole my innocence, and after the unspeakable, unconscionable things he did to me, maybe I really am broken.

I have to be, right?

There's no other explanation for why I not only allowed Sterling to touch me, but liked it, too. Even now, my body is singing his praises while the more logical part of me is scrambling to make sense of any of it.

I mean, how is it possible for one man to affect me so? He can disarm as quickly as he can antagonize me. Truly, the man is infuriating. He's cold. Cruel and calculating. He's told me time and time again; he wants to ruin me.

Even worse, how could I allow it? How could I allow *him* of all people to touch me?

I haven't let a man touch me since Rob. Not a single one.

I swore that the next time I so much as held hands with a man, it would be on my terms, with someone I love and trust.

Not a hate-kiss in a dark office, with a man who's been so cruel.

And what do you know... I let him.

In more ways than one, because how will any other kiss measure up?

I showed him my weak underbelly when I didn't push

him away. My pathetic half-assed protests may as well have been me begging for more.

Which I would've done, if that door wouldn't have slammed.

Sterling is a bully, and everything I despise in a man, and yet my lips still burn with the flames of his kiss.

My tears start anew as I berate myself for being so stupid. It's not like he cares about me. If anything, his kiss is another game, meant to confuse me.

Rob always loved to play games; they were designed to hurt and only he ever won.

Who's to say Sterling is any different? What's that stupid saying... *you are the company you keep?* Yeah, that's it. And Sterling and Rob have been damn near inseparable for as long as I've known them.

Clearly, Sterling Abbot is dangerous. I'm weak for him and now, he knows it.

How could I've let that happen? The question slams into my skull over and over, battering me until I'm on the verge of losing it.

"Just calm down," I mutter to myself, willing my stupid tears to dry. The fact that I'm sitting here crying over him at all is infuriating in and of itself.

He only has power over me because I allow it. The problem is, I don't know how to stop it. I don't know how to wrench myself free from the hold he has over me.

But I will. If it's the last thing I do, *I will.*

Finally, my tears dry and I force myself up from the bench. I shoot Stella a quick text asking her to meet me in our suite, if she can, before creeping out of my hiding place.

Except, before I can step foot back onto the sidewalk, I slam into a brick wall.

"Oof!" I stumble back, clutching my forehead.

"Sweets." *Okay, so not a wall... a Gabe.* "We've got to stop meeting like this."

"What do they feed you?"

He starts to flex, but something stops him. "Have you... have you been crying?"

"It's nothing."

"Zach!" Gabe hollers, and in the blink of an eye, he appears.

"Yeah? Oh, Emmy. Have you been crying?"

Gabe tips his head back, as if to say *see, I told you!*

"I'm fine, guys."

"Tell Daddy what's wrong," Gabe says, linking his arm with mine.

Zach takes up post on my other side. "Whose ass do we need to kick?"

"If I had to guess, I'd say her TA."

I roll my eyes, but don't confirm Gabe's suspicions. "I'm fine. I promise," I say, mostly meaning it. Something about being smooshed between the two of them has me feeling safe and secure.

"Where are you headed?" my blond giant asks.

"My dorm."

The two men exchange a look before Zach says, "We'll walk you."

They pry for more information for the entirety of our walk, but my lips stay sealed.

It's not that I don't want to tell them, it's just... as crazy as it sounds, I can't help but feel like Sterling has eyes and ears everywhere. The last thing I want is for anything to get back to him.

We slow our pace as my building comes into sight. "Thanks, guys," I say right as a flying blonde ball slams into me, wrapping me in a frantic hug.

"Oh my God, Emmy! Where have you been? What happened? Did you let him have it? Who are these two hotties? Tell. Me. Every. Thing!"

"Well, hello there, sunshine," Gabe murmurs as Stella releases me. "Who are you?"

My roomie's big, blue eyes flit between my two escorts. "I'm Stella, Emmy's roommate, and y'all are?"

"Her daddies," Zach says with a twinkle in his eyes.

"What my lovely boyfriend meant to say is we're her friends. I'm Gabe, and that fine piece of meat is Zach."

I zone out, my mind drifting back to the way Sterling played me like a freaking fiddle.

How on earth am I supposed to face him Thursday morning?

"Hello!" Stella snaps her fingers in front of my face. "Are you coming?"

"What? Where?"

"Inside." She draws the word out, the three of them staring at me expectantly. When I don't reply, she adds, "So we can talk. Duh."

"Oh, um. Sure."

The three of them herd me through the door, down the hall, and into the elevator. I fall into an uneasy silence as the elevator car begins its ascent. There's no doubt in my mind they're going to grill me the second we're in our suite. And while the idea of secrets between us unsettles me, I'm not sure I'm ready to face the consequences of what happened between Sterling and me today.

I'm not sure I'm ready to face their judgment either, if I'm being honest.

The elevator jerks to a stop and the doors part. On the other side stands Melanie.

I haven't seen her since the party last weekend, and

after the day I've had, she is one of the last people I feel like dealing with.

"Melanie," Stella sneers, loyal and fierce as ever.

"Flirted with any taken men lately, slut?" my RA hisses, her eyes narrowed in misplaced anger.

Well, only semi-misplaced, I guess, seeing as we made out today.

Oh, God. If they are together, not only did I let my tormentor kiss me, I also helped him cheat.

Lovely.

Gabe and Zach form a protective barrier around me, ushering me past Melanie.

The second we're inside of our suite, Stella is on me, demanding details.

"What happened? Seriously, Emmy. Tell me—*us*—everything."

"Yes, sweets. Spill." Gabe doesn't hesitate, making himself comfy on our couch. His hulking frame makes the room seem ten times smaller, but I'm glad he's here.

Zach lowers himself to the floor in front of where Gabe's seated, leaving the other side of the couch for Stella and me.

Despite being smaller than me, Stella drags me to the couch and plops me down into the middle before claiming the seat beside me.

"Dish, babe. Now."

Tugging on the ends of my hair, I groan. As excited as I am to have true, genuine friends, the thought of telling them what a monumental idiot I am has me wishing a hole would open in the floor and swallow me, if only to spare me my humiliation.

"Look," Zach says, laying his head back onto Gabe's thigh. "We aren't gonna judge you. We aren't gonna think differently of you. No matter what you say, we'll still have your back. Okay?"

Gabe and Stella nod their agreement.

"He.. he kissed me," I mumble. My shoulders instantly sag without the burden of my secret weighing them down.

"What?" Stella shouts, right as Gabe commands me to explain.

I open my mouth to speak, to try and explain myself. But it's no use. All I manage to do is look like a goldfish gasping for air; how can I even begin to explain what happened in that small office?

"He kissed me," I say again, when nothing better comes to mind.

"Yeah, you mentioned that." Stella pins me with a look. "I'm trying to figure out how you ended up locking lips when you left the cafeteria with stabby-stabby-murder-murder in your eyes."

I throw my hands up in the universal *hell if I know* gesture. "I don't know. We were fighting and then, the next thing I know, we were kissing."

"Who kissed who?" Gabe asks, sounding a little too *interested* for my liking.

"Um." I replay the entire sordid ordeal, desperately trying to seek out who was the instigator. "He kissed me. I think. Maybe."

"Emmy!" Stella shrieks my name, bouncing wildly beside me.

"I know." I drop my head into my hands and sigh. "It's horrible."

Truly, it is. Only, I'm not sure which is worse: the fact that we kissed or the fact that I liked it.

"No!" Stella exclaims, pulling my hands away from my face. "It's amazing!"

"What?" Zach and I ask in tandem. At least someone else sees this for what it is—a freaking disaster.

She looks to Gabe for support, but he shakes his head. "I need to hear your reasoning before I can decide if you're insanely smart or just insane."

Stella looks at all three of us like we're as dense as bricks. "Use this to your advantage, babe."

I stare at her blankly. "What?"

Gabe slowly nods his head. "No, she has a point. He's obviously attracted to you. Use your feminine wiles to make him be nice."

"I don't know," Zach murmurs, giving voice to my own thoughts. "Emmy might not be ready for this kind of game."

"That—that's just not me. Not to mention, he probably only kissed me to mess with me. For all I know, it was some power play, just to reinforce how stupid I am."

"No. No way." Gabe leans forward, locking his eyes onto mine. "Remember the second time we met?"

"Um, yeah..." How could I forget? "Why?"

"When you slammed into me outside of your classroom, he was lingering in the doorway, watching us."

"You mean that dude we saw outside of her building?" Zach asks.

"Yeah, him."

"Oh, he's definitely into you." Zach chuckles. "He was stalking your ass like he was a lion and you were a gazelle."

"What? No..."

"Yeah." Gabe nods vigorously. "Swear it. He glared at me so hard when you left with me... let's just say I'm glad looks can't actually kill."

"Truth. After you went inside, Gabe made us walk all the way around the backside of the campus to avoid him. Dude looked like he had a bone to pick."

My brain can't seem to process this new information. Surely there's a logical reason for his strange behavior.

"Maybe it's not about Rob," Stella says, her eyes immediately flaring wide with regret. "Oh my God! Emmy, I'm sorry."

I squeeze her hand. "It's okay. They know about Rob."

"Okay." She eyes me speculatively. "Well, then yeah. Maybe it's not a Rob thing, but like a, jealous-school-boy-play-yard thing?"

"I highly doubt it." I look to Gabe and Zach for support, but they both shrug.

"I was a total ass to Gabe when we first met." Zach looks up at his boyfriend lovingly.

"Yeah, but only because you were still in the closet. You didn't want to admit that my fine-ass-self got your dick hard, so you acted like a macho asshole."

Stella gasps. "Maybe Sterling's in the closet over how he feels about you!"

"Not what that means," I tell her gently.

She rolls her eyes. "I know. I just meant, maybe he's always had feelings for you, but has been in denial."

"He hardly noticed me growing up."

"But—"

I cut her off. "I love you, Stella, but he's not interested in me. He doesn't have a crush. And I can almost guarantee he kissed me with ulterior motives."

I think. Right? Yeah, I have to be right. Don't I?

Indecision turns my stomach.

Thankfully, Stella doesn't keep pushing. At least not about that. "You at least have to tell us, was he a good kisser at least?"

"The best," I say, flopping back on the couch in disgust.

"SERIOUSLY, HOW IS IT ALREADY THURSDAY?" Stella asks as the coffee pot gurgles to life on the counter behind her.

"Ugh," I groan. "Don't even get me started." I'm honestly half tempted to skip class today to avoid Sterling for a little bit longer. But, after the quiz disaster from Tuesday and my unfortunate project pairing, I'm already going to have to bust my ass in that class just to keep my head above water.

Like the heaven-sent angel she is, Stella passes me a mug of coffee. "You gonna be okay?"

"Define okay." I take a long sip, letting the caffeine wind its way through me, warming me and waking me from the inside out.

"Let's set the bar low. Okay, as in you won't shove your pen through his eyeball?"

I can't help but laugh. "Then yeah, I think I'll be okay."

"Atta girl!" Stella clicks her tongue at me. "Now, let's go."

We walk together, chatting aimlessly until we have to go our separate ways. Which, naturally, is when my nerves really set in.

Will he be the same asshole as usual or was our clandestine kiss some type of fucked-up olive branch?

Only one way to find out.

Steeling my spine, I march into the building with my head held high. There're so many things in life we can't control, the actions of others being one of them. Worrying over how he's going to behave won't change anything.

It's out of your control. Just breathe.

I pause outside of the classroom, take a few deep breaths, and then head in.

Like always, Sterling's behind the podium, looking disinterested. Not wanting to draw his attention, I grab the first open seat I see. Unfortunately, it just so happens to be in the front of the classroom, directly in his line of sight.

He glances my way right as my butt hits the seat. My cheeks heat, and he smirks.

So much for not drawing his attention.

I want so badly to move to a desk in the back of the room, but I'm here now, and it would only make me look weak to move now.

Also, I don't want him to think I'm some scared little baby bird. We kissed. So what. No big deal. Or at least, that's the lie I'm choosing to tell myself. Maybe if I say it enough times, I'll believe it, too.

At nine on the dot, Sterling dives into his lecture. As much as it pains me to admit it, I could drown in the deep, smooth pitch of his voice.

The upside is, I'm so tuned in to his every word, that note-taking is a breeze.

I END my lecture with ten minutes to spare. "Please divide yourselves into groups of three and use the remaining time to discuss the four components of social perceptions and how they affect human behavior. This will be the main focus of Thursday's lecture, so please be prepared to share what you discussed today."

My phone vibrates in my pocket with an incoming text for what feels like the hundredth time.

It's Rob, no doubt. Without even looking, I know.

I've gone lately from weekly check-ins to daily. The fact that I've never known him to be patient isn't helping matters, since patience has never been one of Rob's strong suits.

With my class unoccupied, I slide my phone from my pocket and pull up our text thread.

ROB

Fucking answer me, Sterling.

ROB

If you can't get it done, I'll find someone
who can.

Jesus. Talk about escalation. It's like he's gone completely off the deep end, and at this point, I'm not sure if I should toss him a life preserve or let him drown.

ME

Chill out. I've got everything under control.

ROB

Where are you?

ME

In class.

ROB

Fine. I want an update, a real one, by
Sunday, Sterling.

ME

You'll have one.

With less than a minute left, I dismiss everyone and settle back into my seat to wait.

After all, timing is everything.

I watch Emmalyn like a hawk as she packs away her belongings and hefts her messenger bag up, slinging the strap over her shoulder. I wait until she is nearly to the door before calling out her name.

She turns to look at me, her eyes wide with trepidation.

"A word, please." It pains me to tack on that last word, but if she's to believe I'm turning over a new leaf, manners are a must.

Indecision paints her every feature, before she finally turns and comes to me, just like I knew she would.

Summer glares at her as she walks by, intentionally knocking her shoulder into Emmy's.

I cover my smirk with a yawn before adopting a carefully neutral expression, as I file away a reminder to employ Summer's particular brand of bitchy before all's said and done.

"You wanted to see me?" she asks.

I wait until we're alone before replying.

"I did. I wanted to see if you'd like to retake the quiz on Tuesday. That'd give you the weekend to go over the correct materials."

"What's the catch?" she asks, eyeing me suspiciously.

Smart girl.

"Why do you assume there's a catch?"

"Nothing in life is free, Sterling. Especially not your kindness."

I can't help but grin at her candor. "I suppose you're right. This offer does come with strings attached."

Her eyes flit between me and the door as she debates whether or not she should hear me out.

Finally, after what feels like an excruciating eternity, she says, "Name them... your terms, that is."

A pleased feeling stirs inside of me, even as I suppress my grin. "Lunch."

"What?"

"Let me take you to lunch."

"What?" she asks again, parroting herself.

"If you want to retake the quiz next week, let me take you to lunch today. Do try and keep up, Emmalyn. They say you're smart."

She snorts out a derisive laugh. "Definitely smart enough to know going anywhere with you is a bad idea."

"Are you scared?" I ask, half taunting and half genuinely curious.

"Women are taught from a young age not to intentionally put themselves into dangerous situations. Something tells me being alone with you is most definitely dangerous."

"But we're alone now," I press, needing her to take me up on this offer. My entire plan hinges on her cooperation.

"Do you swear this isn't just another game?"

"It's not a game, Emmalyn."

Hook.

"And you swear I'll get to retake the quiz?"

"I guarantee it. I can put it in writing if you'd like."

Line.

"And you're not like... luring me away to murder me?"

I throw my head back and laugh.

"While the idea of my hands around your throat holds merit, I have no intention of killing you," I mutter under my breath, willing my mind to dispel the pretty picture my words are painting.

"What?"

"No, Emmalyn. I am not luring you away to kill you. I simply think we need to have a talk, and lunch seems like a good way to go about doing it."

"Okay. Sure. When?"

Sinker.

"Now's great for me."

"Oh, um. Today. Wow. Um."

"I know you don't have any other classes today. I know you don't have a job or internship. So, whatever bullshit excuse you're concocting in that pretty little head of yours, save us both the trouble and don't."

Her eyes flare at my demanding tone, though with heat or shock, I can't say.

"Okay." She flexes her fingers, clutching and releasing the strap of her bag. She's nervous, and the predator in me likes it. "Today is good."

"Great. I'll drive."

"We're... going off campus?" She gulps, and my eyes hone in on her delicate throat. My brain buzzes at the memory of how soft she is there, how sweet she tastes.

I give her a dull look. "Yes, Emmalyn. Surely you didn't think I was taking you to the dining hall." I rise from my desk and head for the door, not bothering to make sure she's following. I know she is.

No one pays any mind as we traipse across the campus to the parking garage.

Her lips quirk up into a smile when the large structure comes into view. "Fancy."

I roll my eyes but tell her, "You couldn't pay me to park my baby out in the elements. The paint job's custom."

"Of course it is." I grin as I make a big show of opening the door for her.

"It's nice, I'll give you that." She skims her finger over the buttery leather of the seat before buckling her seat belt.

I stroll around to the driver's side, but before I can open the door, my phone buzzes with another incoming text.

Sliding it out, I quickly check the screen. It's Rob. Again.

ROB

Don't fuck this up, Sterling.

ME

Just trust me, man.

I switch off my ringer, pocket my phone, and slide behind the wheel. "Ready?"

Emmalyn chuckles nervously. "As I'll ever be."

I find my attention divided for most of the drive. While I know I *need* to watch the winding mountain roads, I *want* to watch the woman riding shotgun in my F-Type Jag.

The way she squirms in the seat, the way she's so careful not to look my way, the way she's content to sit quietly rather than talk to me. All of these things combined only make me want to push her that much further.

But I'll play nice. For now, anyway.

"Have you eaten here?" I ask, inclining my head toward our destination.

"Café on the Corner." She reads the sign and then shakes her head no. "I haven't really explored town much. I've mostly stayed on campus."

"Why's that?" I whip into a parking spot a few shops down from the café.

She bites her lip and scratches at her chin. *She's nervous.* "Um." She laughs, but it is lacking all humor. "Sorry, I can't help but think you're going to use anything I say against me."

I adopt an understanding expression. "I can see why you'd feel that way. But, believe it or not, I'm trying to turn over a new leaf, Emmalyn."

Her big dark eyes study my face, looking for signs of insincerity. When she doesn't find any, I send up a small thanks and offer her a small, encouraging smile.

"Can new leaves even grow from rotten roots?"

"Guess we'll find out. Now, let's go."

I fall back as we walk down the sidewalk, allowing Emmalyn to walk a step or so ahead of me. My eyes definitely drop to her ass more than once; devious bitch or not, the girl's got a backside you could bounce a quarter off of.

She doesn't wait for me to open the door—not that I was planning to—and marches straight to the hostess stand.

"Hi, how many?"

Before Emmalyn can answer, I step up behind her. "We have a reservation for two, under Abbot."

"Of course. Your table's ready." She grabs our menus and silverware rolls. "Right this way."

We follow her in silence, but I can tell Emmalyn is stewing over something.

"Here you are. Your server will be by shortly. Our specials are listed on the board."

My lunch date glares at me from her seat across from me.

"What?" I lean back into my seat, smirking.

"I just think it's awfully presumptuous of you to make reservations before asking me to join you."

"You're the one being presumptuous."

She crosses her arms over her chest, drawing my eyes to the hint of cleavage her sweater shows off. "How so?"

"For starters, I have a weekly reservation here. You joining me today is pure luck."

"You said it was for two."

"Who's to say I eat alone?"

"Nice." She clenches her jaw and flicks her eyes to the side before studying the menu like it's her own personal bible.

"Jealous?" I ask, more amused than annoyed with the attitude she's throwing my way.

"As if!" She scrunches her nose and damn, if it's not cute as hell. "Why on earth would I be jealous?"

I shrug. "You seem awfully upset over the thought of me bringing someone else to lunch."

"I'm not upset. Or jealous. I just think it's... tacky."

"Well, this isn't a date," I say slowly, watching her face like a hawk. "Just a meal between two... friends."

"Friends?"

"Acquaintances?"

"That's closer." She closes her menu and nibbles her lower lip. "Why are we really here, Sterling?"

"Let's order first and then we can talk, okay?"

"I guess. What's good?"

"The nachos," I answer without hesitation. "They hand-cut the chips and the pico is made fresh for each order."

"Sold."

"We can split an order. The chicken is good, too. Local, free-range, and all of that other shit people like."

"Oh, um. Sure."

Our server walks up at that very moment, and once Emmalyn orders her drink, I order our food.

"Now then, where were we?" I ask once we're alone again.

"You were about to explain your personality transplant."

Unintentional but genuine laughter spills out of me. *Who knew my little mouse was so funny?*

"Maybe I've seen the error of my ways?"

"Sterling, I'm not in the mood for games. Either tell me why we're here or I'll leave."

A million shitty responses sit on the tip of my tongue, but I swallow them down, bitter as they are. "I'm not playing any games." I lean forward, bracing my elbows on the table. "It's just..." I trail off, laying bait.

Which she eagerly eats up. "It's just what?"

"Everything with Rob, no one really bothered to really hear you, and I guess it doesn't sit right with me."

"Oh, sure." She nods thoughtfully. "That totally explains why you've been such a nasty asshole. Because you were upset my voice was minimized. Makes perfect sense."

Swear to God, she wants me to spank her ass.

"Look, I won't deny that I've been... less than welcoming. I'll even go a step farther and admit my behavior is a byproduct of my loyalty to Rob. He's been my best friend my entire life, but that doesn't mean he's telling the truth."

Her eyes are laser focused on me, not quite in a glare, but close. She's angry, but she's eager to hear what I have to say. She's so desperate for someone to buy into her lies that she doesn't even realize she's playing right into my hand.

"And what brought about this change of heart?" she asks after our drinks are dropped off.

I sip from my whiskey, weighing which reply will soften her the most. Another sip, and I decide to go for broke.

"Honestly? Rob's a little unhinged, and I just kept thinking, what if it was *my* sister?"

"You don't have a sister."

"Right." I drum my fingers over the tabletop. "But, *if* I did, I'd want people to listen to her. To be there for her. To support her, to stand with her."

"So you... you believe me?"

Not even a little... at least I don't think I do. She's so convincing, I can't help but wonder who's actually the liar.

"I'm starting to think there's more to it, and I'd really like to hear your side of things, Emmalyn."

Right before my very eyes, she softens. Melts, practically. "Emmy. Call... call me Emmy."

My God, this is almost too easy.

"Okay, Emmy. So, yeah, if you're open to it, I'd like to hear your side of everything. And I'm not saying to spill your heart in the middle of lunch, but in time. Is that okay?"

"I..." She licks her lips and glances around the room. "I think I would like that."

STERLING SMILES like the cat who ate the canary.

At this point, I'm not sure which of us is the dumber: him, for thinking I'm falling for his obvious bullshit, or me for being half tempted to believe him.

Regardless, I'm interested in seeing how this plays out. Even if it blows up in my face, it's not like things can get worse, right? We have no friends as it is, and who knows... maybe I really can get Sterling to see the truth.

I'll never know if I don't try, so here goes nothing.

"I know you're majoring in psychology, but what are you planning to do with that degree?" Sterling asks as a heaping plate of nachos is placed on the table between us.

"I want to be a victims' advocate." I clench and unclench my fists, feeling a whole new kind of vulnerability as I look at him. "I want to help other people... people like me. I want to give a voice to the voiceless."

I expect him to laugh, but instead he nods encouragingly. "I can see you doing that."

"What do you mean?"

He shrugs and pops a queso-laden chip into his mouth. "You just seem the type. Like you'd enjoy helping people."

"Is that a bad thing?" I ask, taking a chip for myself. "Oh my God. This is... whoa."

"Right? Told you."

We eat in silence for a few moments, my question seemingly forgotten. Or so I thought, until Sterling says, "No, it's not a bad thing. It's refreshing, if I'm honest. It's rare to see such selflessness."

Even though his words are most likely nothing more than spoon-fed bullshit, I still feel my cheeks heat all the same.

I only thought my brain and body were at war before, but that was merely a battle. This, him treating me with kindness, this is the war—and I'm going to have to be extra careful spending time with him if I want to emerge the victor.

We exchange silly, inconsequential stories as we eat, and the entire time, I'm struck by how absolutely normal it feels. Then again, he's probably playing me for all I'm worth. Though, joke's on him there, because after the abuse I suffered at his best friend's hands, I'm not worth all that much.

Much to my surprise, and despite my protests to cover my portion, Sterling insists on footing the bill for our meal. "It's the least I owe you after the way I've treated you," he says, sounding so sincere I find myself wanting to believe he really is capable of kindness.

But I know better.

"Can't argue with that," I concede, because a free meal is a free meal.

Even though I have a sizeable inheritance from my father, I try to live frugally, preferring to squirrel most of my funds away for my future. Lord knows my mother doesn't offer support of any kind to me, especially financial support.

I was prepared to pay out of pocket for an in-state school, but then I was offered a full-ride here, and I leaped at the chance to escape.

So, yeah, I'll take a free meal.

"Ready to head back?" he asks as he signs the receipt with a flourish.

"I guess so." I push back from the table. "After all, I have some reading to catch up on."

For a split second, he looks taken aback by my casual joking over his deception. But in the blink of an eye, he schools his features. "I suppose you do. C'mon." He gestures for me to walk ahead of him, but as I pass him, he presses a hand to the small of my back and falls in step beside me.

His palm may as well be a brand on my skin, painfully hot, singeing my skin through the material of my sweater. But I'll be damned if I'm going to acknowledge that his touch is affecting me.

He keeps his hand on me the entire walk back to his car, and even opens the door for me, waiting patiently while I buckle before rounding the hood to the driver's side.

This gentleman act of his is so convincing, it's a miracle he's not majoring in acting. The thought gives me pause, because what *is* Sterling majoring in?

"That's a complicated question," he says, shocking me out of my musings.

"What is?"

"What I'm majoring in." He presses the start button and checks his mirrors before smoothly reversing out of our parking spot.

"I asked that out loud?"

He chuckles under his breath. "Sure did."

"Oh." I duck my head. "Well, tell me."

"I'm finishing B school right now." At my blank stare he continues, "Getting an MBA."

"And you're TA-ing my psych class why?"

He shoots me a cocky grin as he expertly navigates the winding mountain roads. "Simple. I'm the best student the department ever had."

"What?"

"Oh, yeah. Bet you didn't know there was more to me than good looks, huh?"

I snort out a laugh. "Actually, I never realized there was more to you than sharp barbs."

"Funny girl."

"I think so." I lean back against the seat and roll my head to the left to look at him. His profile is so stupidly handsome it sends a rush of flutters through me. "What are you doing with your degrees?"

He sighs. "I'll join dear old mom and dad in the family business."

I blanch at the mention of his parents. Rob lawyered up when I came forward against him, and Mr. Abbot ruthlessly represented him.

Thank God we never went before any kind of judge, mostly because my mom told everyone I was a liar with an overactive imagination. But I don't doubt for a second that he would have annihilated me in a courtroom.

"Right. Why aren't you in law school then?"

"That's a good question," is all he says before changing the subject. "Are you going to the football game this weekend?"

I want to poke and prod him for a truthful answer, but I let it go. "Yeah, we're going to watch Gabe."

He white-knuckles the steering wheel as he turns onto the twisting road that leads back to campus. "Maybe I'll see y'all there and you can introduce me."

Jesus, it's like I'm in The Twilight Zone. "Maybe."

"What? You don't want your friends to know me?"

"I just figured you'd be with your friends."

"Well, maybe I'd rather be with yours."

Yep. Definitely in The Twilight Zone. He's so convincing, it's almost as if he actually wants to hang out with me.

"Okay, Sterling. If that's what you want."

"You have no idea what I want, little mouse," he mumbles under his breath.

We fall into a semi-companionable silence after that, with only the sound of the radio between us.

Before I know it, Sterling rolls to a stop in front of my dorm, proving Gabe and Zach slightly right... because how else would he know where I live?

"Thanks for lunch," I say self-consciously as I fumble to unlatch my seat belt.

"Thanks for joining me." Sterling grins my way and before I can realize his intentions, he leans in and presses his lips to my cheek. "I'll see you Thursday."

I stumble from his car in a daze, wondering not for the first time what his end game is.

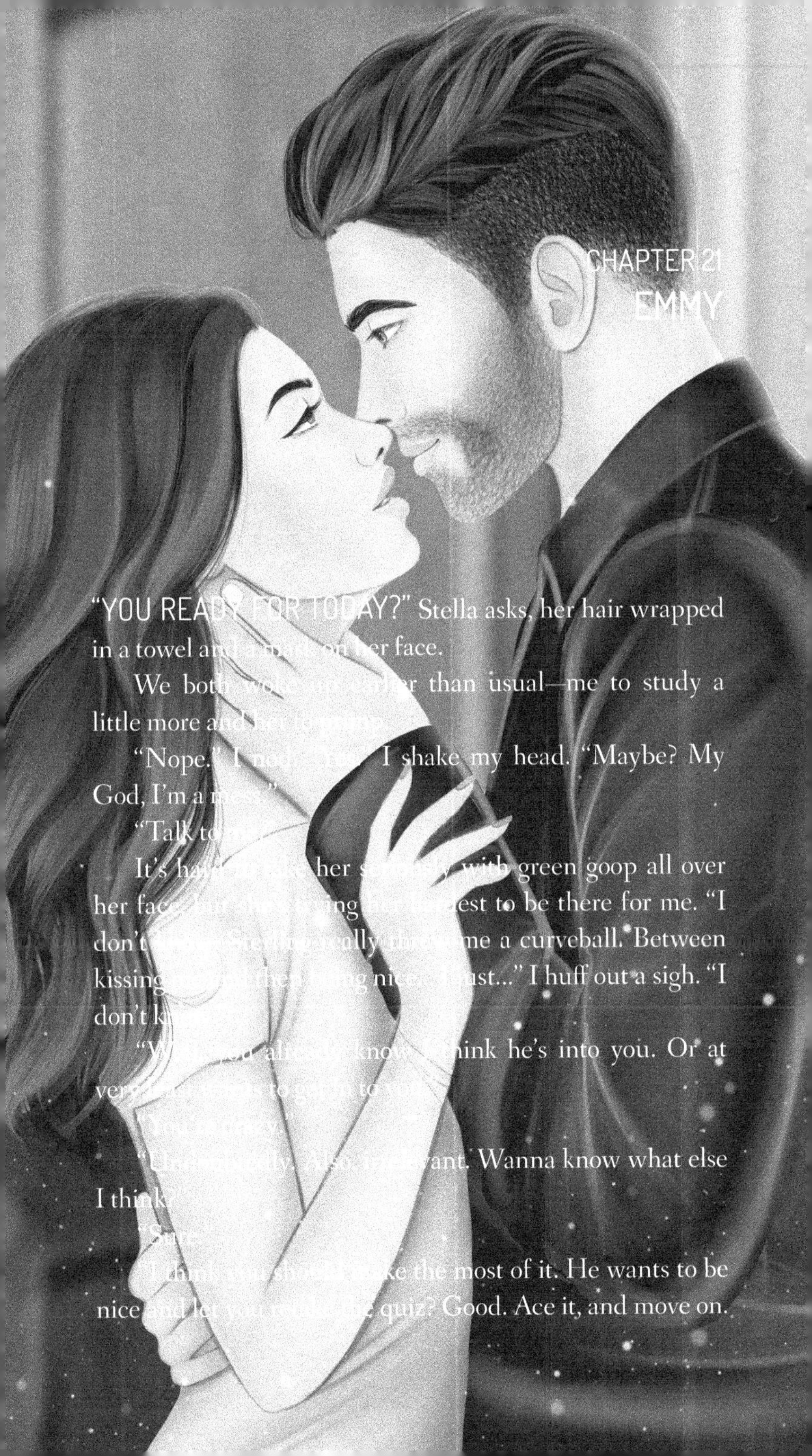

"YOU READY FOR TODAY?" Stella asks, her hair wrapped in a towel and a mask on her face.

We both woke up earlier than usual—me to study a little more and her to—

"Nope." I nod. "Yup." I shake my head. "Maybe? My God, I'm a mess."

"Talk to me."

It's hard to take her seriously with green goop all over her face, but she's still trying her hardest to be there for me. "I don't know. Sterling really threw me a curveball. Between kissing me and then being nice—at last…" I huff out a sigh. "I don't k—"

"Well, you already know I think he's into you. Or at very least he wants to get to you."

"Yes, okay."

"Unfortunately, yes. It's what I want. Wanna know what else I think?"

"Sure."

"I think you should make the most of it. He wants to be nice and let you retake the quiz? Good. Ace it, and move on.

Keep your guard up, but use this to your advantage, you know?"

"Yeah, it's just. Ugh!" I flip my laptop closed and bury my face in my hands. "He's making me crazy." It's true, too; Sterling Abbot is driving me to insanity. Or at the very least, sleep deprivation.

It seems like all I've done over the past day and a half is study and overanalyze every single moment between Sterling and me.

"Babe, don't let him get to you like this. Walls up?"

"Walls up."

"Good. Now, I've gotta rinse this mask. Go forth and kick ass."

"I'll try."

"There is no try, only do."

"Okay, Yoda."

Stella points to the green mask covering her face and winks before flouncing off to the bathroom.

Left to my own devices, there's nothing to do except obsess. At this point, I'm annoying myself. But all I can think about is what if this is just another cruel trick? What if he's setting me up to fail again?

Unable to stand my own whining, I throw on a hoodie, pack up my messenger bag, and head out. If I hurry, I should have time to grab a coffee before class.

Holy Roasters is packed, per usual, but I still have twenty minutes to spare.

For the first time in a long time, it feels like things are finally going my way. If only I could shake off the feeling of waiting for the other shoe to drop.

At the counter, I decide to splurge and get a large iced coffee and a chocolate croissant.

I'm waiting on my order when the door opens and

Melanie walks in with Abigail, one of the other RAs, and a girl I don't know.

Abigail smiles and waves while Melanie glares at me like I just kicked her puppy. I wish I understood her issue with me. Ever since the Sterling-incident at the party, it's like she's a totally different person.

She went from sweet and encouraging to nasty and mean. All because she thought I was flirting with her man.

Oh my God! We ate lunch together yesterday... we kissed...

And it didn't even occur to me to ask him about her. I am officially the worst.

At this point, all I can do is hope that they're not together, because while I've been called a lot of things, homewrecker shockingly isn't one of them. And I'd like to keep it that way.

The barista calls my name, and I pick up my goodies. I still have fifteen minutes left, so I plan to enjoy my breakfast on one of the benches outside.

I square my shoulders and hold my head high as I pass Melanie and company, determined not to show even a hint of fear or hurt. If she and Sterling are together, I'll apologize and own up to my mistakes, and if they're not, how freaking sad that she'd let a guy twist her up like that.

As I near the trio, Melanie's eyes narrow and her lips quirk up into a perfectly evil smile. "Whore," she coughs into her hand, like a middle school bully.

I'm usually not one for confrontation, but for some reason today, I find myself over it. "What is your problem?" I ask, stopping in front of her.

"You are." She drags her eyes over me and curls her lip in disgust. "What kind of woman hits on another's man? It's pathetic, really."

"Listen, I didn't know y'all were together. Furthermore, I'm not interested in Sterling in that way. I'm not your competition, Melanie. He's all yours."

The girl I don't know watches the two of us with wide eyes while Abigail looks concerned, but not shocked.

"Sterling made it official?" the gorgeous redheaded RA asks. "I thought he all but ghosted you."

Melanie's entire face darkens with rage. "You bitch!"

Abigail shrugs. "I'm just saying. No reason to invoke girl code when you're not exactly keeping it yourself. Y'all aren't together, and Emmy couldn't have known you were into him."

"What the fuck? Whose side are you on?" Melanie demands, nearly shouting.

"Girl, it's not a fight. There shouldn't be any sides."

"Whatever." Melanie shoves her way out of the line, intentionally knocking into me.

"Oh my God!" I shout as the ice-cold coffee seeps into my shirt. "What in the hell?"

"Watch your back, slut." She struts out of the coffee shop with a venomous smirk playing on her lips.

So much for the tide turning. My luck's as shitty as ever. I guess now I just have to hope this isn't an omen of what's to come in class.

"Are you okay?" Abigail asks as her friend hops out of line to grab napkins. "I'm so sorry about Mel. I don't know what's gotten into her!"

"Good dick can drive even the sanest girl crazy," no-name says, pressing a wad of napkins into my hands.

"True," Abigail muses. "But I know for a fact they haven't fucked."

Listening to their conversation feels weird, especially since they're semi-talking about me.

Even worse is the spark of hope that flares in my heart at Abigail's words. I really am pathetic.

"Emmy, did you hear me?"

"Huh?"

"I asked if you're okay."

"Oh. Um. I'm..." *Confused. Upset. Sopping wet.* "Fine. I'm fine."

"Are you sure?"

I know she's trying to be nice, and to help, but right now, I just need to get out of this shop. "Thanks, but I–I need to go."

I turn and race out of the coffee shop, chunking my uneaten croissant and mostly empty cup into the trash on my way.

My hoodie is soaked through, but my tank top underneath is mostly dry. On any other day, I'd count that as a win, but it's in the low fifties, which is far too chilly for a damp shirt with no sleeves.

A quick glance at my phone tells me I only have eight minutes to get to class, so going home to change isn't an option. So, tank top it is.

I tug off my hoodie and tie it around my waist, with the wet side facing out before turning and rushing to my class. I'm nearly a popsicle by the time I arrive, but I make it with seconds to spare.

"Emmalyn, a word?" Sterling words it as a question, but his tone tells me it's a command.

"What's up?"

He glares at my exposed shoulders as if they personally offend him. "Where are your clothes?"

"Um. I'm wearing them."

"No. You're not. You have on glorified pajamas." He

notices the hoodie tied around my waist. "Put your jacket on."

"No can do."

"Why?" he asks through gritted teeth.

"Your girlfriend spilled coffee on me."

"My what? I don't have a girlfriend. What are you talking about?"

"Melanie."

Sterling pinches the bridge of his nose and exhales slowly. "Don't move." He bends down and riffles through the bag at his feet. "Put this on."

"What?"

He shoves the shirt, one of *his* shirts, into my hands. "Put this on."

"Why?"

"Emmalyn, don't test my patience. Put on the goddamn shirt and take a seat so we can get started. You're holding up the start of class."

Anger, disbelief, and embarrassment burn my cheeks, but I shrug the button-down on all the same.

Immediately, his scent surrounds me, making me want to inhale deeply and hold my breath all at once.

The implications of our little spat don't really hit me until I turn around to find a desk only to find the entire class gaping at me. Well, except for Summer–she's glaring daggers.

I duck my head and rush to an open seat, sliding my laptop from my bag, determined to ignore the whispers. But Summer isn't content to be ignored. "I heard she's sleeping with him for an A, but after they fucked, he told her the best he could do was a C."

My eyes fill with tears, but I don't speak up in my

defense. If high school taught me anything, it's that giving them a reaction, any kind of reaction, only makes it worse.

Apparently, Sterling's never learned this lesson. "Miss Winters, my desk."

Yes, her name is Summer Winters. I'm completely not surprised.

Summer saunters his way, her hips swaying like a pendulum. He crooks his finger, beckoning her closer.

Something akin to jealousy curls in my gut, but I squash it down. Sterling's free to talk to whomever. He's not mine. Hell, we're hardly even friends. I need to get a grip. Up until this week, he's been a grade-A asshole.

But still, I'm positively green over their nearness. It's in this moment of weakness that I completely cave. As discreetly as possible, I turn my head into my shoulder, pressing my nose into the fabric of his shirt.

Sterling and Summer keep their tones low and their exchange private, but judging from the frown on her face when she turns around, things didn't go in her favor.

She stalks back to her desk, snatches up her bag, and then leaves the classroom altogether, slamming the door in her wake.

"Now that that's over, let's talk more about the four components of social perceptions and how they affect human behavior. Observation provides the primary data of social perception. It's a compound of three sources: persons, situations, and behavior."

As he begins to lecture, I force myself to focus on his words and not the delicious all-male scent surrounding me. Eventually, I get in the groove and my pen flies over my page as I write down every word that leaves his mouth.

His ability to give life to the subject matter is a skill none of my other professors seems to possess. I'm not sure if it's his age, or a passion for the topic at hand, but he teaches in a way that makes you want to learn.

Before I know it, everyone around me is packing up to leave.

Sterling calls my name as I slide my laptop into my bag. I glance his way and he crooks his index finger, beckoning me toward him.

I stand from my desk, and bend to retrieve my messenger bag from the floor. As I straighten, I glance over my shoulder at Sterling, only to find his eyes glued to my ass.

I expect him to look away now that he's been caught. But if anything, he grows bolder, dragging his eyes over every square inch of me.

"See something interesting?" I ask, shocking the hell out of myself. *Guess his boldness is rubbing off on me.*

"Like? Undecided. Want? Abso-fucking-lutely."

"What?"

"Don't play dumb, Emmalyn. You're an attractive woman."

I gulp and then shrug. "So, about that quiz?" A subject change is definitely in order.

He nods toward a sheet of paper on the edge of his desk. "Come and get it."

I can't help but feel his words have a double meaning, one I'm not willing to look any further into. This truce between us is rocky at best, and there's no way I'm about to let something as banal as sexual chemistry dismantle it.

Clearing my throat, I stride toward him, determined to ignore the suggestive look in his eyes and the sensual dip of his voice.

"Thanks again for letting me retake it," I say, regretting the words as soon as I speak them.

Why is it so hard to get things right with him?

Thanking him was pretty much the dumbest thing I could've done. It makes it sound like he's doing me some great favor, by allowing me to retake the quiz, when it's his fault I'm in this predicament to begin with.

A satisfied smile plays on his lips, but I can't decide if it's in response to my slipup or if *cocky-asshole* is simply his default setting.

I'm betting on the latter.

EMMALYN REACHES and grabs the quiz from the corner of the desk and plops herself ungracefully into the seat directly in front of me.

I watch as she presses her pen to the page, oddly enamored by the way her little fingers grip the cylinder.

What in the actual fuck is wrong with me?

I'm not enamored by anything about Emmalyn Price.

Except maybe the look of your shirt, my sex-deprived brain taunts. *Think how much better she'd look in only your—*

I inhale a slow, deep breath through my nostrils, holding it a beat before I exhale. I need to center myself, to ground myself, to remember the fucking plan.

I don't even know what my damn plan was anymore. When I'm not decoding her riddles, I'm lusting after her like a teenage boy with his first Victoria's Secret catalog. The fact that I've jacked off several times in the last few weeks to thoughts of her than I have in the last year is next-level fucked.

There's something about her that twists me up, and it's

bullshit, because I'm supposed to be twisting *her* up. Hence the change of plans. But maybe...maybe I need to up the ante.

I told her I'd ruin her, and I meant it. I just have to try harder. To push harder. Eventually, one way or another, she has to break.

"All done," Emmalyn says, breaking me from my thoughts.

I reach out to take the paper from her, intentionally brushing my fingers against hers. As clear as day, I can see the jolt of pleasure travel through her. And from such a simple touch. Immediately, my mind is brimming with ideas of other ways I could touch her.

Jesus. Christ. What is wrong with me?

She pulls her hand away first. "Thanks for the shirt."

I look back in time to see her shrugging out of it, the smooth skin of her shoulders on display.

Desire pools in my gut. "Let me take you to lunch again?"

"What?" Her question echoes my own thoughts. Because, seriously, *what?*

"When? Now?" she asks.

"Now."

"Really?" She swipes her tongue over her bottom lip, in a move that's far sexier than it has any right to be.

I shove back from the desk, planting my palms on the wooden top. I lean into her space and am instantly taken by her scent mingling with mine. "Say yes," I croak, wondering, again, what it is about her that knocks me so off course. "Say yes and let me spend time with you, let me be in your space, let me prove to you that I'm trying. Trying to be better, to learn, to see. Please?"

My plea seems to shock her as much as it does me. But I

think it's working; she's going to give in, because I think she wants me every bit as much as I want her.

We're both just smart enough not to admit it out loud.

"Okay, yeah. That sounds… great."

I grin, victorious. "Let's go."

As we fall into step with one another, I instinctually bring my hand to the small of her back. There's something about touching her that calms the raging seas in my mind.

"So, where are we going?" she asks as I open the car door for her.

I wait until she's buckled before joining her on the driver's side. "You'll see."

The drive is quiet, with Emmalyn staring at the passing scenery and me lost in my thoughts of… well, her. Until we roll through the main town square without stopping at any of the eateries.

"Where did you say we were going again?" Her voice wobbles with the slightest hint of nerves.

Grinning, I drum my fingers on the wheel. "I didn't." This whole idea is most likely going to explode in my face, and yet I press my foot down more firmly on the accelerator.

"Sterling." Two syllables have never been more full of frustration. I'm delighted.

"Emmalyn," I volley back, keeping my tone light. Jovial, even.

"Please tell me where you're taking me."

"Or…" I drag the word out as I flip my blinker on. "I could just show you."

"This is where you live?" she asks as I key in the gate code.

"Yup." The wrought iron monstrosity swings open, allowing us entry.

"You brought me to your house?"

"That does, in fact, seem to be the case." My voice is rife with humor.

"Why?" Hers is not. If anything, my little mouse sounds about zero-point-two seconds from flinging herself from my car.

She's even edging her right hand ever so slowly toward the door handle, as if she's contemplating bolting at any moment.

"I wouldn't, if I were you."

"Wouldn't what?"

"Run." I nod to her white-knuckled fingers. "Not only would I catch you, but you'd hurt yourself."

"Why are you doing this?"

"I'm just taking you to lunch, Emmalyn." I guide the car into my designated parking space and kill the engine. "I know we had a rocky start, but not everything I do has nefarious motives."

She casts me a doubtful look, so I shoot her my most charming smile.

"Fine. But don't make me regret this, Sterling."

"I won't," I say, all the while thinking, *I'll make you regret so much more than this. I'll make you regret ever crossing my best friend. I'll make you regret it all.*

In sync, we unbuckle and exit my car. "Which is yours?" she asks, eyeing the row of two-story luxury town-homes curiously.

I guide her to the end unit and swipe my fob over the sensor. I give her one last look before swinging the door open and letting her inside.

For the first time in a long time, I take in the space I call home with fresh eyes. From the high ceilings with exposed ductwork and dark stained concrete floors to the floor-to-ceiling glass wall making up the back of my living room, this place is pure masculine splendor.

With a chef's kitchen full of top-of-the-line appliances, three spacious bedrooms, each with their own en suite, and a deck that nearly doubles my living space, there's not a single amenity missing.

And thanks to my designer, it looks lived in. Welcoming, even, if Emmalyn's slack-jawed expression is anything to go by.

"Whoa," she breathes out as she takes in the view beyond the wall of windows. "You live here?"

Then again, it could be the million-dollar mountain view that has her catching flies. It is what sold me on the place, after all.

"I do." I close the door behind us and usher her deeper into my house.

"It's amazing."

"You like it then?" I ask, moving in close behind her.

She shivers at my nearness. "I love it."

For some reason, her approval sends a warm tingle through me.

"Are you hungry?" I know I am, but food is the last thing on my mind. I'm craving another taste of Emmalyn, which is unfortunately not on the menu.

"I could eat."

I swallow down a million dirty retorts, and instead ask her if sandwiches are okay.

"As long as there aren't pickles or onions involved, I'm down."

"I think that can be arranged."

"Such a giver." Her playful tone is a shock to my system, but I decide to roll with it.

"Typically, I prefer to take." I wink. "But something

about seeing you in my space has me feeling particularly hospitable."

"Lucky me."

"Why don't you head out to the deck, and I'll throw these sandwiches together and join you?"

"Are you sure don't need help?"

"I am one-hundred percent sure I can slap meat between some bread."

She hesitates for only a moment, a dopey smile on her face, before the tempting view lures her toward the massive sliding glass doors.

As soon as she steps outside, I take what feels like my first full breath since she walked into class this morning.

Something about seeing her in my shirt, in my space, it feels right. Natural, even. Which is downright terrifying.

Maybe bringing her here wasn't the best idea after all...

I shake the thought off. Too late now.

In the kitchen, I make quick work of plating up some turkey sandwiches, along with some fresh fruit and leftover pasta salad.

"It's beautiful, right?" I step onto the deck, our lunch tray precariously balanced in my right hand.

"Oh!" She tears herself away from the view and rushes toward me. "Let me help you."

I set the tray down onto the table with a flourish. "I've got it. Let me take care of you, Emmalyn. Something tells me very few people have ever bothered to do that."

"To do what?"

I slide out a chair for her and help her into it. "Take care of you." She blushes as she sits, and I help scoot her into the table.

"What makes you say that?"

"Just a feeling I get." I grab two waters from my outdoor fridge and join her. "Am I wrong?"

She drops her eyes to her plate and pokes at the fruit with her fork. "I guess you're right."

"You deserve to be taken care of." I almost gag at the saccharine words leaving my mouth. But I also kind of mean them.

She pops a grape into her mouth and chews it thoughtfully. "I think I do okay taking care of myself." She scrunches her nose. "Most days at least."

"Your mom isn't there for you?" I ask, already knowing the answer. I'm fairly certain if you looked up *gold digger* in the dictionary, Sarah Pearson's picture would be printed beside the definition.

"Um. Well." She sets her fork down and wraps her arms around herself. "She... her marriage... when everything came to a head, she decided her status meant more than my suffering."

"Did you?"

"Did I what?"

"Suffer?"

Emmalyn laughs uncomfortably. "I'm not sure how to answer that."

"It's a fairly simple question." I'm not sure what I'm hoping to gain here, but I keep pushing, hoping for a crack, a fissure, some kind of chink in her armor.

"Yes." She whispers the word with her eyes still downcast. "Every day."

My heart clenches at the pure sorrow in her tone. It constricts at the hurt, the agony—and then, because I'm a sick bastard, it beats a little faster.

"As you probably know, talking to someone can help. Have you... do you talk to someone about your... trauma?"

"I do." She frowns. "Well, I did. I haven't found a therapist here. I do a video call with my old one sometimes, though."

"You should find someone here. I can make a few suggestions, if you want."

"Um. Sure. That... that'd be great."

I want to smile, but I know it'll be all teeth and far from charming, so I bite down on my lower lip and suppress the urge. "And in the meantime, you're welcome to talk to me. You know, if you want."

Emmalyn pushes her plate away, still mostly full, and I worry I've pushed her too far.

"It's okay, you don't have to."

"No, it's..." She trails off. "I think I'd like that, but maybe you could talk to me, too. Open up to me a little? I've known you since I was eight, but you're still virtually a stranger to me."

"You've got yourself a deal, little mouse."

"Why do you call me that?"

I lift one shoulder in a shrug. "At first, because you were always so scared. Now though, it's because I think you're brave."

"That literally makes no sense," she says, laughing. The melodious sound brushes against my skin like a warm caress.

"Makes sense to me."

"So, what now?"

"Coffee with a view? You know, since I inadvertently owe you one."

"I don't know what that means, but I am always down for coffee."

"Be right back."

Back inside, I can't help but smile as I make our coffee.

The thought of her opening up to me is exhilarating. The very idea of Emmalyn sharing her secrets with me, of her freely giving me the very ammunition I've been searching for... it's almost too much to bear.

On the flip side, our little heart-to-hearts could also be the thing that proves her innocence.

I guess only time will tell.

WHILE STERLING MAKES COFFEE, I wander from the table over to the set of chaise lounges on the far end of the deck. *Seriously, who the f—nhomes had decks this size?*

I hesitate for a moment before lowering myself down onto one, reclining myself against the back to enjoy the view.

Fog is slowly descending, both in the air and my mind. Being here, on this side of town, has me second-guessing everything.

Is this a good idea? I was positive of it a few days ago, but now… God, so stupid. I know the smart thing to do is to guard my heart, but instead my is wanting to carve it from my chest as an offering—warm, bloody, and still beating— on a platter for him.

But that's what men like Sterling do. They make level-headed women do idiotic things. They don't just break hearts, they fracture souls and leave while skating through life unscathed.

"Mind if I join you?" Sterling asks from behind me, causing me to jump.

"Depends." I lean forward and twist around to look at him. "Did you bring coffee?"

"Yes." He places another tray, though this one's smaller, down onto the table separating the two chaises. "And cookies, too."

My eyes widen and my belly sings at the sight of a fresh sleeve of Oreos on the tray. "My favorite."

"Would it be weird if I confessed to already knowing that?"

I snatch a cookie and shove it in my mouth. I nod as I chew. "Yes, very."

"The pantry was always stocked with them when I'd come to visit Rob, but he hated them. So, that left you."

"Okay, not so weird."

"So, tell me something," Sterling says.

"Tell you what?"

He sips from his still-steaming mug. "I don't know. Anything. Something true, something meaningful."

I don't know what possesses me to say what I do, but the words topple from my lips before I can think better of them. "I wanted to die. After, I mean. I wanted so badly to stop breathing, to stop *being*. But coming here, it's my fresh start... my salvation."

Sterling swallows roughly and looks away from me. Immediately, I worry I said too much, that he didn't mean it when he said I could talk to him. *God, I'm such an idiot.*

"I'm glad."

Tears prick my eyes. "Glad about what?"

"That you're here. Alive, breathing, in Georgia, next to me."

"Do...do you mean that?"

He hesitates ever so slightly before reaching out and grabbing my hand. "Yeah, Emmalyn, I do."

"SO, Sterling is meeting us at the game?" Stella asks, her back to me as she digs through her closet.

We're in her room getting ready for our first game of the season. Well, she's getting ready—I'm spinning circles in her desk chair, questioning my entire existence.

"Emmy."

"Huh?" I [illegible] my feet, [illegible] the chair's rotation.

"Are you [illegible] listening [illegible]?"

"No[illegible]."

"[illegible] Sterling was meeting us at the game?"

"O[illegible] t su[illegible]."

"He [illegible] tailgate with us [illegible] next him."

"[illegible] that [illegible] number[illegible]"

"[illegible] not [illegible] your [illegible]bus?"

"[illegible] his [illegible] before you even suggest it, I am *not* [illegible] him."

"Fine [illegible] point. Do you need to shower?"

I shake my head [illegible] last night."

"Okay well I'm going to. Be back!" She flits out of the room like a [illegible] and I venture out behind her, planting myself on the couch with a cup of coffee while I wait.

If I lived with anyone else, I'd finish getting myself ready, but I know Stella will want to have a say in everything from my outfit to how I wear my hair.

So, reality television and caffeine it is.

I'm half an episode deep into *Alaskan Bush People* when my phone vibrates on the coffee table. It must be Gabe or Zach, because the only other person who would text me is currently covered in suds.

I pause my show and grab my phone, unlocking it and dragging down my notifications. I tap on the text alert without paying the sender much mind.

MOMMY DEAREST

I assume you're settled in?

No hello, no how are you—nothing.

As I read her text again, I regret even picking up my phone. One of these days, I'm going to block her number. The only reason I haven't already, is there's a small, foolish part of me hoping she'll have a change of heart and start acting like my mom again.

ME

I've been here almost a month.

MOMMY DEAREST

Are you taking your meds?

ME

As prescribed.

Unlike you, I think bitterly to myself.

After Rob assaulted me, I was diagnosed as clinically

depressed with a heaping side of anxiety and a dash of PTSD.

I was distraught upon my diagnosis and utterly terrified of meds. Not entirely surprising, after seeing mood stabilizers all but turn my mother into a mindless Stepford wife.

Luckily my therapy team was able to teach me that, when prescribed and administered properly, meds can be a good thing... a glorious thing.

I still have my good days and my bad. Sometimes, I even think I can skip a day when I'm feeling particularly great. But deep down, I know I can't... so I don't.

MOMMY DEAREST

There's no need to be snappy, Emmalyn. Also, talked to Robert, and we decided it would be best for you to remain on campus over the holidays. You understand, right?

I understand you couldn't pay me to come back there. That's what I understand.

ME

Sure. Got it.

MOMMY DEAREST

Oh, and, Emmalyn, please don't cause any more trouble. Keep your nose clean and your legs closed.

Frustrated tears dot my lashes and hurt grips my heart. A mother should support her child, fight for them. A mother should be a child's number one advocate, and mine... she threw me under the bus in favor of keeping her rich and shiny lifestyle.

"Emmy, you okay?" Stella asks.

I sniffle. "Yeah. Sorry. Didn't realize you were done showering."

"Just got out." She looks at me hard, studying my face. "You sure you're okay?"

I shrug. "I will be."

"Well, you're in luck! I know just the thing to take your mind off of whatever's got you down."

"Oh, yeah?"

"Yes! I'm going to do your makeup!" Her smile is megawatt and her tone pure joy.

Who am I to pop her bubble? "Sounds great, Stell."

If possible, her smile grows wider. "You called me Stell! A nickname. We really are besties now!"

"And we weren't before? Rude."

She rolls her eyes. "Let me get dressed and then it's on!"

"Okay." I click off the television and haul myself up from the couch. "Want me to come to your room when I'm done?"

"Yes. Oh! Wait!" Stella holds up a finger and then darts into her room. She returns before I can so much as blink. "Wear this."

"What is it?" I shake out the silky material and grin when I see what she's handed me. "Where did you get this?"

"Zach had them made."

I snort out a laugh and clutch the jersey to my chest. "Of course he did."

"Just wait until you see them all together."

"Oh, God."

Stella shoos me into my room, where I change into my jersey. I layer it over a white turtleneck, also from Stella, and pair it with distressed jeans and my favorite knee-high boots.

"You're not going to do anything crazy, right?" I ask, stepping into Stella's room.

We're dressed similarly, except she's wearing Uggs and a royal blue zip-up jacket over her jersey.

"Of course not." She pats the seat of her desk chair. "Now, sit."

Stella gets to work, slathering my face with God only knows what. Before Rob, I loved makeup, but now, I typically stick to the basics. It makes me wonder how far Stella will try and push.

After about fifteen minutes, she steps back and appraises her work. "Perfect."

"Can I look?"

She passes me a mirror, and I'm pleasantly surprised with the outcome. I look like a slightly more polished version of me, but with my eyes painted Wildcat gold and lined in Central Valley's signature blue. She even drew a little paw print on my right cheek.

"I love it."

She beams. "Give me twenty and we'll head out."

<hr>

"IT'S a beautiful day for some ball," Stella says as we step outside.

"Cold though," I mutter, rubbing my hands together for a little warmth.

"You'll get used to it." She links her arm with mine. "Where are we meeting Zach again?"

"He said at the wildcat statue."

"Perfect." She tilts her head to look at me. "You think any of his friends are single?"

I laugh under my breath. "You're so boy crazy."

Stella scoffs. "False. I'm only a little boy crazy. You would be too, if you were me. Do you have any idea how hard it is to get laid with an older brother as protective as mine? Orion is like a freaking pit-bull with Spidey senses. Impossible! Hence how I'm still a freaking virgin!"

"Deep breaths, girl. You're not going to die with your V-card."

"I just wanna know what it's like, you know?"

I try to inhale, but it's as if there's an anvil on my chest. "No, not really. My only experience was torture than anything else."

"Oh, shit. Babe." Stella stops and pulls me into a crushing hug. "I am so thoughtless. I am so sorry."

"It's fine," I tell her, mostly meaning it.

It's not that I'm against sex or anything.

I'm just petrified by the thought of actually doing it, by the thought of ever willingly being so vulnerable with a man.

It's really a moot point though, because after Rob, what man would want me anyway? I'm the definition of used goods.

"Twinkies!" Zach's booming voice cuts through my melancholy. "Well, no. What do you call three twins?"

"Triplets," Stella deadpans, making us all laugh.

"Seriously, these shirts are gold." Zach's grin is so infectious, I find myself cheesing right alongside him.

"We need a pic!" Stella exclaims, and Zach grabs a random passerby to snap one.

The front of our jerseys all read *"Ooh that 99, he's so fine"* with a wildcat silhouette. The back has Gabe's name across the shoulders in glittery gold block letters.

"They are perfect," I say as we scroll through the photos.

"Right?" Zach laughs. "Gabe's going to die."

"He doesn't know?" Stella asks.

"Nope."

"This is amazing!"

"C'mon, ladies." Zach wraps an arm around each of us. "There is tailgating to be done." He guides us over to where his friends are already partying hard.

"Ooh, cornhole!" Stella murmurs as we pass a group of fit-looking guys tossing beanbags. "You wanna play?"

"Eh." I shrug. "Hand-eye coordination's not really my thing." You'd think as a former cheerleader it would be, but nope. It seems that was the only exception to the rule.

"Do you mind if I go?"

I nudge her with my hip. "Don't let me stop you from having a good time!"

Stella studies me. "You sure?"

Zach answers her before I can. "Girl, go. I'll keep our Emmy company."

Stella's pink-glossed lips tip up into a huge smile. "Be back soon!" She practically skips away, giddy as can be for her first college football game experience.

"Feeling a little overwhelmed?" Zach asks. He is way too perceptive for my liking. "Let's sit." He weaves through the crowd, leading me to a cluster of chairs.

Or I'm not hiding the anxiety clawing at my skin as well as I thought I was. "Maybe a little." I scan the area, looking for Stella. Sure enough, she's having the time of her life with the cornhole guys.

A particularly muscled specimen currently has his front molded to her back under the guise of helping her with her toss.

Judging from the megawatt grin she's wearing, she's loving every second, the shameless little flirt.

"You want me to grab you a drink? Water, Coke?"

"Water would be great," I say, even though I'm not particularly excited about Zach leaving me on my own.

Maybe I'll just offer to tag along...

But before I get a chance to offer, he cups his hands around his mouth and shouts, "Yo! Renski!"

In the blink of an eye, a ginger-haired guy pops up out of seemingly nowhere. "Yes?"

"Get the lady and me a couple bottles of water."

"On it!" He gives a jaunty salute before hustling away in search of our drinks.

"How'd you manage that?"

Zach bounces his shoulders and smiles. "Must be my award-winning personality."

"Must be."

"Back!" Renski hollers, a condensation-covered water bottle in each hand. "Need anything else?"

"Nah, we're good, my man," Zach says, politely dismissing him.

"Thank you," I call after his retreating form.

Without looking back, he flashes a peace sign our way over his shoulder.

"Now, drink up so we can calm those nerves and get you in the Wildcat spirit."

I shake my head and crack open my bottle of water, sipping from it slowly.

Zach does his best to entertain me, but eventually, I send him off to have fun. Just because I'd rather sit and chill doesn't mean I want to be a wet blanket for my friends. They should still have a good time.

Plus, this is prime people watching if there ever was any. All walks of student-life are here and en masse. It's crazy the way everyone sort of meshes together in a big show of school spirit. Stoners, jocks, nerds—people who wouldn't be caught dead together in high school—are all here.

I'm deeply invested in the Stella-cornhole saga when my phone buzzes in my pocket. After my unexpected and supremely unwanted exchange with my mother earlier, I'm hesitant to check it again.

Another alert buzzes through, and I decide at the very least I can set it to silent.

But when I check the screen, the messages are from an unknown number.

UNKNOWN

Why do you look so miserable?

UNKNOWN

I don't like his name on your body.

What in the ever-loving hell?
My hands shake as I tap out a reply.

ME

Who is this?

UNKNOWN

Who do you think it is?

I suck in air through my teeth as my vision swims.

ME

Answer my question.

UNKNOWN

Who do you want it to be?

It feels like there's a hummingbird trapped inside of my chest, my heart is beating so hard.

ME

This isn't funny.

UNKNOWN

It is a little. Come on. You know who this is...take a guess. If you're right, I'll give you a prize.

ME

Look, I don't know what kind of game you're playing. But I'm about to block your number.

UNKNOWN

Come on, little mouse, live a little.

Oh. My. God.

Instantly, my entire body relaxes. And while that's a concerning reaction in and of itself, I'm choosing to focus on the positives right now.

ME

Sterling.

"You got it, baby."

My eyes fly up, and sure enough, Sterling Abbot stands before me, looking like a god.

"You really freaked me out." I glance down at my lap, where my hands are trembling. "I–I thought it was... not many people have this number..." I trail off, unable to bring myself to say his name.

But Sterling knows exactly whose name was poised on my tongue. "Fuck," he curses under his breath before reaching down and hauling me up from my chair and into his arms. "I'm so sorry, Emmalyn. I wasn't thinking."

It feels weird, him holding me like this, out in the open for all to see. But more than that, it feels... right. Like his strong arms were meant for me.

Which is insane, because I'm still not sure he's not playing some sick, twisted game with me.

"It's okay," I mumble the words against his chest, secretly loving the way the hard planes of his body feel pressed against mine.

What is wrong with me?

Eventually, Sterling pulls away from me. "Truly, I'm sorry."

"It's fine. I-I overreacted."

His gray eyes flash with some unknown, fleeting emotion. "I'll be more careful, okay?"

I try to smile, but then, a thought pops to the forefront of my mind. "Hey, Sterling... how did you get my number?"

"A magician never reveals his tricks." He winks.

"Sterling—" I press, but Zach walks up and interrupts.

"You gonna introduce me to your friend, Emmy?"

"Oh, um." His request flusters me, because I know that he knows exactly whose arms I was just in. "This is... um..."

"Sterling Abbot," he says, reaching past me to shake Zach's hand. "And you are?" There's an edge to Sterling's voice I don't fully understand. If he were anyone else, I would call it jealousy. But that's preposterous.

"Zach Williams." He clasps Sterling's hand in his own, unflinchingly.

"Well, Zach Williams, tell me, how do you know my girl?"

A whole swarm of butterflies take flight within me.

No! Stop it! You aren't his anything, much less his girl.

I open my mouth to tell him just that, but he wraps an arm around my waist and hauls me into his side.

"We're old friends," Zach murmurs cryptically, not giving an inch.

Sterling's chiseled jaw clenches. "As long as you're only friends."

Finally, Zach cracks, and laughter pours from him. "Drop your club, caveman. I'd be more likely to go for you than Emmy. You know, if I weren't already in a committed relationship."

"Oh my God, Emmy!" Stella squeals as she stumbles into our little bubble of testosterone and awkwardness, effectively popping it. "You have to come play—oh, hello there." She drags her glimmering gaze over him, eagerly noting his possessive hold on me. "You must be Sterling."

As soon as she speaks, I want the ground to open up and swallow me whole. Now he knows I've talked about him to her. How mortifying.

"In the flesh."

"I'm Stella, Emmy's suitemate." Her eyes dart down from his to where our bodies touch. "What's up with this?" she asks, gesturing vaguely toward us.

"Just a little show of masculine prowess," Zach replies, his voice full of humor.

"Well, whatever. I'm hungry."

"Grill's this way." Zach nods his head, signaling us to follow him.

"Are you hungry?" I ask Sterling.

He drags his teeth over his lower lip as he regards me. "Sure."

"Okay." I chuckle nervously. "Um, I think they have burgers and stuff."

His steel eyes flare with heat. "Not what I'm craving, but it'll do... for now."

DURING THE FIRST QUARTER, I try to keep my focus on the game, on Gabe and his teammates, but my mind is too busy obsessing over Bradley and his odd behavior.

All day he's been right by my side, attentive and caring and charming. It's honestly freaking me out. Even my brain is starting to question if this is all a game to him. The more time we spend together, the more I find myself wanting to believe him.

Add in all the small touches, and heated looks... yeah, I'm a seriously confused, nervous, and mildly turned-on mess.

By the second quarter, I give up all pretenses of paying attention. Luckily, Sloan and Leah are too engrossed in the game.

Still, even though he's so tuned in to me, my every thought and craving could very well have some kind of sci-fi mind link to keep going on.

"You good?" he asks, bumping my shoulder with his.

"Fine. Just—"

"A million miles away?"

"Maybe only a thousand."

"Wanna talk about it?"

"Here?" I look around the stands, which are packed to the brim with Wildcats fans decked out in gold and blue.

He does this adorable neck-bob-shoulder-shrug thing that makes him look so boyish. "Sure, why not?"

"I'm just trying to figure you out." As soon as I say the words, I wish I would have lied. He probably thinks I'm nuts.

"Tell me what you want to know, Emmalyn."

I've already started digging myself a hole, so I may as well keep shoveling. "Why are you being so nice to me? I know you said you're turning over a new leaf, but I just—I keep waiting for the other shoe to drop."

He tips his head to the side and adopts a wounded look. "You don't trust me?"

"I want to," I confess, since apparently, I've lost my mind.

"Guess I'll have to try harder." His words are the exact same ones he said to me after the quiz incident. I can't help but wonder if it is a coincidence or a deliberate choice.

I smile weakly, not knowing how to reply. He has me flustered to the point of not trusting my own judgment. And when he reaches over and clasps my hand, twining our fingers together, I very nearly stroke out.

"What are you—"

"Shh," he cuts me off, rubbing small circles over my hand with his thumb. "We've got the ball."

The buzzer for halftime sounds, and the players hustle off the field. Stella tries drawing me into conversation, but it's hard to hear her over the marching band doing their thing.

Shaking my head, I point to my ear, but Stella's not

having it. She stares pointedly at mine and Sterling's clasped hands and then slips her phone out of her bag, her fingers flying over the screen.

Sure enough, my phone buzzes two seconds later. With my free hand, I wiggle the device free from my pocket, unlock it, and swipe open our thread.

STELLA

BABE! Dish.

ME

IDK!

STELLA

...

ME

No, really. I have no idea what's happening.
Totally lost. It's weird.

STELLA

Good weird or bad weird? I'll kick his ass if
you want.

ME

Good. I think. Maybe.

STELLA

Well, y'all look good together, If that counts
for anything. Be careful though.

I nod and slip my phone back into my pocket.

Sterling leans all the way into me, pressing his lips to the shell of my ear. "It's definitely a good weird, little mouse."

I hate the way his nearness and that stupid nickname make me shiver, but they do.

They so do.

The third quarter passes in a blur of tackles and

passes. And while I cheer when it's appropriate, I still don't watch the game too closely, thanks to my spinning thoughts.

I will myself to focus on the game, on Gabe and his teammates instead of on Sterling and his personality transplant.

It works for a while, too.

Until a whole new brand of torturous distraction catches my eye.

The cheer squad is now directly in my line of sight, and try as I might to ignore them, my eyes keep drifting toward them.

Their cheers are peppy and their routines are unique, but I can't help but notice some of their counts are off.

Nope. Not my life anymore.

I tear my eyes away and focus back on the game just in time to see Gabe tackle a member of the opposing team to the ground. Cheers sound as Wildcats fans clap and holler and stomp in support of him, and Stella yanks me up onto my feet to join in.

As I sit back down, Sterling pulls me closer to him, so close our sides are completely melded together. "Why don't you cheer anymore?" His warm breath tickles my ear, making me squirm against the hard bleachers.

"Why do you care?"

He looks at me quizzically. "You were really good, it's a shame you quit, that's all."

"How would you even know?"

"Oh, Emmalyn." He grins. "I know all sorts of things about you."

"Creepy, much?" I ask, and he laughs.

"Okay, maybe this does make me a creeper, but I remember your freshman year you were upset because Rob and Sarah never came to any of the home games or your competitions."

"Okay... and?"

"So, I went."

"Went where?" My brow dips in confusion.

"To your games, when I could, and to finals."

"Finals? As in Orlando? You came all the way to freaking Florida to watch me cheer?"

He nods.

"Um. Not to sound rude but, I don't know how to respond to that." At least outwardly I don't; on the inside, I'm cartwheeling.

Seemingly undeterred by my weirdness, Sterling leans in, dipping his face toward mine.

My entire body stills. I'm fairly certain even my lungs stop expanding, and my heart stops beating. Surely, he isn't going to try to kiss me, here, in front of all these people.

And if he does, am I going to let him? The dam breaks and panic floods my system.

However, it seems my freak-out was for nothing, because all Sterling does is gently tuck a wayward lock of hair behind my ear. "Your body tells me everything your words don't, little mouse."

I try to smile, but I'm sure it's more of a grimace.

This man is so totally disorienting that merely being in his presence feels like stepping off a Tilt-A-Whirl.

Before I know it, we're all on our feet cheering and stomping and hollering as one of our players scores the game-winning touchdown.

"What now?" I ask once the roar of victory dies down.

"Now we party!" Zach shouts. "Y'all in?"

"Party where?" I ask, in tandem to Stella shouting, "Hell yeah!"

WE MEET the blond giant in the parking lot, and it takes my all not to knock his ass out cold—or at least die trying—when Emmy flings herself into his arms for a congratulatory post-game hug.

Judging from the shit-eating grin on his face, he knows it, too.

He swings her around a few times before placing her back onto her feet. She sways a little, and I step up to steady her before she—

"This must be Mr. Sterling." He says my name with just enough edge that I know Emmalyn's told them about me.

"Ah, so he speaks." I keep everything from my face to my tone neutral.

His eyes narrow, then travel down to where my hands are still resting on Emmalyn's shoulders. "A friend of Emmy's."

I grit my teeth and force myself to play nice. "And do you happen to have a name, pal?"

His lips twitch in amusement. "Sure I do, but I think

you already know it." He dips his head toward Emmalyn. "After all, your girl's wearing it on her shirt."

"Guys, let's play nice, okay?" Stella says, sidling up next to Emmalyn. "Plus, I was promised a party, and while y'all's dick-measuring competition is entertaining, it's not what I had in mind. 'Kay?"

"I'm with Stella on this one," Zach says. "Let's roll."

Gabe and I lock eyes, each of our gazes loaded with unspoken threats. His, I imagine says, *hurt her and die.* Mine, on the other hand, is telling him to back the fuck off.

"C'mon, Sterling." Emmalyn pries one of my hands from her shoulder and drags me forward. "Let's try to have a good time."

I hold steady though, not budging an inch. "Ride with me?"

She looks back at me and then to her friends' retreating forms. "Okay."

It may be a small victory, but it feels like so much more. She easily could have refused and caught a ride with her friends. But she didn't. She's sitting shotgun in my car. It's a small sign of trust, and I'll gladly take it.

And I damn sure plan on making the most of it.

"Come on, Emmy," Stella calls.

"We'll meet y'all there," Emmalyn replies as we catch up to them.

"Oh." Her friend shoots her a look that's so transparent even I can read it. She's worried about leaving Emmalyn with me. "Okay. Well. I'll text you the address." We break apart and head to our respective vehicles.

"Did you have fun tonight?"

She looks up at me from her peripheral vision. "It was okay. I don't know that it's something I'd want to do regularly."

"Sensory overload?"

"Majorly. And, it's just a long day."

I nod. "That it is. You got an address for me yet?"

"Not yet."

When we make it to my car, I open her door and help her in; this gentleman facade is quickly becoming a habit.

My phone buzzes against my thigh as I walk around to join her, but I ignore it, already knowing who it is. Rob's been texting me every hour on the hour for a few days now. It's safe to say he's gone off the deep end at this point.

Which begs the question—is his fragile mental state and burning anger fueled by her false accusations or is he simply a deranged sociopath?

He's always toed the line of what's socially acceptable, but here lately, it seems he's self-destructing. I can't help but wonder why. Why is he so hell-bent on destroying Emmalyn? Why is her demise worth the cost of his mental health?

That's not to say I don't think she deserves payback; I just don't... *Fuck!* I don't even know anymore. Either way, I need to know, and I mean *really* know, before I do something that can't be taken back.

I slide behind the wheel, liking the look of Emmalyn in my passenger seat a little too much.

"Oh, Stella texted." She flips her screen my way, and I throw the car into gear.

It's time to set phase two in motion.

By the time we make it to the football house, the party is in full swing. There are so many cars that we have to park on a side street, about a block and a half away.

"You ready?" I ask, killing the engine.

"Um. No?" She says it like a question, following it with an uneasy laugh. "I don't... Parties aren't really my thing."

"Is that why I found you holding up the wall at the last one?"

A pained look flashes across her brown eyes at the mention of the last party; and with good reason. I was a real jackass.

"Pretty much."

"The Emmalyn I used to know loved parties. I remember you always going out."

"The Emmalyn you used to know is dead." She turns away from me, but not in time to hide her tears.

"Hey, stop." I reach for her, but she curls her body into the door. "Emmalyn, baby, listen."

"Did you just call me baby?"

"Look at me." Slowly, she relaxes back into her seat. "I'm sorry. For my behavior at that party and for upsetting you now."

"Are you really?" Her voice is equal parts hurt and disbelief.

No, not really. "Of course. I was an asshole. New leaf, remember?"

She sucks in a few measured breaths. "Okay. Let's go."

"Are you sure?"

With a shrug, Emmalyn unbuckles and opens her door. "Nope, but let's go anyway."

I follow after her, catching up a few paces away from where we parked. "I promise to make tonight better, that you'll have fun. Okay?"

"If you say so."

Difficult little mouse. I interlace our fingers and she gasps softly. "I do, and I mean it."

MY EYES WATER as the overbearing scent of too many sweaty bodies, cheap perfumes, and stale pot smoke greet us the moment we open the door. All around us is debauchery at its best.

Bodies writhe together on the dance floor, moving like a mass of tangled serpents while onlookers chug their liquid courage before joining the fray.

"Whoa," Emmalyn whispers, practically skidding to a halt.

I stumble a little at our sudden change in momentum, wrapping an arm around her middle to keep us both standing.

Her soft planes press into my hard ones, and for a moment, I'm lost in her scent, sweet and soft and so fucking feminine, as it overrides everything else around me.

With music pumping, drinks flowing, inhibitions lowering, and Emmalyn Price in my arms, all I can think of is what kind of secrets the tempting little liar might spill, if given the right... *motivation*.

"You okay?" I ask, denying myself the pleasure of burying my face in the crook of her neck.

"Yeah, um. Yes." She wiggles in my hold, her pert ass rubbing against me in a way that sends fire racing through my veins. "This is just a lot to take in."

"Looks like your typical football party." I shrug behind her. "I'm honestly shocked everyone still has their clothes on."

"What?" She sounds so scandalized I can't help but laugh. *Who knew Princess Price was such a prude?*

"Tell me, Emmalyn..." I give in to the temptation and press my lips to the smooth skin of her neck. "Are you really this innocent?"

"I mean, we had parties in high school, but I..."

I can feel her throat work as she swallows.

"I never went to any after my junior year, and those were pretty tame. People drank and smoked and hooked up, but anything really crazy happened behind closed doors. This is so open."

I crowd her, dragging my hand lower from the dip of her waist down to the hem of the stupid-ass jersey she's wearing. "Welcome to the big leagues, baby."

She laughs uncomfortably. "Do you see Stella anywhere?"

"No." I roll my eyes but scan the room all the same. "Maybe they're in the kitchen." Reluctantly, I release her from my hold. "Let's go look."

I grab her hand and pull her toward the kitchen, telling myself it's to keep her close by, and not because I like the way her delicate hand feels in my grasp.

We make it to the kitchen, but the three musketeers are nowhere in sight. "Are you thirsty?"

"Oh, sure."

I walk her back against the far wall, caging her in with my arms. "Wait here."

She blinks up at me with her big doe eyes.

"I mean it. Don't move. Not a single inch."

"Okay."

I turn my back toward her and stalk toward the island, which is serving as a makeshift bar. "Sterling!" Emmalyn calls after me, and I glance her way over my shoulder. "I don't drink alcohol." She bites her lips and drops her gaze toward the floor for a moment before looking back at me. "Just so you know."

The cogs in my brain are turning as an idea takes shape. "No worries. I'll take care of you, Emmalyn."

With a sure hand, I mix us each a drink, making sure to make hers with extra care.

When I return, Emmalyn's in a heated conversation with her friends. "Oh, good," I drawl. "Y'all found us."

"Where were you?" Gabe asks, his voice ripe with accusation.

"Making drinks." I hold my hands up and shimmy the cups before passing one to Emmalyn.

Eyeing me, she sniffs the contents. "What's this?"

"Punch. My own special recipe, just for you." I wink, softening the thinly veiled deception in my words.

She smiles, taking a hesitant sip. "Mmmm, fruity."

Our misfit group lapses into an awkward kind of silence until Gabe looks at me and says, "Let's chat for a minute."

He's not asking.

"Sure thing." If he wants to play this game, we can play it. I come from a long line of lawyers, shit-talking may as well be my third major.

He guides me a few steps away from everyone; close enough to keep an eye on them, but far enough they can't hear us.

"What's your end game with Emmy?"

"I'm not sure what you mean?"

"Don't bullshit me, Abbot."

I grin, liking his protective streak. Too bad he's too late, because after tonight, Emmy will see me as her very own white knight.

"Listen, we clearly got off on the wrong foot." I raise my hands in a placating gesture. "Why don't we start over, yeah?"

He regards me with a snarled lip and keen eye. "You hurt her, and I'll fucking end you, do you understand? I know you've been messing with her out of some sick sense of loyalty to your friend, but that girl? She's already survived a lifetime of pain and betrayal, and if you add even an ounce to her suffering, I'll take great joy in tearing you apart. Got it?"

"Let's take a breath, big guy. No one's going to hurt Emmalyn. I was running a fool's errand and have seen the error of my ways. I'm trying like hell to make up for my less than stellar behavior, but having it pointed out isn't really doing me any favors, you know?"

His facial features relax slightly as he stares me down, waiting for me to crack. But I'm rock solid. "Fine. But I meant what I said."

"I have no doubts."

He tips his head my way before turning and making his way back to where the rest of our group is congregated.

Emmalyn catches my eye from where she's pressed into the wall. I raise my cup to her, signaling I'm getting a refill. She nods and breaks away from her friends and joins me. "Me, too?" she asks, her voice soft.

"Absolutely."

I keep my back to her, using my broad shoulders as a shield, and fix us each another drink, which she readily accepts and tosses back. "So good!"

"Glad you like it."

"I like you," she murmurs before slapping a hand over her mouth. "Oh my God. I don't know why I said that."

"It's okay, Emmalyn, I like you, too."

"You can call me Emmy, you know?"

"Okay, Emmy. Tell me something?"

"What?"

I loop an arm around her waist and draw her in close. "I don't know. Anything."

She shudders against me, her pupils dilating. "I was scared of the dark when I was eight."

Not what I thought she was going to say. "What made you stop being afraid?"

She swallows hard and looks me dead in the eye. "I learned there are far scarier things lurking in the light."

Her words have me reeling. They're so unexpected and so packed full of painful truth, I can't even begin to process them. Not here, anyway.

At my lack of reply, she laughs awkwardly and raises her cup my way. "Refill?"

"Sure are thirsty," I murmur and she shrugs.

Two drinks later, Emmalyn is well on her way to drunk and swaying her hips in time with the music pounding out of the speakers.

"Stell!" Emmalyn shouts loud enough to pierce my eardrums.

"Are you okay, babe?" Her roommate takes in Emmalyn, in all her drunken glory, worry creasing her brow.

"Amazing!" Emmalyn twirls in a wide circle, knocking into more than one person. "I missed you!" She tries pulling Stella into a hug, but the now-angry blonde holds her at an arm's length.

"Have you been drinking?" She turns to me, her eyes narrowed to thin slits. "Has she been drinking?"

"It's a party," I say, as if that explains it all. Hopefully she doesn't push, because I wouldn't put it past her to castrate me for feeding her best friend drinks all night.

"Oh my God! I love this song!" Emmalyn shrieks, waving her arms over her head.

Stella sends a glacial glare my way. "What are you playing at?"

"I'm not sure what you mean."

"She. Doesn't. Drink," Stella grits through clenched teeth.

"It's fine. She's fine."

"I swear, if you let anything—"

Before she can finish her threat, my drunk little mouse stumbles between us, draping herself across my chest. "Dance with me? Please? Let's dance, Sterling!"

I raise my brows at Stella before clasping Emmalyn's hand in mine.

"Show me your moves."

Without even a glance back at her friend, she pulls me out onto the makeshift dance floor, moving with zero inhibitions.

I keep a hand on her hip as she shimmies and rolls her body against mine. She may not cheer anymore, but her body definitely remembers.

It's a little amusing, watching her dance all on her own, until she starts grinding against my dick like a bitch in heat. Suddenly, my logical reason is being replaced with lust.

I can feel my jeans growing tighter as she pops and locks and pretty much uses me as her personal pole.

Fuuuuuck.

I know I mixed her drinks with the intention of loosening her up, but I meant her lips, not her legs.

"You feel so good," she singsongs, grabbing my free hand and placing it on her belly. "So strong and big."

The temptation to sample what she's offering is strong. Really fucking strong.

But, I won't.

Drunk girls never amount to much in the sack, and the thought of taking *physical* advantage of her leaves me with a sick taste in the back of my throat.

"You don't know what you're saying."

"I do!" She stomps her foot and then stumbles into me. "I-I don't feel so good."

"Are you okay? What do you need?"

Her eyes are wide with panic, and her cheeks are no longer glowing, but pale. "I-I don't know. I feel dizzying."

"Dizzying, huh?"

"Everything's spinning. Make it stop." A sliver of regret tugs at my heart as a lone tear rolls her down her cheek. "I don't wanna be here anymore."

"Okay. Let's go."

"Where?"

"My place."

"What? Why?"

"You need someone to look after you, Emmalyn."

"And you're-you are going to?" She hiccups. "Do that?"

"I am."

She mumbles an unintelligible reply and leans farther into me. I loop an arm around her waist for support and walk us toward the exit. She comes without a fight and, by some miracle, we make it to my Jag without any trouble.

Now we just need to make it back to my place without her defiling the leather of my car.

"GIVE ME YOUR PHONE."

Emmalyn groans and rests her head against the passenger window.

"Come on, hand it over."

"Hand what?" she mumbles, her breath fogging the glass.

"Your phone." I'm already over her drunken bullshit, which is unfair, since I only have myself to blame.

"You don't need... kind of..."

I... the bridge of my nose. "Be that as it may, I still need your phone."

"Gah, fine." She flops toward the door, just barely lifting herself from the seat. "It's in my pocket."

...I imagine the next time I'd grab her ass...

I lean over the console to retrieve her phone from her back pocket, taking care to let my hand linger. "Pass-code? Never mind. Give me your hand."

She plants back down and rolls her head my way, flinging her arm into my lap.

"You're a sloppy drunk, Emmalyn."

"Am not!"

"Are, too. You went from tipsy to shitfaced in the blink of an eye."

"Whatever."

I press her thumb over the sensor on her screen, unlocking it. I pull up her text thread with her roommate and fire off a quick message.

> **ME**
>
> It's Sterling. Emmalyn's shitfaced. I'm taking her home with me.

Much to my surprise, she texts back instantly.

> **STELLA**
>
> Hurt her and die.

> **ME**
>
> She's in good hands.

> **STELLA**
>
> To be determined.

By the time I close out of the thread, Emmalyn is fast asleep. Temptation sits on my chest, my fingers itching to snoop.

It's not like she'll ever know...

I tap out of the thread with Stella and scroll through all of her messages.

Stella

Sterling

Mommy Dearest

Gabe

Zach

Five. She has a grand total of five text threads. It's... *fuck*. It's pathetic, really. However, that doesn't stop me from reading through them all.

The texts between Emmalyn and her friends hold little to no useful information, but her thread with her mother is enlightening, to say the least.

I always knew Sarah Pearson was a piece of work, but the way she speaks to her daughter leaves a hell of a bad taste in my mouth. And there's literally been one contact with Emmy since she got here. One.

My dad's been known to be an epic asshole; so much so, that my mother divorced him—*twice*. But even he would never speak to me the way Emmalyn's mom does her. She's cold and dismissive.

It makes me wonder, more than ever, what really went down between her and Rob.

After tossing her phone into the cupholder, I lean back across the center console to buckle her seat belt. She stirs slightly when it clicks into place, mumbles under her breath, and turns away from me.

I punch the start button and drive us back to my place, hoping she's not down for the night. I'd like to ask her a few questions while she's more likely to speak truth—assuming she can sober up enough to hold a coherent conversation, that is.

By the time I make it home, Emmalyn is starting to wake.

"What? Where... Sterling?"

"Let's get you inside." I cut the engine. "Stay put and I'll help you."

I pocket my keys and her phone before moving to the passenger side. She tries to open the door on her own, but can't quite seem to swing it out far enough to stop it from closing on her.

"I said to stay put," I scold her, using my body to keep the door in place.

"I'm tired."

"I'll make you some coffee."

She perks up a little at the mention and allows me to haul her from her seat.

"You steady?" I ask, reluctantly liking the feel of her body tucked into mine.

At her nod, I step away, but she stumbles instantly. "Ugh!"

"Not so much then." I guide her arm around my shoulders and wrap mine around her waist. "Come on."

We make it inside without a hitch, and I deposit her on the couch. "Coffee coming up, little mouse. Don't puke on my couch."

"Ha-ha." She scrunches her nose and flops back onto the overstuffed cushion.

I can hear her grumbles and groans all the way in the kitchen, even over the gurgle of the coffee machine. When she said she didn't drink, I didn't anticipate just how much alcohol would disagree with her.

Then again, I should have expected it. Emmalyn's contrary by nature.

After the drip is done, I pour an oversized mug for Emmalyn. "Drink up."

It takes her a second to sit up, but the second she manages it, she's reaching my way with grabby hands. "Gimme."

Passing it to her, I chuckle and take a seat beside her.

"So good."

"Did you have fun tonight?" I ask, testing the waters.

She sips her drink, tilting her head to the right and then to the left. "I... maybe? Did you?"

"The best time ever." I reach my arms over my head, stretching, before spreading them out across the back of the couch.

"Tell me something, Sterling," she says, throwing my earlier words back at me.

"I think you're beautiful."

She snorts out a laugh.

"You don't believe me?" I lean into her space ever so slightly. We're getting off track from what I had planned, but I'm willing to let this play out.

"I know you're lying," she mumbles the words into her mug. "There's not a soul on earth who'd want me if they knew..."

My eyes snap to her. "Look at me."

She shakes her head, so I reach over and grip her chin, forcing her gaze to mine. Tears are gathered along her lashes and her cheeks and nose are pink, both from alcohol and the gathering emotions.

"If they knew what? Tell me, Emmalyn."

She shakes her head again. "You'll hate me. Everyone will hate me."

Holy shit. Is getting her to open up, to confess, really going to be this easy?

"I swear I won't. Tell me."

"I'm damaged, Sterling. Used and useless. Tainted."

"What does that mean, Emmalyn?"

"He hurt me." Her voice is a hoarse whisper that scrapes against my fucking soul. "He took and took and took until there was nothing left to take."

"What did he take?"

"Everything," she cries, anguish blanketing the entire room. "He took everything."

My skin prickles, both hot and cold, and my gut clenches as the first real thread of doubt weaves its way around my heart. Her words, her pain, her brutal honesty, wash over me, bringing with them a whole slew of emotions I can't even begin to process.

"Are you saying..." My throat flexes as I swallow. "Are you saying he raped you, Emmy?"

She answers me with a heart-wrenching wail instead of words.

"Fuck, baby, come here." I take the coffee mug out of her hands and reach for her. My hand brushes hers, and as if time itself has slowed, I watch in horror as she recoils and scrambles away from me on the couch.

She raises her arms to cover her head and face, all the while sobbing and pleading. "No! No, don't hurt me! Please... please don't hurt me. Stop!"

I'm shaking, my entire body, head to toe, both in anger and sorrow with realization of what Rob did to her and what he tried to put me up to.

She's curled up in a ball, trembling and crying, instinctually making herself as small as possible.

"Shh," I croon, holding my hands up in front of me. "It's me, baby. I'm not going to hurt you. Fuck, Emmalyn. I'm all done hurting you."

Her cries soften and she looks my way from beneath tear-soaked lashes. "St-Sterling?" Her gaze is unfocused and her voice wobbly.

"Yes, baby, it's me."

She flings herself at me, burrowing into my side—and my fucking heart—as I wrap her quaking body in my arms.

"No one's ever going to hurt you again."

HUMILIATION GRIPS me and the burn in my cheeks dries my tears.

Oh, God. I can't believe I said all of that to him.

I can't even begin to imagine what Sterling thinks of me. He's being so nice right now, comforting even, but who knows what's going to happen when I pull away from this little pocket of safety I've found in his arms, of all places.

He's whispering all kinds of things to me, but I can't make any of it out over the sound of my own thoughts.

I just had a full-on meltdown in front of a man who has bullied me relentlessly for the past month. He says he's a changed man, but how am I supposed to believe that? I certainly don't think I said anything that would've inspired a change.

Maybe he was joking, the stupid voice in my head whispers, but it's ridiculous. The mere notion of Sterling changing his tune for me, much less his entire personality, is absurd.

At this point, all I can do is pray he doesn't find a way to turn this back on me.

"Emmalyn." His voice is somehow deep and soft all at once as his fingers weave through my hair to press against my scalp. He massages gently, before gently lifting my head away from his chest. "Are you okay?"

"Um." I honestly don't know how to reply. I'm still a little drunk and a lot embarrassed and kind of feel like maybe I'm dreaming.

"Fuck! That was a stupid question." He pulls me back against his chest. I get the strangest feeling that he needs the comfort just as much as I do.

How bizarre.

"I'm so sorry, Emmy."

"It's not your fault."

"Not directly, but I still feel like I failed you. We all failed you."

"It's..." I can't seem to get my thoughts to connect. "You didn't..."

"I'm going to make up for it."

"What?"

"Just trust me, baby. I'm going to fix this. He was my best friend. I should have known something was off. My dad is the reason he got off scot-free. I'm. Going. To. Fix. This."

I honestly don't know what to make of him right now. It's like a switch has flipped. My bully is now my champion. What a weird night.

"If you say so, Sterling." I'm honestly too exhausted to argue with him over it.

"I do." He speaks those two words in such a way, they weave themselves around my heart like a vow.

"Do you want me to go home?" I ask, pulling away from him.

"I was hoping you'd stay. Here. Tonight."

I want so badly to say yes, but fear keeps me from doing so.

"Please. I just... I'll sleep on the couch if you want." He once again directs my gaze to his. "It's just that what you said fucked me up and I... I'd feel better knowing you were here. Knowing you were safe. But I'm not going to take your choice away. If you want to go home, I'll take you."

It's like his mouth has a direct line to my reasoning abilities, because suddenly, I find myself nodding. "Okay, Sterling, I'll stay."

He places me on the cushion beside him, as if I weigh nothing, before standing. "Let me get you something to sleep in."

The entire time he's gone, I rethink my decision to stay. At this point, the only thing keeping me here is the fact that I have no way home and the utter sense of calm I felt with his arms wrapped around me.

It's a slippery slope I'm walking along, and like the foolish girl I am, I make no move to seek solid ground.

"I hope this'll do," Sterling mumbles as he steps back into the living room, clutching a shirt in his outstretched hand.

"I'm sure it's fine." I take the garment from him. "Where's the bathroom?"

"You can use mine. It's the door at the end of the hall."

"Thanks." I slide off of the couch and slink past him, feeling oddly excited to see his space. I stumble over my feet a little before gaining surer footing.

His room, much like him, exudes a sense of strong masculinity. The walls are a pale gray, save for the back one, which is a black shiplap. His massive bed is centered on the accent wall, with a warm walnut headboard, topped with a duvet fluffy enough to rival a cloud.

The room smells like him, too. So much so, that my head swims as I try to breathe through my mouth, if only not to drown in his scent.

I rush into the bathroom, and unsurprisingly, it's every bit as high-end as the rest of his place. All smooth lines, brushed chrome, and marble, it's a space fit for a king.

The walk-in shower calls to me, with its multiple showerheads, but the thought of being naked in Sterling's space sends a tendril of fear through me. Not because I think he'd hurt me, not anymore at least. It's just...something about it makes me feel unsettled.

I kick off my boots and peel off my socks before ditching both of my tops and jeans. I waffle on my bra, ultimately deciding to keep it on. It may not be comfortable to sleep in, but it's an added layer of protection and modesty, both of which I'm willing to suffer a little for.

The shirt fits well enough, with the hemline falling just past mid-thigh. The real issue though, is it smells like him. If I thought being in his room was bad, it has nothing on this. Every single thread is permeated with his all-male scent, as if it's woven into the very fibers.

I make quick work of folding my clothes then rejoin Sterling in the living room.

Heat flares to life in his gray eyes when he sees me. "Jesus. You look..." He rubs a hand over his face, shakes his head, and then returns his attention to me. "You can set your clothes on the bar if you want."

"Thanks." My eyes drop to my bare toes. I can't help but feel self-conscious. And him leaving me hanging certainly isn't helping. "So, what now?"

"Want to watch a movie?"

"Okay."

"C'mon." He starts leading me back toward his bedroom, and immediately my hackles rise.

"Where are we going?"

"Just trust me, little mouse."

"My, what sharp teeth you have," I mutter under my breath as I follow him, praying with every step it's not to my doom.

"This isn't some ploy to trick you, Emmalyn." He pauses in the doorway to his room, leaning against the frame. "The television's in my room."

"Oh." Come to think of it, I didn't see one in the living room. Weird, but not nefarious. "Okay."

"Go on and get cozy. I'm going to change."

And just like that, my nerves are back full force.

He waltzes into the room, disappearing into his bathroom without sparing me a backward glance. Which, I guess, I'm grateful for. At least I don't have an audience as I wrestle myself into the room and onto his bed.

You can do this. Breathe. Just breathe.

With reluctant steps, I cross the space to his bed. Not even ten minutes ago, I was wondering at the fluffiness of his duvet, and now I'm peeling it back to climb beneath it.

The events of tonight are nearly enough to short-circuit my brain, but when Sterling steps out of the bathroom in nothing but a pair of gray sweats, I'm pretty sure my motherboard fries itself entirely.

"What are you in the mood for?" he asks, moving past me to the other side of the ginormous bed.

"Huh?"

He leans over and pats the mattress. "Movies. What are you in the mood for?"

"Oh. Um." I scramble beneath the covers when his gaze

dips to my legs. It's even softer than it looks. "Something funny, I guess?"

"Have you seen *The Big Lebowski*?"

"I don't think so."

"I think you'll like it." He studies me for a minute. "Unless you'd prefer a chick flick?"

"What's it about?"

Sterling grins. "It's about The Dude."

"What?"

"You'll see."

I settle back against the fluffy pillows, unease still swimming within me, while Sterling queues up the movie.

As the opening scene unfolds, I find myself very much doubting Sterling's taste in movies.

"Just trust me," he murmurs as he scoots closer to me, easily reading my disbelief.

I try my hardest to give the movie my full attention, but my brain isn't having it.

Sure, it's funny, and I laugh when I'm supposed to, but my half-drunk brain is working overtime to process everything.

Not just today, either, but the past month.

The same thoughts have been looping around my brain so often, I'm starting to annoy myself. But how? How did we go from Sterling wanting to destroy me to having movie night in his bed?

I'm so lost in my obsessive internal quest for answers that I don't even notice the movie's over.

"So, what'd you think?" Sterling asks.

"It was good," I answer automatically. It's not a lie, though—the parts I tuned in for were really good. "Not something I would have picked, but I liked it."

"I'm glad. Next time you can pick."

"Next time?" I yawn and snuggle deeper into my pillow, tugging the covers up to my chin.

"This isn't a one-and-done, baby."

"You keep calling me that."

He nods, rustling the sheets. "I do."

"Why?"

"Time will tell." He winks, and I swear to God, I don't know if I want to hug him or suffocate him.

"Or you could tell me. Now." Another yawn slips past my lips, causing Sterling to frown.

"You're tired. Maybe tomorrow."

"How am I supposed to sleep now?" I whine.

"Need me to tuck you in?"

I huff out a laugh. "You're really not going to tell me?"

"Not tonight."

"Fine. Then tell me something else before we go to bed."

"Anything?" he asks, and I nod.

"Is this our thing now?"

I shrug, not that he can see it since I'm wrapped up like a burrito. "Maybe."

"Okay, fine. I..." He shifts a little closer, leaving only a foot between us. "I don't think I want to go to work for my family's firm."

"Really? Why?"

He smiles at me in a way that sends a whole swarm of butterflies fluttering through me. "Growing up, it was always just...expected. You know? And I guess I haven't been feeling it for a while—hence not being in law school— but now, I really can't see myself doing what they do."

"What do you mean? Like, practicing law in general?"

"No." He shakes his head as he reaches out and skims his fingers gingerly over my cheek. "I can't see myself representing people I know are guilty. I can't see myself helping people like Rob. I used to think the money and prestige more than made up for the work, but now…"

"But now what?" I ask, hardly allowing myself a breath.

"But now, I'm realizing there are more important things in life than money."

I smile sleepily, halfway wondering if this conversation is actually happening.

"Sleep tight, Emmalyn," is the last thing I hear before my eyes slip shut and sleep takes me.

I SNUGGLE CLOSER to the warm body beside me, practically plastering my cheek to the warm, muscled chest. Strong arms wrap around me, making me feel safe and protected.

"So cozy," I mumble, as the steady *thump-thump* rhythm of my dream man's heart acts as my own brand of melatonin, calming and comforting me. "Wanna stay here."

"Stay as long as you want."

Something about the warm rasp of his voice sends a happy hum right through me. This is the best dream I've had in God only knows how long.

If I could, my eyes would stay closed forever, just to stay in his embrace.

"I didn't know you were such a snuggly, little mouse."

My eyes pop open and I start to scramble back.

Oh.

I'm not dreaming. I'm in bed. With Sterling Abbot. Wrapped around him like a hungry boa constrictor.

"Don't run from me." He smooths my wild flyaways from my face. "Don't hide from me."

"This is so embarrassing."

"What is?"

"This!" The color in my cheeks rises right along with my voice.

"Baby, there's nothing embarrassing about the way your body is clinging to mine. I'd keep you here full-time if I could, but it's a little soon for all that."

"What?" Clearly, I've woken up in an alternate universe.

"Don't act so surprised. It's pretty clear I'm into you. I think you're into me." I go to speak, but Sterling presses on. "It's okay if you're not there yet. You will be. I'll wait."

"This really isn't a game?"

Before I can process it, Sterling yanks my body flush with his and presses his lips to mine. I panic for a split-second over my morning breath, but the way he sucks on my lower lip chases all worries away.

His kiss is soft—far softer than any we've shared before—and slow. He takes his time, nibbling and tasting and exploring.

Sterling drags his hand up my body to cup my cheek. I sigh at his unexpected tenderness, and he uses the opening to deepen our kiss.

My heart shudders, skipping a beat before pumping into hyperdrive as he slides his tongue against mine.

His erection digs into my belly, yet he makes no move to take things further. His hands don't stray and his hips don't roll. And somehow, his respect and his caution turn me on even more.

Seriously, who even is this man? What happened to the Sterling who took unapologetically... the man who all but slammed me against a wall and demanded my mouth? Not that I'm complaining. If anything, he just got four billion times hotter, and I already had him elevated to a god-like status—looks-wise, at least. If his personality well and truly catches up, I might be totally screwed.

He nips at my lip as he pulls away, ending what was easily the best kiss of my life. "That feel like a game to you, baby?"

"No. Not a game," I sigh and flop onto my back. "But not quite real either."

Sterling rolls, propping himself up so that he's looking down at me. "How so?"

"It feels like I woke up in an alternate universe or something. I don't know how to describe it. Like, my body and my heart are on the same page, but my brain isn't even in the same chapter."

"Are you saying I'm in your heart, Emmalyn?" His voice holds a teasing quality, so I laugh instead of replying with words. God knows, if I spoke my truth and he *was* only joking, I would die.

"Well, how about we ground you in reality with some breakfast? I know a great place down by the river."

"I'm all for breakfast. Two problems though."

Sterling gives me his most indulgent smile. "I'm known to be a real problem solver."

"Well, a shower and toothbrush would be amazing. But also, clothes."

"I just so happen to have a shower, maybe even a spare toothbrush. And, if you can handle last night's jeans, I bet I can find you a shirt."

I nod. "Then you've got yourself a deal."

"We could shower together?"

Panic surges through me, but the twinkle in Sterling's silver eyes chases it away. "Ha-ha. Funny man."

"I'm hilarious, baby." He rolls off of me. "Now go shower. I'll make coffee."

He stands from the bed, making no attempt to hide the *very* prominent bulge hiding beneath his sweats. I'd like to say I avert my eyes, but I'd be lying. And judging from the swagger in Sterling's step, he likes the attention.

Once he's out of sight, I scramble out of the bed and into the bathroom. The sight that greets me in the mirror has me cringing. I look like a train wreck times two.

And yet, he still kissed me. Weird and weirder.

I lock the door and start the shower before undressing. I find a new toothbrush under the sink, all the while telling myself I'm not jealous over who it may have been for. I mean, it could have just been an extra for when his needed replacing, right?

I brush twice and swish with mouthwash before stepping under the spray of the shower. I always thought the rainfall head at my stepfather's house was nice, but this baby makes it seem builder-grade.

The water is the perfect temperature and the perfect pressure. I could give up baths if I had access to this glorious shower every day.

Then again, the tub looks even more amazing. Definitely better than the one we have in our suite on campus. Though, I should probably be glad we even have a tub at all.

I make quick work of washing, even though I could easily spend eternity in here, especially with his scent soaking into my every pore.

Oh, God, I'm going to smell like him all day. How am I supposed to act normal when I'm going to be tempted to sniff myself randomly?

It's not until I am wrapped up in one of his fluffy gray towels that I realize I don't have my clothes in here with me. Which leaves me with two options: I can either face him with only this towel for cover, or in my bra and last night's shirt, because putting on my dirty panties is a no-go.

Finally, I decide the shirt and bra is the lesser of two evils, and slip them both on before wrapping my hair in the towel.

With my panties balled up in my fist, I unlock the door and step out into his bedroom. Luckily, he hasn't returned. As I walk down the hall toward the kitchen, cool air swishes between my legs, reminding me just how vulnerable I am in this moment.

"All clean?" he asks, smirking, when he sees me.

"Yup. Just need my clothes."

He captures his bottom lip between his teeth as he rakes his gaze over me. The sweltering twin flames in his eyes heat me from my core, outward. I shift on my feet, rubbing my thighs together to soothe the ache his unfaltering stare is igniting.

"Better hurry," he growls, sounding very much like the apex predator I know he really is. "Better hurry before I decide you sound like a better breakfast."

A startled squeak escapes me as I lunge for my clothes on the bar, before turning and hightailing it back down the hallway and into his bathroom.

My chest heaves, both from fear and arousal. How is it he can elicit such a response from me? After Rob, just the thought of a man touching me made me feel sick, but with Sterling, I want it. I want him.

The realization robs me of what little breath I have left. I'm not just mildly attracted to him. I'm downright into the man. I trust him, and if given time, I could see myself falling for him, for my former bully.

Definitely an alternate reality. It's the only plausible explanation.

"INSIDE OR OUT?" Sterling asks as we approach our destination, a cute little local place called The Blue Plate.

It takes me a second to process his question; my head is up in the clouds, a million miles away, trying to understand how I got from point A to what feels like point Q.

"Outside, please. It's such a pretty morning."

He snags two menus as we head to an open table.

"What's good here?" I slide my eyes over the menu, slightly overwhelmed by how good everything sounds.

"The pancakes are amazing. But so is the breakfast burrito."

"Which are you getting?"

"Pancakes for sure."

"Then I'll get the burrito."

"Anything to drink?" a blue-apron-clad server says, appearing seemingly out of nowhere.

"Coffee, please," Sterling says smoothly as he passes her our menus.

"You got it."

We chatter mindlessly, talking about small, silly things until our drinks arrive. Except along with our carafe, comes the very unwanted feeling of being watched. It makes my skin crawl, and Sterling notices.

"Are you okay?"

I wrap my arms around myself and discreetly look around. Nothing jumps out as unusual, but the feeling persists. "Yeah. Um." I laugh uncomfortably. "I'm going to sound crazy, but it just...feels like someone's watching us."

Sterling stands and scans the surrounding area, but he, too, comes up empty. "I don't know. I don't see anyone."

"Yeah. Sorry. I get a little paranoid sometimes. It's dumb."

I expect him to laugh, or maybe to poke fun at me, but he doesn't. Instead, concern sparks to life, sharpening his gaze as he leans toward me over the tabletop. "It's not dumb. You've been through hell. You've experienced unthinkable terror at the hands of someone you should've been able to trust. Baby, I'm amazed by the simple fact you're still here and working your ass off to support and help others in similar situations. You're taking your tragedy and turning it into something beautiful. You're beautiful. And—fuck. I got sidetracked."

He laughs under his breath and tucks a wayward strand of hair behind my ear before leaning back into his seat. "My point was, it's totally understandable for you to have a little PTSD. It's not dumb."

I can feel tears well, not because I'm sad, but because for the first time ever, someone from my past is on my side. Someone has my back. It feels better than I ever imagined. "Thanks," I whisper.

Before he can reply, our food arrives, and I dig in, if only to save myself from crying. "Oh my God!" I groan, my tears long forgotten as the flavors of my burrito burst across my tongue.

"Told you." Sterling cuts off a bite of the fluffiest pancakes I've ever seen and holds his fork out for me. "Taste these."

Sterling feeding me feels intimate, maybe even more so than sleeping beside him. But even still, I part my lips, allowing him to feed me.

"Jesus. Where do you find these places? The food is amazing."

He grins and winks. "Eat up."

I dive back into my own meal, barely breathing between bites.

My skin still feels warm and a little too tight under someone's watchful eye, but with Sterling, I feel safe, so I push it to the side and decide to ask a question that's been eating away at me for a while now.

"Sterling?"

His gaze snaps to mine. "Yeah?"

"Did...did you assign Summer as my partner because you knew she'd leave me to do all of the work?"

He has the good sense to look guilty. "Yeah." He nods. "I did."

My throat is suddenly as dry as the desert, as I attempt to process his admission. If you can even call it that. It was pretty obvious why he paired us together. But... was there something more than wanting to break me motivating him?

"Did...were y'all—"

"No!" Knowing where I'm going with my question, he doesn't give me a chance to finish before he's rushing to reassure me. "No. Not ever."

"Nothing? There was nothing between y'all?"

"Why do you sound so disappointed?"

I shrug. "I'm not. I just figured maybe that was why she hated me on sight. It would've explained a lot, you know?"

"She's just an insecure girl. You threaten her."

"What? Me? No."

"Yes, you. You're beautiful, Emmalyn. And you're kind, genuine. Girls like Summer don't know what to do with that."

"If you say so."

"I do, and, Emmy, I need you to know, I'm sorry for assigning you with her. It was shitty of me." He laughs dryly. "One of many shitty things, but I'm going to make up for it. For all of it—each and every sin against you, one way or another."

My cheeks heat as I avert my gaze. The way this man makes me feel has me questioning my own sanity. How is it possible to go from fearing him and dreading his presence to feeling carefree and at ease in his company?

"You ready?" he asks as our waitress drops off our bill.

"Yeah."

"Got any plans?" He leaves a wad of cash on the table to cover our meal.

"Studying. Lots of it."

He grimaces. "Sorry. I'll pull Summer aside and let her know she needs to pull her weight."

I shrug as I stand. "It's whatever. Honestly, I work better alone."

"Well, let me get you home so you can hit the books then."

"Thanks. For today. And last night. And yeah, just thanks."

"I know it sounds like a line, but anything for you. I meant it when I said I was going to make up for all the shit I put you through. Feeding you is the least I can do."

Our hands knock together as we walk back to his car. Each brush of his fingers sends a rush through me, until finally he interlocks our fingers together, holding my hand in his for the rest of our walk.

The drive back to campus passes in a blur, and before I know it, Sterling's pulling to a stop in front of my dorm.

"Text me later?"

The thought of reaching out first sends a spike of

anxiety through me. But friendship is a two-way street, and I guess it's only fair for me to put in some effort as well. "If you want me to, sure."

"I absolutely want you to." He leans over the console and presses his lips to mine in a chaste kiss. "Wouldn't have said it otherwise."

I offer him a small smile. "Okay then."

"Bye, baby."

"Bye," I murmur, slipping out of his car with my head spinning. At this point, I don't even know up from down, much less how to process the way Sterling makes me feel.

I'm so busy trying to dissect all of the revelations and bombs from the last twenty-four hours that I don't notice Melanie lurking.

"You're only a distraction, you know that, right?" she sneers, glaring at me as I pass. "There's nothing special about you. He'll grow bored."

"Whatever you say, Melanie."

"Listen, you bitch!"

I whirl around. "No, you listen. There's no need for this bullshit animosity between us. I know you think I'm stepping on your toes, but I'm not. I've known Sterling since I was eight. That's right, a whole decade. Please stop harassing me because you have a crush. It's not cool and, frankly, makes you look desperate. I don't want problems between us. So, let it go, okay? Just let it go."

Holy shit! I don't know where all of that came from, but I turn and rush into the building before she can reply. I either just cleared the air between us or royally messed things up; my bet is on the latter.

"Oh my God!" Stella shouts the second I step into our suite. "We have so much to discuss!"

"That, we do." A spike of nerves zips through me.

"Starting with why your cheeks are so flushed." She looks me over. "And why you're wearing a man's shirt."

"Um." I collapse down onto the couch. "Well."

"Don't you *um, well* me, babe. I need deets. I spent half the night worried sick about you, you know?"

"Only half?" I ask, trying for humor.

"We'll get to that."

"Okay, fine. I might have just told Melanie off on my way up."

"What?" Stella squeals, flinging herself down onto the cushion next to me. She winces as she makes contact.

"Are you okay?"

Her cheeks burn crimson. "Mmhmm. Totally fine."

"You sure?"

She lets out a dreamy sigh. "Totally fine. Just a little sore."

"Why?"

"After we finish talking about you. About Sterling."

"We talked. About everything. Stell, I think... I think he believes me now. Like for real. At first, I wasn't sure if he was faking nice or what, but after last night and this morning, I think he means it." I drag my teeth over my lower lip, almost scared to speak my next words. "And I think he's into me, or whatever."

My best friend smiles. "Of course he is! You're a total catch. Now, why are you wearing his shirt?"

At her second mention of my outfit, I realize I left my clothes at his place—including my dirty panties. Oh, God. Kill me now.

"Nothing like you're thinking. He just let me borrow a shirt since mine smelled like a day-old frat party." I draw my legs up beneath me on the cushion and rest my head against the back. "Now, your turn."

"Well." She draws out the word. "I ditched my V-card last night!"

"What?" My eyes widen in shock. "With who?"

She looks down at her lap. "You remember my friend Samson?"

"You mean Mr. Mysterious who you'd never spill the details on? That Samson?"

"The one and only."

"Are y'all like an item now?"

The light in her eyes dims a little. "No."

"Oh. Um."

She laughs, but it sounds forced. "It's fine, Emmy. I got what I wanted, and he made sure it was good. What more can a girl ask for, right?"

I reach over and take her hand in mine. "A lot of things, Stell, a lot of things. But if you're happy, then I'm happy for you."

Her lips pull up into a watery smile. "I'm over the moon."

A YAWN ESCAPES me as I stare at my phone waiting for her to reply. My little mouse truly made me sweat it out.

I was half tempted to text her, but something told me she needed time to process all the changes that took place over the last few weeks, and while I wanted to talk to her, I didn't want to scare her off either.

My feelings haven't changed.

As nervous as it sounds, I was fully prepared to wait damn near twelve hours for her text, but I did and it must have been right about that limit to do so because she came to me, willing—

ME

Shit. I truly am sorry. Give me a chance to fix it.

EMMALYN

I know girls like her. I was friends with girls like her. You interfering will only make it worse. Thank you though.

ME

Are you sure, baby? I really want to fix this for you.

No sooner than I hit send does my phone start vibrating with an incoming call.

I answer immediately, embarrassingly eager to hear her honeyed voice. "Decided you needed to hear my voice, little mouse?"

"You've been avoiding me," growls a cold, masculine voice that most definitely doesn't belong to Emmy. "And I don't fucking appreciate it."

"Rob." His name leaves behind a bitter tang in my mouth. "How are you?"

"How do you think I am, Sterling?" His voice is taut with barely concealed rage. "How do you think I am when you've been avoiding me?"

An uneasy laugh lodges in my throat. "Not avoiding you, man. Just busy."

"Busy with what?"

"You know how it is, man."

"No. I don't. Enlighten me. Tell me exactly what's kept you too busy to so much as read my texts."

My mind races as I scramble to think of a plausible excuse. Rob's irrational on a good day, and judging from the hard edge to his voice, it's *not* a good day.

"Just trying to balance it all."

"Hmm," is all he says.

"So, what's new with you?" I ask, hoping he'll let it go.

I should've known better though. "What's new with me is your troublesome lack of communication, Sterling."

"Rob, man—"

"Maybe I should come visit. Remind you where your loyalty lies."

"No need. My loyalty is yours. Just been busy."

"Free up some time, or I'll free it for you."

"Yeah, sure."

"Don't fucking placate me. That little bitch needs to be leashed. And you can either help me or I'll collar you, too."

My insides go molten as he continues to speak. His threats toward me mean nothing, but the way he's speaking about her has me vibrating with fury.

I tune out for the rest of his rant, not even realizing he's finished until the call disconnects.

He definitely knows something's up. I just have to hope I can put him off my trail long enough to devise a plan; a way to keep Emmy safe and by my side.

A bone-weary sigh works its way through me as I toggle back to my text thread.

EMMALYN

I'm sure, Sterling. Thank you though.

ME

Don't thank me. This whole thing is my fault.

EMMALYN

True. I take back my thanks.

ME

What are you up to right now? Do you want to come over?

After talking to Rob, I have this inexplicable urge to see Emmy, to see with my own eyes that she's safe and sound.

EMMALYN

Um. It's like 10! I'm about to go to bed. I have class in the morning and my TA is a real hard ass.

ME

Sleep here?

EMMALYN

Or… I could sleep here. I'm already in my jammies and in bed. I'll see you bright and early though. Okay?

I want to beg her to let me come and get her. No, I want to demand it. But I know I can't.

ME

I guess.

EMMALYN

Goodnight, Sterling.

ME

Goodnight, baby.

I set my alarm and put my phone on the charger, double-checking that my ringer is on in case Emmalyn calls, before climbing under the covers and forcing myself to sleep.

"SUMMER," I call out as she struts past the podium.

She bats her lashes and flashes a coquettish smile my way. "Yes, Sterling?"

"I was hoping to talk to you about your project." I know Emmalyn asked me not to mention it to her, but the guilt is eating at me; I have this driving need to make it right.

A conspiratorial grin lights up her face. "What about it?"

"I'm gonna need you to start pulling your weight."

Her lips flatten, thinning into a hard line. "But you said—"

"I know what I said. And now I'm saying this: pull your weight or fail."

Her eyes narrow as she screws her lips up into a mean snarl. "You don't have the authority to fail me."

"Don't I?" I ask, right as Emmalyn walks in. Her eyes widen at the sight of Summer and me together, but I press on. "In case you missed the memo, Professor Ellison—Uncle Vic to me—doesn't really care what I do."

If looks could kill, I'd be dead twice over thanks to the two infuriated women shooting laser beams at me with their angry eyes. But there's only one I'm concerned with, only one whose reaction I care about.

I slide my phone from my pants pocket as Summer mutters something under her breath and stomps off to her seat. Quickly, I fire off a text to Emmalyn, hoping like hell she reads it and agrees.

ME

I'm sorry for going against what you said. If you let me take you to lunch, I'll explain then.

Students trickle in while I impatiently wait for Emmalyn to check her phone. I manage to catch her eye and try to telepathically signal to her.

Her nose wrinkles as she looks at me like I've lost my

mind. And maybe I have, but either way, she grabs her phone, so I'm counting it as a win.

EMMALYN

I guess. But you better have a good reason
for going behind my back.

Not even two seconds later and another text comes through.

EMMALYN

And dessert, too.

ME

Consider it done.

I go to repocket my phone when another text pings. This time from Rob.

Seeing his name flash on my screen fills me with dread. He's unhinged, and if I don't find a way to nip this whole situation in the bud soon, he's guaranteed to become a problem.

ROB

Tick tock, Sterling. Time's running out.

All throughout class, Rob's threats distract me, weighting me down like cinderblocks roped to my ankles. Finally, I can't take it anymore and dismiss everyone twenty minutes early.

Emmalyn remains seated, taking her time putting her things away, until we're the only people left.

"You ready?" I ask as she stands.

"As I'll ever be."

"Good. Let's go."

Today, I take her to my favorite burger place, Slicks.

"What's good?" she asks, as we wait in line to order at the counter.

"Everything. But the truffle fries are where it's at."

We both order a colossal cheeseburger with an order of fries, plus a decadent slice of cheesecake with raspberry sauce for Emmy.

I guide her to a little corner booth, and as soon as her ass hits the seat, she's on me. "Well, let's hear it then."

"Look, I know you asked me not to say anything to her. And I know I disrespected you by doing it anyway."

"You're not so good at apologizing, huh?"

A smirk threatens to break free at her sassiness, but I roll my lips inward, suppressing the urge. "That's because I'm not apologizing, little mouse."

Frustration colors her cheeks pink. "Then why are we here?"

"I said I'd explain, not apologize. They're not synonyms."

A server runs our burgers out, placing them before us with flourish. I want so badly to dig in, but I know Emmalyn's not going to touch her food without my explanation.

"Look, going behind your back was a shit thing to do, sure. But the thought of her forcing you to do all of the work was driving me insane. I know how much work that project requires, and it's more than you can do on your own. It's my fault you're in the predicament and I just...wanted to make it right."

She rolls her eyes, a sigh escaping her plump lips. "Your heart was in the right place, and what I'm about to say is going to sound pretty rude, but... You didn't talk to her for me, you did it for you. You felt guilty and wanted to ease your conscience. I get it, and I get why you did it. But please stop pretending it was to help me. It wasn't."

Fuck. Why is all this attitude she's throwing my way turning me on?

"Fair enough." I nod. "Can we move past this if I swear to never go behind your back again?" Even as I ask the question, I'm lying. I'm hiding Rob's ongoing threats, but this time, it really is for her.

She contemplates my offer for a minute before offering me a single, decisive nod.

"Good. Let's eat."

"Oh my God!" she exclaims around a mouthful of burger. "How is it this good?"

"Try the fries."

She wastes no time, grabbing one and popping it in her mouth, moaning her delight as she chews and swallows.

Much to my surprise, she puts away her entire meal, plus her dessert. Emmy can eat, and frankly, it's hot as hell. Most of the women in our social circles peck at their salads while longing for the feast their date's eating.

But not Emmy, and this only serves to make me want her a little more. She's different; she refuses to fit the rich girl stereotype, and I love it.

"Oh, another thing," she says, licking raspberry sauce from the tines of her fork.

"Hmm, huh?"

"Professor Ellison is your freaking uncle?"

"Oh, yeah. He's mom's twin."

"That's why you're able to basically run his class, huh?"

"He doesn't really care anymore, to be honest, thanks to his book deal."

"Good for him, I guess." She goes back to her cheese-cake, gathering up the last of the graham cracker crust crumbs onto her fork.

She pops them into her mouth, and like Cupid struck

me with an arrow, I suddenly can't wait a second longer. "Let me take you out."

Emmalyn quirks her head to the side. "Are we not out?"

I grin as I rise from my seat, offering a hand to her. "No, like for real. On a date."

"Oh. Um." Her eyes are as wide as our cleared lunch plates and her cheeks are as red as the raspberry sauce from her dessert. She's flustered, and it's fucking cute.

If I was a smarter man, I'd be more discreet with my interest and affections, but I want her to know I'm into her, and I refuse to let Rob Pearson control me. He's wreaked enough havoc in Emmalyn's life as it is.

He put her destruction in my hands, but instead of hurting her, I'm going to heal her. I'm going to give her back all he took tenfold.

I just have to get Emmalyn on the same page.

"Come on, little mouse. Take a chance on me...on us."

She finally takes my hand, and I haul her to standing from her seat. She allows me to guide her toward the exit and I take full advantage, wrapping an arm around her waist and tucking her into my side as we retrace our steps to where I parked.

"You're not...you really mean it? Like you're serious?" Emmalyn stops at the passenger door and tilts her head my way, staring up at me from beneath her long lashes.

"As can be." I back her into the side of my car, caging her in with my arms. "Say yes. I swear you won't regret it."

Her eyes flit from mine, to the ground, and back again. "I think I probably will, but okay. Yes."

I'm half-tempted to fist pump in my victory, but I rein it in. "Are you free Friday?"

Emmalyn nods.

"Good. I'll pick you up at four." I step back and open her door.

She slides into her seat, a funny look on her pretty face. "Four seems pretty early."

"I have my reasons."

"We'll see."

I grin at her cheekiness as I round the front of my car. Once I'm behind the wheel, I start the engine and throw it into gear. "Guarantee it'll be the best date you've ever been on."

She snorts out a laugh. "It'll be the only."

"What?" Surely, I misheard her. I know she dated in high school. She had a doofy little douche of a boyfriend. Rob complained about him incessantly. *Hello, red flag. Talking about hindsight being twenty-twenty.* "You had a boyfriend though...what was his name?"

"I mean, Aaron and I went out, but it was always group stuff, you know?"

"So, I'll be your first date?"

She shifts in her seat. "Yeah, I guess you will be."

I stop in front of her dorm building, not bothering to park in a space, and slam the gearshift into park. "Friday. Four o'clock."

With a small smile on her face, she unbuckles her seat belt and reaches for the door handle.

"Oh, and, Emmy, pack a bag, because you're spending the night."

She starts to reply, but I reach over the console and pull her back into the seat, pressing my lips to her, silencing her with my kiss.

AFTER DROPPING Emmalyn back at her dorm, I head home. I should probably work on grading for Vic, but the only thing on my mind is getting a jumpstart on planning the best first date ever.

Jesus.

Even thinking that makes me feel like I've lost my balls. But fuck it, because something tells me Emmalyn Price is worth it.

I wait until I'm over the threshold on my door. The light flashes green as I shoulder the door open, kicking off my shoes and eagerly make headway back to my bedroom to change into something more comfortable.

I'm so tempted to shower, but I know the second I get under the hot spray I'll end up with my hand wrapped around my cock as I jerk off to thoughts of Emmalyn.

As tempting as that sounds, it's not conducive to my end goal...making her mine. So, instead, I swap my jeans for sweats and head back down the hall toward the kitchen in search of coffee.

Armed with my laptop and caffeine, I make my way to the couch.

"I was wondering when you'd get here."

"What the fuck!" I shout, as my laptop goes flying across the room, and my mug drops to the floor, shattering on impact, splashing scalding hot coffee all over my bare feet. I stumble back, slipping and sliding, in an attempt to escape the scorching liquid.

"Don't be so dramatic, Sterling."

With fury and fire still racing through my veins, I give him my back, stalking off in search of a towel to clean up the mess.

I return in a new pair of sweats and a whole slew of questions for my former best friend. "Why in the hell are you inside my house?"

Rob tsks. "Is that any way to greet your best friend?"

"I'd probably be a bit more hospitable if I had known you were coming." I cross the room to retrieve my laptop; thankfully it's in one piece. "It also would've helped had you knocked and I let you in. It's a little disconcerting to find someone inside your locked home. Breaking and entering isn't a good look."

He scoffs loudly. "Step down from your soapbox, Sterling. We both know you gave me a key. I simply used it."

"Without my consent." I flip open my laptop and exhale a relieved breath when it powers up with no problem.

"You giving me the key is implied consent."

Not for the first time, I want to slam my fist into his face. But I remain seated, with a carefully neutral look on my face. "Shouldn't be surprised. Consent's not really your thing."

Rob's on his feet in a flash. "What did you just say?"

"You heard me." I place my laptop down on the cushion

and stand as well. Only, my movements are slow, methodical.

"I was really hoping my eyes had deceived me. That you weren't cozying up to that little bitch."

"Watch your mouth." My voice is a growl, feral and vicious, a warning.

Rob barks out a sharp, mirthless laugh. "Whatever for? Surely you haven't fallen for the whore's innocent victim act."

"I swear to God, Rob—" I advance toward him, fully prepared to forcibly remove him from my home.

"You have." He shakes his head, his disappointment evident. "I was torn at first, you know? I thought maybe you were having sleepovers and taking her out as a way to gain her trust. But instead, she somehow gained yours."

I stop halfway to him as his words sink in, ratcheting my anger up to uncharted levels. "You...you've been following us. Spying."

A grin that can only be described as evil splits his cheeks. "Had to make sure my *best friend* was staying loyal. I should've known better. What's the saying...if you want a friend, get a dog?"

"Get out."

Instead of leaving, Rob unceremoniously drops back down in the chair I found him in. "I don't think I will. We have things to discuss."

"No." I continue on my path toward him. "We don't. You've outstayed your welcome and need to leave."

"Sterling, Sterling. Surely we're not going to let some pussy come between us. Especially one as subpar as Emma—"

"Don't you dare speak her fucking name." I'm on him in seconds, yanking him up by the front of his shirt as my fist slams into his face. Blood trickles from both his nose and lip, and I welcome the sight of it. A busted-up face is the least he deserves after the things he's done.

He makes no move to retaliate, but I'm too busy dragging his sorry ass toward the door to lend more thought to why. "I don't understand your fucking obsession with her, but it ends *now*. You will not seek her out, watch her, follow her, nothing. You won't contact her, and you're damn sure not going to hurt her."

I shove him against the solid wood of the door, holding him in place with my arm pressed to his throat, as my heart tries to beat its way out of my chest. "Do you understand me? Forget she even exists. She's dead to you."

He glares at me, malice burning in his usually dead eyes. "You're making a mistake."

Pressing my arm tighter against his throat, I look him dead in the eyes as I officially end our lifelong friendship. "My only mistake was believing you." He shoves me off of him and throws the door open, leaving of his own accord.

I slam and deadbolt the door in his wake as a million-and-one different emotions flood my system. Fear, panic, regret, anger. But more than any of those, I have a driving need to check on Emmalyn. To hear her voice, to *know* she's safe.

But when I grab my phone to call her, there's already a text waiting for me from Rob.

ROB

You're going to regret this.

Worry like I've never felt before shoots through me, but I squeeze it into submission long enough to block his number and dial hers.

My concern surges with every ring. Before I can think it

through, I'm shoving my feet into a pair of shoes and heading for the door.

I won't let that piece of shit hurt her again. I have this overwhelming need to protect her, and I will—at all costs—even if that means kidnapping her ass and bringing her here where I can keep an eye on her at all times.

I'm about to hang up and dial her again when she answers. "Hey."

"Emmalyn," I breathe her name as relief flows through me. "You're good? You're okay?"

"Um. Yes. Are you? Not to be rude, but you sound a little..." She trails off, but I know exactly what she's thinking. I sound crazed.

"I am now." I toe my shoes back off and sink down onto my couch, my entire body melting into the cushions as the sound of her breathing through the line soothes me.

"You're kind of freaking me out, Sterling. What's going on?"

"Fuck. Nothing. Sorry."

"Obviously it's something. Please talk to me."

Sighing, I pinch the bridge of my nose and drop my head onto the back of the couch. "I-I'm overreacting. That's all."

"But over what?" Frustration drips from her every word.

"I... Rob called."

Her sharp intake of breath somehow robs me of my air as well. "What...what did he want?"

"He's...how did I ever call him a friend?"

Emmalyn sighs sadly. "He's a skilled liar. A master manipulator. Don't beat yourself up about it."

"How can I not, baby? Just one person in your corner could've changed everything."

"You're here now," she whispers.

"I am." I nod even though she can't see me. "I am, and I'm not going anywhere."

"Thanks for calling me. For checking on me. For caring."

"I need to ask a favor before we hang up, okay?"

"Sure, Sterling. What?"

"I want you to promise me you won't leave your dorm tonight. Lock the door, stay in. Have a girls' night. Can you do that?"

"Freaking me out again."

"I know, baby. I'm not trying to, but will you do that? For me, please?"

"Okay."

"Promise?"

"Yeah, Sterling. I promise."

"ARE YOU NERVOUS?" Stella asks, clipping my long hair into three even sections while she waits on her curling wand to heat up.

"Yeah. No. I don't

"But it's your first date, right?"

"That's weird, right? That I'm eighteen and just now going on my first date?"

"I don't She as she releases the first clip and combs out my hair. What do I know? My brother sure as hell never let anyone me out."

"I lost my V-card before you even went on first A as I say it, a sobering thought sees m "Well guess we both did."

Stella her onto mine in the reflection of the her ma'am."

I true.

"Go only is a good day, and tonight is going to be better

"You think so as she begins carefully wrapping sections of hair around the barrel of the wand.

"Yup. Physics says so."

"Physics?" I try to turn my head to look at her, but she pops me with the comb.

"Yeah. Like, you've had so many awful things happen to you, it's time for good. I'm pretty sure it's a universal or karmic law or something."

I can't help but giggle at her attempt to rationalize the universe. "You're a mess."

"And yet, you love me."

"More than you know."

"Do you want me to do your makeup, too?"

"No. I'll do it. But you can definitely help me pick an outfit. I have no clue what we're doing, so..."

"Babe. Say no more. I've got this."

Stella darts out of her room and into mine, while I move to the bathroom to start on my makeup.

Since I'm completely in the dark about our plans, I keep my makeup neutral. If I still lived at home, my mother would have pushed for a heavier hand. She is of the belief that natural beauty doesn't exist. Which probably explains why she's so pumped full of silicone and injectables; the only natural thing about her is her selfishness.

When I join Stella in my room, it looks like a laundry-filled bomb went off—clothes are everywhere.

"Um. Stell."

She half sighs, half giggles. "I know. I'll clean it up. But I think I've narrowed it down."

"Let's see it."

"Two options: casual cute," she says, nodding to a pair of jeans and a sweater. "Or classy cute." She gestures to a long-sleeved cotton maxi dress with a gauzy overlay.

"Jeans for sure."

She steps out while I change, and after I'm dressed, I

take stock of my appearance in my full-length mirror.

I look like me, only different.

It's not my outfit, my makeup, or my hair. It's my heart.

For the first time, in a really long time, hope is beating in tandem to the organ in my chest, pumping my veins full of possibility.

My tummy flutters as Stella whistles when I step out of my room. "So?"

"It's gonna be great, Emmy," Stella says right as a knock sounds through our suite.

"Oh! I still need to pack."

My best friend grins. "I took care of it."

And sure enough, my bag's sitting on the coffee table in front of the couch.

Sneaky girl.

"Thanks. I think."

Stella flings herself at me, wrapping me in a hug. "Have so much fun! And remember, I'm only one call away."

"You're the best," I whisper as I head for the door, grabbing my overnight bag and phone along the way.

My heart hopscotches in my chest as I swing the door open. My skin tingles at the mere sight of him. But unlike me, Sterling is the picture of composure, leaned against the doorjamb with his muscled arms crossed over his chest.

"Emmalyn." His eyes light up at the sight of me. "You look gorgeous."

My cheeks burn under his scrutiny. "Thanks."

"You ready?" He reaches for my bag, tugging it from my grasp.

I nod.

"Then let's go."

"Where?" I ask, hoping he'll give in and tell me.

"You'll see."

OUTWARDLY, I'm calm and collected; but inside, I'm second-guessing the hell out of the plans I made for us.

For the first few minutes of the drive, Emmalyn asks questions, trying to get me to slip up and spill the details of our date. But, much to her dismay, my lips are sealed.

Eventually, the mountain view steals her attention as we drive down the winding road toward the valley. "It's just so...beautiful."

"It is," I agree. Though she doesn't know it, I'm referring to both her and the view.

Eventually, our final destination comes into view.

"A grocery store?" Emmalyn asks, a dubious look on her face as she takes in our surroundings.

"I know a little grocery shopping doesn't sound like a good date."

"Um—"

"I'm kidding, baby."

"Oh, good." She laughs, and I kill the engine.

I rush out of the car and around to her side so I can open her door. It's weird, this sudden need I have to take care of her. But at the same time, it feels so natural that I don't question it much.

"This way." I tip my head toward a wooden stairway nestled in the foliage surrounding the lot.

She walks a step ahead of me, and I'd be lying if I didn't say my eyes were glued to her ass the whole way down.

I'm so distracted by the jiggle and sway she's got going on that I almost miss her trying to walk into the pizza place.

"Whoa," I murmur, hooking two fingers through one of her belt loops, dragging her back into me.

"Oh, okay. Not here then."

There's a little whine to her voice, and I can't help but wrap her in my arms. "I know. Mr. T's makes the best pizza, but it's not where we're headed."

I guide her to the crosswalk, linking our hands together as we dash to the other side of the street.

"The Incline Railway!" Her gaze flits from the stairs in front of us, to me, and back again. "Is this where we're going?"

"It's our first stop."

She jumps once and pumps her fist. "This is on my to-do list! I'm so excited."

"What else is on your list?" I ask, as we follow the painted-on train track up the stairs to the ticket window.

"Not much." She laughs. "Stella inspired me to make it. She has a whole college plan of things she wants to do. So I figured I'd make one, too."

"Anything I can help cross off it?"

"You already are."

"Anything else?" I ask as I hold up two fingers at the window before sliding my card beneath the glass divider.

"I'll have to think on it."

"You do that and then let me know. I'll help you check every box."

She rolls her eyes like she thinks I'm joking, but I'm dead-fucking-serious. Emmalyn's missed out on so much, and if I can help her create some memories, some *good* memories, then I'll gladly do it.

Tickets in hand, I guide her around to where we board the cable car, stopping along the way to take a touristy green screen picture.

"Oh, whoa!" she whispers as we step into the back of the car. "It's freaking slanted!"

"Cool, right? The best seats are the front. Be careful going down."

She stumbles a little on the way to the front, but I steady her from behind. "Thanks."

"I know it seems sudden, but I'll always catch you, Emmy."

She slides into the front seat, her cheeks rosy as she processes my words.

Once the car is at capacity, the overhead speakers crackle and we begin our ascent up the mountain.

"Oh, wow," she breathes out in amazement. "What a view."

"Sure is," I murmur, staring directly at her, once again finding myself far more taken with the woman beside me than the majestic scenery all around us.

Fuck. I sound like a wus. Yet somehow, I can't find it in me to care.

I watch Emmalyn the entire climb, hyper-focused on her as she takes in the views. I can't pinpoint what exactly, but something about her calls to me. Even when I was trying to ruin her, I was drawn to her.

Maybe that's why I was never able to fully wreak the havoc Rob intended for me to.

Maybe, deep down, I knew she was innocent but didn't want to let go of Rob's friendship.

Now, though? Now, I not only want to cut ties, I want to burn the fucking bridge.

I'm so caught up in my mind, in her, that I don't notice we've reached the top until the car jerks to a stop, jolting me forward.

"What now?" Emmalyn asks as everyone begins to stand and walk to the back to exit.

"Follow me."

Once on the platform, I ask if she wants to go into the gift shop.

"No, not really." She cocks her head to the side. "Do you?"

"Come on," is all I reply, taking her hand and guiding her to the stairwell.

I guide her all the way to the highest observation deck, and immediately, she's at the rail, oohing and aahing over the view. "Man, this is so much prettier than Texas."

"You don't think Texas is nice?"

"I mean, it's not bad, other than the memories associated with it. But there's something about the mountains that just calls to me, you know? It feels like...home."

"C'mere." I crook a finger at her as I step back into a shady corner of the deck.

"What's up?"

"There's something I need to do."

"What?"

As soon as she's within reaching distance, I hook my arm around her waist and draw her body flush to mine. "This." And then I crush my lips to hers.

She gasps in surprise, and I seize the opportunity to deepen the kiss. Our tongues slide together in a sensuous dance as I tangle my free hand in the hair at the nape of her neck.

I use my grip on her hair to gently leverage her into the exact position I want her in. Her taste is heaven, like she was made specifically for me, and I can't help but wonder if she'd taste this amazing if I were to kiss her somewhere else, somewhere much more intimate.

Emmalyn smooths her hands over my chest, gripping the material of my shirt as she loses herself to our kiss.

I'm already as hard as the stone wall at my back when she presses in closer to me and rocks her hips against mine, a soft moan slipping past her lips. That sound, that singular breathless whimper, nearly has me ready to strip her down and claim her here and now.

Luckily, the sound of voices trickles our way on the breeze, reminding me we're in public. We're both breathless as I pull away, ending our kiss with a few small pecks.

"Thank you for this, Sterling."

"For what?"

"For this date, for being so gentle, so sweet."

Fuck. This woman. Her capacity to forgive is beyond me. If I were her, I wouldn't give my sorry ass the time of day, but here she is thanking me. I don't deserve her, not in the least, but I'm damn sure not letting her go.

"We're just getting started, baby."

"I CAN'T BELIEVE you set all of this up for me. It's been the best first date ever."

He grins. "I don't think you have much to compare it to."

His words, while blunt, aren't meant to be mean. "You're right, I don't. But I stand by what I said. I can't imagine anything that would've been better than this."

"We're not done yet," he says. "We still have one more thing to do."

I stare at him in disbelief. What more could there possibly be? Suddenly? We rode the incline railway, an amazing dinner, dancing, and now ice cream. I can't think of a single thing that would make tonight better than it already is."

"There's no need to analyze me, little mouse. Trust that I know what I'm doing and that I know how to make you happy."

"I don't doubt that," I murmur, dropping my gaze to my lap.

Stellan reaches across the table and skims his index finger beneath my jaw, tilting my face back up to his. "Don't do that. Don't hide from me. I want to know how you feel and what you're really thinking. I want us to be transparent with each other, Emmalyn. We started with so much dishonesty and distrust that I think it's the only way we can be successful."

His words give me pause. There's such earnest truth behind them that I know he means what he's saying. "Okay, Sterling. I trust you, and I'll do my best not to hide from you."

"Good. Now let's go."

"Where?"

He stands and chucks our empty bowls and spoons into the trash. "Trust, remember?"

I roll my eyes, but follow him back to the car all the same.

Fifteen minutes later, we pull up outside of what appears to be a rundown warehouse. I shoot Sterling an apprehensive glance. "Are you sure we're in the right place?"

Looking at me from the side of his eyes, he smirks. "Remember that talk we had about trusting me? It wasn't that long ago."

"I do trust you, smartass. But come on, this place looks shady."

He rolls his eyes, but there's a smile on his face, so I know he's not put out by my skepticism. "You're right, it does look a little sketchy. Weren't you taught not to judge a book by its cover?"

"Sterling Abbot, this place is not a book! It's a seedy building." I throw my arms in the air, motioning toward our surroundings. "This is the kind of place people get kidnapped or mugged!"

"I promise you're not going to be kidnapped or mugged. In fact, if you come inside with me, this will be a step to ensure none of these things happen to you, or at the very least you'll be able to handle yourself if they do."

His words are just ominous enough to be intriguing, or maybe they're just intriguing enough to be ominous. I'm not sure, but either way I find myself nodding and getting out of the car.

He guides me toward a garage-style door that's rolled up just enough for people to walk under. To say I'm not prepared for what we find inside is an understatement. This definitely isn't a seedy warehouse, but a state-of-the-art gym.

The space is unlike any gym I've ever set foot in before. The back wall is made up entirely of mirrors, giving patrons a clear view of the entire space. Punching bags, ropes, heavy mats, and more fill the space. There are even a few fighting cages.

Off to the right there's a desk, and I'm shocked to see Abigail sitting behind it. "Hey, you two. Welcome to Full Contact."

"Hey, I didn't know you worked here."

"I don't, not really. It's my brother's gym, and his receptionist called out." She grins. "So, what can I help you with?"

Good question, Abigail. Why are we here?

Sterling steps slightly in front of me. "I want to sign her up for self-defense classes."

A warm feeling moves through me at his declaration. My heart is basically a pile of goo in my chest. The fact that he cares enough about me to make sure I'm able to protect myself is almost unfathomable.

"Really?" I ask, emotion clogging my throat.

"Really, baby."

"Thank you." I throw myself into his arms, forcing him to hug me.

"It's as much for me as it is for you. I want to know you'll be able to take care of yourself when I'm not around."

His words cause something inside of me to break a little,

but in the best possible way. This man is nothing like what I thought he was. In fact, he may very well be everything I never knew I needed; he's damn sure everything I've ever wanted.

Somehow, he's morphed from my own personal nightmare into a dream come true.

"SO, you're cool with me bringing you here?" I ask, feeling particularly nervous. I can't even pinpoint why I'm so on edge over her being here. But I am. "You're not upset or anything?"

"Sterling, how could I ever be upset at you for wanting to protect me?"

"True," I shoot a cocky smirk her way. "I do what I can."

She leans into me, the subtle sends zips of molten energy through

"I genuinely owe me

I grin at her because even if there's a thread of truth to it. "Are you ever going to stop bringing up what an awful shit

She probably no

"Ha. Never. New friends you signed up."

Once the paperwork is complete, she turns to me with a timid smile. "Seriously though, thank you for an absolutely amazing night. I know I keep repeating myself, but I truly couldn't have asked for anything better for my first date."

I brush a strand of hair off of her face, tucking it behind her ear. "You deserve all of this and more, and it might sound crazy, but if I have any say in it, I'm damn sure going to be the one to give it to you."

Her eyes get a faraway look as we walk back to my car. I can't help but wonder what she's thinking. Deciding to go for it, I ask.

She laughs nervously. "Nothing."

"No, not nothing."

"It's nothing," she insists.

"It's something." I open her door and help her into her seat.

"Sterling, please." She turns her face away from me. "Can we talk about it later?"

I debate pushing the issue, but eventually decide that she's right; we can talk about it later.

"So, what next?" she asks once I'm behind the wheel.

"Well, we can either find something else to do or we can go back to my place...if you're still okay with staying over. If not, I'll take you home."

"No!" she blurts, whipping around to face me. "No, please take me back to your place...that's where I want to be."

Feeling like I've won the lottery, I don't waste a second starting the car and pulling into traffic. The drive home passes like molasses. Every mile feels like ten with her shooting me these nervous, coy looks, nibbling on her lip, and squirming in her seat.

It's obvious there's something on her mind, possibly even something dirty, but I don't want to push and risk her shutting down completely.

Once we're safely inside of my house, I offer her some after dinner coffee, which she readily accepts. I'm starting to think she might be as addicted to caffeine as I am, if not more so.

"Do you want to drink it on the deck? I can light the fire pit."

"That sounds perfect." Her voice has an almost dream-like quality to it that sends an appreciative chill down my spine.

"Great. Do you think you can handle making the coffee while I start the fire?"

"Pretty sure I can handle your fancy coffee maker, Sterling. It's not exactly rocket science."

I laugh at her smart mouth, loving the little bit of spirit that's starting to break through.

She's no longer the subdued, meek little creature from the start of the semester, instead she's a woman with fire and sass and a will stronger than steel. I love the woman she's becoming, and I'm fucking thrilled that I get to be a part of it. It's an honor, one I'll never take for granted—especially since I know I don't deserve it.

The fire is lit by the time she joins me outside, and we decide to sip our coffee on the small loveseat facing the mountain peaks in the distance.

When I set up my deck, romance was the last thing on my mind, but suddenly I'm glad I let my designer do her thing. Because having Emmalyn this close has me feeling content in a way I've never known before.

"Are you sure tonight was good?" I know I'm a shit, fishing for compliments, but my ego demands it. Something about hearing her tell me it was good settles the part of my soul that screams I'm not good enough and don't deserve her.

"It was perfect, Sterling. I'll be honest, I was really

apprehensive, but you made tonight better than anything I ever could've imagined."

I nod my head, feeling proud that I was able to give her this, as small as it may be. "The next one will be even better."

"It's not a contest, stop trying to one up yourself. Honestly, I don't even think you could."

"Tonight was that perfect, huh?"

Her teasing smile turns serious. "Sterling, I need to ask you something."

Apprehension and dread collide inside of me in a head-on collision. "What?"

"Can I kiss you?"

"Baby, that's not something you ever have to ask for."

Her brown eyes glint in the firelight as she leans forward, setting her mug down onto the table. I place mine on the deck at our feet, waiting anxiously for her next move.

I'm expecting her to lean in for a gentle kiss, so imagine my surprise when she turns toward me and swings one leg over mine to straddle my lap.

"Fuck, baby," I groan, but she swallows the sound, boldly pressing her lips to mine, flicking her tongue against the seam until I open for her.

In the span of a breath our kiss goes from tame to heated, with her tunneling her fingers through my hair and rolling her hips against mine.

My hands roam her body, squeezing her ass. She trembles in my arms as I drag my hands across her hips and over the dips in her waist.

"Sterling," she moans, and I swear, between the sound of her voice and the way she moves against me, it feels like I'm in paradise.

But I'm worried she's not ready for where this is headed.

"Baby." I move my hands back to her hips, stilling her movements. "Stop. Slow down. Let's talk about this."

But she doesn't let up. "I want this, I want you," she murmurs, her lips never breaking from mine.

"I want this, too, Emmalyn, but I also want to make sure we're on the same page."

The amount of self-control I'm displaying right now impresses even me. Because while I would love nothing more than to flip her onto her back and claim every square inch of her delectable body, I refuse to take more than she's willing and ready to give.

I refuse to take anything more before getting complete consent.

"Just kiss me, Sterling!" She leans back in, frantic for my touch in a way that sets my teeth on edge.

"Slow down and talk to me, little mouse."

She huffs and flings herself from my lap, moving to the chair beside me. "Sure, Sterling," she bites out my name. "Let's talk."

"Are you mad at me?"

"It's not every day that a girl gets rejected in the heat of the moment. Especially on her first date."

"Whoa, hold up. I am *not* rejecting you. I just think we need to talk before we go any further. You're more to me than some cheap fuck. I see the possibility of a future between the two of us, and I don't think slowing down to talk is a bad thing. Can we please...I just want to understand where you are, what you want, and to make sure that everything is what it should be."

She instantly deflates. "Okay."

"It's not that I didn't like where this was going, but it seemed sudden."

Her shoulders curl forward and she wraps her arms

around herself. "I guess you're right. It's just..." Tears well in her eyes, and my heart clenches at the sight of the droplets clinging to her lashes.

I don't ever want to see her cry ever again, and yet here she is, on a night that was supposed to be magical, with tears dripping from her chin.

"Talk to me, baby, you're breaking my heart."

A broken sob spills from her lips. "It's...I... He's the only man to ever touch me, and I don't want the memory of his touch to linger. I want you to erase it...I *need* you to. I don't want to think about sex and see his face. I want to think about pleasure and happiness. I want to think about you, about your touch and the way you say my name. Please, Sterling, please make it better. Touch me, brand me. Make me yours."

And just like that, my heart absolutely shatters in my chest.

I mean—fuck—who am I to deny her?

"C'mere, baby," I whisper, opening my arms wide.

"Really?" she asks, a slight tremble to her voice. "You really want to do this with me? Even knowing...everything?"

My tongue darts out, swiping across my lower lip, savoring the lingering taste of her kiss. "Baby, want is not a strong enough word."

She wipes away the last of her tears. "Okay, then," she whispers as she stands, stepping into my waiting arms.

I guide her through the house, straight back to my bedroom. I can feel the nervous energy pouring off of her. Or maybe it's me, because I'm damn sure a wreck, hoping like hell I can make this good for her, that I can indeed erase his touch and replace it with mine.

That I can submerge and drown her in so much plea-sure, she'll never think of his hands on her again. I want to purge that piece of shit from her system until she associates sex with pleasure, and pleasure with me, with my body, my touch, and my voice.

Once we cross the threshold into my room, Emmalyn pops up on her toes and kisses me softly.

I brush my lips against hers twice before pulling back with a smile. "It's not too late to change your mind," I tell her. "It's never too late to change your mind. If at any point it's too much or you don't want to continue, all you have to do is say the word and everything stops. This is about you, okay?"

Her hair falls into her face as she nods; I reach out and brush the strands so I can see her eyes. "I mean it, baby; I won't get upset. I won't get mad. You set the pace, you're in charge."

She smiles up at me with so much faith in her gaze that my knees nearly buckle. "I trust you, Sterling. I know you'll take care of me."

I WENT into this date hopeful yet apprehensive. Given our twisted history, it seemed wise to be at least a little guarded. But after all of the thought and effort Sterling put into tonight, I know he's worthy of me. That he will cherish me, and treat me right.

By the time we made it back to his place, I was confident in my decision. Eager for his touch even. Ready and willing.

As foolish as that sounds, I stand by it, even as my body quakes with muted anticipation for what's to come.

It's not that I'm scared of him, how he'll react to me once it's over.

What if he finds me lacking? What if I'm not good enough for him? A guy like Sterling has plenty of experience. How could someone like me ever satisfy him?

A gentle touch through my hair as he smooths his index finger along my jaw and over my cheek. "Where did you go, little mouse?"

"Sorry."

He kisses my forehead. "Let me into those thoughts.

Remember what I said about not hiding from me? How can I take care of you if I don't know what you're thinking?"

I laugh ruefully. "How did I get so lucky to have you?"

"I don't think luck had anything to do with it. I'm pretty sure you were meant to be mine. The wires of the universe just got crossed along the way. But I'm here now, baby, and I'm gonna make up for everything."

Unable to help myself, I loop my arms around his neck and pull him down for another kiss that quickly turns heated as Sterling walks us back toward his bed.

"I want to touch you here." He whispers the words against my lips as he reaches up to cup my breasts. "To taste you here."

I try to capture his lips again, but he pulls away, making me whimper. I crave his touch; I long for it more than I've ever longed for anything. It honestly feels like I'll die if he doesn't put his hands on my body.

"Can I take this off?" he asks, pulling at the material of my sweater.

I nod, unable to form words as desire unlike anything I've ever known crashes into me, nearly knocking me sideways.

He removes my shirt, and I quickly follow with my bra, too lust-drunk on him to remember to be nervous.

"God, you're beautiful." He presses a kiss to my collarbone before moving his mouth to the valley between my breasts. His warm lips blaze a trail, sucking and licking and nibbling, until he draws my right nipple into his mouth.

The combined suction and the heat of his mouth is almost too much for me to bear as he lavishes my breast with attention.

A whimper breaks free as he pulls away and moves to the other side. "Let's lay you down," he murmurs, positioning me just so against the mountain of pillows at the headboard before crawling up the bed, coming to rest between my thighs.

"I want to taste all of you," he says, his voice deeper than usual, as he trails his fingers, feather soft, down my abdomen to the waistband of my jeans.

Fear and excitement strum through me like an electric current, but still, I nod.

"Take your pants off," he says as he reaches around to pull his shirt over his head. My eyes are glued to the hard planes of his chest and the dips and valleys of his abs. The man's a work of art, a god among men, and yet here he is making all of my dreams come true.

Piece by piece, he removes his clothing, until all that's left is a pair of skintight black boxers.

His arousal is evident through the thin material. I fist my hands at my sides as I fight the urge to reach out and touch him, to cup him through the fabric, to explore him as thoroughly as he did me.

I can barely process that he's hard and hot for me, yet the proof is staring me right in the face, quite literally.

He smirks when he sees me staring. "Are you gonna finish taking off those jeans or do you need a little help?"

Wordlessly, I lie back and lift my hips, allowing him to pull them down the rest of the way, taking my underwear with them.

"Fuck, baby," he groans at the sight of me laid bare before him. "You're sure this is okay?"

"I'm positive, Sterling."

He licks his lips as he lowers himself back between my thighs, kissing his way down my stomach. A sudden bout of shyness has my hips shifting as I try to clamp my thighs shut.

Sterling pauses, but at my urging continues, sliding his hands under my ass while pressing his thumbs into my thighs. Using his newfound leverage, he pushes my legs wider, making room for his shoulders before lowering his mouth to my tender, needy flesh.

He sucks my clit into his mouth, and I nearly scream from the toe-curling sensation. "You like that?" he murmurs, cocky as hell.

I try to respond, but words are beyond me; all I can do is moan and nod.

"Yeah, you fucking love it." He dives back in, licking me from bottom to top, like I'm the best and last meal he will ever eat.

In a matter of minutes, I'm screaming my pleasure as I come violently against his face. "Oh my God," I murmur when I come down from my oxytocin high. "I never knew it could feel like that."

Sterling grins, popping up to his knees. "Just wait, baby, we aren't anywhere close to done."

My eyes dart down to his still hard dick. "Can I touch you, too?"

He flops onto his back beside me. "You can touch me anytime you want."

Hesitantly, I roll to my side and reach out, pressing my hand to the bulge straining against the front of his boxers. He jerks beneath my touch and I grin, delighting in the knowledge that I affect him just as much as he does me.

"Take off your boxers."

"You do it," he challenges.

If he thinks I'm going to back down, he's wrong. I've set my mind to this; I'm ready, and I want to know how he feels inside of me. God knows, he's already found his way into my heart.

I move so that I'm between his knees and begin working the material down to his feet. He takes over from here, kicking his boxers off and onto the floor.

I knew he was large, but seeing it face-to-face is a whole new experience. My eyes widen with trepidation as I ask, "Are you sure it'll fit?"

"Like a fucking glove, baby."

"Can I kiss it?"

He chuffs out a laugh. "Again, you never have to ask to put any part of your body on mine. You have carte blanche when it comes to me."

I nibble on my lower lip as I lean forward. Gingerly, I flick my tongue against the tip of his dick, and he shudders as an animalistic groan spills from his lips.

Feeling emboldened by his response, I lean down and suck the crown into my mouth, sucking softly.

"Fuck. A little harder."

I follow his guidance, sucking harder.

"Now move your lips down my cock, baby."

Again, I do as he says, causing his hips to flex and a myriad of curses to fall from his lips.

"So good, Emmy. So. Fucking. Good. I love that mouth."

Internally, I grin, beyond pleased with myself.

Somehow, even while he's the one getting pleasure, Sterling takes great care to make sure I know I'm the one in control.

That notion spurs me on and turns me on as I add my hand into the mix, fondling his balls.

"Baby, you gotta stop," he croaks out.

Immediately, I worry I've done something wrong and scramble away from him. "Are you okay?" I ask, uncertainty lacing my tone.

"I'm more than okay, but if we don't stop now, I'm gonna finish in your pretty little mouth."

"Oh." My cheeks flame as his meaning sinks in. "Right. Okay. How do you want to do this?" I ask, immediately regretting it when I realize how completely idiotic I sound.

Sterling just smiles though. "Any way you want. What do you think you'll be most comfortable with?"

I think on it for a minute. "Can I be on top?"

"Baby, are you asking if you can ride me?"

"Um." I shift nervously. "I guess so."

"Go for it, cowgirl."

His joke, while cheesy, is precisely what I need to relax. I don't know how, but this man always seems to know the exact right way to ease my anxiety.

"Do you have a...a condom?" I ask.

"In my drawer."

I move away from him to grab one, ignoring the pinch of jealousy at the thought of him here with someone else.

"You want to put it on or do you want me to?"

I look back to him, and my brain nearly short-circuits at the sight of him pumping his fist leisurely over himself.

"I'll let you do it," I say, passing him the foil packet, which he eagerly rips into before rolling it down his shaft.

Sterling pats his thighs, signaling for me to climb on top of him. I hesitate momentarily, wondering if I'll be too heavy.

His lips tilt up in a knowing grin, as if he can read my mind. "Baby, I can take it."

I suck in a deep breath, mentally hyping myself before swinging my leg back over his, landing right below his abs.

Immediately, I feel stupid. Obviously, he can handle my weight, as proven earlier tonight. Not to mention, the man's packing pure muscle beneath his clothes.

"Get out of your head and give me a kiss." He hooks his index finger beneath my chin and draws my face to his, mashing our lips together. I open for him and his tongue invades my mouth, pushing away all of my worry until only he remains.

He nips at my lips as his hands roam up and down my body before finally settling on the swell of my ass. "You feel so good. I can't wait to be inside you."

The sensual growl of his voice has me rolling my hips on instinct, desperately searching for friction to alleviate the ache he's created.

"Yes, baby, fuck."

Acting on instinct once again, I lift my hips and he reaches between us to help guide himself inside of me. I wince as the broad head of his dick pushes against my opening.

"Take it as slow as you need to. You set the pace."

I know he means what he is saying, but I can hear the strain in his voice. He wants to feel me wrapped around him just as badly as I want to feel him filling me up.

I take another deep breath and plunge myself downward, seating him fully inside of me.

"Fuck! Goddamn, baby."

My body is caught between ecstasy and agony; it feels like he's ripping me apart from the inside, and yet, I don't want to pull away.

"Let me make you feel good," he begs, and I bob my head in agreement. "I'm going to touch you," he warns seconds before pressing his index and middle finger against my clit, rubbing the sensitive nub in small, tight circles.

I cry out and rock my hips, causing his to buck beneath me. He continues his ministrations until finally that lingering pinch of discomfort ebbs away, leaving nothing but pleasure in its place.

I try to move faster, but his hands move to my hips, stilling me.

I whine as frustration washes away the high I was chasing. "I thought I set the pace. I thought I was in control."

"You are," he rushes to assure me.

"Then quit treating me like I'm made of glass. You won't break me."

A feral grin splits his cheeks as he palms my waist on both sides. "Well, let's see what you got, then."

The challenge in his voice is oddly enticing. Planting my hands on his chest, I lift myself off of him before slamming back down, impaling myself all over again.

Fire burns through me, radiating out from my core at the sensation, and then I start moving against him in earnest, moaning and groaning until the only sounds in the room are that of our pleasure and our skin slapping together in an erotic rhythm.

"I'm so close," I whisper, a desperate edge to my voice. I don't sound like myself, but I can't find it in me to care. "Help me, Sterling. Oh, God, please." I don't even care that I'm begging.

"I've got you." He leans up and presses a kiss directly over my heart. "Hang on, baby." He begins thrusting into me from below and our once-coordinated rhythm is now sloppy and uncontrollable as we both desperately seek our climax.

By some miracle, we finish together, both calling out the other's name. I collapse against his chest, feeling wrung out and yet so, so sated.

"Is that how it always is?" I ask against his chest. "How it's always supposed to be?"

"Baby." He presses a kiss to my forehead. "I have never felt anything like that in my life. That's just...*us.*"

I revel in his words, feeling positively elated to know my rapidly growing feelings aren't one-sided...to know that he still wants me...that it wasn't a one and done.

To know that I'm his...*and he's mine.*

SUNLIGHT PEEKS THROUGH THE CURTAINS, slowly waking me.

Emmalyn murmurs in her sleep beside me, confirming that last night wasn't just a dream. She really is here, sprawled across me, her skin pressed to mine and hair fanned out across my pillow. She looks every bit like the angel she is.

Unable to stop myself, I lean down and press my lips to her forehead, murmuring in her hair. "Did you sleep okay?"

"Everything's okay," she yawns. "Better than ever before, honestly."

"Go back to sleep."

She curls up beside me with her eyes still closed. "Did I wake you. Are you sure?"

She cracks her eyes open, fighting to see. "Only a little."

"God, I never want to hurt you. I don't ever want to hurt you," I ramble before I could, and I quickly amend my statement. "Everything. If I could change the past, believe me, I would. But I swear to you, little mouse, never again."

"A girl could get used to waking up next to you. What

are your plans for the day?" she asks, her voice soft, maybe even a little guarded.

"The only plans I have are the ones that allow me to spend time with you."

"The only thing I have to do today is study and work on my project a little. Typically, Stella and I have a girls' day, but I think she'll be okay with me making an exception just this once."

"Why don't you text her and find out while I warm up the shower?"

Her cheeks burn scarlet. "For both of us?"

"That's right, for both of us."

She swallows roughly. "Oh, okay."

"Is it okay with you?" I ask, hoping I'm not pushing her too far.

The little vixen wiggles her hips again, this time brushing against my erection. "Yes, Sterling, I think it's okay."

I pull the covers off and stand from the bed, making no attempt to hide my nakedness as I pad into the bathroom. In fact, I fucking love the way her eyes are locked onto my cock, watching it with a hungry smile as she takes me in.

"Better hurry...wouldn't want the water to get cold."

She cracks a grin. "Surely a place as fancy as this has a water heater that lasts longer than a minute."

I laugh. "You're right, I just don't want to miss you."

"I'll be right here," she promises, with hearts in her eyes as she reaches for her phone.

The water is hot and the bathroom steamy by the time Emmalyn joins me.

"Thought you said you only be a minute," I tease.

"Sorry." She flashes a sweet smile. "Stella was on the warpath for details."

I reach for her and she steps into the shower and then into my arms. "What'd you tell her?"

"I didn't tell her anything, I promise."

I spin us so she is standing beneath the warm spray. "I wouldn't be mad if you did, as long as it's good things."

She runs her hands up my chest and locks them behind my neck. "Of course it would be good things, thanks to that new leaf of yours."

Momentary guilt spears through me, but I push it down because this time I really am a changed man. Thanks to her, my eyes are open. From here on out, I will always put her first, come hell or high water.

"Can I wash your hair?"

Her eyes jump from me to the shampoo bottle and back again. "I guess. If you want."

"Oh, I want."

She scrunches her nose like she thinks I'm weird, but I'll show her. I lean over and reach past her to grab the shampoo bottle, intentionally brushing my fingers over the dip in her waist.

Emmalyn shivers and I get myself a mental pat on the back. By the time her hair's clean, she'll be ready to get down and dirty.

I squeeze a dollop of shampoo into my hand, rubbing them together before tunneling my fingers into her hair and pressing them into her scalp.

"Oh, wow, I forgot how nice this feels. Except you're better than any hair salon."

I lean down and kiss her lips. "That's because mine comes with a happy ending."

She smacks my chest but there's mirth dancing in her eyes.

"I'm just saying. Think about it." And judging from the

quick rise and fall of her chest and the way her pupils are blown wide, she's doing just that.

I step aside and let her rinse the suds from her hair before repeating the process with conditioner.

"Can I wash yours?" she asks.

"I washed it while you were checking in with Stella."

Disappointment blooms across her every feature and I feel like a piece of shit, simply for washing my hair. I should have waited.

"What about your body?" She looks up at me from beneath wet lashes, looking far too sexy for her own good.

Wordlessly I pass her my bottle of shower gel, content to let her get to work.

"Actually, I don't need this." She passes the bottle back to me and I turn and place it back on the shelf.

"What do you—oh, God." Before I can fully process what's happening, Emmalyn's on her knees and wrapping her pretty pink lips around my cock. "Fuck, yes."

Gone is the nervousness from last night. She sucks me like a pro, swirling her tongue and flicking it as she works the base with one hand and my balls with her other.

I try to maintain my composure, fisting my hands at my sides, determined to let her set the pace.

Until she pulls off of me and says, "Fuck me. Fuck my mouth. I...I want it."

"Baby, are you sure?" I ask, not missing the slight tremor in her voice.

"Yeah, I'm sure." She leans in and presses a kiss to my right thigh. "I want to make you feel good."

"You make me feel good just being here," I murmur as she kisses my left thigh.

She laughs, but it sounds off. Different. Not at all like her normal laugh. "Emmalyn, look at me."

With a shake of her head, she tries to draw me back into her mouth.

Unease wars within me as she bobs her head up and down my length. She doesn't make it more than two passes before I reach down and pull her up to standing.

"Why'd you do that?" she asks, her cheeks splotchy as tears mingle with the water raining down on both of us.

"Why are you crying?" I fire right back, reaching past her to turn off the water.

"I'm not."

"You are."

I step out of the shower and wrap a towel around my waist before grabbing another, wrapping it around her and pulling her into my arms. "Talk to me, baby. You're not acting like you and it's freaking me out."

She sniffles and my heart clenches, desperately wanting to fix whatever is wrong.

I dry her off and scoop her up in my arms, carrying her back to my bed, where I pull the covers up over both of us and hold her close.

"Talk to me, little mouse."

"It's nothing."

"It's something."

"It's stupid."

"It's not."

She cries softly against my chest. "It's...it's just that..."

"It's what, baby?"

"It's just you have all this experience, and while last night was amazing, I know you're probably used to something more...something better. And I wanted—*God, this sounds so stupid now*—I wanted to make you feel so good that you forgot every girl that came before me."

My heart squeezes before dropping to my gut. "Jesus,

Emmy." I pull back just enough to look her in the eye. "You outshine any other woman I've ever known and any I've yet to meet, just by being you. You don't need to impress me with your sexual prowess, Emmalyn. You don't need to blow my mind with orgasms. All I need is you. Y-O-U. That's it."

"Really?"

"Really."

"I feel like such an idiot."

"No need to."

"You're sweet to pretend."

"Not pretending, either. You're human, and sometimes humans do foolish, weird, messy things." I huff out a laugh. "Like bully the girl they love, albeit, I didn't know I loved you then."

Emmalyn sucks in a sharp breath. "You love me?"

Shit. Fuck. Am I doing this? "Yeah...I guess I do."

"Wow." She blinks twice. "Really? You're not just saying it to make me feel better?"

I cup her cheek, rubbing the tips of my fingers over her smooth skin. "I'm just as surprised as you are."

She cracks a smile at that, trying to suppress a laugh, but it breaks free.

"You know laughter is not typically the response one wants upon telling someone they love them."

She drops her eyes, releasing my gaze. Immediately I feel bad, wishing like hell I could take the words back. "Hey, I was only joking. There's no pressure for you to feel any certain way about me. Just like everything else, it's on your time."

"No. I do...I do love you. So much that it scares me. I mean, how is it even possible to feel this way about you, given our history?"

Once again I'm hit with guilt, but I deserve it and I own it. "Honestly, and this might sound crazy, but I think our past is why we feel so strongly connected in the present. It wasn't an ideal beginning, but it was our beginning, plain and simple. There's never been anything typical about us, nor do I want there to be."

I shift and pull her a little closer. "Well, I would've preferred not to hurt you, but you know what I mean."

"As crazy as it sounds, I do love you, Sterling. Does this...does this mean...are we..."

A giant, smug grin breaks out across my face as she stumbles over her words. "Little mouse, are you trying to ask me if we're dating?"

Her cheeks turn a brilliant shade of pink. "Yeah, I guess so."

"Yes, we are. And we're dating exclusively."

"Exclusively?" There's an undercurrent of surprise in her tone, and I hate it. I'll just work that much harder to assure her of our status.

"That's right, baby, exclusively. Unless that's not what you want?"

"It's exactly what I want, it's just hard to believe you do. Surely you know that you're so out of my league—"

I cut her off. "No. That's where you're wrong. It's you who's out of my league."

She laughs; any other time the sound would be music to my ears, but the fact that it's full of self-deprecation rubs me the wrong way. This woman is wonderful and she needs to know it, which is why it's now become my new mission to prove it to her.

"How about some breakfast?" she asks, very obviously changing the subject.

"I could eat." I wag my brows.

"You're insatiable," she says with a small laugh.

"Only for you."

She rolls her eyes, trying to downplay my words.

"I mean it. This thing between us might take some time for you to get used to, but I need you to know I'm in this for the long haul. This isn't a game, and you aren't some passing fancy. I want a future with you, whatever that looks like. Anything and everything you're willing to give me, I. Fucking. Want. It."

Her eyes shine with emotion as she smiles up at me, her earlier sadness melting away. "I want you to have all of me, Sterling Abbot, every single drop."

She leans in and kisses me then, moving her lips against mine in a way that sets my heart soaring, and before I know it, the covers are pushed away and our towels are on the floor as we come together—body, mind, and soul—two hearts finally beating as one.

"DO YOU HAVE EVERYTHING PACKED?" I holler to Stella from my room.

"I think so," she grunts back, her voice strained.

Curious, I wander into her room, only to find her kneeling over a duffel bag, squeezing it together with her knees as she tries to force the zipper closed.

"Um, how much do you need for an overnight trip?"

She glares up at me, and I have to cover my smile with my hands.

"Emmy, there's no such thing as being too prepared."

"Okay, Park Ranger Stella, is there anything useful in that besides clothes?"

"Don't knock your mouth. There's also snacks, drinks, sunblock, bug spray. I even brought some Oreos. But if you want to complain, I guess I'll take them out to make room."

I hold my hands up in surrender. "Let's not make any hasty decisions."

We both laugh, knowing good and well if she took the Oreos out of her bag, they'd only end up in mine.

"It sucks we can't ride together." She looks at me with big, puppy dog eyes.

"Yeah, it does."

"Damn Sterling and his two-seater car." She knocks her shoulder into mine. "You'd think with all that money he could afford a back seat."

"Oh my God, you're such a mess."

"I'm delightful."

"A delightful mess," I deadpan before busting out laughing.

"What time is he supposed to be here?"

"Should be any minute." I check the time on my phone, and, sure enough, there's a knock at the door.

Except when I open the door, it's not Sterling waiting on the other side.

"Do you need something?" Stella asks, all sass, as our RA cranes her neck, trying to peek into our suite, looking for God only knows what.

"Just stopping by to check on things, ladies." While her words are typical, her tone is caustic.

"Are you ever gonna give this a rest?" I ask, beyond exasperated with her antics.

"Give what a rest?" She cuts her eyes at me, and Stella throws her hands in the air.

"You know exactly what she's talking about. Stalking isn't a good color on you and neither is petty."

Melanie glowers. "I can make y'all's lives very hard here, so tread carefully, ladies."

"Did I just hear you threaten my girlfriend?" Sterling asks from behind her. It's been two weeks since we made it official, and my heart still flutters every time I hear that word.

"And her best friend," Stella grumbles.

"Oh, Sterling." Melanie bats her lashes, her personality switching in an instant. "It's *so* good to see you."

Sterling looks down his nose at her. "I can't say the same."

Melanie rolls her eyes and swats at his chest like he's joking. "You're so funny."

He takes a step back, and she tries to follow. "Melanie, enough is enough. This has to stop."

"I don't know what you're talking about," she whines, trying to deny any wrongdoing. "She started it!"

"I didn't start anything!" I shout, my temper getting the better of me.

"When he comes to his senses and leaves you, I hope you know he'll come crawling back to me." Melanie flips her hair, like she's hot shit, once again focusing her gaze on Sterling.

I go to reply, but he steps around her, placing himself between us, creating a buffer with his body. "Melanie, I need you to listen to me, and I need you to listen carefully." She nods eagerly, like a puppy begging for scraps. "There is no us. There has never been an us and there never will be. What you're doing is considered harassment, and if you don't leave Emmalyn and Stella alone, you will force my hand in pursuing this with the dean."

She tries to laugh, like he's joking, but we all know he isn't.

Before she can say anything else, Sterling turns around to face me, clearly dismissing her. "Are you ready to go, baby?"

"Yup." I pass him my bag and turn to Stella. "I'll see you there. What time is Gabe coming to pick you up?"

"Oh, he texted me five minutes ago that he was waiting outside, but I wasn't packed yet."

"Well, then let's go," I say, and together all three of us head downstairs, blatantly ignoring a fuming Melanie as we all file past her.

"EXACTLY HOW FAR AWAY IS THE campsite?" Stella asks, looking apprehensively at the woods in front of us.

"Not that far, princess," Gabe replies with a deep, masculine chuckle.

"Listen, you outdoorsy giant, camping is not my thing, but I'm here and I'm making the best of it."

Gabe grins, pleased he was able to get a response out of her. The two of them realized quickly they could rile one another up within seconds and have been playfully at each other's throats ever since.

"Retract your claws, kitten," Zach says, slinging his arm around Stella's shoulders. "You know Gabe can't help himself. Every now and then he has to prove how big and manly he is."

Gabe puffs out his chest. "I'll show you big and manly."

Zach's eyes widen and he licks his lips. "You don't have to prove anything to me, babe."

"And that's enough of that," Sterling says, approaching our little group with both of our backpacks slung over his shoulder. "Let's go."

We hike about a mile through the woods, down a well-marked trail, until we come to a circular clearing. The guys immediately set to work pitching our tents while Stella and I gather wood for a fire. Ever the gentleman, Sterling sets up Stella's for her as well.

"Are you sure about sleeping out here?" she asks, glancing around like a bear's going to pop out and gobble us up.

"We're gonna be fine, Stell."

"Says you! You and Sterling get to share a tent together, and Zach and Gabe have their tent together. Where does that leave me?" She throws her hands in the air. "Bait! That leaves me as bait!"

"I'll sleep with you, and Sterling can sleep alone."

Judging from the pained sound Sterling makes, he must've overheard me and is not a fan of the decision, but I know he won't fight me on it because my happiness means more to him than a night of sleeping alone.

After our camp is set up, Stella asks, "Okay, so who brought food?"

I snicker, knowing that she has an entire pantry of snacks in her bag.

Gabe looks back at her with comically wide eyes. "What do you mean *brought* food?"

Stella tilts her head to the side. "You know, that stuff you eat?"

Sterling moves in closer behind me, bringing his lips to my ear and whispers, "You've got something I want to eat."

I elbow him in the ribs, but I'm laughing.

Gabe continues giving Stella a blank look, somehow keeping a straight face as he says, "I thought we were gonna like hunt and gather...you know, everyone gets their own food."

"Like on those TV shows," Zach says, catching on to his boyfriend's plan. He begins pulling his shirt over his head. "You know, like *Naked and Afraid!*"

Stella's cheeks blush brightly at the sight of Zach's abs. "You stop right there!" she shouts, but it's no use.

Gabe joins in and whips his shirt off as well, despite the fact that it's cold outside. "What's wrong, Stella? You don't want to play with us?"

My best friend is now the color of a tomato, and if I know her like I think I do, she's wishing the ground would swallow her whole.

Finally, I can't take watching her be tortured any longer. "Y'all leave her alone."

"Spoilsport." Gabe rolls his eyes, but he's smiling. "I brought the stuff to roast hot dogs over the fire."

"And s'mores," Zach pipes up.

"Thank God. How long until we eat?"

"Girl, we just got here. Slow your roll, enjoy the fresh air."

Stella huffs, causing both Gabe and Zach to laugh.

"You really don't like nature, do you?" Gabe asks.

"I like nature just fine, thank you very much. I just happen to prefer it to be on the TV screen."

"Okay, city girl. Think you can handle a hike?"

Stella tilts her chin defiantly. "Of course I can!"

"All right, let's go."

The three of them immediately set off toward one of the trails while Sterling and I hang back a little. "Are you sure this is a good idea?" he asks, his voice strained. God love him, while Stella has grown on him, he's still getting used to spending time with Gabe and Zach. But he's friendly...for the most part.

"I'm sure everything will be fine."

"Remind me why your friends came with us?"

"Because I wanted to do this, and those three are the best friends a girl could ever ask for. Simple as that. Plus, I don't think you get to complain, Ster. You bullied me just because your friend wanted you to. My friends, on the other hand, come camping with me."

A resigned sigh leaves his lips. "Touché, little mouse, touché."

"Now, let's go." I start walking after the others.

"Okay, but first—" He snags my hand and pulls me back into him, pressing his lips to mine in a sudden but passionate kiss.

But before it can heat up too much, Gabe interrupts us. "Come on, lovebirds!" he shouts from the tree line.

"So," Sterling hedges, drawing out the word. "Are we gonna talk about that nickname you just called me?"

"What nickname?"

"You called me Ster."

"Oh. It just slipped out."

"I like it."

I link my arm with his and rest my head on his shoulder as we approach my friends. "Good."

"I've camped here before," Gabe says, "and if we take this path, there's a really beautiful waterfall."

We all nod our agreement, and Gabe leads the way. We talk and bicker collectively as a group, generally just having a good time as we traipse down the trail.

The nature all around us is so serene and beautiful, so untouched and untroubled by the modern world, that it gives me pause. It makes me really stop and think about where I am and who I am...and who I want to be.

As always, Sterling is totally tuned into me and notices the change in my attitude. "What's on your mind, little mouse?"

"Just thinking about life." I shrug.

"Talk to me," he urges, his voice low, meant only for me.

"Just thinking about the future, I guess."

He grins. "Am I a part of that future?"

My heart soars in my chest, as it does every time he mentions a future between the two of us. "I hope so," I tell him honestly.

"I do, too, because, Emmalyn, you're mine."

I bite my lip to stop myself from smiling at his cocky alpha tendencies. "I am yours, for as long as you'll have me."

"Settle in for the long haul, baby."

"It should be just up here on the left!" Gabe hollers, bringing both Sterling and me back into the moment.

We hear the waterfall before we see it; the sound of rushing water is louder than I ever could have imagined.

"Oh, wow! It's beautiful," Stella murmurs, awe evident in her voice.

Zach wraps an arm around her slim shoulders. "Better than television?"

"Holy shit, one hundred percent. I would literally get married here if I could."

"There's an idea," Gabe says. "Who knows, maybe I'll get ordained just so I can officiate."

She laughs. "You're just extra enough to do it."

"Birds of a feather..."

"Are you calling me extra?"

"Babe, you're the definition," I say, coming to stand beside her.

Together, we peer over the rail, to where the fall crashes into a pool below, sending spray into the air.

She smiles. "Yeah, I am. Now, let's take a selfie."

We take turns snapping pictures in front of the waterfall before finally heading back toward camp.

"WERE YOU A BOY SCOUT?" Stella asks, teasing Gabe as we all stand around the fire roasting our hot dogs.

"For fifteen years."

She giggles. "That explains *so* much."

"Not quite sure what you're trying to insinuate, but there's absolutely nothing wrong with being a scout. They taught me a lot of invaluable lessons."

"Don't get your panties in a bunch, Gabriel. I'm only teasing."

"I'll show you teasing." He tosses his roasting stick down, hot dog and all, and charges toward her.

Stella screeches and throws her stick to the ground as well, breaking out into a run. She squeals as he gains on her, the two of them playing their own demented game of duck-duck-goose.

"You take it back!" he shouts.

"Take what back?" She stumbles a little but keeps going.

It's obvious Gabe's not really trying to catch her; not that you'd know it from the way Stella's running. She's like a chicken with her head cut off, flapping her wings as she sprints circles around the campfire.

"Take back that I have my panties in a twist. I don't wear panties, Stella!"

Gabe's face reflects the humor we're all feeling as we crack up at their antics. That is, until Stella trips and goes down hard.

"Ouch!" she wails, and we all rush to check on her.

"Are you okay?" I ask.

"No! It hurts. God, it hurts." She clutches her ankle as she rolls to her side, tears welling in her eyes.

"What do we do?" I ask, feeling helpless.

"Let's try and stand you up," Gabe says.

"No." Zach tugs his boyfriend back. "We need to check her ankle first."

Gabe nods and kneels next to her, letting Zach take over.

"Can you rotate it?"

Stella tries and cries out, her pain so apparent that I swear I feel it, too. "N-not really."

"What about your toes—can you wiggle your toes?"

Again she cries out, her chest heaving with the effort.

"Okay. Shit. Let's get you up and see if you can put any weight on it."

Gabe scrambles to help her to stand, but the second she tries to put weight on it, she immediately crumples.

Luckily Zach catches her before she hits the ground.

I take her hand in mine, trying to comfort her. "I hate to say it, but I think you need to go to the hospital."

"But then I'll ruin your camping trip!"

"Stell, we can camp anytime. You getting to a doctor is way more important."

"Why don't you and Sterling stay and we will take her?" Gabe offers.

"Are you sure?" It feels weird to stay while she's hurt. But Sterling, Zach, and Gabe all nod.

I turn back to Stella, because right now her opinion is the only one that matters.

"Babe. Stay and have a good time. I know this is something you've been wanting to do, and it'll be too cold pretty soon."

"Are you sure?"

"Positive." She tries to smile, but it's more of a wince. "Bright side, now there's no worry over who sleeps where. It'll just be you two out here."

"Jesus, Stell. You didn't have to break your ankle to avoid sleeping alone."

She shrugs and immediately hisses in discomfort. "Like Gabe said, I'm extra."

"Let's see if I can stabilize your ankle," Zach says, grabbing two sticks and a T-shirt. He rips the shirt into three strips and sets to work while the rest of us pack up their things.

We help them back to the parking lot. "Text me updates. And if you decide you want me with you, just let me know and I'll be there. Okay?"

"Don't worry about me, babe. Go have fun with your man."

"Emmy, why don't you and Zach help Stella into the car?" Sterling says.

He's clearly up to something, but I go along with it, rushing ahead of them to pull open the door.

"You take care of her," Gabe says, his attention focused on Sterling. I'm not sure he means for us to hear him, but the wind carries his words to us loud and clear.

"She's in good hands," Sterling replies, his voice as stiff as his posture.

"You know, a month ago I would have trusted wild dogs more than you."

Sterling smirks, not rising to Gabe's bait.

"But now...as much as it pains me to admit this...you're good for her."

"You're goddamn right I am."

"So swoony," Stella sighs, her head lolling back against the seat back.

"Text me," I remind her before shutting the door.

Gabe breaks away from Sterling and I hug both him and Zach bye, much to Sterling's displeasure.

"Ready, baby?" he asks.

I smile up at him, my heart torn between excitement over a night beneath the stars with him and worry over my best friend.

"Ready."

"DID YOU GET ENOUGH TO EAT?" I ask Emmalyn, knowing her mind is a million miles away. She's worried about her friend, and it pains me that her camping trip has been derailed, though I'm not sorry to have her to myself.

"Yeah, I think so."

"You tell me if you get hungry. I brought snacks."

She cracks a smile. "So did Stella. I'm pretty sure half her bag was—"

"That must be why it was so heavy when I carried it to the—"

"I hope she's okay." The worry in her voice gnaws at my heart.

"She will be, baby. It's probably just a bad sprain."

"I know, I do, but I can't help feeling guilty. I'm the reason we were even out here."

"Don't do that. Don't place blame on yourself when there's no reason for it."

Her slim fingers slur. "Logically I know that, but..."

I pull her off the couch she's sitting on and onto my lap. "I know, baby, but the heart isn't very logical."

"Tell me something," she says, "take my mind off of it."

"Hmm. I could tell you that I love you."

She snuggles closer to me, pressing her cheek to my chest. "Tell me something I don't already know."

Here goes nothing... "I told my parents about us."

She sucks in a sharp breath and tries to pull back from me. I tighten my hold, forcing her to stay put. "You did what? My God, Sterling, why? Your parents hate me!"

"That's not true." And really, it's not. They don't feel any certain way about her at all. "They just love money. Well, my dad does. But yeah, I told them about you, and I told them that we needed to have a long talk about a lot of things. They were both receptive to the idea."

"Really?" I can't discern where her mind's at from her tone.

"I know it's easy to think that because they're both lawyers that they are both callous assholes. But really, they're not. Not in their personal life, anyway. They're just way too good at their jobs."

"I guess that makes sense, but I'm still nervous."

"Well then, why don't we go check out the inside of our tent and see if I can't ease your nerves?"

"Really?" she asks, sounding far more eager than anxious.

"Would I ever lie about wanting to make you feel good?"

The firelight illuminates the pretty blush staining her cheeks. "Okay." She wiggles free from my hold and stands. "Let's go."

Emmalyn turns and heads toward the tent, surprising the hell out of me when she pulls her shirt off and lets it drop to the ground halfway there. I'm frozen, raptly watching as her pants quickly follow.

"Don't tease me," I warn.

She pauses right outside of our tent and turns to look at me over her shoulder. "Who's teasing who, Ster? You promised me a good time, and here I am heading to bed all alone."

Over the last two weeks, Emmy's definitely gotten braver sexually, but this little vixen before me has me staring slack-jawed.

"Seriously, are you coming or not?"

"We both are, if I have anything to say about it," I mutter, as I spring up from my chair and take off after her.

With a delighted squeal, she darts into the tent. I can hear her rustling around inside—hopefully ditching the rest of her clothes—but I stop on my way to grab her discarded clothing before quickly shucking mine off and joining her.

"Took you long enough," she says with a coy smile.

"Didn't mean to keep you waiting." My eyes rove over her naked body hungrily.

"I'm sure you can make up for it." She reclines back onto the mound of sleeping bags, propping herself up on her elbow. Her pose is casual, effortlessly sexy in a way that is wholly unique to Emmy.

"Oh, I'm sure I can."

"What are you waiting for?" This playful side of her is my favorite.

"For you to spread those sexy legs." My voice is a growl as the predator in me surges to the surface.

Emmalyn's eyes widen and her cheeks go scarlet, but she complies, lying flat and hooking her hands beneath her knees, pulling her legs wide and bearing herself to me.

The soft skin of her thighs is slick with her arousal, and I can hardly restrain myself from diving down for a taste.

"So damn beautiful." I kiss her ankle and then her calf

before switching to the other leg, dragging my lips from her knee all the way up to her thigh. "So damn tempting."

I skim my mouth up and over, pressing a searing hot kiss to her pussy lips. She sighs and her back arches.

"So damn mine."

"Your mouth," she moans.

"What about it?"

"I love it."

"Tell me what you love," I demand before darting my tongue inside and then licking all the way up to her clit.

"I...I, oh!" She loses her train of thought as I slide my middle finger inside while simultaneously sucking her clit into my mouth.

"Oh, God. Ster. Fuck!"

Her soft pleading sounds have me grinding my erection into the pallet beneath us, searching for friction of my own.

I want inside of her more than I've ever wanted anything else, but I'm not moving from this spot until her release is dripping down my chin.

Emmy doesn't make me wait long.

A mixture of moans and praises fall from her lips as I figure-eight my tongue over her clit. She's so close I can feel it. I curl my finger inside of her, stroking her sweet spot.

She detonates, her chest heaving and legs shaking as she wails my name.

Before she's even finished coming, I'm on my knees, sliding on a condom, and guiding myself inside of her. She clenches around me, and my back bows from the mind-blowing pleasure.

"Fuck, baby, yes," I encourage her as she begins to meet my thrusts.

She's beyond words as she once again dances on the

edge of release. I'm right there with her, ready to topple over. "Come for me, Emmy. Come so I can."

She cries out and I lean down, drawing her nipple into my mouth while also applying pressure to that little bundle of nerves.

Like a fucking landslide, we crash furiously over the edge together into oblivion.

"TWIRL," Stella says, and I move back into the line of sight of my computer camera. I spin a little circle, and the skirt of my black dress flares out around me. "Yes! That's definitely it."

"Are you sure it's not too short? It's pretty cold outside."

"Keyword: outside. You will be inside with like a hundred other people. It's going to be hot."

"I guess you're right."

My best friend laughs. She's always right. *Ugh.* I wish I was there so I could help you get ready. And so I could go with you. This is basically the biggest party of the year."

"I wish you were there, too, but you wouldn't want to miss your parents' twentieth anniversary dinner, would you?"

"Right now? The answer is yes, I would."

We both laugh.

"Okay, I better get going. I need to go help Mom chop vegetables for the salad."

"She's making the salad?"

"Oh, girl, yes, the salad for everything. I'll have to bring you over for dinner one night. Mom's food will blow your mind."

"Any home-cooked meal will blow my mind. I grew up eating food made by our chef or the highly talented Marie Callender."

Stella gives me a sad look before masking it with a smile. "Talk later, babe." She ends the call, and I close my laptop.

A swipe of berry-tinted lip gloss and a spritz of hairspray later, and I'm ready to go. I fire off a text to Sterling to see how far out he is. I don't want to wait out in the cold, and I damn sure don't want to wait in the lobby and risk a Melanie run-in.

ME

How long until you're here?

STERLING

Waiting out front, baby.

I head downstairs to meet Sterling, and sure enough, he's waiting in front of my building. Dressed in a pair of dark wash jeans and a form-fitting sweater, he looks like a freaking model as he leans back against the passenger door.

He lets out a wolf whistle when he sees me, his eyes moving up and down my body.

"Can't wait to get that dress off of you later," he says as soon as I'm within hearing distance.

I roll my eyes and nudge him out of the way so I can get in the car. "Come on, let's get this over with."

He laughs. "Don't sound so excited."

"Hey, I'm trying. Parties just aren't my thing."

"Do you want to stay home?"

"No, it's fine. Let's go."

"Okay... If you're sure?"

"I'm sure. Plus, I think Stella might actually murder me if I don't go and give her a play-by-play report since she has to miss it."

He puts the car in drive, and within minutes we reach our destination. This house is somehow even grander than the football house. It's old and ornate looking, save for the plastic cups and dry-humping couples scattered about the lawn.

Inside it's like every other party I've been to this year—the drinks are flowing, the bass is pounding, and people are making questionable decisions on every available surface in every room.

"What do you want to do first?" Sterling asks.

"Consider yourself my tour guide for the night."

He winks. "First up, something to drink. Nonalcoholic for you, of course."

"I could probably handle one drink." For some reason, I feel keyed up. Maybe a few sips of liquid courage will be just what I need to take the edge off.

"Are you sure? Don't feel pressured, baby."

"No, I think I'm okay. I really would like a drink."

"Then to the kitchen we go!"

I wait patiently near the edge of the room while he mixes us each a drink. Knowing him, he'll most likely be light-handed with mine. I think he still has some residual guilt for feeding me alcohol at the last party we attended together. And while it was a shitty thing for him to do, at least it had a happy ending.

"Slut."

Great. I was hoping to avoid her tonight. Still, I pivot around to face her.

"Melanie." Surprisingly, Summer is also with her.

"Nice to see y'all," I say, employing the years of etiquette classes my mother insisted I take.

"Everyone's going to know the truth about you," my RA hisses, sounding like a drunk snake.

"Can we not do this? Please. Let's call a truce, just for tonight."

Summer laughs. "Oh, wait, you were being serious?"

I nod, hoping they'll agree.

"Yeah, no." Both women cackle. "Good luck tonight."

"Good luck with what?" I ask, but they both turn and flounce away.

"Miss me?" Sterling asks, and I whirl back toward the kitchen in time for him to drop a kiss to my cheek before passing me my drink.

I sip from it, determined to put Melanie and Summer's strange behavior out of my mind. "Mmm, fruity."

"How about we take these to-go and head to the dance floor?"

I down the rest of my drink along the way, abandoning my cup on a table before Sterling pulls me into the throng of dancers.

The tempo of the music is sensuous and the rhythm heavy as we rock our hips together, swaying in time to the beat. We stay that way, in our little cocoon, dancing for several songs, before I announce that I need a break.

"Oh, look!" I point toward the far side of the room. "There's Gabe and Zach. Wanna go say hi?"

"You go ahead, baby. I'll wait here."

He swears he's not, but I think he's still salty about me wearing Gabe's name. Regardless, at least they don't hate each other. That would be miserable.

"Gabe! Zach!" I rush up to them and they squish me between them in a bear hug.

"Where's Stella?" Zach asks.

"Anniversary dinner for her parents," I inform him.

Suddenly my ears heat and my skin prickles. I glance up, expecting to find Sterling looking my way, but he's right where I left him, messing with his phone. *Weird,* I think, shaking off the odd sensation.

"Oh, man, that was tonight?" Gabe says.

"I know, it sucks. She's really bummed."

Gabe snaps his fingers. "We one-hundred-percent need to send her a selfie."

The three of us pose, our cheeks squished together with smiles on our faces. Gabe sends her the picture, chuckling evilly.

"If that doesn't set her FOMO off, I don't know what will," Zach says.

Gabe's phone dings almost instantly. "Guess we're about to find out," he says as he whips it up to his face to look at her response.

He swallows roughly, glancing from his screen to me. "Um, Emmy."

"What?" I ask, his tone setting me on edge.

Before he can answer, Zach's phone pings.

"Jesus-fucking-Christ," he mutters, looking like he's going to be sick.

"Guys, y'all are freaking me out."

"You need to get out of here, Emmy. You need to leave and go straight home."

"What?" I ask, my eyes prickling with unshed tears. "Why?"

"Just go, Emmy!" Gabe snaps, turning and stomping off to God knows where.

I sniffle, turning to look for Sterling so I can ask him to take me home. I don't know what I did to suddenly make

Gabe mad, but I clearly did something.

Frantically, I move through the crowd, looking for Sterling, but he's nowhere to be found.

I reach for my phone, but then remember it's in his car. It's not like this dress has pockets.

"Hey, baby," an unfamiliar voice calls out as I pass.

"What?"

"Wanna go upstairs? My cell has a great camera."

"No. Oh my God. No!" I shove away from him, only to be jostled into another leering face.

"I'll fuck your mouth any day!"

I reel back, the panic washing over me as people move closer. It feels like everyone is looking at me, laughing at me, mocking me. Some have pity in their eyes, while others size me up like they know exactly what's under my dress.

It feels like I'm in a waking nightmare.

"Come on, Emmy," Zach murmurs, alerting me to the fact that he's still with me. "Let's get you out of here."

"What's going on?" I ask, on the verge of tears. "Why's everyone looking at their phones?"

"Fuck!" Zach pinches the bridge of his nose. "Come on."

It's too much. I sway on my feet, thankful I wore boots and not the heels Stella claimed I needed. "Sterling..." I whimper his name.

"I'll find him," Zach says, alerting me to the fact that he didn't storm off with his boyfriend.

Finally, I see him, but before I can make it to him, the music gets cut and a familiar voice crackles over the PA system.

My voice. It's *my* voice.

"*You won't break me.*" I hear myself say as sounds of sex fill the room.

Filthy sounds.

Animalistic grunts and pleading groans. The sound of skin slapping skin.

"I'm so close. Oh, God, please."

My gut churns and bile crawls up my throat at the sound of my begging.

I don't even realize I'm crying until the tears dripping from my chin splash against my chest.

My heart races and my legs shake as the obviously and poorly edited sound clip plays.

I spin, looking for the nearest exit, only to find something so horrific, it renders me immobile.

On the far wall, there's a projection screen, with my very own and very non-consensual porno playing for all to see.

It feels like everything is closing in around me, and for the first time since Rob raped me, I feel like I want to die.

It's too much. Everything's too much.

My watery gaze clashes with Sterling's from across the room. He looks stricken, but I know better than most just how deceiving looks can be.

He said he wanted to break me.

His words from the first week of class bombard me, crashing into me so hard I nearly collapse to the floor.

"Poor little Princess Price. So eager to ruin the lives of others but whimpers and whines when she's paid back in kind."

That's what this is. That's what this has always been.

Payback.

Oh my God. How stupid could I be?

My throat constricts as I try desperately to suck in much needed air, but it's no use. Even my body is turning on me.

He told me. Sterling told me, again and again, and like the stupid little girl I am, I didn't listen.

He played me.

A handful of weeks of being nice and I was eating out of his palm, falling in love with him and letting him into my bed...into my body. Only for him to betray me in the worst way.

He's nearly to me when Melanie steps in front of him, blocking his path. He leans in as she speaks to him, and that's all the confirmation I need.

I was nothing to him. A sweet little nothing. This was all a ploy.

With ice in my heart and a sinking emptiness in my gut, I turn and flee.

"Emmy!" Zach calls after me, but I don't turn back. I just run.

I run through the crowd, out the door, and down the street.

I run and I run and I run, blind from tears and locked in my head.

I run until I'm safely back inside my dorm. Once inside I lock the door and shove the coffee table in front of it.

Pain unlike anything I've ever known lances through me, piercing what's left of my tattered, barely beating heart.

There isn't a single cell of my body that doesn't ache.

It's the kind of hurt that pierces your skin and sinks into your veins, your bones, your fucking soul. It's the kind of pain that eats away at you like poison, consuming all of the good within you until all that's left is a shell.

I stumble, tripping over my own feet as I cross the living room. "Stupid, so stupid," I mutter, righting myself. I flip on the lights as I enter my bathroom, recoiling at the bright light. God, even my eyes hurt.

I guess crying as hard as I have will do that, huh?

My fingers tangle in my now limp and dirty hair. I

wince as I tug on the ends, my past and my present colliding in my mind, morphing into a single mangled nightmare.

"Stop, stop, stop!" I plea, the words a garbled cry to the universe. I want it all to go away, for the memories of then and the horrors of now to all stop. But I learned long ago there's no one out there listening. Not for me, anyway. My own mother didn't even have time to hear my story.

"Not enough." I pivot in a wide circle, clipping my hip on the vanity. "Never enough. Stupid!"

Tears cloud my vision as I struggle to breathe. I want... *I need* the pain to stop. For my past to stop haunting me. For the taunts and leers to go away.

I'm a top spinning out of control, desperate for someone —*anyone*—to save me from the path my own self-loathing is shoving me down. If I'd have been stronger—*smarter*—none of this would've happened to me.

My breaths heave in and out of my lungs as a humorless laugh slips past my trembling lips. God knows, there's not a single person on this planet who cares enough to try and pull me from the murky depths of my misery. *If anything, they'd press their boots to the back of my head and hold me under.*

My hands shake as I press down on the lid, pushing to the right.

"Dammit!" I cry as the orange bottle slips and my blessed relief falls to the floor. The tablets scatter and roll around my feet as I fall to my knees in a desperate attempt to gather them.

With one hand clutching pills, I grip the edge of the vanity and pull myself back to standing with the other. The reflection staring back at me is the face of a stranger. She looks like me, but different, too. The face in the mirror is how I feel inside—worthless...empty...hollow.

Already gone.

I watch as she raises her hand and jams the pills into her mouth. The plasticky outer-coating quickly gives way to a bitter taste. Her face puckers, and so does mine.

She is me, but she's more than me. She's all of my hurt and bitterness and suffering personified. She's the part of me that's broken beyond repair—used up and dirty, unwanted and unloved. She's the voice urging me to end it all. I've fought her for so long, but now, my fight is gone.

AFTER DANCING WITH EMMY, her body so close, grinding against mine, I want nothing more than to find us somewhere private and dance.

Or better yet, leave.

But I dragged us here, so I might as well see it through. Although, I'm not even sure why I wanted us to come, other than it being part of that tradition.

"Oh, look. There's Gabe and Zach." I look to where she's pointing and see standing head and giant in the crowd. "Want to say hi?"

My phone buzzes in my pocket for the fifth time in as many minutes. "You go ahead of me. I'll wait here," I tell her, keeping my eyes trained on her until she makes it across the room to her friends.

The moment her back is to me and I look away, sliding my phone from my pocket already knowing who it is. Foolishly, I thought ignoring his messages would be enough.

UNKNOWN

You brought her to bed... and now you can
both lie in it.

UNKNOWN

She stained my sheets red when I choked
her, and she turned blue. You took what's
mine, now I'm coming for you.

Jesus Christ. He's actually lost his mind.

UNKNOWN

Don't fucking ignore me, Sterling. You
owe me.

UNKNOWN

You took from me. You lied to me. What
happens next is on you.

UNKNOWN

You have received a video message, tap to
play.

I know I shouldn't click the link. I fucking know I shouldn't, but I do.

Anger, bright and hot, burns through me as Emmalyn's body fills my screen. I close the link before the sound can start, my body practically vibrating in rage.

My anger turns to dread as all around me people start checking their phones, nudging the person next to them and sharing their screen.

That dread turns to panic as the guy next to me shows me his screen, confirming my worst fears: the link wasn't only sent to me, it was sent to everyone.

Every single person at this party is now watching what should have been a beautiful and *private* moment, and to make matters worse, the fucker edited the video to paint my

Emmy in the worst light, showing all of her and hardly any of me.

My brain can't even begin to comprehend how Rob pulled this off, but I fucking know it was him, and there will be hell to pay.

"Fuck. Fuck. Fuck!" I yell, causing several heads to turn my way.

I search for her, but she's not with Gabe and Zach anymore. Or, if she is, they aren't where they were.

Finally, after what feels like an eternity, I spot her. Except, before I can get to her, the music cuts out and the sounds of sex—our sex—blast from the speakers.

She stands frozen, with tears dripping from her chin. Her entire body is shaking like a leaf, and Gabe and Zach are nowhere in sight.

My vision goes red as people shout and leer at her; a few even try to touch her, and I commit their faces to memory, fully prepared to make them pay later, once I know she's okay.

I start shoving my way through the crowd, determined to make it to her, to explain, to save her.

She turns to flee, and like time itself has slowed down, we both notice the movie playing on a giant projector screen at the same time.

We're both frozen as our gazes meet. She looks so hurt, so broken, so utterly betrayed that, in this moment, I hate myself.

"Get the fuck out of my way!" I roar to the idiots blocking my path.

I don't make it more than two steps before Melanie and Summer stop me.

Melanie bats her eyes as she nods toward the screen. "I told you so."

It's then I realize, that somehow, these two were in on this.

"I will fucking ruin you," I sneer, leaning in close to make sure she hears every word, as well as the promise behind them.

When I look back to Emmy, she has this dead, vacant look in her eyes, and it instantly sets me on edge. But before I can make it to her, she turns and runs.

I feel like the biggest piece of shit on earth as I run after her, now violently shoving party-goers out of my way. Because, deep down, I know this is my fault.

If I wouldn't have agreed to help Rob, this wouldn't be happening. I told her I would protect her, and yet, I basically led her to slaughter.

I'm nearly to the door when Gabe steps into my path. Before I can get a single word out, his fist flies toward my face, crunching against my cheekbone on impact. "You sorry ass motherfucker! I told you! I told you I would kill you if you hurt her!"

I shake my head, despite the pain ricocheting through my skull. "It wasn't me! This isn't me."

"That's not you in that video?" he asks, even though we both already know the answer.

"That's me, but I'm not behind this."

"How convenient."

"Look, you can either help me find her or you can get the fuck out of my way."

Gabe looks ready to hit me again, but before he can, Zach appears out of nowhere and steps between us.

"Stop. Both of you, stop. Y'all can fight later, but right now we need to find Emmy."

"Fuck." Gabe scrubs a hand over his face. "You're right."

"Let's go. Gabe, you check with Stella. I'll look on campus, and, Sterling, you check her dorm."

"You trust him to go there?" Gabe demands.

"I do," is all Zach says. "Now let's go."

We split up, going our separate ways, agreeing to check in every fifteen minutes.

I haul ass to my car, flinging open the driver's side door and slamming myself into the seat. "Why the fuck is the light on?" I mutter, mashing the start button. Only, nothing happens.

I jab my fingers into it again and again, my foot pressing the brake so hard it feels like it might punch straight through the floorboard.

But still, my engine doesn't start.

"Stupid fucking battery." It feels like the entire universe is conspiring against me.

I throw my door back open and grab my phone. I start to call Emmalyn, but see her phone sitting in my cup holder. My shoulders slump and defeat sits heavy on my chest. But I won't give up. Not on her, not ever.

I pull up the Uber app, but it's peak hours, and I don't have that kind of time to wait.

The drive here was about fifteen minutes, so maybe thirty on foot. I don't even think twice; I just start running. I would fucking crawl over hot coals if that's what it took to get to her right now.

By the time I reach her building, I'm a panting, sweaty mess, despite the chill in the air. My legs feel like jelly and my heart is like it's on the verge of stalling out.

I bang on the door before slamming my hand down onto the buzzer. "Geez, what's the—Sterling, are you okay?" asks Abigail, the redhead from the gym.

"Emmalyn. I need Emmalyn."

She eyes me curiously, more questions on the tip of her tongue, but I don't have time to waste. I have a gut feeling she's here.

I shove past her, bypassing the elevator, heading straight for the stairs.

"What's going on?" she asks, huffing as she struggles to keep up.

I beat on her door so hard my fist aches. "Emmalyn!"

"Sterling, this is...you can't do this. What is going on?"

"Emmalyn!" I try the knob. Locked.

I pound even harder, barely pausing to think through the consequences of my actions, before slamming my shoulder into the door.

Abigail screams as the wood splinters. I try to shove the door open, but something's blocking me. Which means she's here. She's fucking *here*.

I kick my foot into the small space between the door and jamb and make contact with something hard. A few more kicks, and I manage to move whatever she blocked the door with out of the way.

I step into the dark space and flip the lights on, still shouting her name. Abigail checks the bedrooms while I head for the bathroom.

What I see stops me in my tracks, my heart lodging into my throat, choking me as grief and guilt rain down on me.

"Oh my God. Baby!" I drop to my knees and pull her limp body to me, cradling her head in my lap. "Baby!" I press two fingers to her throat and shout for Abigail. "Call 911!"

She flies into the room, her phone already pressed to her ear. "Help, please help. One of the girls in my dorm... I think... she overdosed." Her words are rapid fire as panic consumes her, just as it is me.

"Put it on speaker," I order, and she does.

"I need you to calm down," the dispatcher says in a mild voice. "Is she breathing?"

"Yes, barely."

"Conscious?"

"No."

"Do you know what she took, sir?"

"No, I don't. I don't know."

Abigail rattles off the address, before collapsing to the floor beside me where she buries her face in her hands and cries.

Seconds feel like minutes and minutes like hours while we wait. "What's taking them so long?"

My entire body shakes as the woman I love slips further away from me, succumbing to whatever it was she took.

"Campus police!"

"In the bathroom!" I yell.

"Sir, please move away so we can work."

"I'm not leaving her," I grit out through clenched teeth.

"We need you to move back," he reiterates. "It's in her best interest, we're trained first responders."

At those words, I gently slide out from beneath her and retreat to just outside the door with Abigail.

The other officer immediately springs into action, crossing Emmy's arms over her chest and rolling her to her side.

"Do you know what she took?"

"No."

"Do you know when?"

"I don't know. An hour? Maybe?"

"Does she have a history of mental health issues?"

"Yes," I admit, feeling like I'm somehow betraying her.

"A history of suicidal thoughts?"

"I'm not sure." I swallow roughly. "She... her stepbrother abused her most of her life and tonight..."

"What happened tonight?"

I rehash the sordid details for the campus police. By the time I'm done, Abigail is sobbing inconsolably. "Oh my God."

"Got a pill bottle!" the officer in the bathroom yells. "Benzos."

"I'll let 'em know."

The officer who has been questioning me reaches up and speaks into the mic clipped to his shirt. "We've got a suspected benzodiazepine overdose."

The radio crackles. "10-4. We're about five out."

The paramedics make it in less than five—*thank fuck*— and from there, it's a flurry of activity, with them checking her vitals and loading her onto a stretcher.

A million-and-one questions sit on the tip of my tongue, but the officer's earlier words about being in the way keep me from asking any of them.

"Let's roll," one of the paramedics says, and I spring into action, following them out into the hall.

"I-I'll clean up here," Abigail says, tears still falling.

I nod my thanks and take off behind them, once again taking the stairs so that I'm on the first floor waiting when the elevator arrives.

"Which hospital are you taking her to?"

"Who are you?"

"Her boyfriend."

"We're taking her to Central North," he says, as the other maneuvers the stretcher into the back of the ambulance.

I try to follow them, but the paramedic stops me with a hand to my chest. "Not so fast."

"Please," I beg.

He offers a sympathetic look. "Sorry, family only."

Those words are an arrow through my already tattered heart.

"Please take care of her," I whisper.

"Let's go," one of the other workers calls.

He gives me a nod before turning and heading for the truck.

As they pull away, I realize I don't have my car. "Fuck!" I yell for what has to be the hundredth time tonight.

I scramble to grab my phone from my pocket, dialing Gabe.

He answers on the first ring. "Did you find her?"

"Yes, but I need you to come pick me up."

"What's going on, Sterling?"

"Just come get me. I'm outside of her dorm."

"I'll be there in five."

I pace back and forth until I hear the sound of squealing tires. I look up just in time to see Gabe's truck jerk to a stop.

Wordlessly, I run and jump into the cab. "Tell Zach to meet us at Central North."

He whips around in his seat, glaring at me. "I'm sorry, what? Why are we going to the hospital?"

Even as he asks, he's shifting the truck into gear.

"She overdosed."

He curses under his breath and peels out of the parking lot. "If anything happens to her, if she doesn't pull through this, I'll fucking kill you."

I want to argue, to plead my case but, deep down I know he's right, so I don't. Instead, I pull my seat belt across my lap and say, "Just hurry, man."

THE DRIVE to the hospital passes in a blur.

Gabe tries to ask me questions, but my mind is completely shut down. All I can think of is the way Emmalyn laid limp in my arms, her breaths so shallow I'm almost convinced I imagined them.

Before I know it, we're pulling up outside the emergency department. "Zach should be here any minute," Gabe says as he swings his truck into a parking space.

I nod to let him know I heard him, and together we exit his truck and head for the double doors beneath the illuminated red cross.

I'm half tempted to storm the desk, but Gabe yanks on the back of my shirt and whispers for me to chill.

"Can I help you?" the nurse asks.

"Has Emmalyn Price been brought in? She came by ambulance."

"Are you family?"

I don't make the same mistake I did with the ambulance. "Yes, her husband."

Gabe nearly chokes on air, garnering him a few strange looks.

The woman behind the desk gives me a soft smile. "She was brought in about ten minutes ago. That's all I can tell you at this time. You fellas can take a seat in the waiting area, I'll do my best to keep you updated."

"Thanks," I say tersely, balling my hands into tight fists by my sides.

"Hopefully the doctor will be out to speak with you soon."

Gabe grabs the back of my shirt and tugs me toward the waiting area.

"Husband?" he asks, as we each drop down into a too-small yellow chair.

The unforgiving plastic bites into my side, another painful reminder of where I am and why I'm here. "Told the paramedics I was her boyfriend and he shut me out."

Gabe nods. "At least you did something smart."

"Listen, I get you're upset—"

"Upset?" Gabe bellows. "Try furious! You're nothing but bad news."

"Listen," I say, my voice deadly calm, despite wanting to shout and rage. "I love her. I. Fucking. Love. Her. We had a fucked-up start and a crooked journey, but she is everything to me. Do you hear me? Everything. And you can blame me all you want, you can hate me all you want, but it'll never be more than I hate myself."

I hunch over, propping my elbows on my knees, burying my head in my hands.

"You love her?" Gabe asks quietly from beside me.

"Yeah, man. I love her."

***

"WHERE IS SHE? What's happening? Is she okay?" Zach demands as he approaches where we're seated.

"We don't know anything yet," Gabe says, opening his arms for his boyfriend.

Zach leans down and pulls him close before releasing him. He then leans over and hugs me, too, shocking the hell out of me.

"So how is it your boyfriend over there punched me and you're hugging me?"

Zach smiles, but it doesn't reach his eyes. "Because he didn't see the look on your face when that video came on for everyone to see. He didn't see how utterly devastated you were. I did. A man doesn't fake a look like that, especially when he doesn't have an audience. Now, what happened?"

"Overdose."

"Damn. I hate to be the bearer of bad news, but it's about to get worse."

I sit upright in my seat. "Why? What do you know?"

"Nothing. It's just... one of us has to call Stella."

"Shit. Not me!" Gabe says. "There's no way I can break my sunshine's heart."

I sigh and pinch the bridge of my nose and then pull my phone from my pocket. "I'll do it," I say, dialing her number.

"Hey, Sterling?"

"Yeah, it's me."

"What's going on?"

"Listen, have you gotten any weird texts tonight?"

"Yeah, how did you know?"

"Did you look at it?"

"No. It came during dinner, and Mom hates phones at the table. Plus, I typically ignore unfamiliar numbers. Why?"

"Okay, good." A fraction of the weight on my chest eases. At least Stella didn't see the video with her own two eyes.

"You're freaking me out."

"There was an accident."

"What kind of accident?" she asks, a wobble to her voice.

"Emmalyn overdosed." The words sound as unfathomable and foreign now as they did the first time I said them.

"What? Wait, what?"

"We don't know anything yet. We're at Central North."

"I'm on my way," she says and the line goes dead.

I slide my phone back into my pocket and lean my head

back against the wall, wondering how tonight went so sideways.

Rob. It all comes back to Rob.

While I'm not exactly spotless, he's the real reason we're here. He's utterly unhinged and is in need of some serious help.

With the way money talks, I doubt he'll ever see any jail time, but I'm damn sure going to push for him to face the consequences of his actions to the fullest extent possible. Be that from a rehab facility, or monetarily, he will pay.

Fifteen minutes later Stella, along with a man I don't know, bursts into the waiting area. "Have you heard from the doctor?"

"Not yet," Gabe says.

Her friend takes a seat but she begins pacing anxiously in front of the row of chairs we've claimed as our own.

Back and forth she paces, well as best she can her walking boot, until the man she brought with her reaches out and grabs her by the shoulder and forcibly seats her down onto his lap.

"Let me up!" She struggles against his hold.

"Sit down, Luna."

"So help me God, if you don't let me up right now—!"

He bands his arms around her, making an X over her chest. "You'll what?"

Before she can reply, a man in a white coat walks out from the double doors behind the desk. He's heading straight for us, and I stand so quickly my chair rattles. "Are you the family of Emmalyn Price?"

"I'm her husband," I say, the lie falling smoothly from my lips.

He nods. "Come with me please."

I follow behind him, back through the double doors he

came out of, down a hall and around a corner, finally stopping outside of a closed door. "How is she?" I ask, unable to wait for him to speak first.

"Stable. We administered charcoal, and she's now stable."

"Is she awake?"

"Sleeping."

"Can I see her?"

"I'd like to ask you a few questions first."

"Yeah." The hope that was growing within me turns to ash. "Of course."

"Does she have any history of mental illness? Has she ever attempted suicide before?"

"Yes, and no." My heart aches for her, knowing she's lying in that bed, alone. What if she wakes up and there's no one with her?

"Elaborate, please."

"She was abused, for years, by a family member," I tell him, proceeding to give him all of the pertinent details. "So, can I see her now?" My voice cracks, but fuck if I have it in me to care.

"Yes, just one last thing."

"What?"

"Once we have a room for her, we will be moving her upstairs and placing her on an involuntary psych hold."

"Seventy-two hours, yeah, I figured."

The doctor eyes me speculatively. "I TA a psych class and she's a psych major."

"Got it." He pushes the door open. "You're welcome to stay with her until they take her upstairs."

"Thanks." I swallow roughly and head into the room.

I pause at the foot of her bed, the sight of her lying there, looking so small and fragile, hooked up to a plethora of monitors and wires, hits me harder than finding her on her bathroom floor.

As gently as possible, I take her hand in mine, careful not to bump the IV line. "Oh, God, baby. I'm sorry. I'm so, so sorry."

She stirs, humming under her breath, but she doesn't wake.

"I love you, Emmalyn. I know I messed up. God, do I. I was supposed to protect you and now look." I shake my head, disgusted at myself for not working harder to keep her safe.

I've known Rob practically forever. I, better than anyone, know what he's capable of. I should have seen this coming.

"I'm going to fix this. I know, I know. I've said that before. But this time, I'll fix this or die trying. I love you, Emmy. Today, tomorrow, and always. And I'll work tirelessly to prove it to you."

I lean down and press a kiss to her forehead, inhaling her scent, before pulling away, content to sit with her until they force me to leave.

CONSCIOUSNESS FILTERS in bit by bit, slowly waking me from the deepest sleep of my life.

I groan as I try to shift to a more comfortable position. There's a rhythmic humming filling the room, and the sound is an affront to my already pounding head.

Where the hell am I? I wonder to myself as I try to open my eyes. The light is so bright, it's like looking into the sun. I whimper and immediately keep my lids closed.

"Are you awake?" some man, asks.

I mumble something incoherent back.

"Let me see if I can dim some of these lights." I hear him shuffle around the room as I try to take stock of my body and its aches. "Okay, try again."

Slowly, I blink my eyes open, and while it's still an adjustment, it's easier than it was the first time.

"Stop." My strained rasping vibrates in my chest as I whisper the word, but I don't know why. "Where are we? What—what happened?"

"You don't remember?" he asks, his brow dipping in concern.

Little tidbits trickle in, falling like raindrops, slowly watering my brain with the missing pieces. "We were at a party."

He swallows roughly and nods.

The memories rain down a little harder, until finally, a full-on tsunami is taking place inside the dome of my skull.

Sex tape.

Sterling lied.

Pills.

These fragments come together, flashing through my mind like lightning. But the one that hurts the most is knowing the man seated beside my bed played a part in it all.

"Why are you here?" I croak, refusing to look at him.

"Little mouse, I'm so sorry."

"Don't call me that." I sniffle. "I want you to leave."

"I can't do that."

"I don't want you here." Tears gather behind my lashes; I don't bother to try to stop them from falling. "Please go."

"Baby," he says, right as a scrub-clad nurse walks into the room.

"Glad to see you're awake, Mrs. Price. How are you feeling?"

"Peachy," I deadpan.

"Good to see your sense of humor is intact. Let's see what's what." She pushes a rolling trolley in front of her, stopping at the side of my bed. After checking my vitals, she asks, "Do you know where you are?"

"Obviously in the hospital."

"Correct. You're actually in the intensive care unit. Do you know why?"

"Yes," I whisper. "Yes, I know."

She gives me a sympathetic look. "Do you know what day it is?"

"Saturday, right?"

"Almost Sunday. What year is it?"

I huff and rattle off the four digits she wants to hear.

"Great. How's your pain?"

"Everything hurts."

"I can get you some Tylenol..."

"No, thank you. I just... can I have some water please?"

"Very small sips." She nods as she passes me a cup with a straw.

Sterling rushes to help me sit up and I flinch ever so slightly, shying away from him. "Please don't touch me."

He looks crestfallen, and I don't understand why. He should be happy...

This *is* what he wanted, after all. Or maybe he's just upset that I pulled through.

He looks helplessly from me to the nurse, and she gives him a sad smile. "This is normal, sweetie. She'll come around."

"I want him to leave."

"Oh, hun, your husband hasn't left your side since you got here. Why don't you try and get some rest," she says, dismissing me. "The doctor will be in to see you shortly."

I lie back against the flimsy pillow, shifting in search of a comfortable position, but it's no use.

"Emmy, I'm so sorry. I'm so, *so* sorry."

"Sorry for what? Sorry I'm still here?"

"What? No!" He paces at the foot of my bed, tugging on the ends of his hair before turning to me. "God, when I found you on your bathroom floor, I thought..." He looks tortured, absolutely anguished, but how do I know he means it? Sterling's nothing if not a good liar, and my brain is far too foggy to make heads or tails of him right now.

" I didn't protect you! I'm sorry I didn't see what was coming. That I didn't prevent this. God, I could have fucking prevented this. I should have known when he came by—"

"When who came by?" I ask, already knowing the answer.

"Rob."

Those three letters, that single syllable, rob me of my breath. It takes me a minute to ask, "When? That night you called me and were acting weird?"

He nods, his cheeks burning with something akin to shame. "Yeah."

"Why didn't you tell me?"

"I thought I handled it. I thought I was keeping you safe." He laughs brokenly. "I fucked up. God, baby, I'm sorry."

I try to shrug, but my shoulder only lifts a fraction of an inch. It feels like someone beat me with a baseball bat and left me for dead. "You really expect me to believe you had nothing to do with this?"

He pinches his eyes shut and tips his head back. "You have every reason to believe I'm guilty, but I wasn't, and I'm gonna do everything in my power to prove it to you. I'm going to make those responsible pay."

Sterling lowers his gaze, locking his eyes onto mine. "I'm calling every favor I'm owed. Rob will not get away with this. He won't."

He sounds so sincere, so broken, but still, I'm hesitant to believe him. I mean, he lied about Rob stopping by, how do I know he isn't lying to me now as well?

"Why do they think you're my husband?"

He offers a sheepish smile. "Only immediate family can come back here."

I try to nod, but the motion makes my head swim. "Do you want some more water?"

"Sure."

He crosses the room, and picks up my cup, guiding the straw to my lips. "I know you don't believe me, but I love you, and I'm gonna fix this."

He truly is distraught looking, with his rumpled clothes, pale face, and tired eyes. My heart wants so badly to believe him, but my brain knows I'm not ready to make those kinds of decisions.

I swallow and turn my head, looking away from him. A lone tear falls as I ask, "Why is it every time you try to fix things, they seem to get worse?"

I can tell Sterling wants to say something, to defend himself, to plead his case. The pulsing of his clenched jaw is a dead giveaway. But he doesn't. Instead, he retreats back to his chair beside my bed.

The silence between us is thick and awkward, but before either of us can make a move, there's a knock.

"Come in," I say, bringing a hand to my throat; even speaking hurts.

"Mrs. Price, it's so nice to see you awake and alert. How are you feeling?"

"Like I tried to die."

The doctor hums thoughtfully under her breath. "Indeed you did." She checks something on the stationary computer in the corner of the room before coming to stand beside my bed. "Is this the first time you've tried to take your own life?"

"Yes."

"Do you regularly have suicidal thoughts?" The weight

of her words and their implication are almost too much for me to bear. If Sterling wouldn't have found me, I really might have died. The thought is as sobering as it is terrifying.

Still, it feels so weird to talk about this in front of Sterling, but they all think he's my husband, so of course, no one bats an eye.

"I've, um... I've thought about it before, but this was the first time I've ever tried anything."

"I see. Your husband told me a little bit about your past and the abuse you suffered. Given your circumstances, we're going to place you on a seventy-two-hour hold."

Shame and regret and a little bit of panic race through me as my eyes move from the doctor to Sterling. "You talked to people about me?"

"Your husband wanted to make sure you received the best care possible. Now you can enter the hold on your own volition or I can mandate it. Do you understand what I'm saying?"

I nod.

"The choice is yours."

"Not much of a choice," I muse. "Go to the psych ward by choice or go by force."

She offers a sympathetic smile.

"It's fine."

"So, you're agreeing to go?"

I lift one shoulder in a half-shrug. "Sure."

"Now, I have to ask, do you still feel like harming yourself, Mrs. Price?"

"No. No, I just want to sleep."

She nods thoughtfully. "I'll get the ball rolling on that and we'll get you moved shortly. If you need anything at all, just press the call button and until then enjoy some time with your husband."

It's on the tip of my tongue to shout that he's not my husband, but I don't have the energy to fight this or anything else. Hell, I barely have the energy to keep my eyes open.

"YOU ALL READY TO head home, honey?" Kelsey, my favorite nurse, asks.

"As ready as I'll ever be."

She smiles warmly. "That's the right attitude to have! The paperwork's all signed, we're just waiting on your ride." She checks her watch. "That husband of yours should up any second."

I lift my lips in some semblance of a smile at the mention of *my husband*. I've had a lot of time over the last three days to think—and talk—about everything that happened.

I see some things a little more clearly, but I have questions about a lot of things, too.

But... I'm fairly certain that Sterling wasn't involved. Sure, he's not perfect, but I don't believe he was plotting against me either.

I'm actually of the belief that someone set him up. And I *know* that someone is Rob.

All the way down to the deepest depths of my soul, I know it.

If nothing else, I guess Sterling and I at least have one thing to talk about on the drive back to my dorm.

"He brought some clothes by a little earlier so you'd have something to wear home."

"Oh, that's nice." I want to smile, but I don't have the energy.

"He's called to check on you multiple times every day." Her tone implies just how swoony she thinks that is.

Me, though? I'm not sure how I feel about it.

"So I've been told."

"You must be so excited to see him!"

"Ecstatic."

She smiles again. "I'll step out and let you get changed. I'm sure you don't want to wait any longer than you have to."

I grab the bag she left on the chair and dump it on the bed, inspecting the contents.

He grabbed all of the essentials, including my favorite sweatshirt. For some reason, the thought of him riffling through my panty drawer gives me pause. It's silly, given our level of physical intimacy, but still.

Five minutes later, Kelsey sticks her head back into the room. "He's here."

"Like, here-here?" I ask, tipping my head in her direction.

"Waiting right outside of the unit." She pushes the door all the way open. "Come on, I'll walk you out."

"Thanks."

Apprehension builds inside of me with every step toward the double-doors leading to my freedom. Or maybe it's seeing Sterling that has my heart rioting in my chest.

Either way, I guess I'm about to find out.

We pause in front of the doors, and Kelsey turns to me. "Take care of yourself, hun."

"I will. Thanks."

She nods. "Your discharge paperwork has a few options listed for continued treatment. I really hope you'll consider it."

My eyes burn, but I blink back the tears. "I will."

"Good. Glad to hear it." She presses the buzzer on the wall and the doors swing open.

My eyes land on Sterling immediately. He looks as nervous as I feel.

Deciding to offer an olive branch, I lift my hand in a silly wave. "Hey, Ster."

He's as still as a statue as he takes me in.

"So, you, um...you ready to take me home?"

At that, he springs into action. "Yeah. Yes." He steps forward as if he's going to reach for me, but draws up short, awkwardly stuffing his hands into his pockets. "Let's go."

There's this tension between us, an awkwardness. It's as if a rift the size of an ocean has suddenly opened, and we're each standing on opposite sides.

"You look good, Ster," I say, biting my lip.

"Thanks."

I drop my eyes to my feet and move toward him as an awkward silence settles over us.

It's weird. Neither of us seem to know what to say or how to act.

Gone is the confident-to-the-point-of-cocky man I fell in love with and in his place is this unsure replica. He looks like my Sterling, but doesn't act like him. And I worry it's my fault.

"I parked out front."

"Great."

Neither of us speak again until we're a few miles down the road, when I say, "I want you to know, I realize you didn't have anything to do with...*everything*. I know that now."

"Really?" The hopeful edge in his voice flutters through

my belly, but I tamp them down. I'm not ready to tackle the issue of *us* quite yet.

Lord knows, I need to work on me before I can even think about being a part of an us.

"Really."

"There's a lot we need to talk about."

"Yeah." I glance his way, before returning my gaze to the curvy mountain road. "But can it maybe wait?"

From the corner of my eye, I see his fingers tighten around the steering wheel. "Yeah. Of course. Whenever you're ready."

"How is Stella? And Gabe and Zach?"

"They're okay. Good. Worried about you. But I've kept them in the loop."

"Thanks, I guess."

I hate this distance between us. I want so badly to reach over the console and take his hand in mine, to comfort him and to let him comfort me, but now I'm second-guessing every decision I make.

Plus who's to say he's even interested in me anymore? I can't imagine he would be, not when he can have anyone.

Why on earth would he settle for me, especially now that he knows just how weak I really am?

A deep melancholy wraps itself around me. I'm so lost in my woe-is-me despair that I don't even notice we're parked outside of my dorm until he cuts the engine.

"Can I walk you up?"

"Sure, if that's what makes you happy."

I won't admit it out loud, but I'm secretly glad he's going to walk me. The last thing I want is to chance running into Melanie alone. A shiver rolls through me at the mere thought.

Sterling gives me a long look, one loaded with some deeply felt emotion I can't quite pick apart. "You," he says, opening his door and climbing out of his car. "You make me happy."

I follow after him, not quite knowing how to reply. I want to tell him that he makes me happy, too, but I can't.

How can I, when I'm not even happy with myself?

I'm on pins and needles until we step inside my suite. "Where is Stella?" I ask, scanning the empty suite, looking for any evidence of what took place here only a few short days ago.

"She should be back in just a bit. She didn't want you to be overwhelmed right when you got home."

"Oh. Okay." I walk farther into the space, my hands shaking slightly. "When will she be back?" For some reason the thought of being here alone makes me feel jumpy as hell.

"I...I could wait with you, if you want."

"Please. If you don't mind."

Sterling's eyes light up. "There's nothing more important than you."

I don't know how to respond to him, so I don't.

"Come sit with me," he says, dropping down onto the couch, patting the cushion beside him.

I do, and we once again lapse into a stilted silence.

"Can we... can we talk?" Sterling asks, finally.

"About what?"

"God, so much. We can start slow, I guess."

I nod, waiting for him to continue.

"First things first. I just want to get this out of the way, and please know, you don't have say anything back, but I love you. That hasn't changed, and it's not gonna change. If anything, my feelings have only grown stronger. My heart beats for you, Emmalyn. I'm sure you need time to process everything, but I'm willing to wait."

He laughs through his nose. "I'm not typically a patient man, but for you, I can wait."

I flex my fingers, clutching the hem of my sweatshirt. I want so badly to reach out to him, to pull him to me to hold him close. To press my chest to his and feel our hearts beating together, but I force myself to remain seated.

"Sterling, I..."

"You don't have to say anything."

"No. I-I love you, too. I do. I just need time."

Before he can say anything else, the door opens and Stella walks in.

"I guess that's my cue to leave." He leans in, as if he's going to hug me, but stops short.

Deep breaths, I tell myself before I lean in, closing the distance between us, pulling him to me so our foreheads touch.

We sit like this for a few moments, content to just soak each other in.

"Thank you, Sterling," I whisper.

"Anything for you." He softly kisses my forehead before releasing me. It feels like a piece of me is missing as he stands and heads for the door. "See you soon."

Tears threaten to fall, but Stella claims his vacated seat before they have a chance.

She takes my hands in hers. "Don't you ever scare me like that again!"

"I'm sorry."

"No need to apologize. Just get better, you know? Get healthy."

"I will. Promise."

"I know you will."

"How's Gabe and Zach?"

"They're good. They've been really worried about you, but Sterling has made sure to keep everyone updated."

Stella laughs.

"What?"

"Babe. You don't even know."

"Tell me then."

"I think a lot of it he needs to tell you. But trust me when I say you are his priority. He's been at the hospital every day, almost all day, and when he wasn't, he's been fighting to make sure that piece of shit stepbrother pays for what he did."

"Really?" A small thrill runs through me. "What about his classes and his TA duties?"

Stella gives my hand a squeeze. "I guess I'll tell you since you're gonna find out anyway. He stepped down from his TA position. He told his uncle he couldn't do it anymore, and he's been doing his classes remotely."

An indescribable feeling—some odd combination of joy and sadness and a whole lot of love—settles into my chest, sinking through my heart and into my soul. The fact that he's willing to basically put his entire life on hold... *for me* has me feeling some kind of way.

"That man definitely loves you."

"I love him, too."

She beams. "Good. Are you hungry?"

"Starving. Hospital food is the worst."

Stella crinkles her nose. "I don't know. I kind of like it."

"Gross."

"How about I order us a pizza and we invite your daddies over to eat?"

I very nearly choke on a laugh. "That sounds perfect."

"IS IT DONE?" I ask, skipping over any and all pleasantries.

"Son, do you have any idea how late it is?"

"I do."

"And this couldn't have waited until tomorrow?"

"Dad," I growl.

"Sterling," he growls right back. As much as I sometimes hate to admit it, my dad and I are a lot alike. "Yes. It's done."

Immediately, a weight lifted off my chest. "Tell me everything."

He sighs, and I can just picture him pinching the bridge of his nose as he paces in front of his desk. Because, as late as it might be, I know for a fact he wasn't in bed. Harold Abbott is nothing if not a workaholic.

"I called Robert Sunday night. He wasn't very receptive at first, but I threatened to pull my support of his businesses, and when that wasn't enough, I also threatened to advise other clients to walk away as well. Pearson Enterprises is nothing without my money, and the wheels I grease, so he agreed to my terms."

"When does he...

"Rob was on the first flight Monday morning. He's already gone."

"Where?"

"To a place he can't hurt anyone ever again."

"How do you know?" I ask, because damn if this doesn't all sound too good to be true.

"Some things are better left unsaid, son. But he knows the consequences he'll face if he ever comes back."

"Which are?"

"He'll be not only disowned, but also disinherited. All of the money in his trust would be forfeited to Emmalyn."

"And you have this in writing?"

My dad scoffs. "I'm not an amateur, son."

"I know." I stand and begin to pace. My apartment feels so lonely without her here. Hell, my whole life feels lonely, sad as it sounds. "Thank you."

"That's not all," he says, immediately putting me on edge.

"What's that supposed to mean?"

"The remainder of Emmalyn's college has been paid for. And Robert and Sarah will be making quarterly donations to several charities that help battered women."

"Why?" I ask, even though I'm overjoyed at what he's saying.

"I've made a lot of mistakes in the name of money, son. A lot of mistakes period. But I'm trying to make it right. I never should have helped that slimy little shit the first time around. I've never liked that kid."

"Then why did you?"

He sighs, and I answer for him.

"Money?"

"Money."

"Thanks for helping me, Dad."

"It's the least I could do. And, it's got your mom talking to me again, so that's another plus."

My phone beeps, and I go on high alert when I see it's Stella.

"Dad, I—I gotta let you go."

I accept the incoming call before he can say another word.

"Stella, what's wrong?" There has to be a reason for her to be calling so late. It's nearly ten o'clock. "Is everything okay?"

"I don't know." Her distress bleeds through loud and clear. "She's having a nightmare, and I can't wake her up. I don't know what to do!"

"I'm on my way," I say, flying out of the house barefoot and shirtless. The cold doesn't even phase me as the wind whips across my skin. I only have one thing on my mind, and that's getting to Emmalyn.

I don't remember anything about the drive to campus. I have no clue if I passed another car, saw a deer, nothing.

My sole focus was on getting to my girl.

The second I throw the car in park, I shoot off a text to Stella, and she rushes down to let me in. Wordlessly, we both rush back up to the third floor to their dorm.

I hear her before I see her, but I'm still stricken by the sight of her thrashing and crying. She's begging someone to stop, for them not to hurt her.

Rage, scalding liquid rage, pours through me, because I know exactly who she's dreaming about.

Stella looks at me helplessly. "I tried to calm her down. Tried to wake her up. It was no use. She just screamed louder anytime I touched her."

I nod so that she knows I hear her, fully entering the bedroom.

My little mouse whimpers, and my heart cracks a little more. "It's okay. I'm here."

She moves fitfully beneath the covers, and on instinct I lie down beside her. Immediately she turns and curls into me. "Sterling," she whispers, still asleep.

Thank you, God. Instinctually, her body recognizes mine. "It's me, baby."

I hold her close as she sighs, snuggling into me and falling into a peaceful sleep.

"Thank you," Stella whispers before heading back to her own room.

I tell myself I'm only going to lie with her for a little while, just long enough to make sure she's truly okay, and then I'll move to the couch so that I'm here if she needs me again.

Except the next thing I know, it's morning, and we're both blinking ourselves awake.

"Sterling?" She yawns, confusion swirling in her brown eyes. "What are you doing here?"

"You don't remember?" I ask, and she shakes her head.

"Remember what?"

"Stella called me last night because you were having a nightmare and she couldn't calm you down."

"Oh." She looks away from me.

Ever so softly, I reach over and grasp her chin between my thumb and index finger, bringing her gaze back to mine. "What have I told you about hiding from me? Don't be embarrassed. You've been to hell and back more than once and somehow come out stronger every time."

"I don't feel very strong."

"You are. So fucking strong. You just can't see it yet, but you will."

"So Stella called you? I'm sorry."

"Don't be sorry. Don't you know I'd do anything for you?"

"Thanks, I guess." She pushes the covers off of her and sits up. "Might as well make you breakfast since you're here. It's the least I can do."

"What's on the menu?" I ask, following her into the kitchenette.

She swings open the fridge door, and I shamelessly check out her ass as she bends over and looks inside. "Well, unless you want water and bread, we better order in."

I laugh at her put-out tone. "Or, I can run out and get us something from Holy Roasters."

"Really? You'd do that?"

"You know I would."

She closes the fridge and wraps me in a hug, shocking the hell out of me. "Thanks, Ster."

"Anything for you, baby." And I fucking mean it...

Anything.

AFTER STERLING LEAVES, I head back into my room to get changed out of my pajamas. When I emerge, Stella's at the counter pouring herself a cup of coffee.

"So... I had—"

Stella yelps and rocks back on her heels, clutching her mug to her chest. "Damn, you did. You scared me."

Guilt and something are forming on me, making me feel about an intrusion the fact my best friend doesn't miss.

"Don't worry, it's Emmy, it's understandable, you know?"

"I understand," and I do, but that knowledge does nothing to make me feel any better. "Why did you call Sterling?"

"I didn't know who else to call. But, babe, the second he was here and touching you, I mean, down. You stopped thrashing and everything. You screamed and you curled into him and went right to—"

"Really?"

"Yes, and then when I tried to comfort you, it just made things wor—

I'm not quite sure how to process what she's saying, so I stay quiet.

"Speaking of, where is he?"

"Oh, he went to get us breakfast. For you, too."

A cheek-splitting grin overtakes her face. "I'm telling you, that man is a keeper."

I glance down at my feet, wriggling my toes over the plush rug. "I know he is. I'm just worried I'm not."

"Emmy. He loves you, and you are so worthy of his love. Do you hear me? You deserve good things and to be happy and healthy. Are you gonna..." She swallows and looks away.

"Am I going to what?"

"Are you gonna see a therapist or anything?"

My eyes water. There's such a freaking stigma surrounding mental health, and in my family, it's better swept under the rug. And certainly never talked about. It's part of the reason, aside from the hell Rob put me through, that I wanted to go into the psych field.

Still, it feels strange to talk about it all so openly. "Yeah. Yes, I am. I know I need to."

"Good. I'm really glad. So where is he getting breakfast from?" she asks, mercifully changing the subject.

"Holy Roasters."

Stella does a little fist pump and drains the last of her coffee. "Don't need this anymore, but don't want to waste it either."

I can't help but laugh at her antics. "Never waste coffee."

"Precisely," she says, right as someone knocks on the door.

"That must be Sterling," I say as she heads to the door. "His hands are probably full."

Stella opens the door, but it's not Sterling on the other side.

"Abigail, is everything okay?" Stella asks, but the red-headed RA rushes past her and wraps me in bone-crushing hug.

"Oh, my God! I am *so* glad you're okay, Emmy!"

"Um." I glance at Stella over her shoulder. "Thank you."

"I was there," she whispers, nodding her head toward the bathroom door. "With Sterling, when he...when we..."

Realization dawns. "Oh wow. Um." Embarrassment now trumps all other emotions warring inside me. "I'm so sorry you had to see that."

"Emmy." She grasps my shoulders and waits until I'm looking her in the eye. "You have nothing to apologize for. Just focus on getting better and know if you ever need an ear, I'm here for you. Okay?"

I nod, feeling as hopeful as I do awkward. "Thanks, Abigail."

"Anytime."

There's another knock. "That *has* to be Sterling," Stella says, rubbing her hands together, no doubt already envisioning gobbling up her food.

"That's my cue." Abigail hugs me once more before turning for the door. Except, when she opens it to leave, it's to a man who is most definitely not Sterling.

"Where would you like these?" asks the uniformed delivery man.

My roomie turns to look at me. "Where would I like what? I didn't order anything."

"Are you Emmalyn Price?"

"Yes, but—"

"Your name's on the label," he says, cutting me off.

"I guess put it on the coffee table."

He nods and then turns around, stepping back into the hall, only to return with the largest bouquet I've ever seen.

"Good Lord! Who do you think it's from?"

Stella gives me a droll look. "You know who it's from."

"They're gorgeous." But why would Sterling send me these?

The delivery man turns back toward the door and I move to close it behind him, but he stops me. "Not quite finished yet, ma'am."

I cast a confused look Stella's way, expecting her to be equally as mystified. But she's not. Nope, my secret-keeping roommate sports a very knowing look.

He makes two more trips in and out; once with a standard, nondescript brown package, and once with a humongous cellophane-wrapped gift basket. "That's it," he says, shutting the door behind himself.

"Thanks," I murmur dazedly, but he's already gone.

Stella, meanwhile, is grinning like a loon. "Girl, just wait. He actually tried sending this stuff to the hospital while you were there, but they told him he couldn't. So, he arranged this instead."

"Why?"

"Babe." Stella looks at me like I'm utterly clueless. "He's got it bad for you, and he did all of this when he thought you were never gonna speak to him again. So..."

"I-I don't even know how to process this, much less where to begin."

The front door swings open, and Sterling walks in.

"Might I suggest starting with the card attached to the flowers, then the package, and then the basket." He winks. "Go on, dig in, and I'll heat up our breakfast sandwiches. I told them not to so they wouldn't get soggy."

Stella gives him a thumbs up. "Smart man."

I move to the couch as if on autopilot, perching myself on the edge of the cushion. My hands tremble as I reach for the envelope. It's larger than your standard bouquet-card. *Much larger.*

My hands tremble as I slide my finger beneath the flap and slide the contents from within it into my hands.

EMMALYN,

I HAVE SO MUCH I WANT TO SAY TO YOU. SO MUCH I NEED TO SAY.

BEFORE I PLEAD MY CASE, I NEED YOU TO KNOW SOMETHING...

WHILE YOU WERE IN THE HOSPITAL, I TOOK CARE OF THINGS. I TOOK CARE OF ROB. THAT JACKASS WILL NEVER HURT YOU AGAIN. I MADE SURE OF IT, WITH A LITTLE HELP FROM MY DAD.

THAT MIGHT HAVE CROSSED SOME BOUNDARIES, BUT I'D DO FUCKING ANYTHING TO KEEP YOU SAFE. ANYTHING.

I UNDERSTAND, AFTER EVERYTHING THAT'S HAPPENED, IF YOU NEVER FORGIVE ME, BUT PLEASE KNOW I WILL LOVE YOU ALWAYS, AND I'LL BE HERE FOR YOU NO MATTER WHAT.

IF YOU FIND IT WITHIN YOUR HEART TO GIVE ME A SECOND CHANCE, I'D COUNT MYSELF THE LUCKIEST MAN ON EARTH.

YOURS,

STERLING

"He...he's gone?" I ask as a whole host of emotions dive-bomb my heart.

Sterling stops what he's doing and turns to fully face me. "Yes, Emmy, he's gone."

"And he's not coming back? Not ever?"

"Not ever."

I debate asking him more, but honestly at this point, I'm so relieved to know I'm out of Rob's reach, I just...don't. I'm sure I'll eventually grow curious, but today's not that day.

"Thank you," I whisper, sagging back against the couch. "For everything." I swipe my index fingers beneath my eyes, wiping away my tears. "The flowers are beautiful."

"I'm glad you like them. I picked each bloom myself."

"Why?"

"Well," he says, taking one sandwich from the microwave and swapping it for another. "The purple hyacinth, because it symbolizes asking for forgiveness. Yellow lilies because I'm thankful you're still here. The roses, I imagine are fairly obvious. And, the daffodils are for new beginnings. I know they don't really go together—the florist damn sure tried talking me out of it—but they all mean something and, yeah." He shrugs, trying to play it cool.

Meanwhile, I'm on the verge of tears over his thoughtfulness.

"The package next," he reminds me.

I don't know how anything could top the flowers, but I tear into it all the same.

A delighted smile lights up my face when I see the contents inside of the box. "Are you serious?" I ask.

"Very much so."

"Sterling!"

"What? I know you like them."

"This is too much," I say, gesturing to the package, which

contains at least six packs of Oreos, all in different seasonal flavors.

"Speak for yourself," Stella says tartly. "I'll gladly help you eat them."

I roll my eyes at her and thank him. "Seriously, this is too much."

"There's no such thing as too much when it comes to you. Now, onto the basket."

I untie the bow from around the top of the gift basket, letting the cellophane fall away. Inside, there's an insulated mug with mountain peaks etched into it, along with the words *feels like home.* There are also several bags of coffee from Holy Roasters along with a gift card and a new hoodie that's softer than anything I've ever felt before.

"Thank you. So much."

"I think there's one more thing," he says, trying to sound nonchalant.

I glance back down to the basket, and sure enough there's a lanyard of some sort. As I grab it, I notice there's a key dangling from the end. "What's this?"

"A key to my place."

"What? Why?"

"Don't panic, baby. Consider it a safe space if you ever need to get away. The locks have been changed, and that key there is the only spare. I also have a new security system."

My heart pitter-patters, doing a happy little dance in my chest. "Thank you."

He simply smiles in response.

The microwave dings, and Sterling grabs the final sandwich. Stella and I quickly move everything to the floor so we can eat. A happy quiet settles over us, and for the first time in a long time, contentment flows through me.

"What do you have planned for today?" Sterling asks once we finish eating.

I shrug. "I guess I need to find a therapist. And figure out stuff for my classes. Oh, God, I can only imagine how behind I am."

"Hey, I'll help you get it sorted out, okay?"

I smile gratefully. "But before any of that, I need a shower. I was too tired yesterday, and I swear, I can *feel* the hospital on my skin."

"We'll clean up out here," Stella says, gathering our plates.

"Thanks." I grab my new hoodie before darting into my room for a pair of jeans and a bra.

I'm already anticipating the relief the hot water will bring to my sore muscles, but the second I'm inside, panic floods my system.

My skin feels too tight for my body, and the walls feel like they're closing in on me. My vision pinpricks, and I can't seem to take in a full breath.

Suddenly, flashes of me lying on the floor, fading away to nothing, assault me.

A broken sob spills out of me as I crumble to the floor. "Oh my God," I cry, holding my knees to my chest as I rock in the fetal position.

The bathroom door bursts open, and Sterling rushes in and pulls me up into his strong arms. "Oh, baby. I'm so sorry."

I'm crying too hard to respond.

He walks us out to the couch and sits, keeping me on his lap and his arms locked tightly around me. His touch is the only thing grounding me right now, the only thing keeping me from completely breaking down.

"I can't do this. I can't do this. I can't do this," I whisper over and over, clutching at his shirt.

He whispers soothing words into my ear, while Stella watches on helplessly.

Sterling continues to hold me, rocking and whispering, until finally, I regain some sense of composure.

"How am I supposed to stay here?" I wail.

"Don't," Sterling says, "don't stay here."

My heart sinks. He wants me to leave.

"Move in with me."

Just as fast, my heart soars, buoying itself to the surface. My brain, however, quickly shuts it all down. "I don't know if that's such a good idea. It seems really sudden, and I don't want to make any rash decisions." I'm trying to be logical, but it's hard when my entire being is practically begging me to say yes.

"I don't know...maybe a change of scenery would be good," Stella says. "I know I'm not a therapist, but I don't know how conducive to your healing it will be to stay here."

Sterling nods in agreement.

"I don't know. I just... don't know."

"How about this?" he says, easing me onto the cushion next to him. "The unit next door just went on the market. Why don't you rent it?"

"It's probably really expensive."

He grins like he knows something I don't. "I know the landlord personally. Something tells me he'd give you a deal. And if it's too much for you and Stella, y'all could get a third roommate."

Stella nods eagerly. "I think we should consider it, babe. I really do."

"I'll think about it. That's the best I can offer."

I WATCH in rapt fascination as Emmalyn wakes.

It's the fifth time in as many days that she's woken up to me in her bed, thanks to her recurring nightmares. As much as I love the fact that my presence calms her, I'd do about anything for the nightmares to just stop.

"Sterling." Her voice is thick with sleep.

"Good morning, little mouse."

She looks up at me and blinks once...twice...and then sighs. "Another nightmare, finally gone, chasing away any and all vestiges of sleep."

"A—"

She lifts her head and rolls to face me, burying her head in my chest. How many times is that now? God, I just want—

"I think I know why. If that even."

"You're broken inside. That much I know."

"I think you might be right. Staying here isn't good for me. I think I need to get away."

"I think that's a good idea. Do you mean for a while or for good?"

She doesn't answer me right away, so I know she's taking my question to heart. "Both, I think."

"My family has a cabin in Tennessee. We could go there."

"Really?"

"Really. And, if you're serious about getting away for good, maybe while we're gone Gabe and Zach could help Stella move y'all into the unit next to mine?"

"I'd have to talk to Stella."

"Talk to me about what?" asks Stella, popping her head into the room.

"Stalk much?" I ask, but I'm laughing.

"Hey, I was making coffee and heard my name."

"Emmalyn and I were talking about y'all moving in next to me. I suggested Gabe and Zach could help you move everything while I took our girl to my family's cabin."

"And I"—Emmalyn cuts her eyes at me—"was telling him I couldn't make those kinds of decisions without talking to you."

"Oh, I am totally down. Let's blow this popsicle stand."

"Are you sure?"

"One-hundred-and-ten percent. And I know the guys will be down to help me move our stuff. You just take care of you. Go to the cabin, relax and recharge. Read a book on a bearskin rug in front of the fire."

"I thought you were supposed to make love in front of the fire?" Emmalyn asks.

"Now, there's a thought," I murmur in her ear.

"Oh my God! I cannot believe I just said that."

"I'm just saying, baby. You want to give that a go, I'm down." My tone is light and teasing, but I'm half serious, too.

It's only been five days since Emmy came home, and I'm respecting her need for time. But it is driving me fucking insane to sleep next to her every night without touching her.

I've got blue balls like a motherfucker, but I know she'll return to me. I also know that when she does, it'll be mind-blowing and oh-so-worth the wait.

"Okay, let's do it."

"There's no rug here. Or fireplace."

She rolls her eyes and laughs. "I meant let's go to the cabin. And...let's move."

It takes everything in me not to fist pump. "Y'all want to get started on packing and I'll head home and pack a bag for the cabin?"

Stella answers for them both. "Yup. It's basically just clothes and a few odds and ends."

"Oh!" Emmalyn cries. "We don't have furniture."

"You're in luck," I say, lying through my teeth. "It comes furnished."

Emmy and Stella exchange grateful glances and then Stella says, "Sounds like it was meant to be."

"Something like that," I mutter, wondering how fast I can get furniture delivered. And if I can get the blond giant and his boyfriend to set it all up.

Something tells me I can; I'm pretty sure those two would do anything for my girl. And if they were anyone else, that notion would piss me the hell off, but with them, I don't mind.

"Well, at least I'll never have to see Melanie again." She frowns. "Unless I run into her on campus."

"Baby... Did no one tell you?"

"Tell me what?"

"Jelly Melly isn't here anymore," Stella says, sounding ridiculously pleased.

"What?"

"Turns out when Rob was here, he followed you for a few days and somehow made friends with her. She helped him with stuff. And yeah, she was relieved of her RA duties. Her parents were so furious they pulled her from school."

"She's practically grown," Emmy says, furrowing her brow. "Why would her parents care?"

"Rich people." Stella shakes her head. "They didn't want her ruining their good name. Sent her ass to Europe. Poor thing."

Emmalyn rolls her eyes. "Sounds about right."

"Summer was in on it, too. She quit, but no one knows where she went."

"Good riddance, if you ask me," Stella mutters.

I stand from the bed.

"Where are you going?" Emmalyn asks, pouting.

"To pack a bag. I'll be back in two hours to pick you up."

"Okay. Drive safe."

"I will." I pause right outside her door. "Oh, and, Emmy?" She looks up at me. "I love you."

Her cheeks go pink. "I love you, too."

"I'M REALLY proud of your progress, Emmy," says Holly, my therapist. "You've come leaps and bounds."

I laugh softly under my breath. "Still got a long way to go."

"And that's okay. This is a marathon, not a sprint. Do you remember what we discussed about what to do when you feel overwhelmed?"

"Yeah. I remember."

"Good. Employ the things we've discussed, and I think you'll be pleasantly surprised with the results, okay?"

I nod.

"Great. Same time next week?"

"Yep. See you then." I do an awkward little finger wave before ending the video call and packing up my laptop.

I linger for just a moment before taking a deep breath and stepping out of the bedroom.

"How'd it go?" Sterling asks, standing from the chair he was seated in.

"It was good. We talked about a lot today. Unpacked a lot, too."

"I'm so proud of you, baby."

I can tell he wants to say more, to reach for me, to kiss me and touch me. There's a longing in his steely gray gaze that reflects that of my own.

Ever since coming to his family's cabin two weeks ago, we've been dancing around each other, but neither one of us has made a move.

Aside from sleeping wrapped around one another and a few soft kisses, we may as well be completely platonic friends.

At first, it was to protect myself, and then it was to protect him—I didn't want to jump back with both feet only to have another breakdown and drown him right along with me. But now...now I'm ready.

My heart, brain, and body are all on the same page, and they're shouting for me to claim my man and my happily ever after.

Holly thinks it's okay, too. Not that her opinion is the be-all-end-all, but it's nice to have her on board.

"So, I have a surprise for you tonight." He rocks back on his heels, a boyish look flitting across his handsome features.

"Do you?"

"Well, since it's our last night at the cabin, I figured I could grill us a nice steak dinner and maybe we could check out the hot tub."

I have to bite my lips to stop from grinning. Looks like we're both ready to take things up a notch, because I know for certain neither of us brought a swimsuit.

"That sounds really nice," I murmur, and he leans in, pressing a soft kiss to my lips.

I'm half-tempted to deepen the kiss here and now, but Sterling pulls away before I can. The man must have the self-control of a saint. I know he's been trying to respect me, but I also know he's got blue balls like whoa.

But tonight... Tonight everything's going to change.

Tonight, we're going to get back on track.

Tonight, I'm going to show him exactly how much I love him, how much I trust him, and how much I want to be his.

Not that I ever really stopped being his. Not really.

"Do you mind if I take a bath first?"

"Go for it, baby. I'm gonna go ahead and start grilling, if that's cool with you?"

"It's perfect."

He leans in and kisses me once more. "Come find me when you're done."

"MMM." I inhale deeply as I step out onto the deck. "Something smells good."

"Gonna taste good, too." Sterling winks at me from behind the grill. "You want to run inside and grab us some plates and the salad I made?"

"So fancy."

His lips quirk up into a smile. "Your therapist said a healthy diet's good for your physical and mental health."

"That she did," I say, secretly touched by his thoughtfulness, before turning and heading back into the house.

When I step back outside, I'm blown away. Somehow, in less than five minutes, Sterling's managed to light like a bajillion candles.

Okay, so like, twenty. But still.

They're spread out, with a few along the deck rail, two tall ones on the table, and the rest scattered around the hot tub.

"Ster," I breathe. "This is magical."

He smiles, but doesn't say anything. Not about the candles, at least. "Ready to eat, little mouse?"

I nod, and he takes the plates and salad from me before pulling out my chair. I serve us each some salad while he pulls the steaks from the grill. "Made some eggplant, too."

"It smells and looks so good."

"Dig in."

I saw off a bite of steak and moan as the flavors of butter, garlic, and rosemary burst across my tongue. "Oh my God."

Our eyes meet over the flickering candlelight, and a calm settles over me. Being here, with him, just feels right.

"How are you feeling about everything, about school?"

"Mixed emotions. A little sad, but also like it was the right choice."

"An incomplete is better than failing out."

"Agreed."

"And you get to start fresh next semester."

"Also true."

"I'm proud of you, Emmy. Truly. You're amazing. An inspiration, really."

I roll my eyes, but I'm smiling. "Flattery will get you everywhere, Sterling Abbot."

"Everywhere, you say?"

"Everywhere."

"Well, then, let's finish up dinner and let that flattery take us to the hot tub."

We push back our chairs and stand at the same time, both of us clearly ready for what's to come.

Without any preamble, I shove my leggings and panties off, followed by my sweatshirt and bra. Sterling stands, slack-jawed, as I climb into the bubbling water.

"Aren't you going to join me?" I ask, pouting out my lower lip.

"Fuck yes." He scrambles to undress, nearly tripping in his haste to get to me.

As soon as he's seated, I climb onto his lap, straddling him.

His hands move to my hips, holding me in place. "Emmy, baby, are you sure?" he asks, his voice an octave or two deeper than usual.

"So." I lean in and kiss him. "Very." Another kiss. "Sure." This time, I lick across the seam of his lips, seeking entrance to his mouth.

He opens for me, and the moment our tongues touch, he takes over.

Sterling yanks my body flush to his with one hand while burying the other in my hair. He tugs, positioning my head to just the right angle for him to devour me with his mouth.

"God, baby. I've missed this, you." He speaks the words against my mouth, and I greedily swallow them down, rolling my hips against his.

"Yes, Ster. Me, too. God, me, too."

"I need to be inside you, baby. I need to feel you all around me."

"Then what are you waiting for?"

He stands from the water, and I cling to him as he steps over the edge of the hot tub.

"What are you doing?"

"Taking you to bed, little mouse, so I can fuck you right."

I press my lips to his neck in reply, kissing up and down the column of his throat.

Inside, he lays my dripping wet body down onto the mattress. "You look so fucking good with your skin all pink and your pussy all wet for me."

"Please touch me," I beg, feeling like I might actually die if he doesn't put his hands back on my body.

He moves to lower his head between my legs, but I stop him. "No."

"Baby."

"No, I just want you inside of me. I want you to fill me up and make me feel whole. Please. Can you please do that?"

He rakes his teeth over his lower lip and stalks over to his suitcase to retrieve a condom. "You know damn well I can't deny you anything."

"Then give me what I want. What I need."

He crawls up the bed, settling between my legs and pushes into me. We both moan as my body stretches to accommodate his.

"Fuck, baby, you feel...this feels..."

"Like coming home," I whisper, wrapping my arms and legs around him.

"Yeah," he grunts as he pulls back before thrusting into me again and holding his hips to mine. "Just like that."

I whimper, digging my nails into his back, urging him to move.

He gets the hint and begins fucking me in earnest. "I love you, Emmalyn."

"I love you, too, Sterling." I wrap my legs around his waist and his back bows as I meet him on every downward stroke. "So, so much."

My heart is thundering in my chest, my entire body shaking with need, as Sterling works me over, hitting all the right spots and whispering filthy promises into my ear until we're both *right there*, clinging to each other as we both find our release.

"GOOD MORNING," Sterling whispers, jostling me softly until my eyelids flutter open. "Are you ready?"

"Ready for what?" I stretch my arms over my head as I yawn.

"For your first real day of college."

Outwardly, I'm all sass as I roll my eyes, but inside, I melt. "As ready as I'll ever be."

"You still feeling like taking last semester off was the right idea?"

I nod, my head rubbing against the pillow. "Yeah. I feel healthier and stronger. I'm still a work in progress, but I'm definitely getting there."

"I'm so proud of you," he murmurs, his eyes heating as he takes me in.

"No sex, Sterling. None of that."

He groans. "Why not?"

"Sterling, I cannot be waltzing into my first class with sex hair."

"You better hop in the shower then, or you'll be going in with bedhead, and everyone will think it's sex hair anyway."

I narrow my eyes at him and he smirks.

"Fine." I kick off the covers and force myself out of his warm, cozy bed. "I'll be back."

"You know," he starts, following behind me, "you could just move in with me and then you wouldn't have to run next door all the time. You're practically here every night anyway."

"Not until Stella finds a roommate," I say, instantly slapping my hand over my mouth.

"Wait, what was that?"

"Um." I dart my eyes from side to side. "Nothing."

"No. I definitely heard something. It sounded a lot like you considering moving in."

I planned on surprising him once Stella found someone to cover my share of the rent. Though, with Sterling as our landlord, I'm not sure it really matters. But she's proud and refuses to take a handout from him.

But, I guess the cat's out of the bag now.

"Fine. I planned on packing my stuff and bringing it over once Stell found a roomie."

"Baby, let's put an ad on Craigslist."

"Shut up."

"You act like I'm bluffing. I'll take out a damn billboard if it gets your clothes in my closet, your smelly-good shit in my shower, and your fine-ass self in my bed every night."

"You're too much."

"Sometimes I worry I'm not enough," he says, letting his guard all the way down. "Sometimes I worry you'll realize you're too good for me and tell me to kick rocks."

"Never. You hear me? Not ever."

"Go shower before I toss you back down onto the bed and never let you leave."

I steal a quick kiss and dart out the door.

"Stell?" I call out as I enter our place.

"Babe!" she hollers back, rushing into the foyer to greet me. "Are you stoked for today?"

"Y'all are making such a big deal!"

"Um, because it is a big deal, sweets," Gabe says, scaring the hell out of me.

"Where did you come from?"

"My mother." He wobbles his head from side to side. "Or maybe my father. Depends on how you look at it. The chicken or the egg, am I right?"

"I—what?"

"Ignore him," Zach says, joining our weird little impromptu entryway party. "You here to get ready?"

"Yep, and y'all are here why?"

"To support you!" Gabe says, like it should be obvious.

"And by that he means we came for coffee."

"I am always down for coffee."

The four of us catch up over steaming hot mugs, laughing and cutting up, until I have to hop in the shower. "Thanks for coming," I say, getting misty eyed.

"Wouldn't be anywhere else," Zach says, hugging me before passing me over to his boyfriend, who redefines the term *bear hug*.

"Good luck today, sweets. You're going to kick all of the ass."

"Thanks, guys."

Stella sees them out while I hop in the shower. I soap up and rinse off in under five, tossing my wet hair into a braid before tugging on a pair of jeans and the hoodie Sterling bought me when I was in the hospital.

I like to think of it as my lucky hoodie and wear it pretty much all the time.

Stella's waiting for me in the kitchen when I finish getting ready. "I have something to tell you."

A million different scenarios bombard me. *Deep breaths,* I remind myself, *you can only control what you can control.*

"What's up?" I ask, pleased when my voice comes out smooth and even.

"I found someone to take over your portion of the rent."

"Really?" The worry that tried to trip me up morphs into excitement.

"Yeah. A girl named Frankie. She's in my art class. Oh, wait. Sterling won't mind a kid staying here, right?"

"She has a kid?"

Stella nods. "Yeah. She's a single mom and is trying to make a life for her and her son."

"He totally won't mind."

"I'll let her know today." She smiles. "Now, go forth and kick ass, babe."

Quick as lightning, I wrap my arms around her and hug her tight. "I'm so glad you're in my life. I'd be lost without you, Stell."

"Back at you, Emmy." She breaks our embrace. "Now, go get a good luck kiss from that man of yours."

"You don't have to tell me twice."

I grab my bag and dart back to Sterling's place, the smell of bacon greeting me.

"Made you some breakfast." He holds a piece of bacon out toward me, and I snatch it from him. "Most important meal of the day, you know?"

"False. That's coffee."

"You're an addict."

"Truth."

"You want me to drive you or..."

"I'll drive myself. Gotta assert my independence over the universe and whatnot."

"Okay, little mouse. I'm proud of you."

"I love you." I wrap my arms around his neck and pull his face down to mine, sealing our lips together in a toe-curling kiss.

"I love you, too."

"Oh, and before I forget," I say as I head for the door, "Stella found a roommate."

"Does that mean what I think it does?"

I nod.

"You're not fucking with me?" He steps closer, his face full of hope. "You're moving in?"

I nod again and he rushes me, wrapping his arms around me and twirling me around.

"Hell yes! This is the best day ever!" he exclaims before crushing his lips to mine.

I can't help but agree. Today is the best day ever.

It's my *real* fresh start and the official first day of the rest of my life with Sterling Abbot at my side.

STANDING in front of the full-length mirror, I smooth my hands over the front of my pretty white dress. My makeup is perfect, and there isn't a single strand of hair out of place.

Just breathe. I tell myself, trying to settle the swarm of nerves twisting through me.

My phone buzzes, and I grab it from the table.

STELLA

Today's the day! Are you excited?!

ME

I'm mostly just nervous. You know?

STELLA

You'll knock all their asses! Promise!

ME

If you say so…

ME

I wish you were here!

STELLA

Ugh! Me, too, babe. But noooo, I'm at a
family reunion in the middle of BFE.

ME

It's fine.

STELLA

It's not. Send me a selfie. I want to see you
in your gown.

ME

Will do. Love you!

STELLA

Love you more!

God love her, she always knows the right thing to say. And today of all days, I need the extra help.

Holly says bad days are normal, but luckily, they're few and far in between. But today, I can feel it itching to take hold and derail my plans.

Deep breaths. Today is going to be a good day. I will not allow my past to derail my future.

I feel marginally calmer after repeating the affirmations Holly taught me.

Some days, it's a little hard to believe that I've made it this far—that *we've* made it this far—but we have, and I know that together, Sterling and I are going to do great things.

It wasn't easy getting here, and it definitely wasn't always fun. But I know I'm exactly where I am meant to be, and damn if that doesn't feel good.

"Knock-knock," Sterling says before entering the room.

Scowling playfully at him in the mirror, I ask, "What are you doing in here?"

He hitches his thumb over his shoulder. "It's time to go."

"Already?" I ask, turning to fully face him.

His gorgeous gray eyes eat me up as he takes in every little detail. "You look beautiful, Emmalyn. So fucking beautiful."

"Thanks. I'm almost ready."

"You look perfect to me."

I roll my eyes and turn back to the mirror. Of course he would say I look perfect; he loves me and would think I was hot dressed in a potato sack.

"I just need to put on my necklace."

His eyes spark, and he steps completely into the room, moving with purpose until he's at my back. "Let me help you."

I pass him the necklace—a stunning family heirloom his mother passed to me on the second Christmas we celebrated together as a family—and he sweeps my hair out of the way and fastens the delicate chain around my neck before leaning in and pressing a soft kiss to the sensitive skin there.

"There," I say, assessing myself one last time.

"Perfection," he growls. "You're perfection."

I turn to face him. He's standing so close I have to look up to make eye contact. "Is it dumb that I'm nervous?"

He settles his hands on my shoulders, giving them a gentle squeeze before sweeping them down my arms to interlock our fingers. "You're going to do amazing. Just remember when you walk down the aisle, keep your eyes straight ahead."

"What if I trip?" I ask, kicking out my right foot to emphasize the heels Stella talked me into.

"Then look down and avoid eye contact at all cost."

I laugh, breaking his hold on one hand so I can smack his chest. "A lot of help you are!"

"But, I made you smile. So..."

"You are something else, Sterling Abbot."

"But you love me."

"With my whole heart."

He leans in to kiss me, but pulls back at the last minute. "Don't wanna ruin your lipstick."

"You better kiss me right this very instant!"

With his lips curled up into a smirk, he gives into my command, kissing me like his life depends on it.

"Better?"

"So very much."

"Good. Now, come on, little mouse, the ceremony waits for no one."

The drive to the venue is a quick one—just enough time to fix my lipstick—and by the time we're there, my nerves have settled, because I know that this is the first step in achieving the many things I want out of my life.

We park near the back of the very full lot. "Do you have everything?"

"Just need to get my bag from the trunk."

"I'll get it, baby."

Sterling grabs my garment bag from the trunk and drapes it over his left arm, wrapping his right around my waist. He walks me all the way to the side door, where we have to go our separate ways. "You've got this!"

"Where will you be?"

"In the very first row." He hands me my bag. "And when they call your name, I'll be the one cheering the loudest."

"Love you!" I say, darting inside before I get too emotional.

STERLING

"Is it still on?" Gabe asks from where he's seated beside me.

"Yeah." I nod decisively. "Definitely."

"Are you nervous?" Zach asks, peeking around his now husband.

"Nope. Not at all." I lean back into my seat, resting my ankle on my knee.

"My, my." Gabe shoots me an amused look. "Aren't you confident, Mr. Abbot?"

"Fuck yeah, I am!" I exclaim, causing someone in the row behind us to shush me. All three of us turn around and glare. *Like they've never heard someone drop an F-bomb before.*

"You're positive she's gonna say yes?" Gabe asks, playing the devil's advocate like he loves to do.

It took a long time for us to warm up to each other, but now we're so close that we talk daily.

"How could she say no?" I ask, just as the lights overhead flicker, alerting us that the ceremony is about to begin.

I zone out for most of it. Graduation is graduation. I'm only here for one thing, and that's to watch my little mouse claim her diploma. Although, I guess she's not much of a mouse anymore.

No. She's bold and vibrant and the bravest person I know and, if everything goes right today, she'll eventually be my wife. *Emmalyn Abbot has a ring to it, and I'm about to put a ring on it.*

I'm so caught up in my thoughts that I almost miss them call her name.

"Emmalyn Price."

I jump to my feet, along with Zach and Gabe, clapping

and whistling and cheering like we're at a football game, as she walks across the stage.

She looks my way, and I wink, mouthing the words *proud of you, baby.*

"PROUD OF YOU, SWEETS," Gabe says, shouldering me out of the way so that he can hug her first.

The blond giant is also a giant asshole.

"Thank you!" She smiles up at him and then hugs Zach.

I'm practically pouting by the time she makes it to me. "Best for last," she whispers in my ear, before slinging her arms around my neck.

"Damn straight, baby."

"Are y'all joining us for dinner?" Emmy asks.

"Ah, no can do," Zach says. "Gabe here has an interview."

"This late?" Emmalyn's eyes widen. "Where? With who? Why didn't you tell me?"

"It's online because of time differences." He shrugs. "And, I didn't want to jinx it."

"Okay, well. Good luck! Break a leg. Whatever applies."

Gabe shakes his head. "You're too much, sweets. I'll let you know the outcome."

They hug again and then it's just the two of us. "You ready?"

"Starving. Wanna tell me where we're eating?"

"Why do you always want to ruin my surprises?"

She rolls her eyes. "Fine."

We drive with the windows down and the radio on, enjoying the fresh mountain air.

"Oh!" A smile flashes across her face as recognition sets in. "Café on the Corner, huh?"

I park the car and cut the engine. "That's right. This is where I took you on our first date, so it seemed like the right choice for today."

"Hmmm." Emmy climbs out of the car and I follow.

"What?"

"I'm pretty sure you made it quite clear that our lunch here was *not* a date."

"Fair enough. But if I wouldn't have brought you here, I don't think we would've ended up here."

She smiles softly. "Here's a good place to be."

I stop her from reaching for the door and pull her off to the side, wanting a private moment before we head inside. "Anywhere is a good place if you're there."

Emmalyn laughs...*loudly*. "Who knew big-alpha-macho-man Sterling Abbot was such a softy?"

"You're the only person I'm soft for."

She licks her lips and drops her eyes. "I like it better when you're hard for me."

"Dammit, baby, if you keep this up, we're not gonna make it to lunch."

"I've got something you can eat." She bats her lashes and steps in closer.

"That's enough." I place my hands on her shoulders and nudge her back a step. She's too damn tempting, and while I'd love nothing more than to take her home and devour her, I've got fucking plans.

"Okay, fine. But only if you get me nachos."

"I can handle that." I clasp her hand in mine and pull her back toward the door.

She glares at me as I pull it open. "Cheesecake, too."

"Consider it done."

"Your same table?" the hostess asks.

Emmy nods, but I say, "Actually I was hoping we could sit outside today."

"What? Why?" Emmy cocks her head to the side.

"It's a beautiful day," is all I say in reply, glad everyone is sticking to the script.

"I guess." She crinkles her nose. "You're acting weird."

"If y'all will follow me?" The hostess leads us out onto the patio, which I've rented out just for us.

Fairy lights twinkle overhead, casting a romantic glow over the whole space, while soft music pumps from the speakers.

On cue, "No One's Gonna Love You" by Band of Horses starts up right as the sun dips below the horizon.

"Sterling!" Emmalyn whips around to face, accusation evident in her big, brown eyes.

"Yes, baby?"

"What is all of this?" She throws her arms wide, gesturing to the patio. "What are you doing?"

"This," I murmur, dropping down to one knee.

Tears fill her eyes, but a smile splits her cheeks. "Ster."

"I love you. All of you. Every single part of you." I reach up and take her hand in mine. "I love you on your good days and on your bad. You're easily the best part of my life, Emmalyn Price. I didn't deserve a chance with you, and yet you gave me one. So, here I am now, once again asking for something I probably don't deserve."

I lean back ever so slightly on my heel and slide the velvet box from my pocket. "Marry me? Marry me and make me the happiest motherfucker on the planet?"

She nods, her tears freely falling.

"Words, baby. I need your words."

"Yes! Oh my God. Yes!"

I slide the ring onto her finger before standing and pulling her into my arms for a searing kiss. "I love you, little mouse."

"I love you, too." She squeezes me to her once more. "You will always be my home."

RESOURCES

If you or anyone you know is having suicidal thoughts, please know you are so very loved and so very wanted. Your life matters. **YOU MATTER.**

Help is available, free of cost, at the resources below.

Call the National Suicide Prevention Lifeline at 1-800-273-8255

This is a free 24-hour hotline.

(Press 1 for a dedicated line for Veterans and their families.

Para español, oprima 2.)

https://suicidepreventionlifeline.org/

The website above also offers a chat feature.

To Write Love on Her Arms is a non-profit movement dedicated to presenting hope and finding help for people struggling with depression, addiction, self-injury, and suicide. TWLOHA exists to encourage, inform, inspire,

and also to invest directly into treatment and recovery.
https://twloha.com/

LK'S OTHER TITLES

All of LK's titles can be read as standalones & are available with Kindle Unlimited. An asterisk next to the title denotes it is also available in audio.

*Dirty Little Secret** (an older brother's best friend/second chance romance)

*Pretty Little Thing** (a single mom/forced proximity/mistaken identity romance)

*Best Laid Plans** (an older brother's best friend/secret baby romance)

*Best of Intentions** (a friends-to-lovers/little sister's best friend romance)

*Best of Me** (a second chance at love/forbidden twin romance)

Rebel Heart (an enemies-to-lovers jock/tutor rom-com)

Rebel Soul (an arranged baby/friends-to-lovers rom-com)

Rebel Desire (an unrequited soulmates/surprise single dad rom-com)

*Coming Up Roses** (a small-town/single mom romance)
*An Uphill Battle** (a frenemies-to-lovers romance)
Weather the Storm (a second chance at love romantic suspense)
Come What May (an age gap/single dad romance)

My greatest fear with every single book, and I mean this *every single book,* is that I'll forget to thank someone important. And there are *so* many people who deserve my gratitude. So many people who have helped me, not only with this book, but with my entire author journey.

Thank you to the many amazing, kind souls who have gone out of their way to help me, to lend an ear, or a kind word on a down day. You, my friends, are the light in this world and I'm more grateful for you (and your friendship) than words can adequately express.

A major thanks to my amazing Alpha & Beta team. You ladies are an invaluable part of my creative process.

I also need to thank my editing team—Kiezha, Ellie, and Julie, the fact that y'all haven't fired me is amazing. And a blessing, because I couldn't do this without y'all.

To my PA's, you ladies keep me sane. Seriously, never leave me.

Candi, and the whole Give Me Books crew, thank y'all for all of your hard work in getting the word out about this book.

But maybe the most important group I need to thank is the book lovers! Whether you're a reader or a blogger, *you* are the reason I am able to do this. Your support means more to me than I'll ever be able to articulate. I am thankful for each and every one of you.

And last but not least, my family. Y'all are my everything and I'm incredibly grateful for the glorious chaos y'all
bring.

ABOUT THE AUTHOR

Known by Kate to most, LK Farlow is an Amazon Top 40 bestselling author of more than a dozen romances, ranging from sweet, to sexy, to rip your heart out, and everything in-between.

She has a heart built for happily-ever-afters, which is lucky since she found hers at the young age of nineteen. Now, at thirty-something, she is the wife to one hunky man and the mother to four semi-feral humans, three lizards, a chameleon, a tortoise, and a handful of stray cats.

Kate often jokes that her life is all out chaos on most days, but she wouldn't trade it for the world.

www.authorlkfarlow.com

www.ingramcontent.com/pod-product-compliance
Lightning Source LLC
Chambersburg PA
CBHW070403310726
48977CB00003B/542